TERRY and the Pirates

by MILTON CANIFF

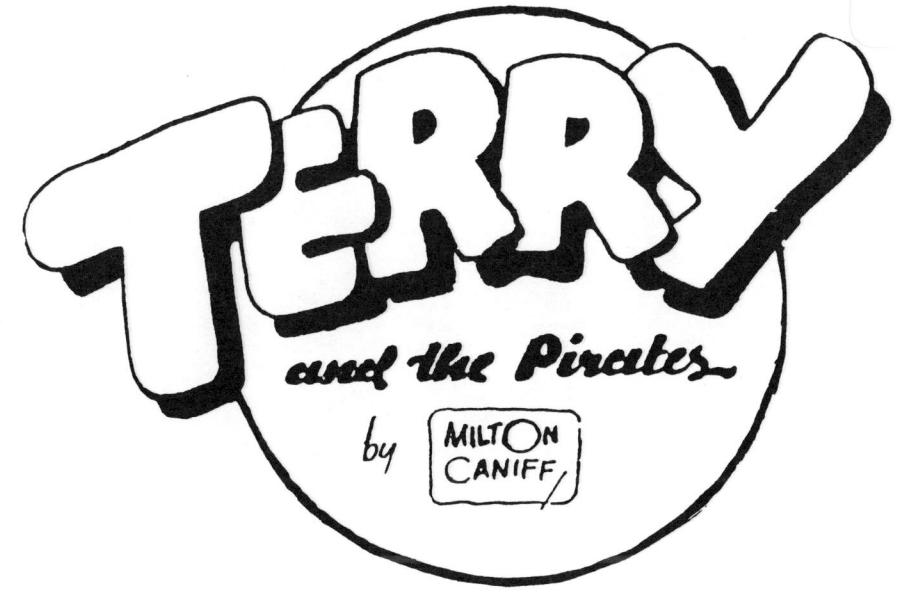

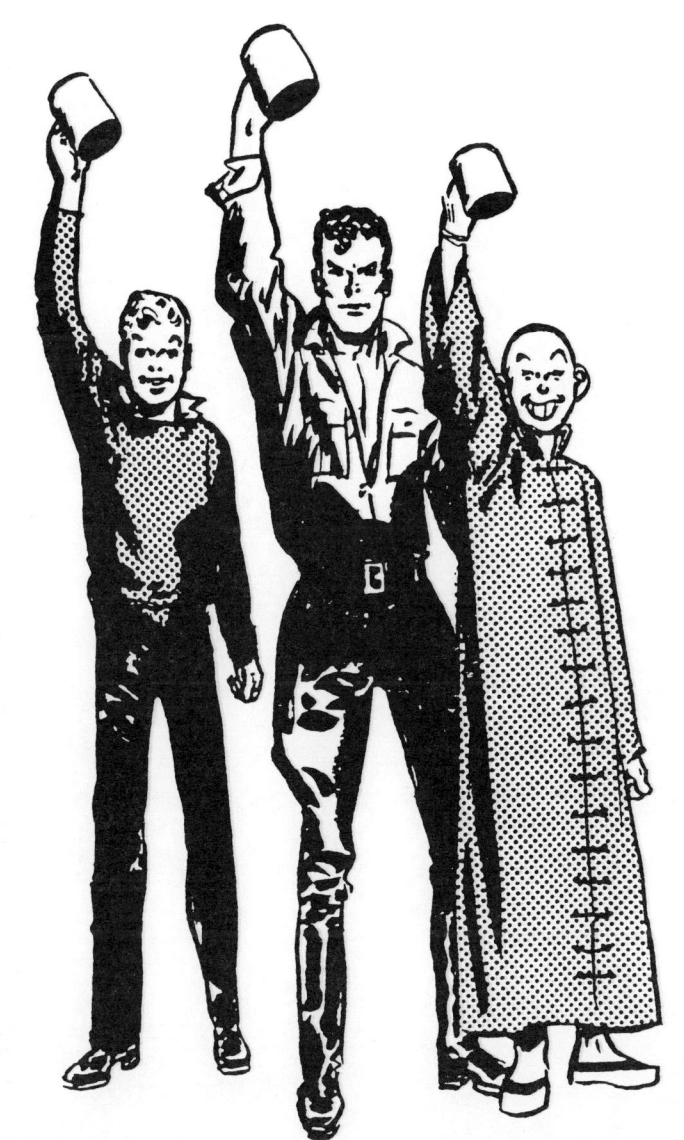

TERRY
and the Pirates
by MILTON CANIFF

DRAGON LADY'S REVENGE

FLYING BUTTRESS
Classics library

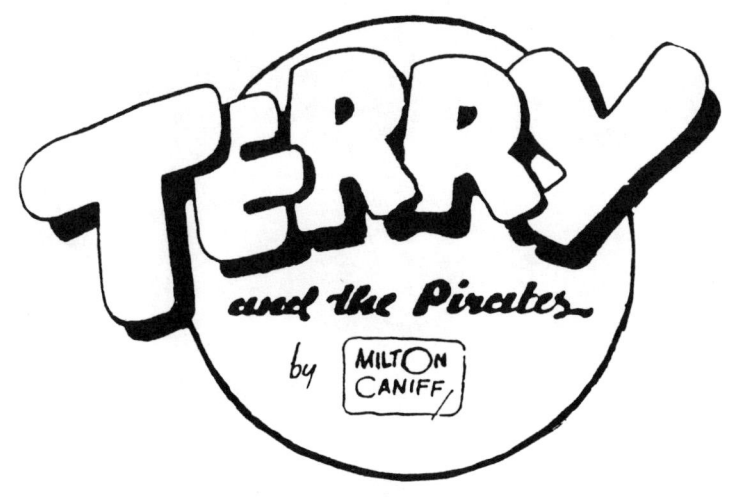

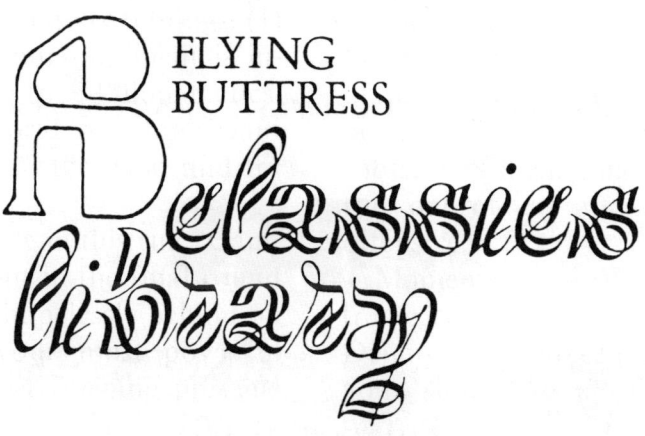

COPYRIGHT 1986 NBM PUBLISHING
COVER DESIGNED AND PAINTED BY RAY FEHRENBACH
ISBN# 0-918348-26-9

Terry & The Pirates is a registered trademark of Tribune Media Services, Inc.

THE FLYING BUTTRESS CLASSICS LIBRARY is an imprint of:

NANTIER · BEALL · MINOUSTCHINE
Publishing co.
new york

Our Story So Far: Terry Lee and his guardian Pat and their servant Connie have been wandering the China coast for about a year. In ***MAROONED WITH BURMA*** (vol. 2 in this series) they meet a blonde adventuress named Burma on a desert island, who is a member of a pirate gang. Burma falls in love with Pat, but when the pirate chief, Capt. Judas, discovers their romance he imprisons everyone but Burma. Burma and our heroes escape in a motor boat to what they think is the mainland. As we pick up the story, Pat and Terry begin to question Burma about her pirate past.

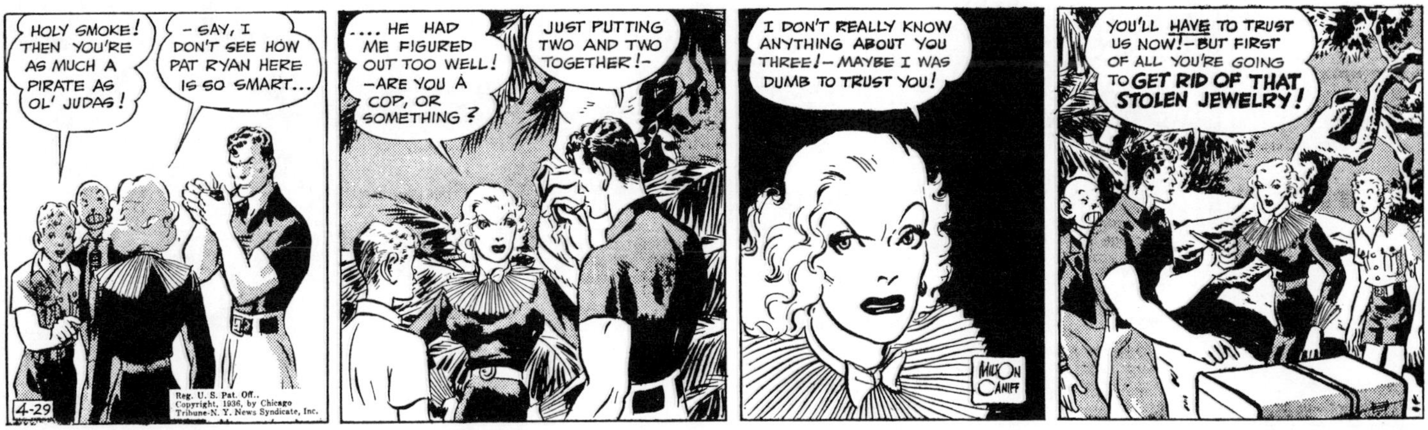
HOLY SMOKE! THEN YOU'RE AS MUCH A PIRATE AS OL' JUDAS!
- SAY, I DON'T SEE HOW PAT RYAN HERE IS SO SMART...
4-29
Reg. U. S. Pat. Off., Copyright, 1936, by Chicago Tribune-N. Y. News Syndicate, Inc.
.... HE HAD ME FIGURED OUT TOO WELL! -ARE YOU A COP, OR SOMETHING?
JUST PUTTING TWO AND TWO TOGETHER!-
I DON'T REALLY KNOW ANYTHING ABOUT YOU THREE! - MAYBE I WAS DUMB TO TRUST YOU!
MILTON CANIFF
YOU'LL HAVE TO TRUST US NOW! - BUT FIRST OF ALL YOU'RE GOING TO GET RID OF THAT STOLEN JEWELRY!

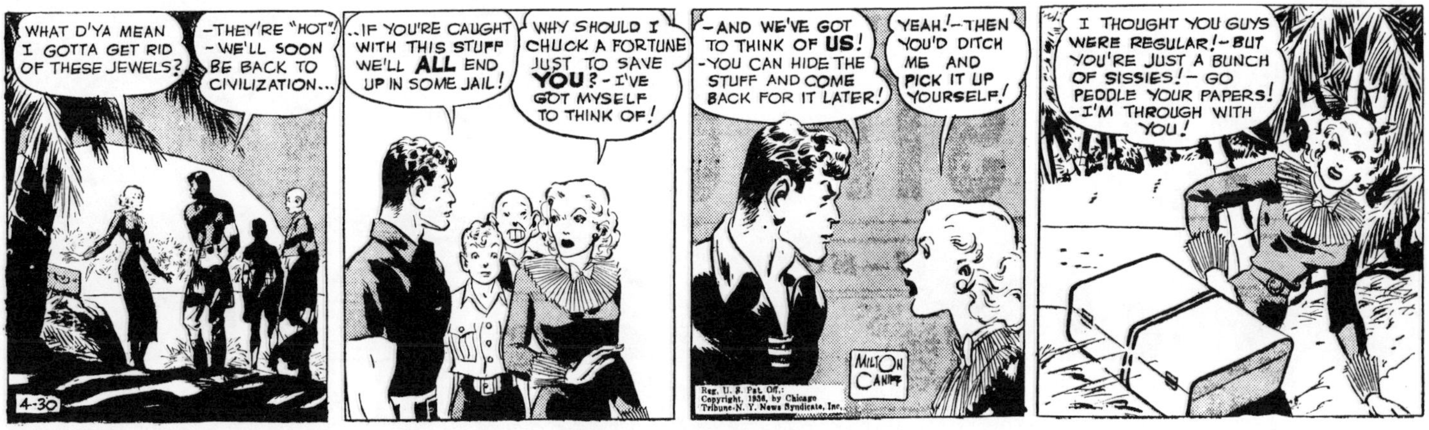
WHAT D'YA MEAN I GOTTA GET RID OF THESE JEWELS?
-THEY'RE "HOT"! - WE'LL SOON BE BACK TO CIVILIZATION...
4-30
..IF YOU'RE CAUGHT WITH THIS STUFF WE'LL ALL END UP IN SOME JAIL!
WHY SHOULD I CHUCK A FORTUNE JUST TO SAVE YOU? - I'VE GOT MYSELF TO THINK OF!
-AND WE'VE GOT TO THINK OF US! -YOU CAN HIDE THE STUFF AND COME BACK FOR IT LATER!
YEAH! - THEN YOU'D DITCH ME AND PICK IT UP YOURSELF!
Reg. U. S. Pat. Off., Copyright, 1936, by Chicago Tribune-N. Y. News Syndicate, Inc.
MILTON CANIFF
I THOUGHT YOU GUYS WERE REGULAR! - BUT YOU'RE JUST A BUNCH OF SISSIES! - GO PEDDLE YOUR PAPERS! -I'M THROUGH WITH YOU!

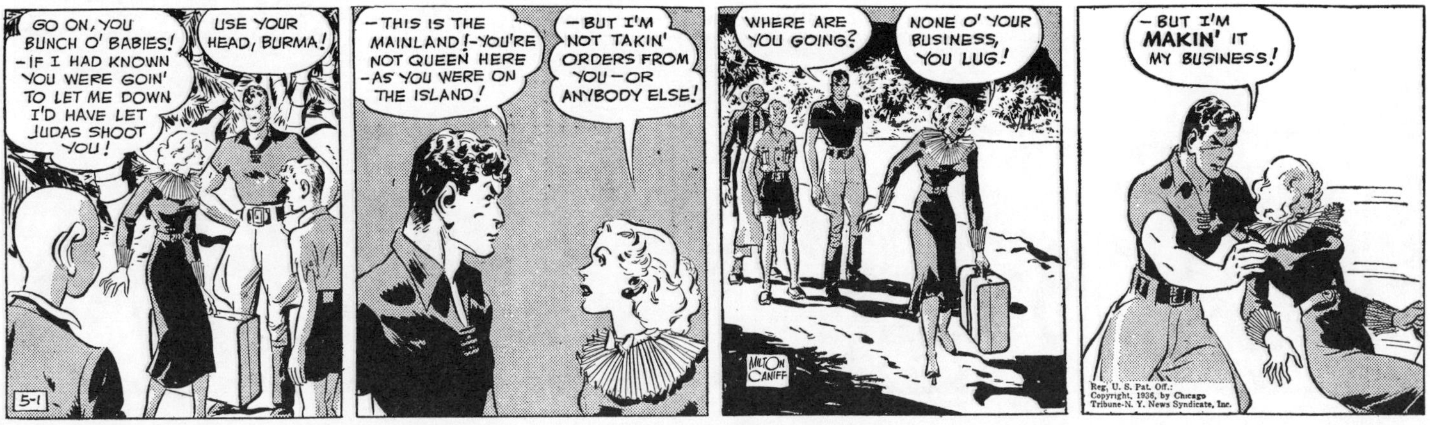
GO ON, YOU BUNCH O' BABIES! -IF I HAD KNOWN YOU WERE GOIN' TO LET ME DOWN I'D HAVE LET JUDAS SHOOT YOU!
USE YOUR HEAD, BURMA!
5-1
-THIS IS THE MAINLAND! - YOU'RE NOT QUEEN HERE -AS YOU WERE ON THE ISLAND!
-BUT I'M NOT TAKIN' ORDERS FROM YOU - OR ANYBODY ELSE!
WHERE ARE YOU GOING?
NONE O' YOUR BUSINESS, YOU LUG!
MILTON CANIFF
- BUT I'M MAKIN' IT MY BUSINESS!
Reg. U. S. Pat. Off., Copyright, 1936, by Chicago Tribune-N. Y. News Syndicate, Inc.

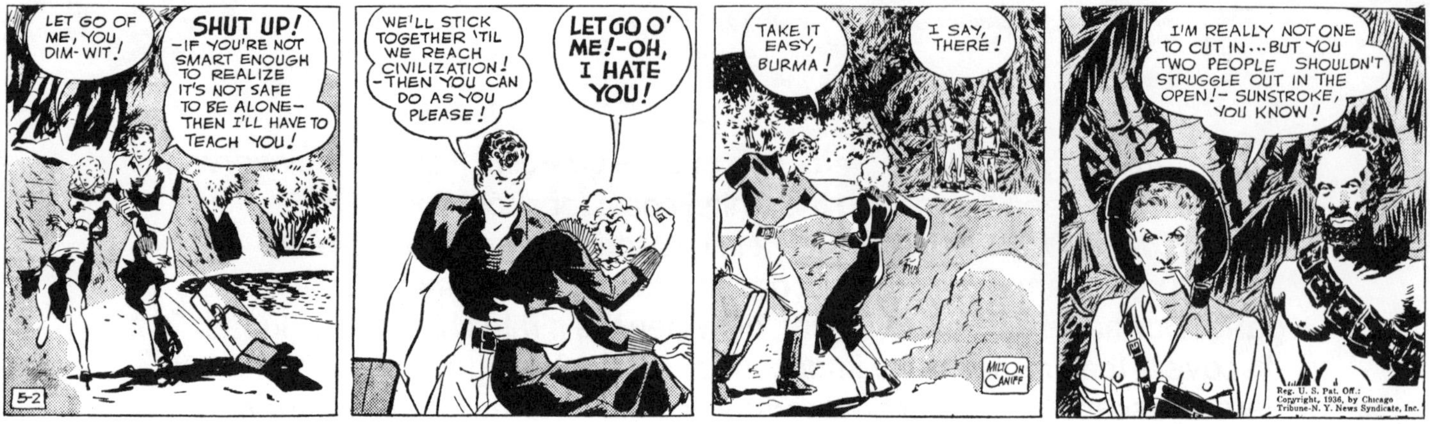
LET GO OF ME, YOU DIM-WIT!
SHUT UP! -IF YOU'RE NOT SMART ENOUGH TO REALIZE IT'S NOT SAFE TO BE ALONE- THEN I'LL HAVE TO TEACH YOU!
5-2
WE'LL STICK TOGETHER 'TIL WE REACH CIVILIZATION! -THEN YOU CAN DO AS YOU PLEASE!
LET GO O' ME!-OH, I HATE YOU!
TAKE IT EASY, BURMA!
I SAY, THERE!
MILTON CANIFF
I'M REALLY NOT ONE TO CUT IN...BUT YOU TWO PEOPLE SHOULDN'T STRUGGLE OUT IN THE OPEN!- SUNSTROKE, YOU KNOW!
Reg. U. S. Pat. Off.: Copyright, 1936, by Chicago Tribune-N. Y. News Syndicate, Inc.

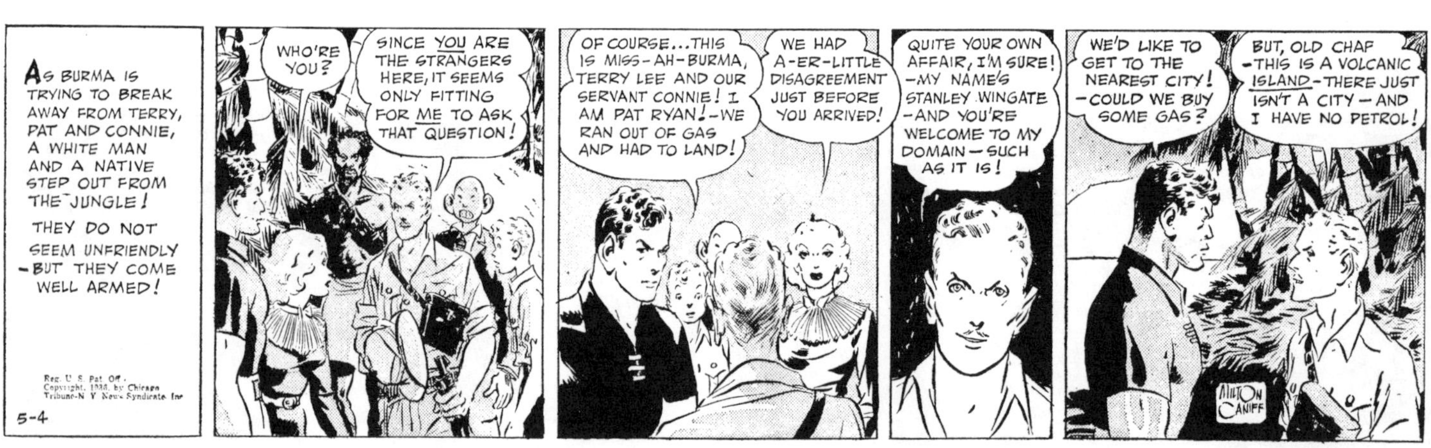
AS BURMA IS TRYING TO BREAK AWAY FROM TERRY, PAT AND CONNIE, A WHITE MAN AND A NATIVE STEP OUT FROM THE JUNGLE!
THEY DO NOT SEEM UNFRIENDLY -BUT THEY COME WELL ARMED!
Reg. U. S. Pat. Off. Copyright, 1936, by Chicago Tribune-N. Y. News Syndicate, Inc.
5-4
WHO'RE YOU?
SINCE YOU ARE THE STRANGERS HERE, IT SEEMS ONLY FITTING FOR ME TO ASK THAT QUESTION!
OF COURSE...THIS IS MISS-AH-BURMA, TERRY LEE AND OUR SERVANT CONNIE! I AM PAT RYAN!-WE RAN OUT OF GAS AND HAD TO LAND!
WE HAD A-ER-LITTLE DISAGREEMENT JUST BEFORE YOU ARRIVED!
QUITE YOUR OWN AFFAIR, I'M SURE! -MY NAME'S STANLEY WINGATE -AND YOU'RE WELCOME TO MY DOMAIN-SUCH AS IT IS!
WE'D LIKE TO GET TO THE NEAREST CITY! -COULD WE BUY SOME GAS?
BUT, OLD CHAP -THIS IS A VOLCANIC ISLAND-THERE JUST ISN'T A CITY-AND I HAVE NO PETROL!
MILTON CANIFF

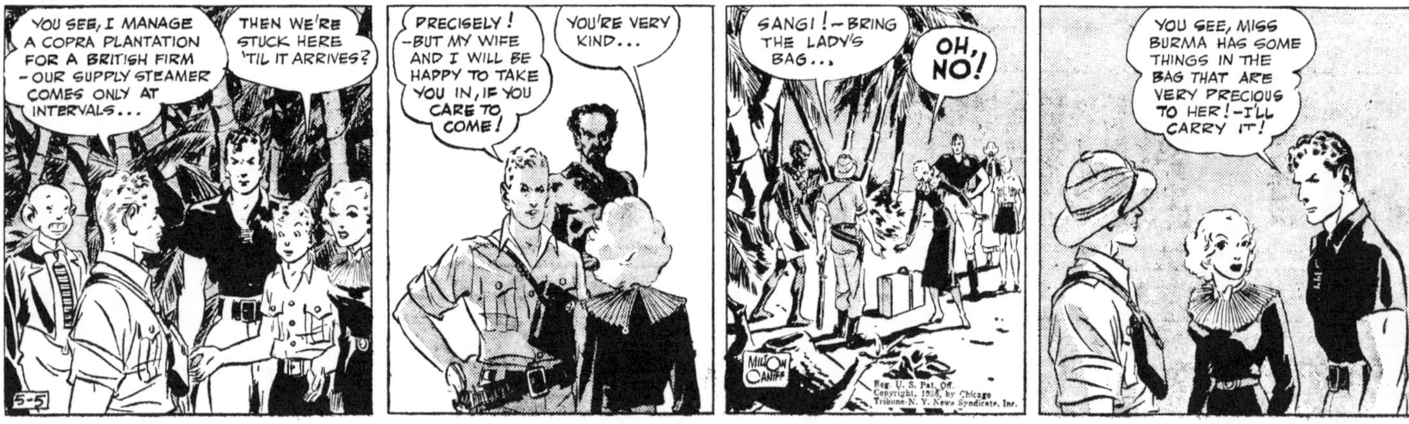
YOU SEE, I MANAGE A COPRA PLANTATION FOR A BRITISH FIRM -OUR SUPPLY STEAMER COMES ONLY AT INTERVALS...
THEN WE'RE STUCK HERE 'TIL IT ARRIVES?
5-5
PRECISELY! -BUT MY WIFE AND I WILL BE HAPPY TO TAKE YOU IN, IF YOU CARE TO COME!
YOU'RE VERY KIND...
SANGI!-BRING THE LADY'S BAG...
OH, NO!
MILTON CANIFF
Reg. U. S. Pat. Off. Copyright, 1936, by Chicago Tribune-N. Y. News Syndicate, Inc.
YOU SEE, MISS BURMA HAS SOME THINGS IN THE BAG THAT ARE VERY PRECIOUS TO HER!-I'LL CARRY IT!

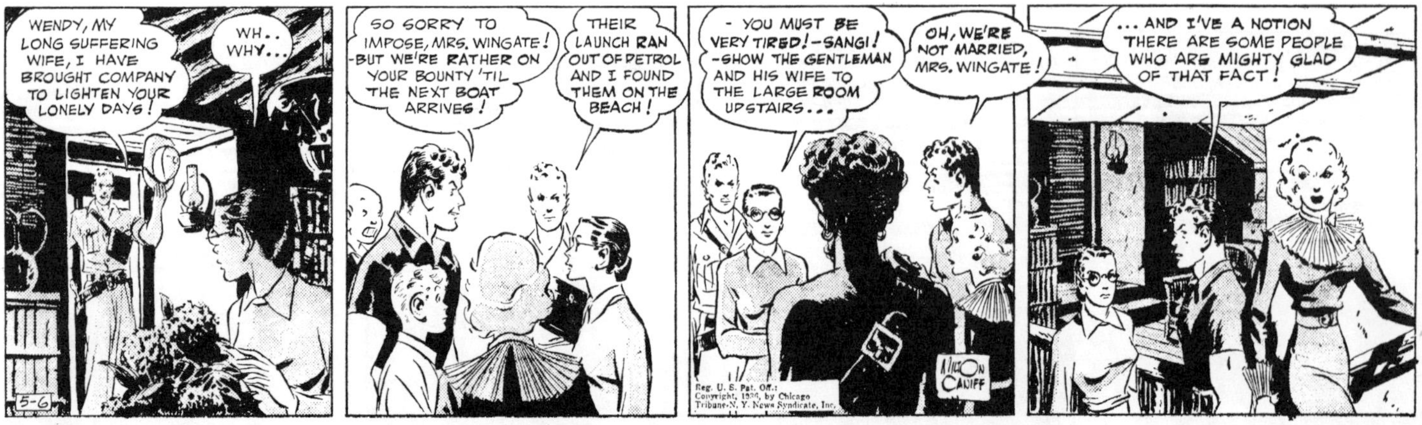
WENDY, MY LONG SUFFERING WIFE, I HAVE BROUGHT COMPANY TO LIGHTEN YOUR LONELY DAYS!
WH.. WHY...
5-6
SO SORRY TO IMPOSE, MRS. WINGATE! -BUT WE'RE RATHER ON YOUR BOUNTY 'TIL THE NEXT BOAT ARRIVES!
THEIR LAUNCH RAN OUT OF PETROL AND I FOUND THEM ON THE BEACH!
-YOU MUST BE VERY TIRED!-SANGI! -SHOW THE GENTLEMAN AND HIS WIFE TO THE LARGE ROOM UPSTAIRS...
OH, WE'RE NOT MARRIED, MRS. WINGATE!
Reg. U. S. Pat. Off.: Copyright, 1936, by Chicago Tribune-N. Y. News Syndicate, Inc.
MILTON CANIFF
...AND I'VE A NOTION THERE ARE SOME PEOPLE WHO ARE MIGHTY GLAD OF THAT FACT!

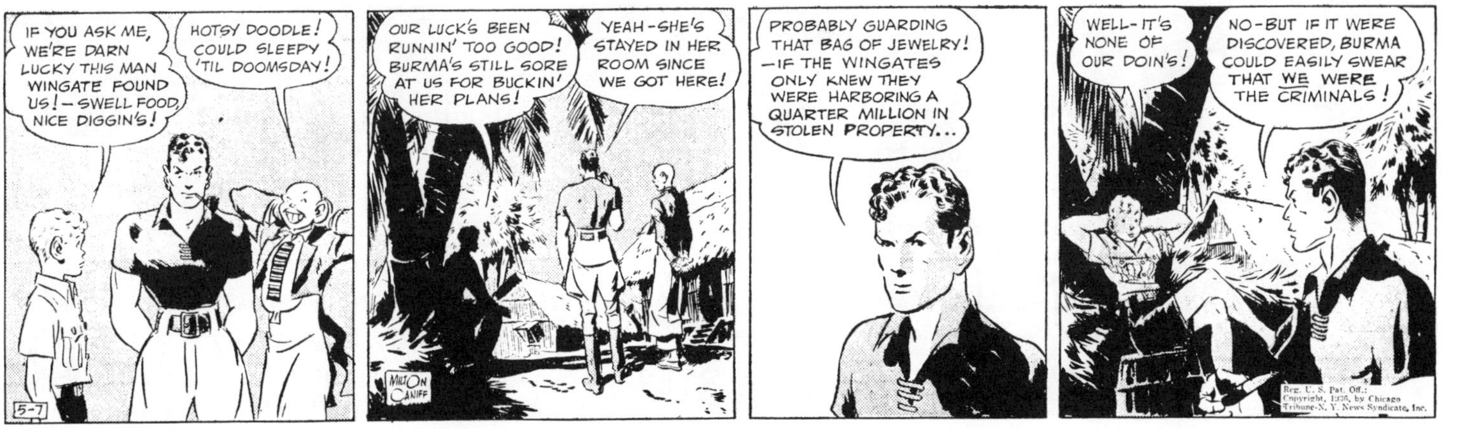
IF YOU ASK ME, WE'RE DARN LUCKY THIS MAN WINGATE FOUND US! — SWELL FOOD, NICE DIGGIN'S!
HOTSY DOODLE! COULD SLEEPY 'TIL DOOMSDAY!
5-7
OUR LUCK'S BEEN RUNNIN' TOO GOOD! BURMA'S STILL SORE AT US FOR BUCKIN' HER PLANS!
YEAH - SHE'S STAYED IN HER ROOM SINCE WE GOT HERE!
MILTON CANIFF
PROBABLY GUARDING THAT BAG OF JEWELRY! — IF THE WINGATES ONLY KNEW THEY WERE HARBORING A QUARTER MILLION IN STOLEN PROPERTY...
WELL - IT'S NONE OF OUR DOIN'S!
NO - BUT IF IT WERE DISCOVERED, BURMA COULD EASILY SWEAR THAT WE WERE THE CRIMINALS!
Reg. U. S. Pat. Off.: Copyright, 1936, by Chicago Tribune-N. Y. News Syndicate, Inc.

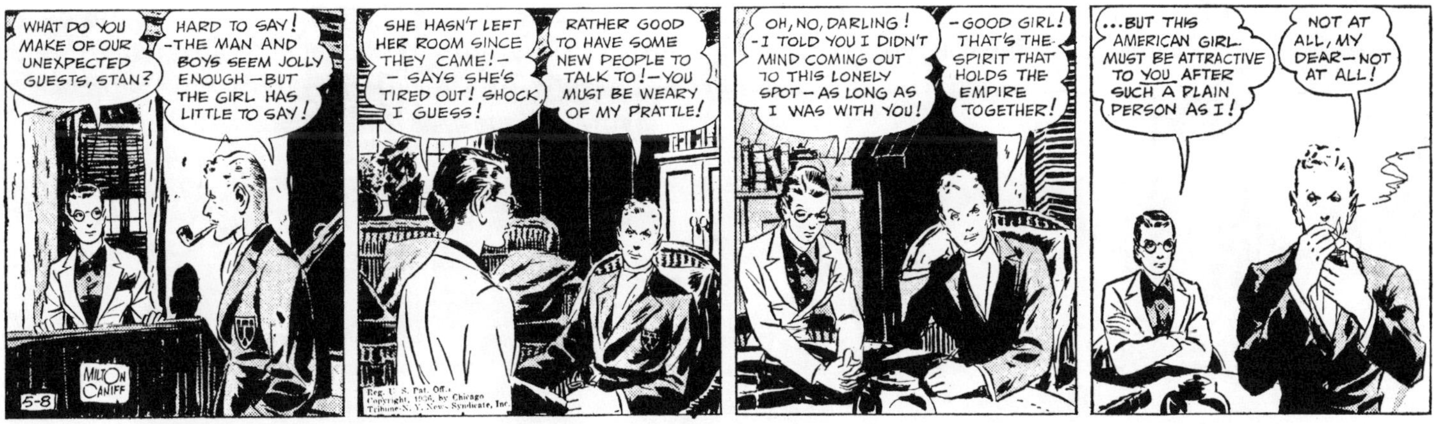
WHAT DO YOU MAKE OF OUR UNEXPECTED GUESTS, STAN?
HARD TO SAY! — THE MAN AND BOYS SEEM JOLLY ENOUGH — BUT THE GIRL HAS LITTLE TO SAY!
MILTON CANIFF
5-8
SHE HASN'T LEFT HER ROOM SINCE THEY CAME! — — SAYS SHE'S TIRED OUT! SHOCK, I GUESS!
RATHER GOOD TO HAVE SOME NEW PEOPLE TO TALK TO! — YOU MUST BE WEARY OF MY PRATTLE!
Reg. U. S. Pat. Off.: Copyright, 1936, by Chicago Tribune-N. Y. News Syndicate, Inc.
OH, NO, DARLING! — I TOLD YOU I DIDN'T MIND COMING OUT TO THIS LONELY SPOT — AS LONG AS I WAS WITH YOU!
— GOOD GIRL! THAT'S THE SPIRIT THAT HOLDS THE EMPIRE TOGETHER!
...BUT THIS AMERICAN GIRL MUST BE ATTRACTIVE TO YOU AFTER SUCH A PLAIN PERSON AS I!
NOT AT ALL, MY DEAR — NOT AT ALL!

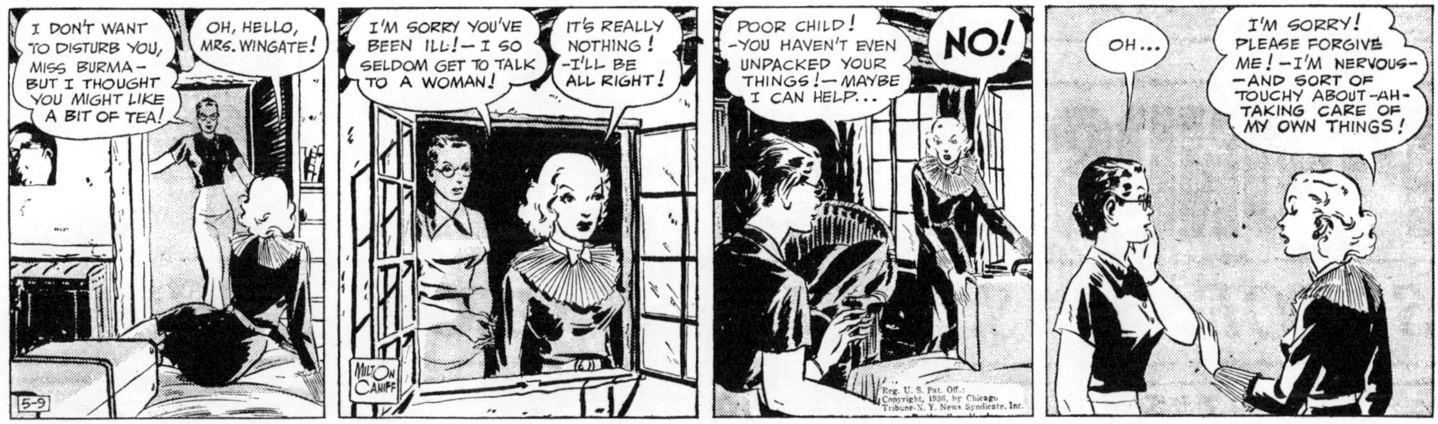
I DON'T WANT TO DISTURB YOU, MISS BURMA — BUT I THOUGHT YOU MIGHT LIKE A BIT OF TEA!
OH, HELLO, MRS. WINGATE!
5-9
I'M SORRY YOU'VE BEEN ILL! — I SO SELDOM GET TO TALK TO A WOMAN!
IT'S REALLY NOTHING! — I'LL BE ALL RIGHT!
MILTON CANIFF
POOR CHILD! — YOU HAVEN'T EVEN UNPACKED YOUR THINGS! — MAYBE I CAN HELP...
NO!
Reg. U. S. Pat. Off.: Copyright, 1936, by Chicago Tribune-N. Y. News Syndicate, Inc.
OH...
I'M SORRY! PLEASE FORGIVE ME! — I'M NERVOUS — AND SORT OF TOUCHY ABOUT — AH — TAKING CARE OF MY OWN THINGS!

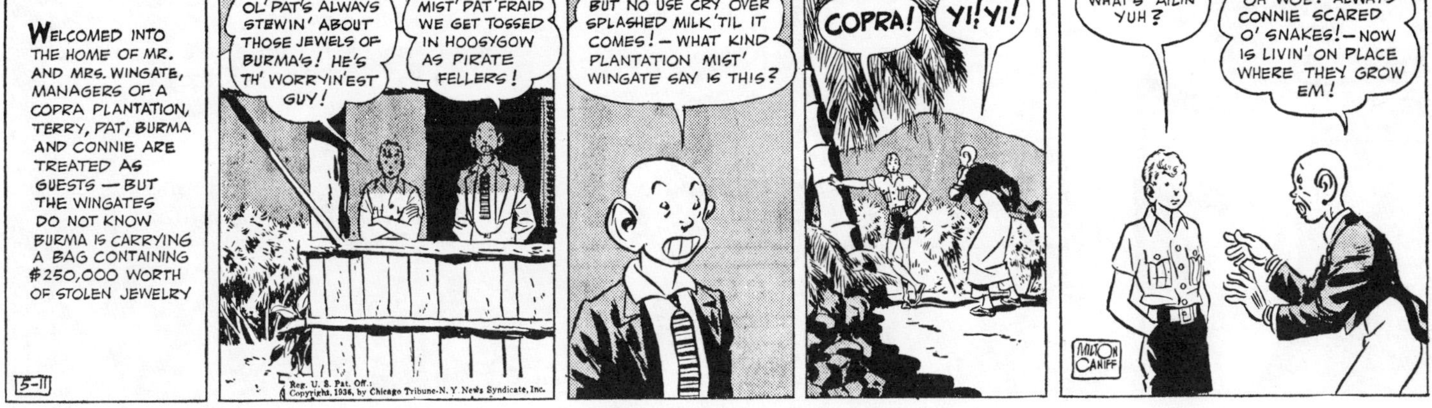
WELCOMED INTO THE HOME OF MR. AND MRS. WINGATE, MANAGERS OF A COPRA PLANTATION, TERRY, PAT, BURMA AND CONNIE ARE TREATED AS GUESTS — BUT THE WINGATES DO NOT KNOW BURMA IS CARRYING A BAG CONTAINING $250,000 WORTH OF STOLEN JEWELRY
5-11
OL' PAT'S ALWAYS STEWIN' ABOUT THOSE JEWELS OF BURMA'S! HE'S TH' WORRYIN'EST GUY!
MIST' PAT 'FRAID WE GET TOSSED IN HOOSGOW AS PIRATE FELLERS!
Reg. U. S. Pat. Off.: Copyright, 1936, by Chicago Tribune-N. Y. News Syndicate, Inc.
BUT NO USE CRY OVER SPLASHED MILK 'TIL IT COMES! — WHAT KIND PLANTATION MIST' WINGATE SAY IS THIS?
COPRA!
YI! YI!
WHAT'S AILIN' YUH?
OH WOE! ALWAYS CONNIE SCARED O' SNAKES! — NOW IS LIVIN' ON PLACE WHERE THEY GROW EM!
MILTON CANIFF

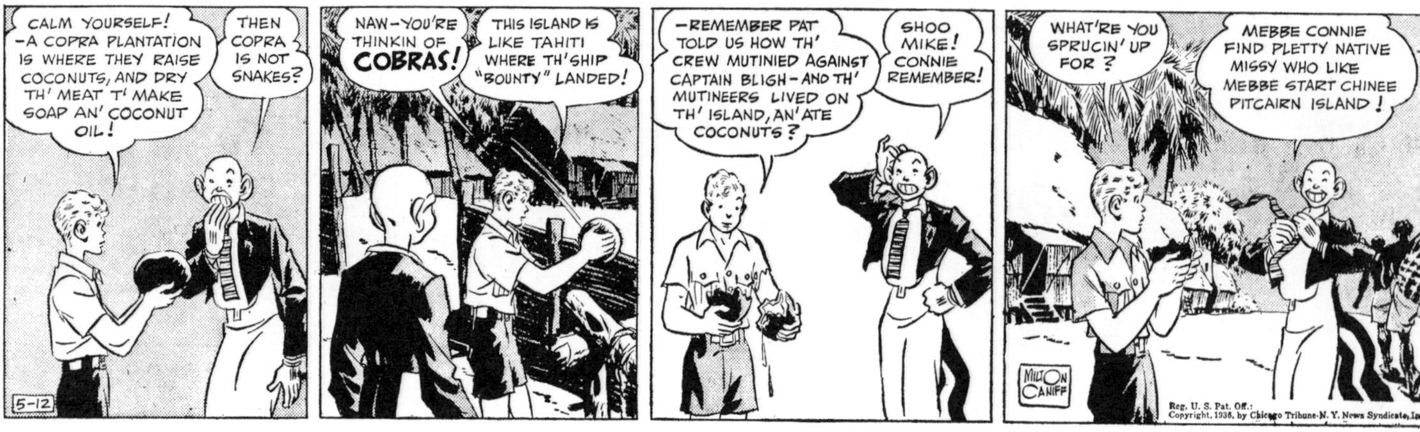
CALM YOURSELF! -A COPRA PLANTATION IS WHERE THEY RAISE COCONUTS, AND DRY TH' MEAT T' MAKE SOAP AN' COCONUT OIL!
THEN COPRA IS NOT SNAKES?
NAW-YOU'RE THINKIN OF COBRAS!
THIS ISLAND IS LIKE TAHITI WHERE TH' SHIP "BOUNTY" LANDED!
-REMEMBER PAT TOLD US HOW TH' CREW MUTINIED AGAINST CAPTAIN BLIGH-AND TH' MUTINEERS LIVED ON TH' ISLAND, AN' ATE COCONUTS?
SHOO MIKE! CONNIE REMEMBER!
WHAT'RE YOU SPRUCIN' UP FOR?
MEBBE CONNIE FIND PLETTY NATIVE MISSY WHO LIKE MEBBE START CHINEE PITCAIRN ISLAND!
5-12
MILTON CANIFF
Reg. U. S. Pat. Off.: Copyright, 1936, by Chicago Tribune-N. Y. News Syndicate, Inc.

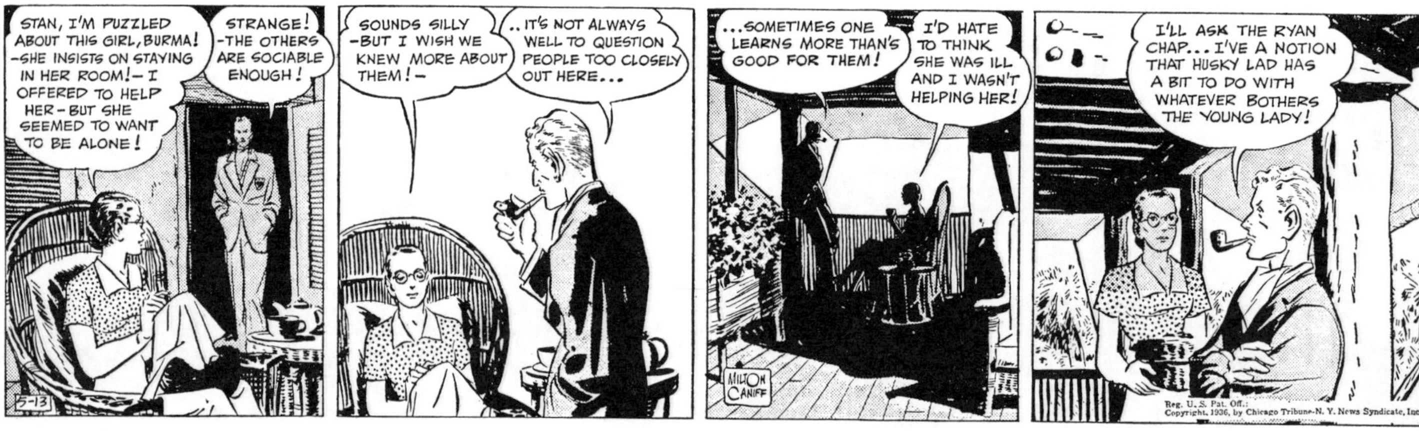
STAN, I'M PUZZLED ABOUT THIS GIRL, BURMA! -SHE INSISTS ON STAYING IN HER ROOM!-I OFFERED TO HELP HER-BUT SHE SEEMED TO WANT TO BE ALONE!
STRANGE! -THE OTHERS ARE SOCIABLE ENOUGH!
SOUNDS SILLY -BUT I WISH WE KNEW MORE ABOUT THEM!-
..IT'S NOT ALWAYS WELL TO QUESTION PEOPLE TOO CLOSELY OUT HERE...
...SOMETIMES ONE LEARNS MORE THAN'S GOOD FOR THEM!
I'D HATE TO THINK SHE WAS ILL AND I WASN'T HELPING HER!
I'LL ASK THE RYAN CHAP... I'VE A NOTION THAT HUSKY LAD HAS A BIT TO DO WITH WHATEVER BOTHERS THE YOUNG LADY!
5-13
MILTON CANIFF
Reg. U. S. Pat. Off.: Copyright, 1936, by Chicago Tribune-N. Y. News Syndicate, Inc.

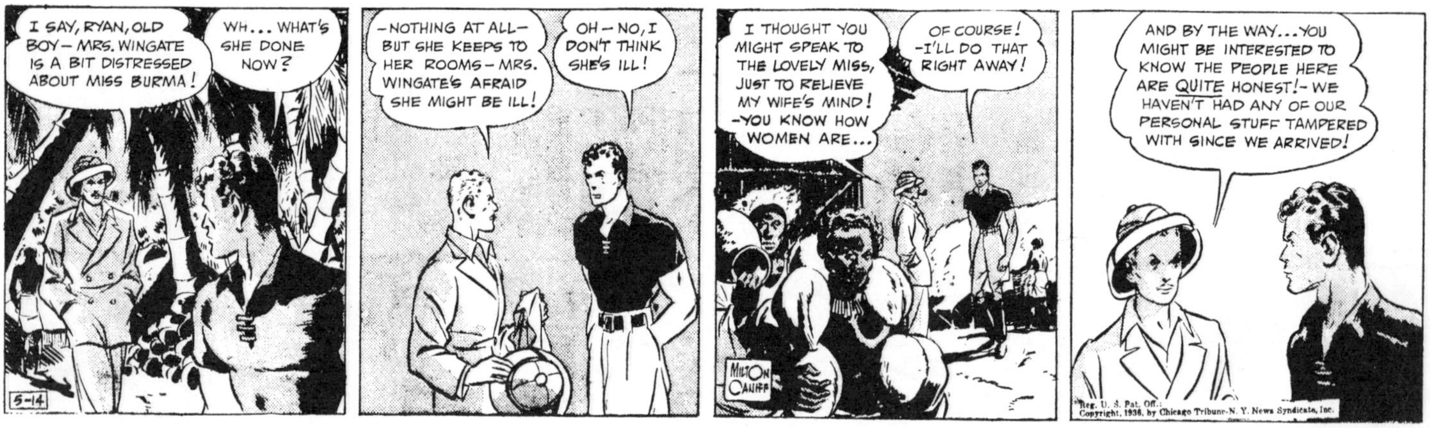
I SAY, RYAN, OLD BOY-MRS. WINGATE IS A BIT DISTRESSED ABOUT MISS BURMA!
WH... WHAT'S SHE DONE NOW?
-NOTHING AT ALL-BUT SHE KEEPS TO HER ROOMS-MRS. WINGATE'S AFRAID SHE MIGHT BE ILL!
OH-NO, I DON'T THINK SHE'S ILL!
I THOUGHT YOU MIGHT SPEAK TO THE LOVELY MISS, JUST TO RELIEVE MY WIFE'S MIND! -YOU KNOW HOW WOMEN ARE...
OF COURSE! -I'LL DO THAT RIGHT AWAY!
AND BY THE WAY... YOU MIGHT BE INTERESTED TO KNOW THE PEOPLE HERE ARE QUITE HONEST!-WE HAVEN'T HAD ANY OF OUR PERSONAL STUFF TAMPERED WITH SINCE WE ARRIVED!
5-14
MILTON CANIFF
Reg. U. S. Pat. Off.: Copyright, 1936, by Chicago Tribune-N. Y. News Syndicate, Inc.

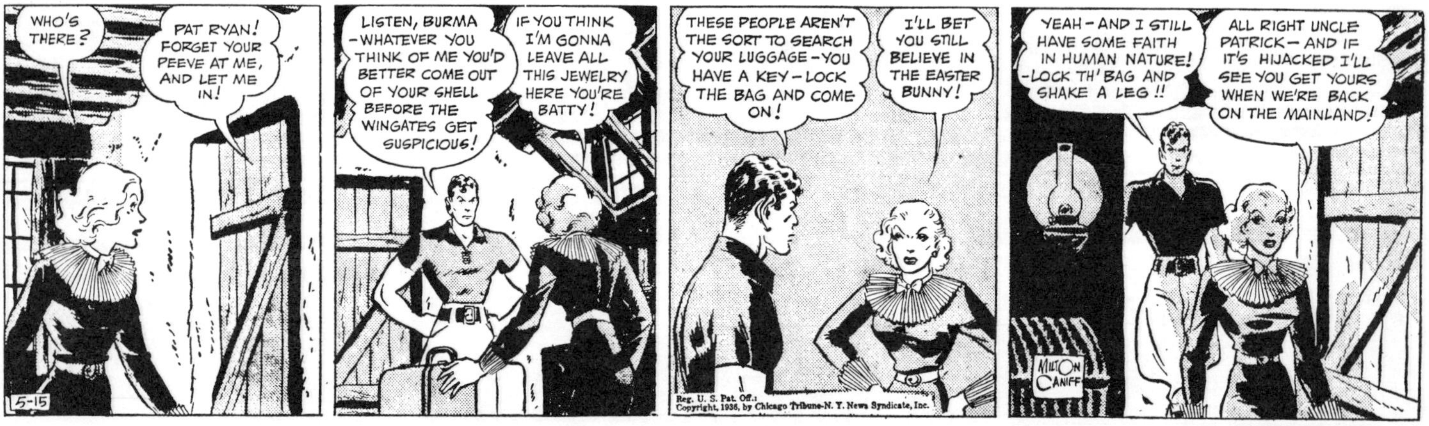
WHO'S THERE?
PAT RYAN! FORGET YOUR PEEVE AT ME, AND LET ME IN!
LISTEN, BURMA -WHATEVER YOU THINK OF ME YOU'D BETTER COME OUT OF YOUR SHELL BEFORE THE WINGATES GET SUSPICIOUS!
IF YOU THINK I'M GONNA LEAVE ALL THIS JEWELRY HERE YOU'RE BATTY!
THESE PEOPLE AREN'T THE SORT TO SEARCH YOUR LUGGAGE-YOU HAVE A KEY-LOCK THE BAG AND COME ON!
I'LL BET YOU STILL BELIEVE IN THE EASTER BUNNY!
YEAH-AND I STILL HAVE SOME FAITH IN HUMAN NATURE! -LOCK TH' BAG AND SHAKE A LEG!!
ALL RIGHT UNCLE PATRICK-AND IF IT'S HIJACKED I'LL SEE YOU GET YOURS WHEN WE'RE BACK ON THE MAINLAND!
5-15
Reg. U. S. Pat. Off.: Copyright, 1936, by Chicago Tribune-N. Y. News Syndicate, Inc.
MILTON CANIFF

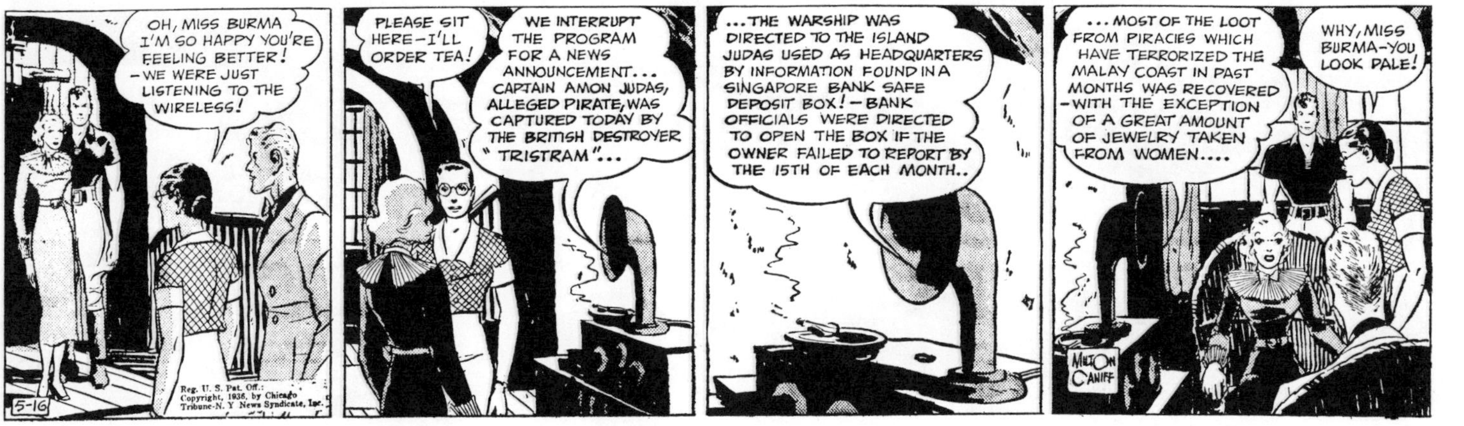
OH, MISS BURMA I'M SO HAPPY YOU'RE FEELING BETTER! -WE WERE JUST LISTENING TO THE WIRELESS!
5-16
Reg. U. S. Pat. Off.: Copyright, 1936, by Chicago Tribune-N. Y. News Syndicate, Inc.
PLEASE SIT HERE-I'LL ORDER TEA!
WE INTERRUPT THE PROGRAM FOR A NEWS ANNOUNCEMENT... CAPTAIN AMON JUDAS, ALLEGED PIRATE, WAS CAPTURED TODAY BY THE BRITISH DESTROYER "TRISTRAM"...
...THE WARSHIP WAS DIRECTED TO THE ISLAND JUDAS USED AS HEADQUARTERS BY INFORMATION FOUND IN A SINGAPORE BANK SAFE DEPOSIT BOX! -BANK OFFICIALS WERE DIRECTED TO OPEN THE BOX IF THE OWNER FAILED TO REPORT BY THE 15TH OF EACH MONTH..
...MOST OF THE LOOT FROM PIRACIES WHICH HAVE TERRORIZED THE MALAY COAST IN PAST MONTHS WAS RECOVERED -WITH THE EXCEPTION OF A GREAT AMOUNT OF JEWELRY TAKEN FROM WOMEN....
WHY, MISS BURMA-YOU LOOK PALE!
MILTON CANIFF

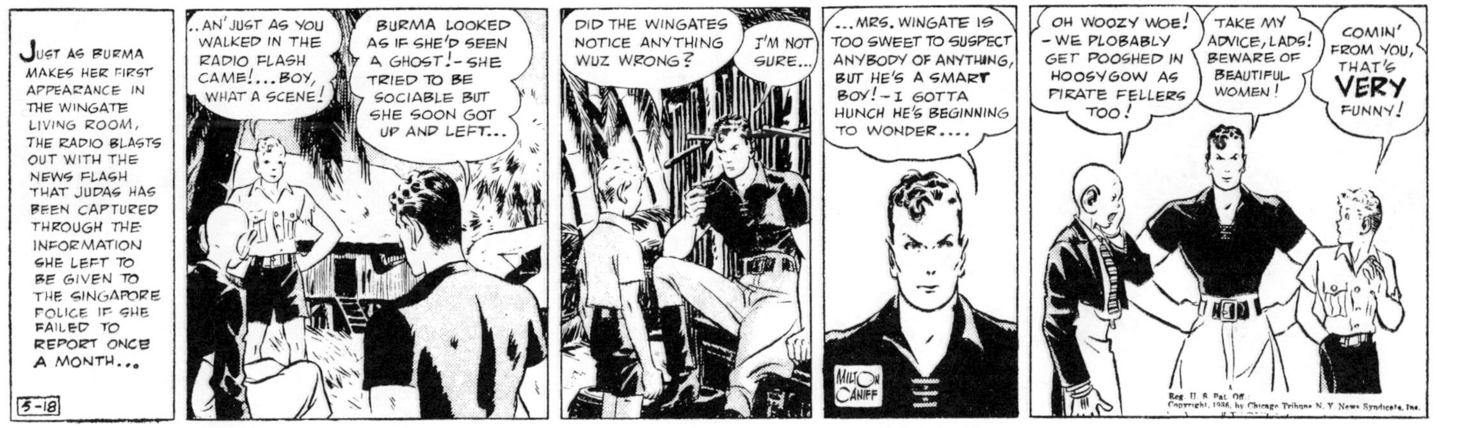
JUST AS BURMA MAKES HER FIRST APPEARANCE IN THE WINGATE LIVING ROOM, THE RADIO BLASTS OUT WITH THE NEWS FLASH THAT JUDAS HAS BEEN CAPTURED THROUGH THE INFORMATION SHE LEFT TO BE GIVEN TO THE SINGAPORE POLICE IF SHE FAILED TO REPORT ONCE A MONTH...
5-18
..AN' JUST AS YOU WALKED IN THE RADIO FLASH CAME!...BOY, WHAT A SCENE!
BURMA LOOKED AS IF SHE'D SEEN A GHOST!-SHE TRIED TO BE SOCIABLE BUT SHE SOON GOT UP AND LEFT...
DID THE WINGATES NOTICE ANYTHING WUZ WRONG?
I'M NOT SURE...
...MRS. WINGATE IS TOO SWEET TO SUSPECT ANYBODY OF ANYTHING, BUT HE'S A SMART BOY!-I GOTTA HUNCH HE'S BEGINNING TO WONDER....
MILTON CANIFF
OH WOOZY WOE! -WE PLOBABLY GET POOSHED IN HOOSYGOW AS PIRATE FELLERS TOO!
TAKE MY ADVICE, LADS! BEWARE OF BEAUTIFUL WOMEN!
COMIN' FROM YOU, THAT'S VERY FUNNY!
Reg. U. S. Pat. Off. Copyright, 1936, by Chicago Tribune N. Y. News Syndicate, Inc.

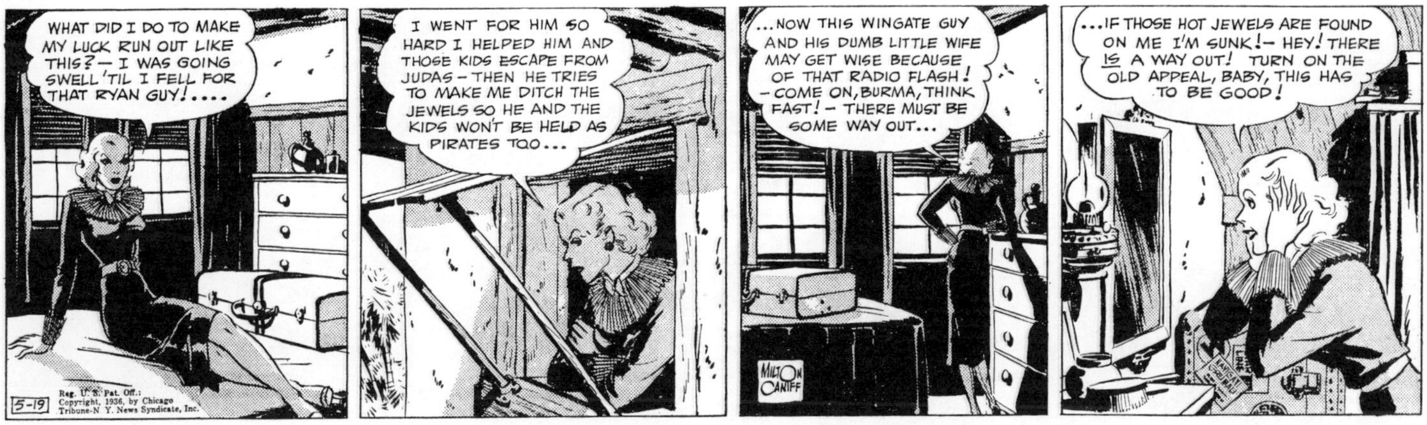
WHAT DID I DO TO MAKE MY LUCK RUN OUT LIKE THIS?-I WAS GOING SWELL 'TIL I FELL FOR THAT RYAN GUY!....
5-19
Reg. U. S. Pat. Off.: Copyright, 1936, by Chicago Tribune-N. Y. News Syndicate, Inc.
I WENT FOR HIM SO HARD I HELPED HIM AND THOSE KIDS ESCAPE FROM JUDAS-THEN HE TRIES TO MAKE ME DITCH THE JEWELS SO HE AND THE KIDS WON'T BE HELD AS PIRATES TOO...
...NOW THIS WINGATE GUY AND HIS DUMB LITTLE WIFE MAY GET WISE BECAUSE OF THAT RADIO FLASH! -COME ON, BURMA, THINK FAST! -THERE MUST BE SOME WAY OUT...
MILTON CANIFF
...IF THOSE HOT JEWELS ARE FOUND ON ME I'M SUNK!-HEY! THERE IS A WAY OUT! TURN ON THE OLD APPEAL, BABY, THIS HAS TO BE GOOD!

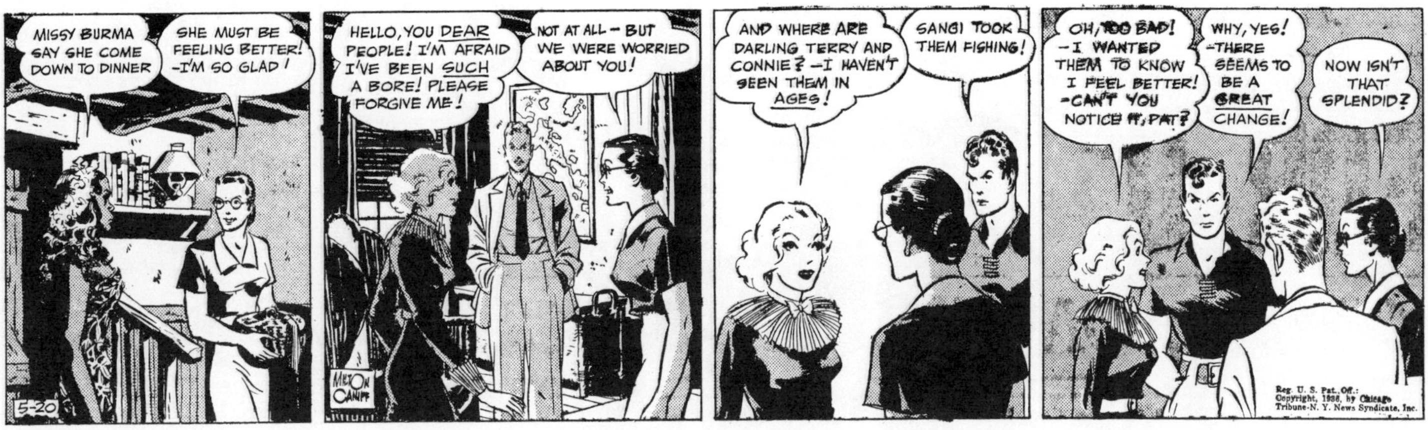
MISSY BURMA SAY SHE COME DOWN TO DINNER
SHE MUST BE FEELING BETTER! -I'M SO GLAD!
5-20
HELLO, YOU DEAR PEOPLE! I'M AFRAID I'VE BEEN SUCH A BORE! PLEASE FORGIVE ME!
NOT AT ALL-BUT WE WERE WORRIED ABOUT YOU!
MILTON CANIFF
AND WHERE ARE DARLING TERRY AND CONNIE?-I HAVEN'T SEEN THEM IN AGES!
SANGI TOOK THEM FISHING!
OH, TOO BAD! -I WANTED THEM TO KNOW I FEEL BETTER! -CAN'T YOU NOTICE IT, PAT?
WHY, YES! -THERE SEEMS TO BE A GREAT CHANGE!
NOW ISN'T THAT SPLENDID?
Reg. U. S. Pat. Off.: Copyright, 1936, by Chicago Tribune-N. Y. News Syndicate, Inc.

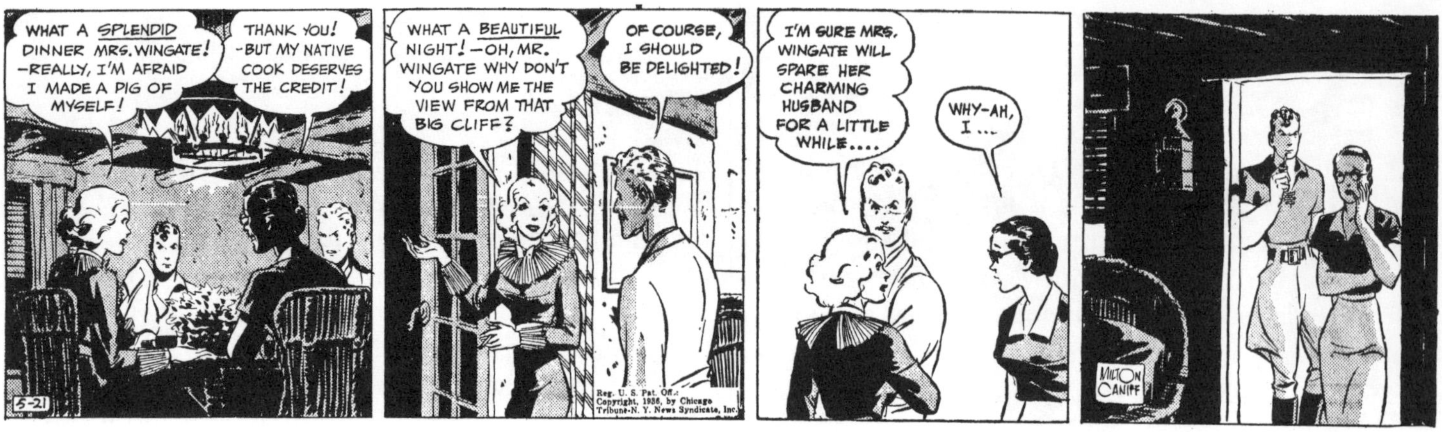
5-21
WHAT A SPLENDID DINNER MRS. WINGATE! —REALLY, I'M AFRAID I MADE A PIG OF MYSELF!
THANK YOU! —BUT MY NATIVE COOK DESERVES THE CREDIT!
WHAT A BEAUTIFUL NIGHT! —OH, MR. WINGATE WHY DON'T YOU SHOW ME THE VIEW FROM THAT BIG CLIFF?
OF COURSE, I SHOULD BE DELIGHTED!
Reg. U. S. Pat. Off.: Copyright, 1936, by Chicago Tribune-N. Y. News Syndicate, Inc.
I'M SURE MRS. WINGATE WILL SPARE HER CHARMING HUSBAND FOR A LITTLE WHILE....
WHY-AH, I...
MILTON CANIFF

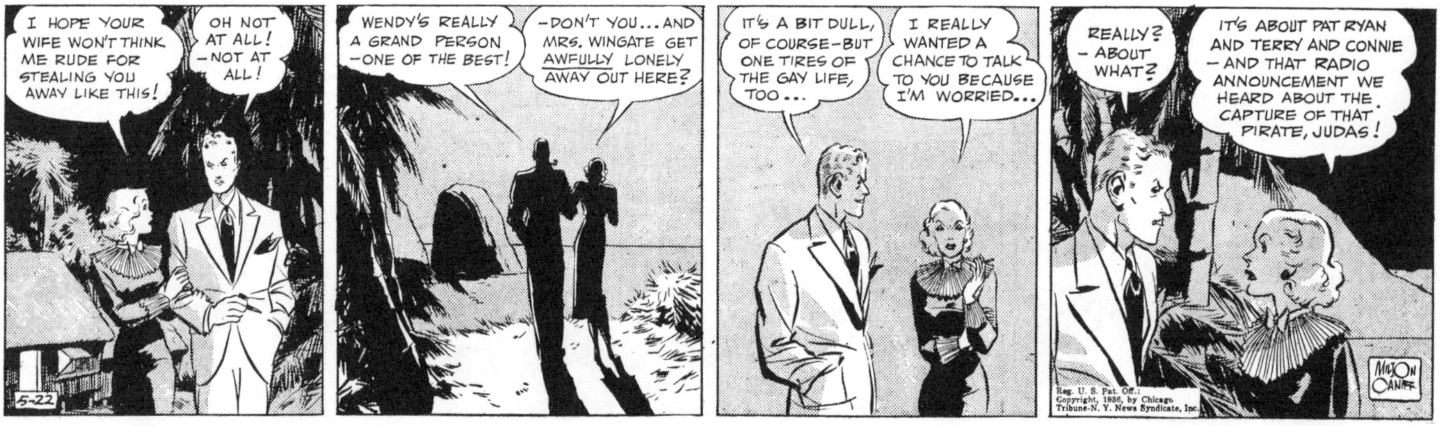
5-22
I HOPE YOUR WIFE WON'T THINK ME RUDE FOR STEALING YOU AWAY LIKE THIS!
OH NOT AT ALL! —NOT AT ALL!
WENDY'S REALLY A GRAND PERSON —ONE OF THE BEST!
—DON'T YOU... AND MRS. WINGATE GET AWFULLY LONELY AWAY OUT HERE?
IT'S A BIT DULL, OF COURSE—BUT ONE TIRES OF THE GAY LIFE, TOO...
I REALLY WANTED A CHANCE TO TALK TO YOU BECAUSE I'M WORRIED...
REALLY? —ABOUT WHAT?
IT'S ABOUT PAT RYAN AND TERRY AND CONNIE —AND THAT RADIO ANNOUNCEMENT WE HEARD ABOUT THE CAPTURE OF THAT PIRATE, JUDAS!
Reg. U. S. Pat. Off.: Copyright, 1936, by Chicago Tribune-N. Y. News Syndicate, Inc.
MILTON CANIFF

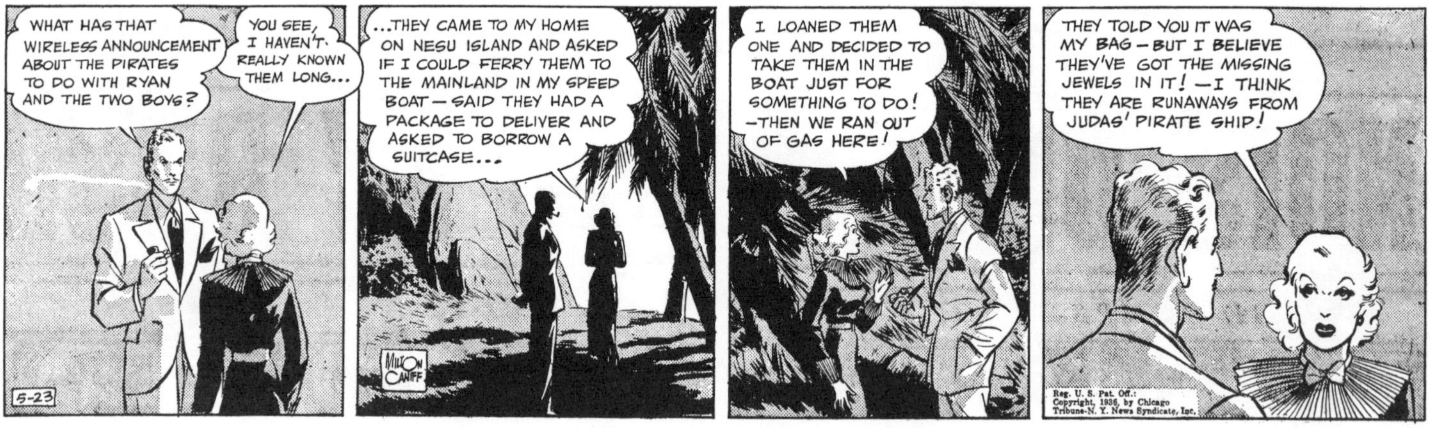
5-23
WHAT HAS THAT WIRELESS ANNOUNCEMENT ABOUT THE PIRATES TO DO WITH RYAN AND THE TWO BOYS?
YOU SEE, I HAVEN'T REALLY KNOWN THEM LONG...
...THEY CAME TO MY HOME ON NESU ISLAND AND ASKED IF I COULD FERRY THEM TO THE MAINLAND IN MY SPEED BOAT—SAID THEY HAD A PACKAGE TO DELIVER AND ASKED TO BORROW A SUITCASE...
MILTON CANIFF
I LOANED THEM ONE AND DECIDED TO TAKE THEM IN THE BOAT JUST FOR SOMETHING TO DO! —THEN WE RAN OUT OF GAS HERE!
THEY TOLD YOU IT WAS MY BAG—BUT I BELIEVE THEY'VE GOT THE MISSING JEWELS IN IT! —I THINK THEY ARE RUNAWAYS FROM JUDAS' PIRATE SHIP!
Reg. U. S. Pat. Off.: Copyright, 1936, by Chicago Tribune-N. Y. News Syndicate, Inc.

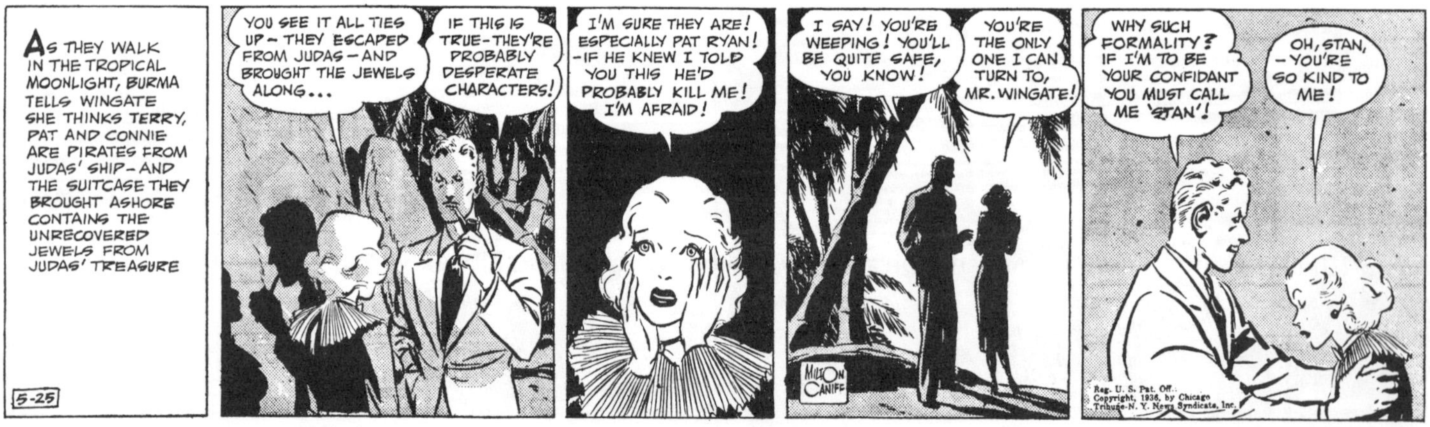
AS THEY WALK IN THE TROPICAL MOONLIGHT, BURMA TELLS WINGATE SHE THINKS TERRY, PAT AND CONNIE ARE PIRATES FROM JUDAS' SHIP—AND THE SUITCASE THEY BROUGHT ASHORE CONTAINS THE UNRECOVERED JEWELS FROM JUDAS' TREASURE
5-25
YOU SEE IT ALL TIES UP—THEY ESCAPED FROM JUDAS—AND BROUGHT THE JEWELS ALONG...
IF THIS IS TRUE—THEY'RE PROBABLY DESPERATE CHARACTERS!
I'M SURE THEY ARE! ESPECIALLY PAT RYAN! —IF HE KNEW I TOLD YOU THIS HE'D PROBABLY KILL ME! I'M AFRAID!
I SAY! YOU'RE WEEPING! YOU'LL BE QUITE SAFE, YOU KNOW!
YOU'RE THE ONLY ONE I CAN TURN TO, MR. WINGATE!
MILTON CANIFF
WHY SUCH FORMALITY? IF I'M TO BE YOUR CONFIDANT YOU MUST CALL ME 'STAN'!
OH, STAN, —YOU'RE SO KIND TO ME!
Reg. U. S. Pat. Off.: Copyright, 1936, by Chicago Tribune-N. Y. News Syndicate, Inc.

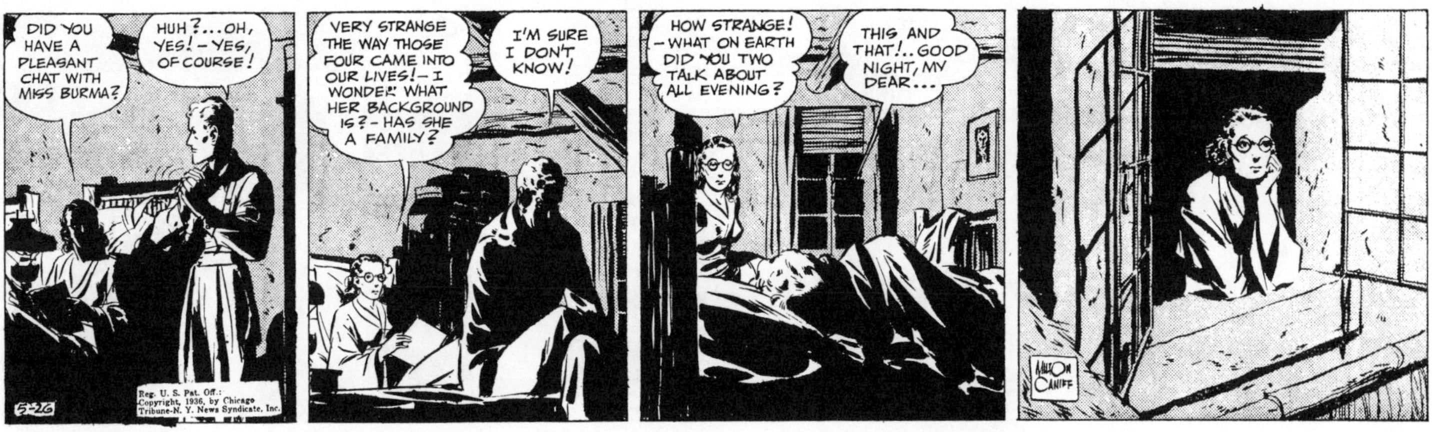
DID YOU HAVE A PLEASANT CHAT WITH MISS BURMA?
HUH?...OH, YES! – YES, OF COURSE!
5-26
Reg. U. S. Pat. Off.: Copyright, 1936, by Chicago Tribune-N. Y. News Syndicate, Inc.
VERY STRANGE THE WAY THOSE FOUR CAME INTO OUR LIVES! – I WONDER WHAT HER BACKGROUND IS? – HAS SHE A FAMILY?
I'M SURE I DON'T KNOW!
HOW STRANGE! – WHAT ON EARTH DID YOU TWO TALK ABOUT ALL EVENING?
THIS AND THAT!.. GOOD NIGHT, MY DEAR...
MILTON CANIFF

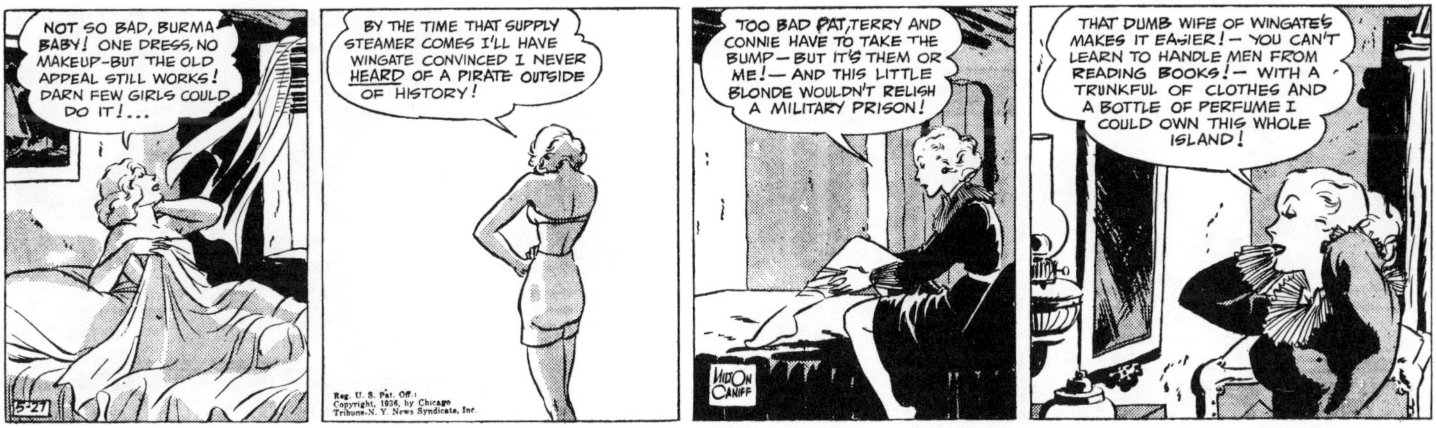
NOT SO BAD, BURMA BABY! ONE DRESS, NO MAKEUP – BUT THE OLD APPEAL STILL WORKS! DARN FEW GIRLS COULD DO IT!...
5-27
BY THE TIME THAT SUPPLY STEAMER COMES I'LL HAVE WINGATE CONVINCED I NEVER HEARD OF A PIRATE OUTSIDE OF HISTORY!
Reg. U. S. Pat. Off.: Copyright, 1936, by Chicago Tribune-N. Y. News Syndicate, Inc.
TOO BAD PAT, TERRY AND CONNIE HAVE TO TAKE THE BUMP – BUT IT'S THEM OR ME! – AND THIS LITTLE BLONDE WOULDN'T RELISH A MILITARY PRISON!
MILTON CANIFF
THAT DUMB WIFE OF WINGATE'S MAKES IT EASIER! – YOU CAN'T LEARN TO HANDLE MEN FROM READING BOOKS! – WITH A TRUNKFUL OF CLOTHES AND A BOTTLE OF PERFUME I COULD OWN THIS WHOLE ISLAND!

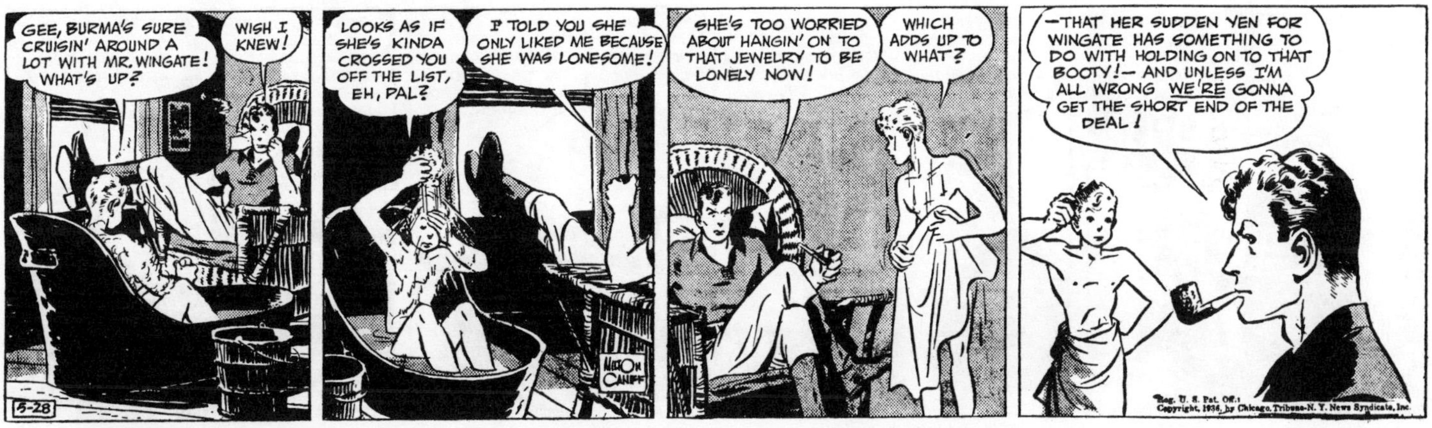
GEE, BURMA'S SURE CRUISIN' AROUND A LOT WITH MR. WINGATE! WHAT'S UP?
WISH I KNEW!
5-28
LOOKS AS IF SHE'S KINDA CROSSED YOU OFF THE LIST, EH, PAL?
I TOLD YOU SHE ONLY LIKED ME BECAUSE SHE WAS LONESOME!
MILTON CANIFF
SHE'S TOO WORRIED ABOUT HANGIN' ON TO THAT JEWELRY TO BE LONELY NOW!
WHICH ADDS UP TO WHAT?
– THAT HER SUDDEN YEN FOR WINGATE HAS SOMETHING TO DO WITH HOLDING ON TO THAT BOOTY! – AND UNLESS I'M ALL WRONG WE'RE GONNA GET THE SHORT END OF THE DEAL!
Reg. U. S. Pat. Off.: Copyright, 1936, by Chicago Tribune-N. Y. News Syndicate, Inc.

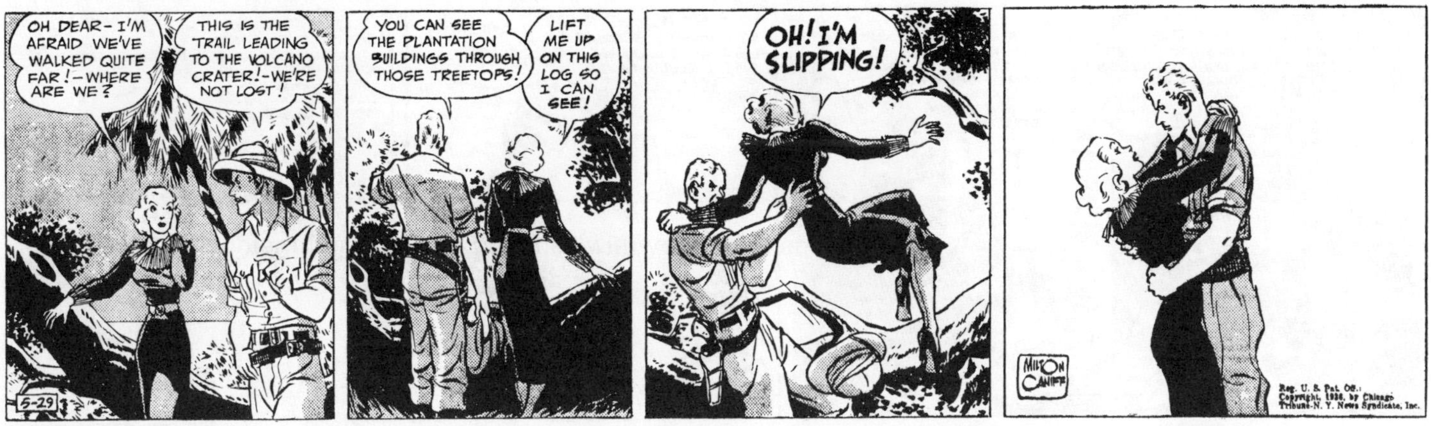
OH DEAR – I'M AFRAID WE'VE WALKED QUITE FAR! – WHERE ARE WE?
THIS IS THE TRAIL LEADING TO THE VOLCANO CRATER! – WE'RE NOT LOST!
5-29
YOU CAN SEE THE PLANTATION BUILDINGS THROUGH THOSE TREETOPS!
LIFT ME UP ON THIS LOG SO I CAN SEE!
OH! I'M SLIPPING!
MILTON CANIFF
Reg. U. S. Pat. Off.: Copyright, 1936, by Chicago Tribune-N. Y. News Syndicate, Inc.

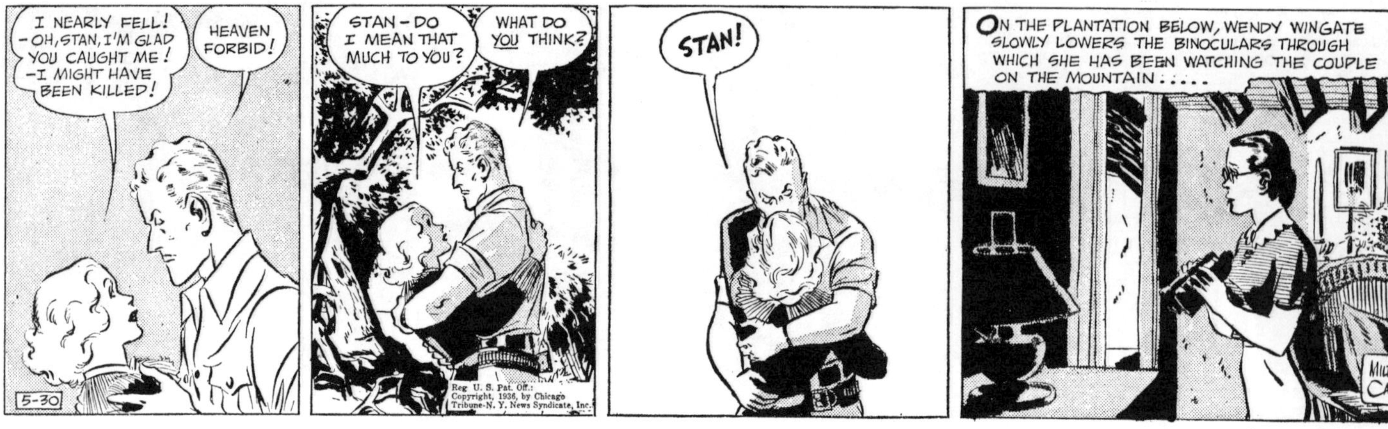
I NEARLY FELL! -OH, STAN, I'M GLAD YOU CAUGHT ME! -I MIGHT HAVE BEEN KILLED!
HEAVEN FORBID!
5-30
STAN-DO I MEAN THAT MUCH TO YOU?
WHAT DO YOU THINK?
Reg. U. S. Pat. Off.: Copyright, 1936, by Chicago Tribune-N. Y. News Syndicate, Inc.
STAN!
ON THE PLANTATION BELOW, WENDY WINGATE SLOWLY LOWERS THE BINOCULARS THROUGH WHICH SHE HAS BEEN WATCHING THE COUPLE ON THE MOUNTAIN.....
MILTON CANIFF

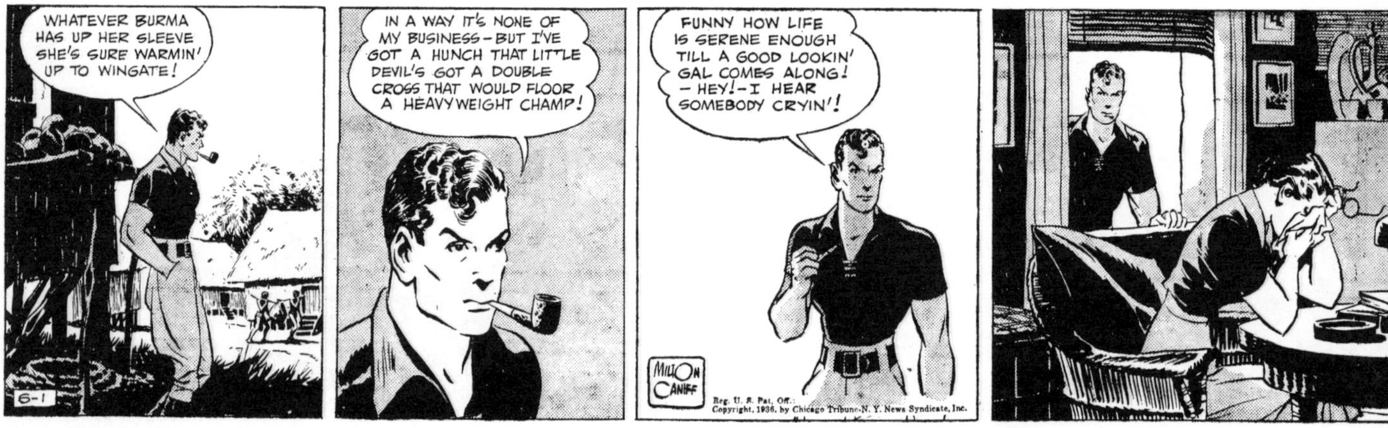
WHATEVER BURMA HAS UP HER SLEEVE SHE'S SURE WARMIN' UP TO WINGATE!
6-1
IN A WAY IT'S NONE OF MY BUSINESS-BUT I'VE GOT A HUNCH THAT LITTLE DEVIL'S GOT A DOUBLE CROSS THAT WOULD FLOOR A HEAVYWEIGHT CHAMP!
FUNNY HOW LIFE IS SERENE ENOUGH TILL A GOOD LOOKIN' GAL COMES ALONG! -HEY!-I HEAR SOMEBODY CRYIN'!
MILTON CANIFF
Reg. U. S. Pat. Off.: Copyright, 1936, by Chicago Tribune-N. Y. News Syndicate, Inc.

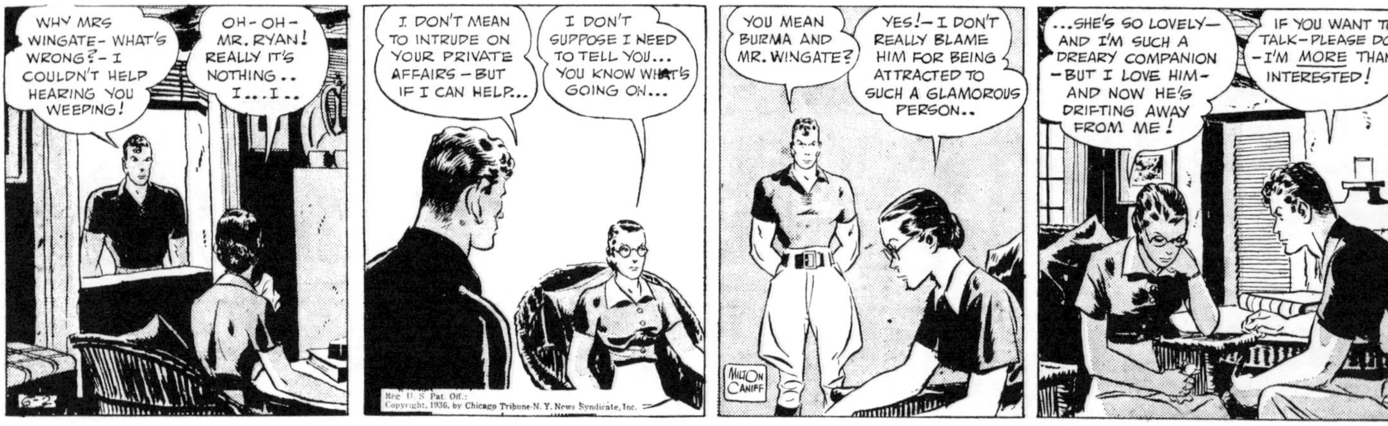
WHY MRS WINGATE- WHAT'S WRONG?-I COULDN'T HELP HEARING YOU WEEPING!
OH-OH- MR. RYAN! REALLY IT'S NOTHING.. I...I...
6-2
I DON'T MEAN TO INTRUDE ON YOUR PRIVATE AFFAIRS-BUT IF I CAN HELP...
I DON'T SUPPOSE I NEED TO TELL YOU... YOU KNOW WHAT'S GOING ON...
Reg. U. S. Pat. Off.: Copyright, 1936, by Chicago Tribune-N. Y. News Syndicate, Inc.
YOU MEAN BURMA AND MR. WINGATE?
YES!-I DON'T REALLY BLAME HIM FOR BEING ATTRACTED TO SUCH A GLAMOROUS PERSON..
MILTON CANIFF
...SHE'S SO LOVELY- AND I'M SUCH A DREARY COMPANION -BUT I LOVE HIM- AND NOW HE'S DRIFTING AWAY FROM ME!
IF YOU WANT TO TALK-PLEASE DO! -I'M MORE THAN INTERESTED!

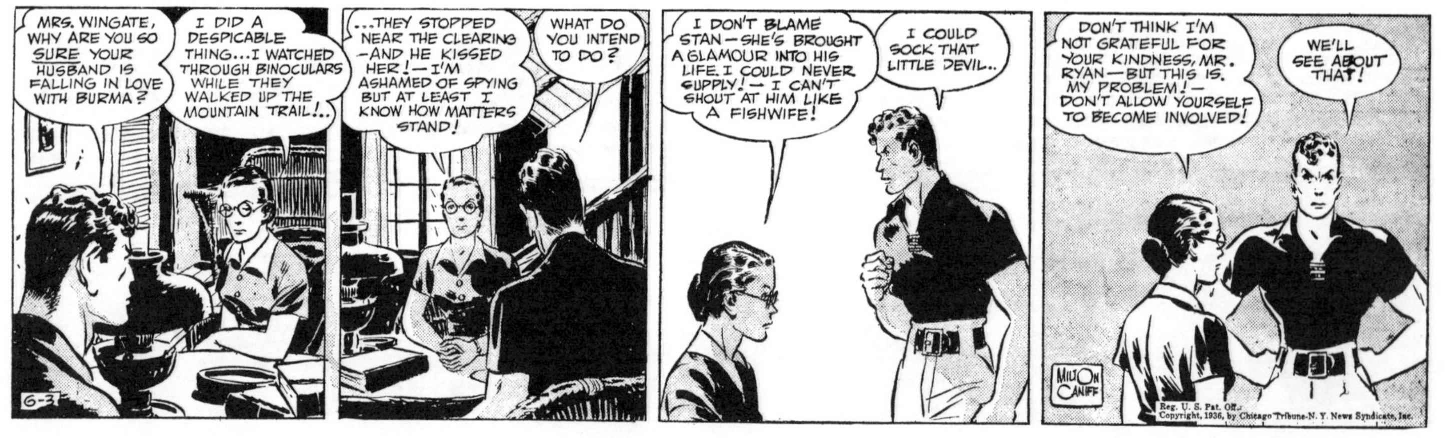
MRS. WINGATE, WHY ARE YOU SO SURE YOUR HUSBAND IS FALLING IN LOVE WITH BURMA?
I DID A DESPICABLE THING...I WATCHED THROUGH BINOCULARS WHILE THEY WALKED UP THE MOUNTAIN TRAIL!..
6-3
...THEY STOPPED NEAR THE CLEARING -AND HE KISSED HER!-I'M ASHAMED OF SPYING BUT AT LEAST I KNOW HOW MATTERS STAND!
WHAT DO YOU INTEND TO DO?
I DON'T BLAME STAN-SHE'S BROUGHT A GLAMOUR INTO HIS LIFE. I COULD NEVER SUPPLY!-I CAN'T SHOUT AT HIM LIKE A FISHWIFE!
I COULD SOCK THAT LITTLE DEVIL..
DON'T THINK I'M NOT GRATEFUL FOR YOUR KINDNESS, MR. RYAN-BUT THIS IS MY PROBLEM!- DON'T ALLOW YOURSELF TO BECOME INVOLVED!
WE'LL SEE ABOUT THAT!
MILTON CANIFF
Reg. U. S. Pat. Off.: Copyright, 1936, by Chicago Tribune-N. Y. News Syndicate, Inc.

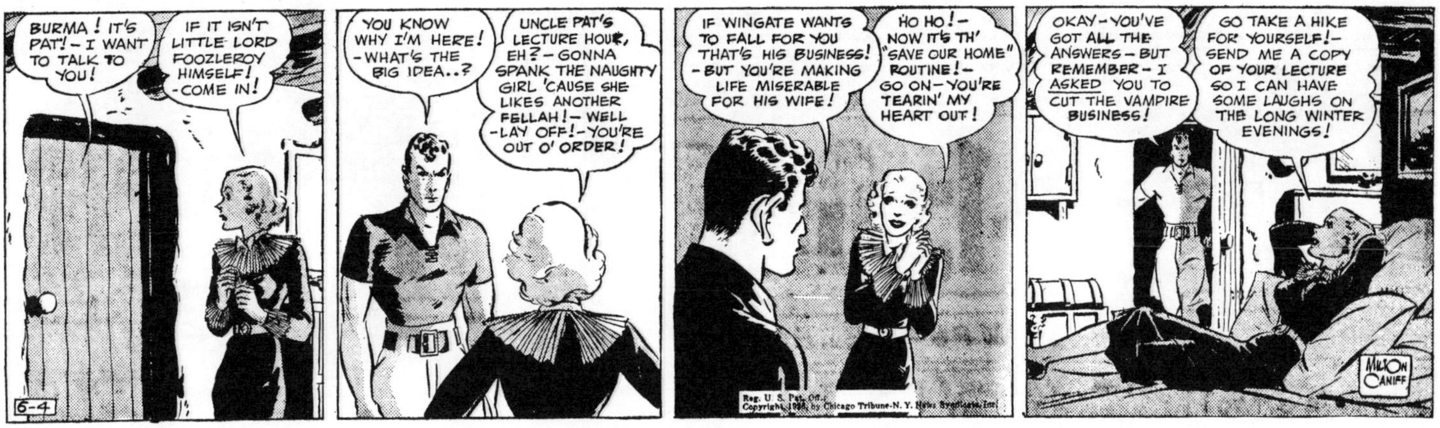
6-4
BURMA! IT'S PAT! – I WANT TO TALK TO YOU!
IF IT ISN'T LITTLE LORD FOOZLEROY HIMSELF! – COME IN!
YOU KNOW WHY I'M HERE! – WHAT'S THE BIG IDEA..?
UNCLE PAT'S LECTURE HOUR, EH? – GONNA SPANK THE NAUGHTY GIRL 'CAUSE SHE LIKES ANOTHER FELLAH! – WELL – LAY OFF! – YOU'RE OUT O' ORDER!
IF WINGATE WANTS TO FALL FOR YOU THAT'S HIS BUSINESS! – BUT YOU'RE MAKING LIFE MISERABLE FOR HIS WIFE!
HO HO! – NOW IT'S TH' "SAVE OUR HOME" ROUTINE! – GO ON – YOU'RE TEARIN' MY HEART OUT!
Reg. U. S. Pat. Off.: Copyright, 1936, by Chicago Tribune-N. Y. News Syndicate, Inc.
OKAY – YOU'VE GOT ALL THE ANSWERS – BUT REMEMBER – I ASKED YOU TO CUT THE VAMPIRE BUSINESS!
GO TAKE A HIKE FOR YOURSELF! – SEND ME A COPY OF YOUR LECTURE SO I CAN HAVE SOME LAUGHS ON THE LONG WINTER EVENINGS!
MILTON CANIFF

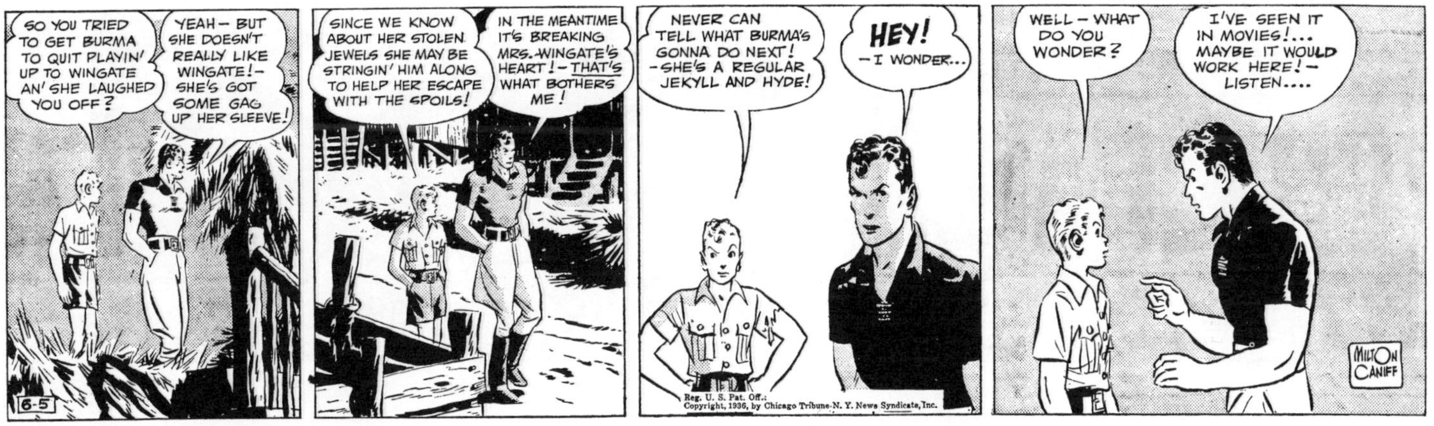
6-5
SO YOU TRIED TO GET BURMA TO QUIT PLAYIN' UP TO WINGATE AN' SHE LAUGHED YOU OFF?
YEAH – BUT SHE DOESN'T REALLY LIKE WINGATE! – SHE'S GOT SOME GAG UP HER SLEEVE!
SINCE WE KNOW ABOUT HER STOLEN JEWELS SHE MAY BE STRINGIN' HIM ALONG TO HELP HER ESCAPE WITH THE SPOILS!
IN THE MEANTIME IT'S BREAKING MRS. WINGATE'S HEART! – THAT'S WHAT BOTHERS ME!
NEVER CAN TELL WHAT BURMA'S GONNA DO NEXT! – SHE'S A REGULAR JEKYLL AND HYDE!
HEY! – I WONDER...
Reg. U. S. Pat. Off.: Copyright, 1936, by Chicago Tribune-N. Y. News Syndicate, Inc.
WELL – WHAT DO YOU WONDER?
I'VE SEEN IT IN MOVIES!... MAYBE IT WOULD WORK HERE! – LISTEN....
MILTON CANIFF

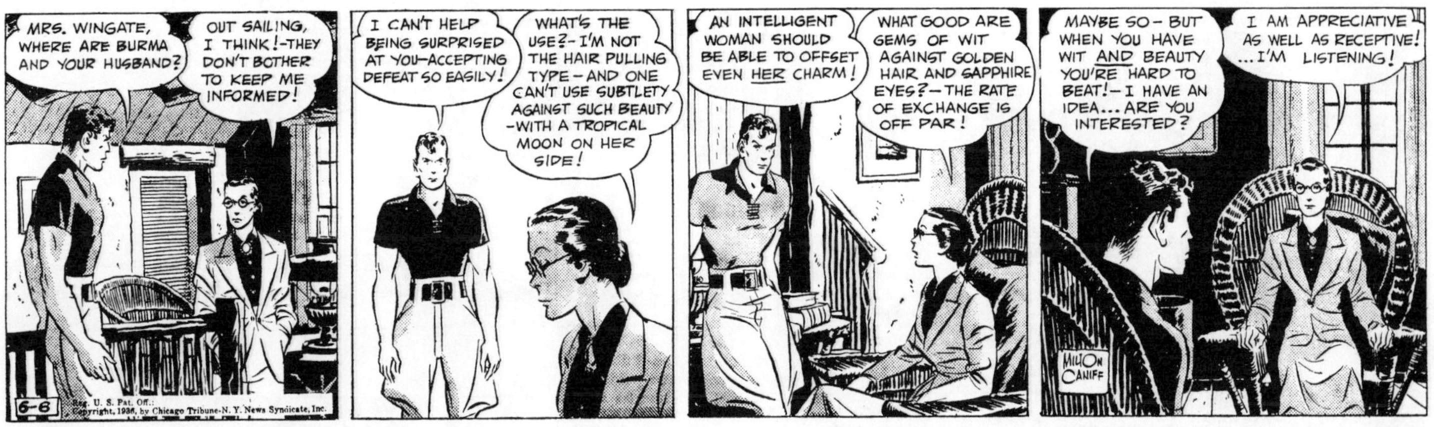
MRS. WINGATE, WHERE ARE BURMA AND YOUR HUSBAND?
OUT SAILING, I THINK! – THEY DON'T BOTHER TO KEEP ME INFORMED!
6-8
Reg. U. S. Pat. Off.: Copyright, 1936, by Chicago Tribune-N. Y. News Syndicate, Inc.
I CAN'T HELP BEING SURPRISED AT YOU – ACCEPTING DEFEAT SO EASILY!
WHAT'S THE USE? – I'M NOT THE HAIR PULLING TYPE – AND ONE CAN'T USE SUBTLETY AGAINST SUCH BEAUTY – WITH A TROPICAL MOON ON HER SIDE!
AN INTELLIGENT WOMAN SHOULD BE ABLE TO OFFSET EVEN HER CHARM!
WHAT GOOD ARE GEMS OF WIT AGAINST GOLDEN HAIR AND SAPPHIRE EYES? – THE RATE OF EXCHANGE IS OFF PAR!
MILTON CANIFF
MAYBE SO – BUT WHEN YOU HAVE WIT AND BEAUTY YOU'RE HARD TO BEAT! – I HAVE AN IDEA... ARE YOU INTERESTED?
I AM APPRECIATIVE AS WELL AS RECEPTIVE! ...I'M LISTENING!

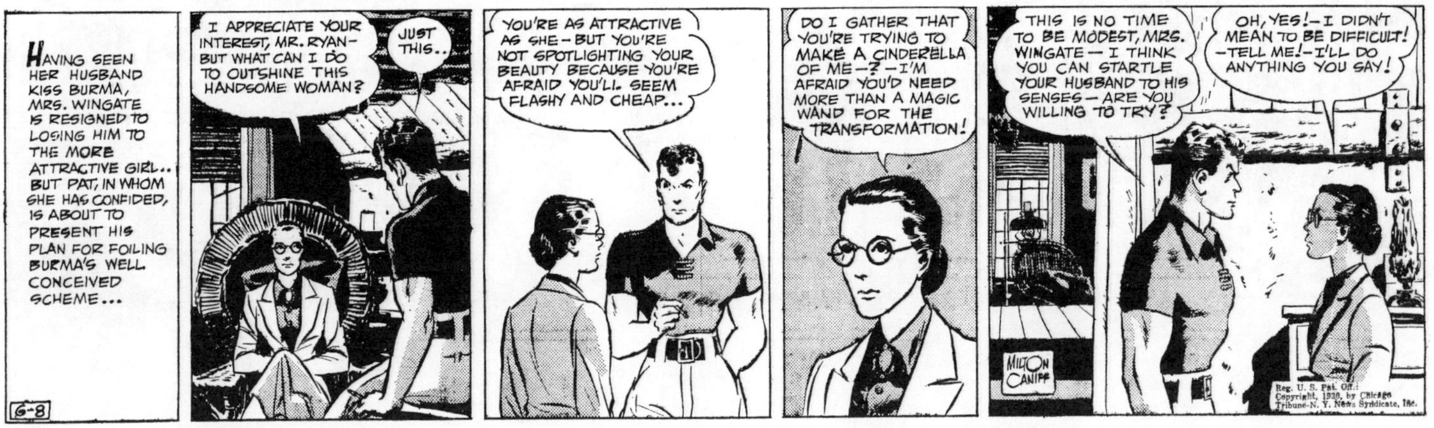
HAVING SEEN HER HUSBAND KISS BURMA, MRS. WINGATE IS RESIGNED TO LOSING HIM TO THE MORE ATTRACTIVE GIRL.. BUT PAT, IN WHOM SHE HAS CONFIDED, IS ABOUT TO PRESENT HIS PLAN FOR FOILING BURMA'S WELL CONCEIVED SCHEME...
6-8
I APPRECIATE YOUR INTEREST, MR. RYAN – BUT WHAT CAN I DO TO OUTSHINE THIS HANDSOME WOMAN?
JUST THIS..
YOU'RE AS ATTRACTIVE AS SHE – BUT YOU'RE NOT SPOTLIGHTING YOUR BEAUTY BECAUSE YOU'RE AFRAID YOU'LL SEEM FLASHY AND CHEAP...
DO I GATHER THAT YOU'RE TRYING TO MAKE A CINDERELLA OF ME – ? – I'M AFRAID YOU'D NEED MORE THAN A MAGIC WAND FOR THE TRANSFORMATION!
MILTON CANIFF
THIS IS NO TIME TO BE MODEST, MRS. WINGATE – I THINK YOU CAN STARTLE YOUR HUSBAND TO HIS SENSES – ARE YOU WILLING TO TRY?
OH, YES! – I DIDN'T MEAN TO BE DIFFICULT! – TELL ME! – I'LL DO ANYTHING YOU SAY!
Reg. U. S. Pat. Off.: Copyright, 1936, by Chicago Tribune-N. Y. News Syndicate, Inc.

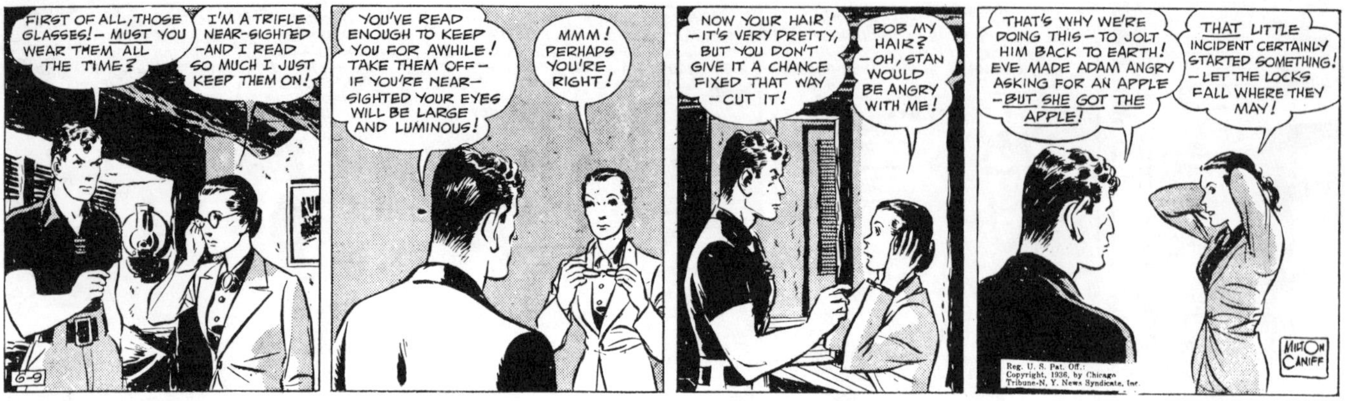

6-9
FIRST OF ALL, THOSE GLASSES! – MUST YOU WEAR THEM ALL THE TIME?
I'M A TRIFLE NEAR-SIGHTED – AND I READ SO MUCH I JUST KEEP THEM ON!
YOU'VE READ ENOUGH TO KEEP YOU FOR AWHILE! TAKE THEM OFF – IF YOU'RE NEAR-SIGHTED YOUR EYES WILL BE LARGE AND LUMINOUS!
MMM! PERHAPS YOU'RE RIGHT!
NOW YOUR HAIR! – IT'S VERY PRETTY, BUT YOU DON'T GIVE IT A CHANCE FIXED THAT WAY – CUT IT!
BOB MY HAIR? – OH, STAN WOULD BE ANGRY WITH ME!
THAT'S WHY WE'RE DOING THIS – TO JOLT HIM BACK TO EARTH! EVE MADE ADAM ANGRY ASKING FOR AN APPLE – BUT SHE GOT THE APPLE!
THAT LITTLE INCIDENT CERTAINLY STARTED SOMETHING! – LET THE LOCKS FALL WHERE THEY MAY!
Reg. U. S. Pat. Off.; Copyright, 1936, by Chicago Tribune-N. Y. News Syndicate, Inc.
MILTON CANIFF

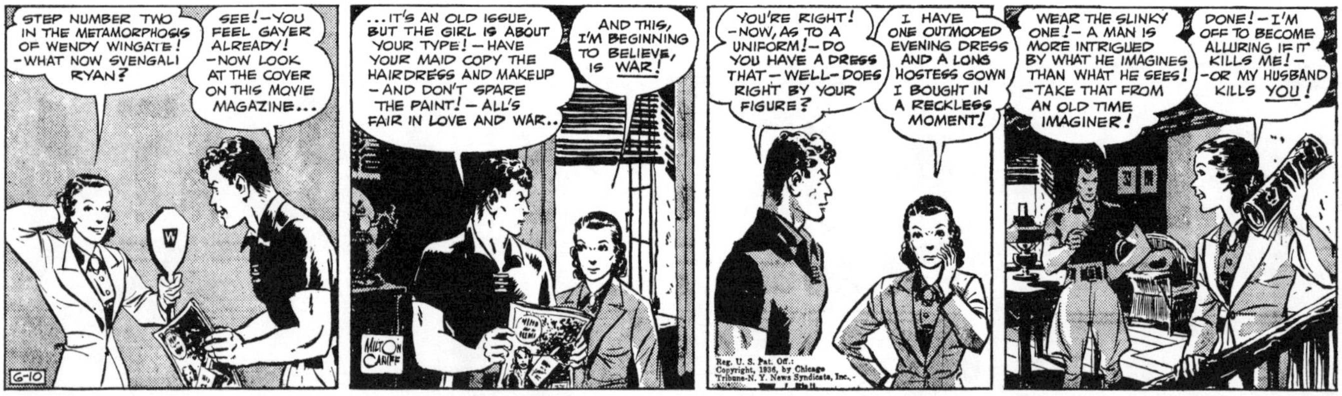

6-10
STEP NUMBER TWO IN THE METAMORPHOSIS OF WENDY WINGATE! – WHAT NOW SVENGALI RYAN?
SEE! – YOU FEEL GAYER ALREADY! – NOW LOOK AT THE COVER ON THIS MOVIE MAGAZINE...
...IT'S AN OLD ISSUE, BUT THE GIRL IS ABOUT YOUR TYPE! – HAVE YOUR MAID COPY THE HAIRDRESS AND MAKEUP – AND DON'T SPARE THE PAINT! – ALL'S FAIR IN LOVE AND WAR..
AND THIS, I'M BEGINNING TO BELIEVE, IS WAR!
MILTON CANIFF
YOU'RE RIGHT! – NOW, AS TO A UNIFORM! – DO YOU HAVE A DRESS THAT – WELL – DOES RIGHT BY YOUR FIGURE?
I HAVE ONE OUTMODED EVENING DRESS AND A LONG HOSTESS GOWN I BOUGHT IN A RECKLESS MOMENT!
Reg. U. S. Pat. Off.; Copyright, 1936, by Chicago Tribune-N. Y. News Syndicate, Inc.
WEAR THE SLINKY ONE! – A MAN IS MORE INTRIGUED BY WHAT HE IMAGINES THAN WHAT HE SEES! – TAKE THAT FROM AN OLD TIME IMAGINER!
DONE! – I'M OFF TO BECOME ALLURING IF IT KILLS ME! – OR MY HUSBAND KILLS YOU!

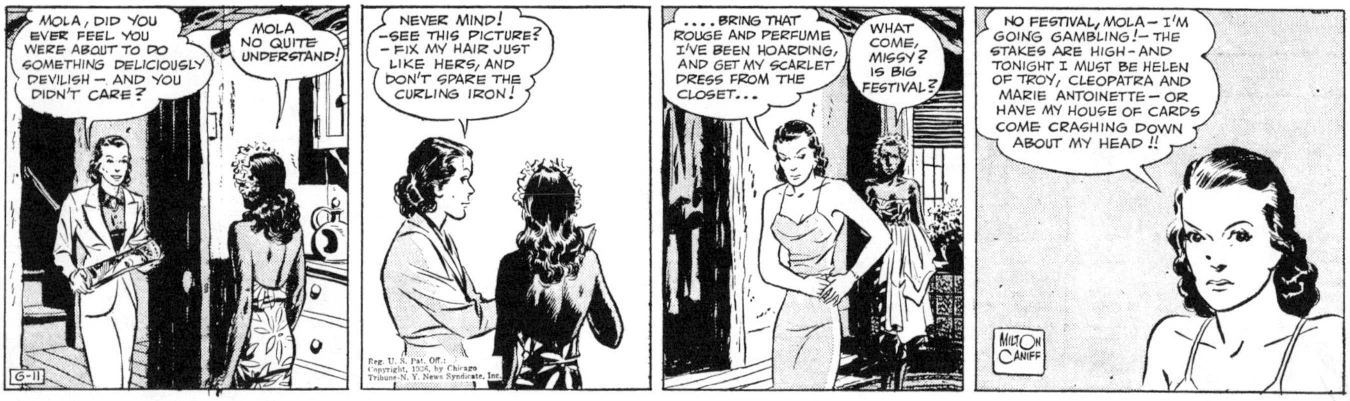

6-11
MOLA, DID YOU EVER FEEL YOU WERE ABOUT TO DO SOMETHING DELICIOUSLY DEVILISH – AND YOU DIDN'T CARE?
MOLA NO QUITE UNDERSTAND!
NEVER MIND! – SEE THIS PICTURE? – FIX MY HAIR JUST LIKE HERS, AND DON'T SPARE THE CURLING IRON!
Reg. U. S. Pat. Off.; Copyright, 1936, by Chicago Tribune-N. Y. News Syndicate, Inc.
....BRING THAT ROUGE AND PERFUME I'VE BEEN HOARDING, AND GET MY SCARLET DRESS FROM THE CLOSET...
WHAT COME, MISSY? IS BIG FESTIVAL?
NO FESTIVAL, MOLA – I'M GOING GAMBLING! – THE STAKES ARE HIGH – AND TONIGHT I MUST BE HELEN OF TROY, CLEOPATRA AND MARIE ANTOINETTE – OR HAVE MY HOUSE OF CARDS COME CRASHING DOWN ABOUT MY HEAD!!
MILTON CANIFF

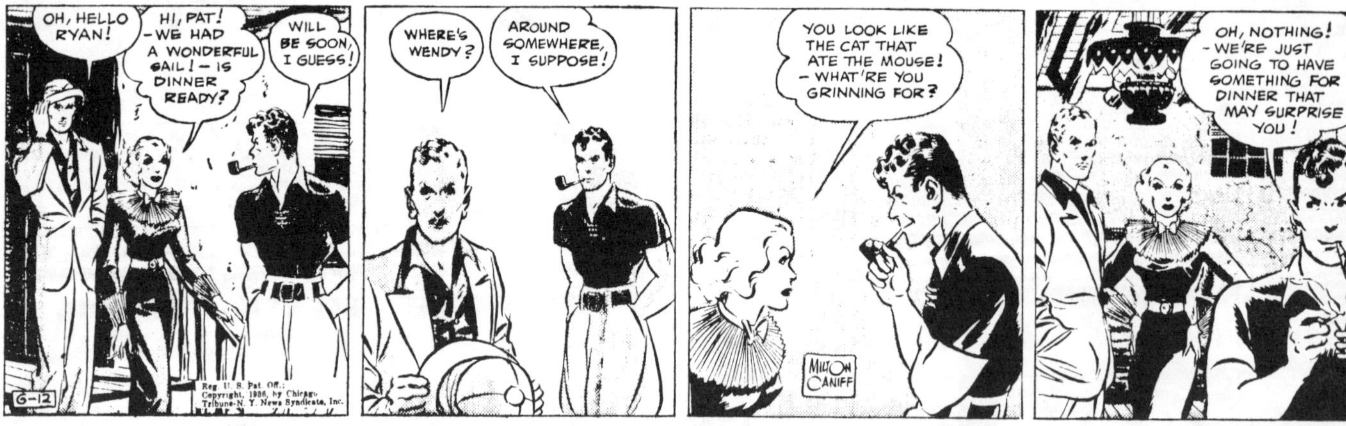

6-12
OH, HELLO RYAN!
HI, PAT! – WE HAD A WONDERFUL SAIL! – IS DINNER READY?
WILL BE SOON, I GUESS!
Reg. U. S. Pat. Off.; Copyright, 1936, by Chicago Tribune-N. Y. News Syndicate, Inc.
WHERE'S WENDY?
AROUND SOMEWHERE, I SUPPOSE!
YOU LOOK LIKE THE CAT THAT ATE THE MOUSE! – WHAT'RE YOU GRINNING FOR?
MILTON CANIFF
OH, NOTHING! – WE'RE JUST GOING TO HAVE SOMETHING FOR DINNER THAT MAY SURPRISE YOU!

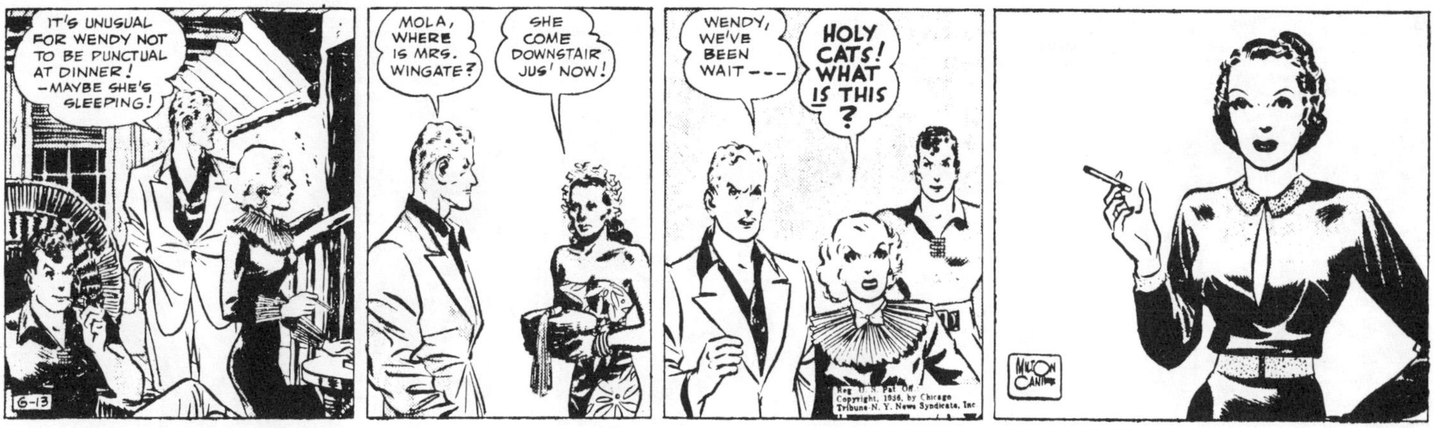
6-13
IT'S UNUSUAL FOR WENDY NOT TO BE PUNCTUAL AT DINNER! —MAYBE SHE'S SLEEPING!
MOLA, WHERE IS MRS. WINGATE?
SHE COME DOWNSTAIR JUS' NOW!
WENDY, WE'VE BEEN WAIT---
HOLY CATS! WHAT IS THIS?
Reg. U. S. Pat. Off. Copyright, 1936, by Chicago Tribune-N. Y. News Syndicate, Inc
MILTON CANIFF

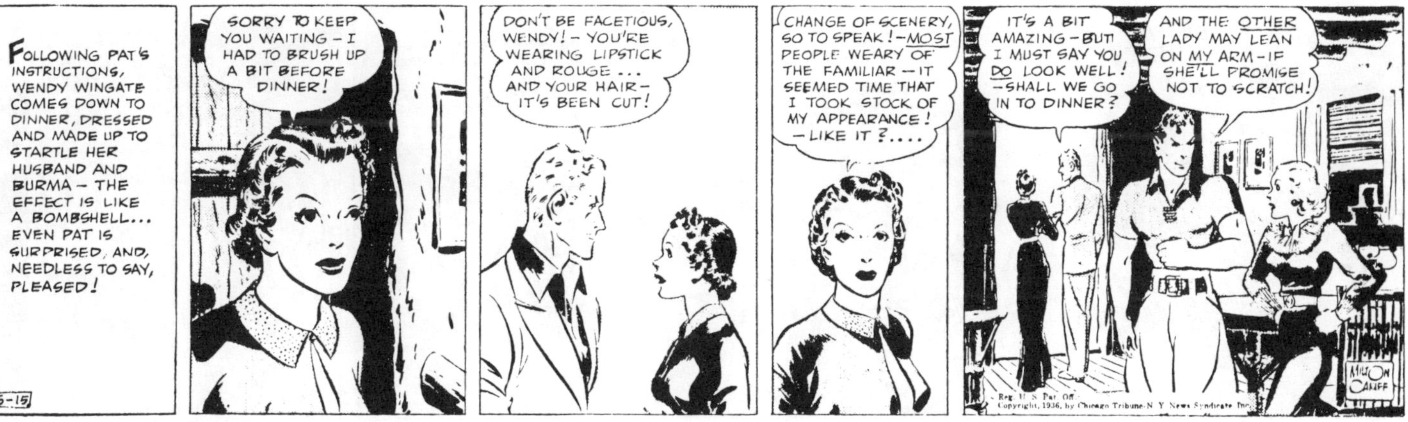
FOLLOWING PAT'S INSTRUCTIONS, WENDY WINGATE COMES DOWN TO DINNER, DRESSED AND MADE UP TO STARTLE HER HUSBAND AND BURMA — THE EFFECT IS LIKE A BOMBSHELL... EVEN PAT IS SURPRISED, AND, NEEDLESS TO SAY, PLEASED!
6-15
SORRY TO KEEP YOU WAITING — I HAD TO BRUSH UP A BIT BEFORE DINNER!
DON'T BE FACETIOUS, WENDY! — YOU'RE WEARING LIPSTICK AND ROUGE... AND YOUR HAIR — IT'S BEEN CUT!
CHANGE OF SCENERY, SO TO SPEAK! — MOST PEOPLE WEARY OF THE FAMILIAR — IT SEEMED TIME THAT I TOOK STOCK OF MY APPEARANCE! — LIKE IT?....
IT'S A BIT AMAZING — BUT I MUST SAY YOU DO LOOK WELL! — SHALL WE GO IN TO DINNER?
AND THE OTHER LADY MAY LEAN ON MY ARM — IF SHE'LL PROMISE NOT TO SCRATCH!
Reg. U. S. Pat. Off. Copyright, 1936, by Chicago Tribune-N. Y. News Syndicate, Inc.
MILTON CANIFF

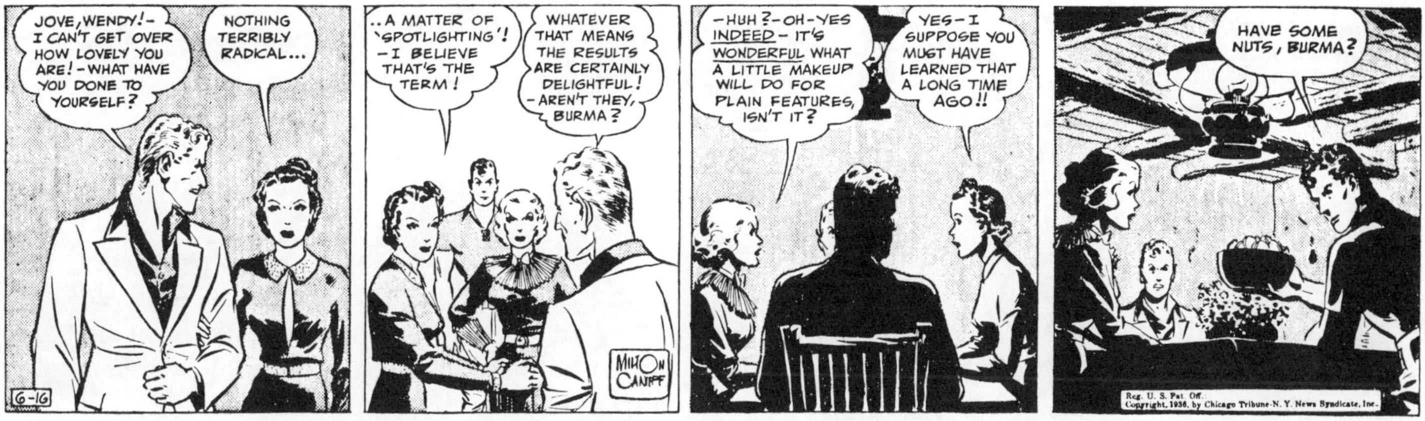
JOVE, WENDY! — I CAN'T GET OVER HOW LOVELY YOU ARE! — WHAT HAVE YOU DONE TO YOURSELF?
NOTHING TERRIBLY RADICAL...
6-16
..A MATTER OF 'SPOTLIGHTING'! — I BELIEVE THAT'S THE TERM!
WHATEVER THAT MEANS THE RESULTS ARE CERTAINLY DELIGHTFUL! — AREN'T THEY, BURMA?
MILTON CANIFF
— HUH? — OH — YES INDEED — IT'S WONDERFUL WHAT A LITTLE MAKEUP WILL DO FOR PLAIN FEATURES, ISN'T IT?
YES — I SUPPOSE YOU MUST HAVE LEARNED THAT A LONG TIME AGO!!
HAVE SOME NUTS, BURMA?
Reg. U. S. Pat. Off. Copyright, 1936, by Chicago Tribune-N. Y. News Syndicate, Inc.

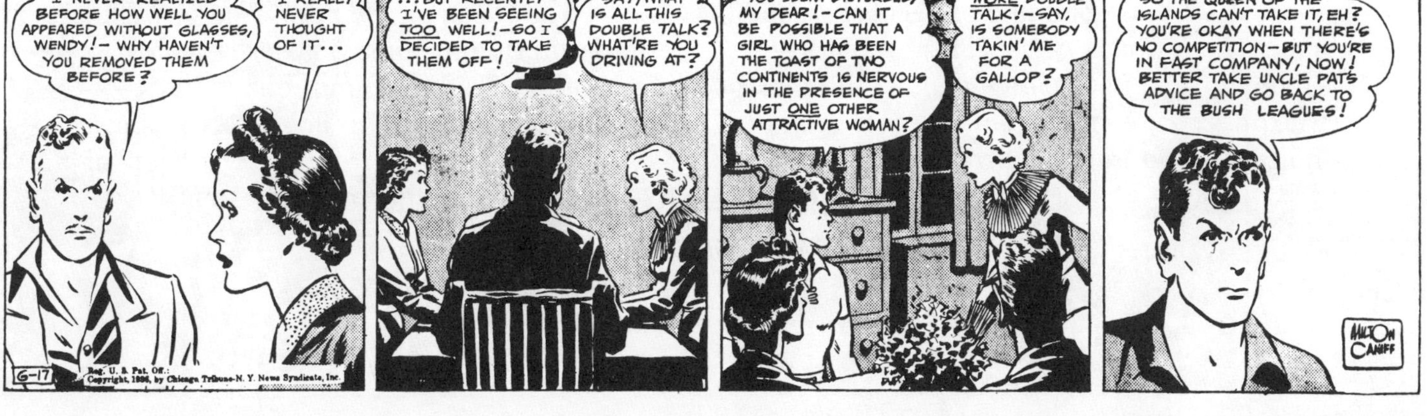
I NEVER REALIZED BEFORE HOW WELL YOU APPEARED WITHOUT GLASSES, WENDY! — WHY HAVEN'T YOU REMOVED THEM BEFORE?
I REALLY NEVER THOUGHT OF IT...
6-17
Reg. U. S. Pat. Off. Copyright, 1936, by Chicago Tribune-N. Y. News Syndicate, Inc.
...BUT RECENTLY I'VE BEEN SEEING TOO WELL! — SO I DECIDED TO TAKE THEM OFF!
SAY, WHAT IS ALL THIS DOUBLE TALK? WHAT'RE YOU DRIVING AT?
YOU SEEM DISTURBED, MY DEAR! — CAN IT BE POSSIBLE THAT A GIRL WHO HAS BEEN THE TOAST OF TWO CONTINENTS IS NERVOUS IN THE PRESENCE OF JUST ONE OTHER ATTRACTIVE WOMAN?
MORE DOUBLE TALK! — SAY, IS SOMEBODY TAKIN' ME FOR A GALLOP?
SO THE QUEEN OF THE ISLANDS CAN'T TAKE IT, EH? YOU'RE OKAY WHEN THERE'S NO COMPETITION — BUT YOU'RE IN FAST COMPANY, NOW! BETTER TAKE UNCLE PAT'S ADVICE AND GO BACK TO THE BUSH LEAGUES!
MILTON CANIFF

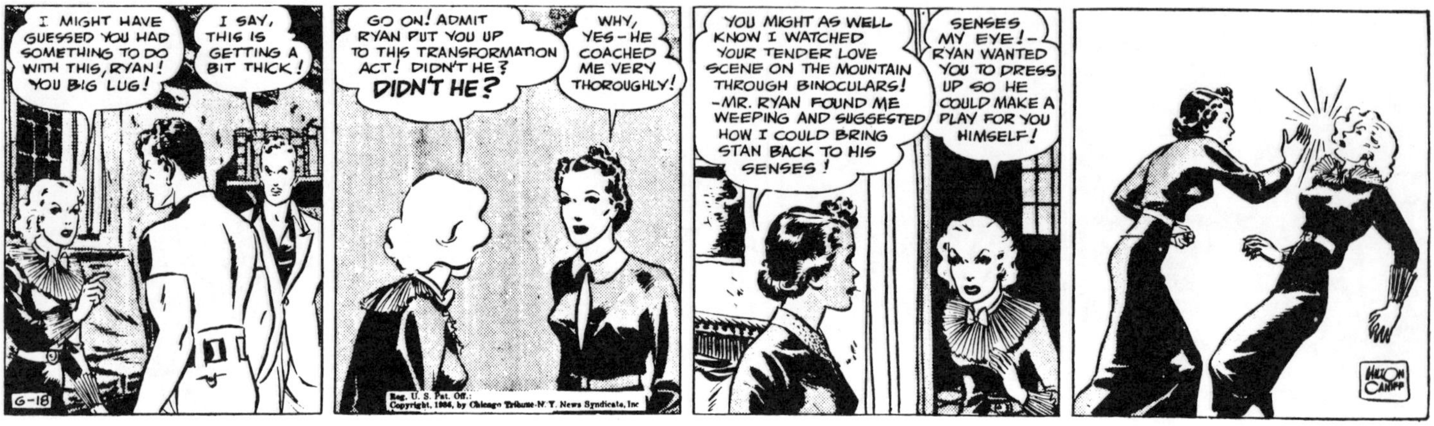
6-18
I MIGHT HAVE GUESSED YOU HAD SOMETHING TO DO WITH THIS, RYAN! YOU BIG LUG!
I SAY, THIS IS GETTING A BIT THICK!
GO ON! ADMIT RYAN PUT YOU UP TO THIS TRANSFORMATION ACT! DIDN'T HE? DIDN'T HE?
WHY, YES—HE COACHED ME VERY THOROUGHLY!
YOU MIGHT AS WELL KNOW I WATCHED YOUR TENDER LOVE SCENE ON THE MOUNTAIN THROUGH BINOCULARS! -MR. RYAN FOUND ME WEEPING AND SUGGESTED HOW I COULD BRING STAN BACK TO HIS SENSES!
SENSES MY EYE!—RYAN WANTED YOU TO DRESS UP SO HE COULD MAKE A PLAY FOR YOU HIMSELF!
MILTON CANIFF

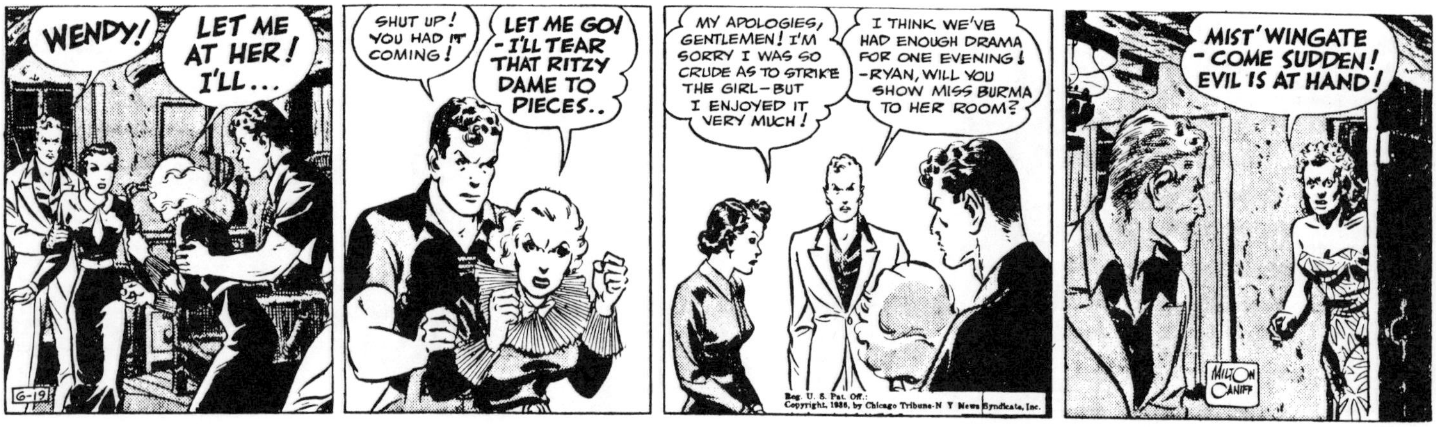
6-19
WENDY!
LET ME AT HER! I'LL...
SHUT UP! YOU HAD IT COMING!
LET ME GO! -I'LL TEAR THAT RITZY DAME TO PIECES..
MY APOLOGIES, GENTLEMEN! I'M SORRY I WAS SO CRUDE AS TO STRIKE THE GIRL—BUT I ENJOYED IT VERY MUCH!
I THINK WE'VE HAD ENOUGH DRAMA FOR ONE EVENING! -RYAN, WILL YOU SHOW MISS BURMA TO HER ROOM?
MIST' WINGATE -COME SUDDEN! EVIL IS AT HAND!
MILTON CANIFF

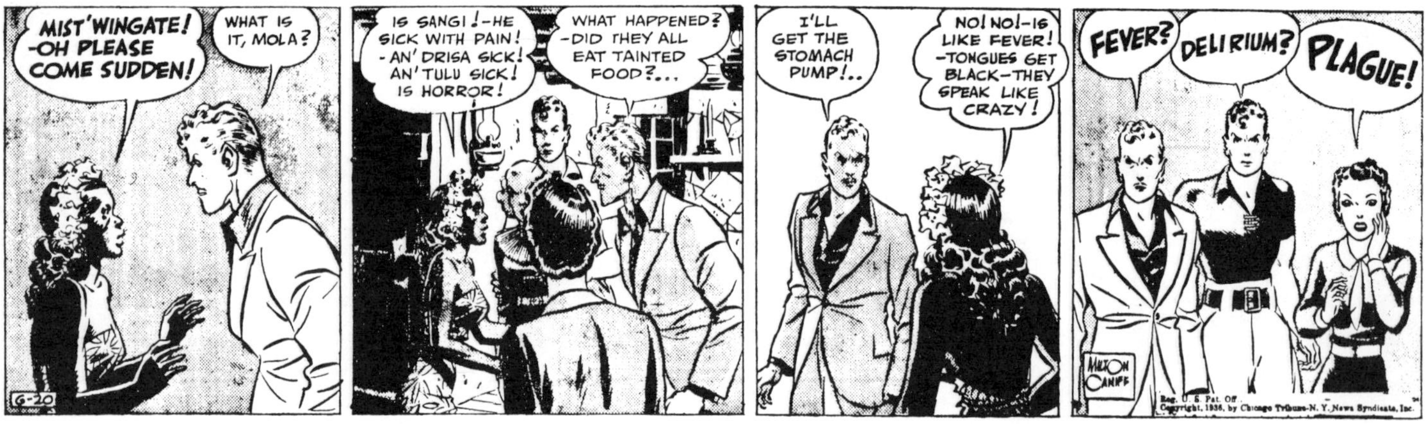
6-20
MIST' WINGATE! -OH PLEASE COME SUDDEN!
WHAT IS IT, MOLA?
IS SANGI!—HE SICK WITH PAIN! -AN' DRISA SICK! AN' TULU SICK! IS HORROR!
WHAT HAPPENED? -DID THEY ALL EAT TAINTED FOOD?...
I'LL GET THE STOMACH PUMP!..
NO! NO!—IS LIKE FEVER! -TONGUES GET BLACK—THEY SPEAK LIKE CRAZY!
FEVER?
DELIRIUM?
PLAGUE!
MILTON CANIFF

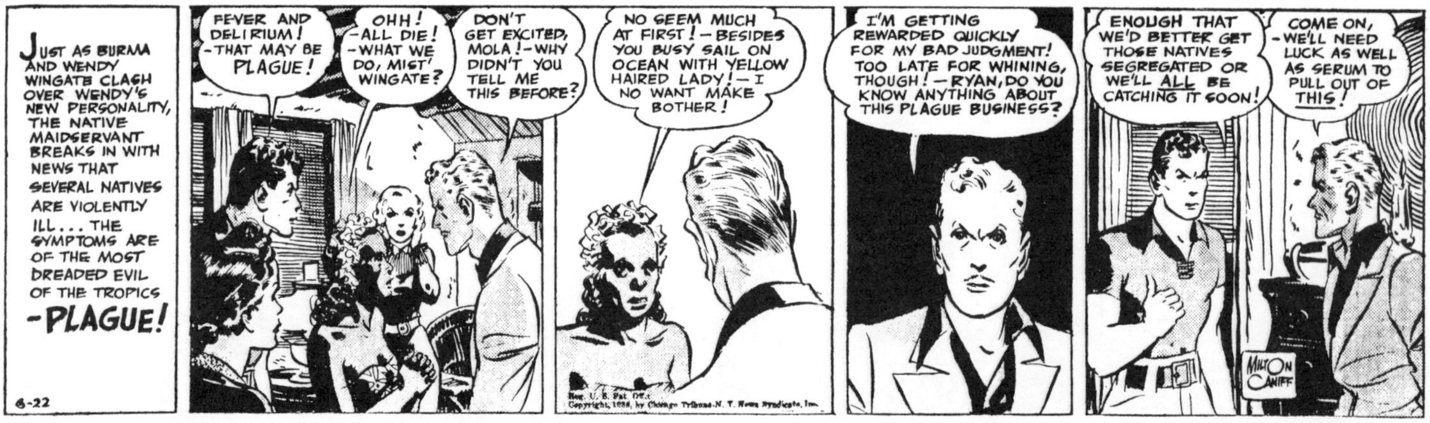
JUST AS BURMA AND WENDY WINGATE CLASH OVER WENDY'S NEW PERSONALITY, THE NATIVE MAIDSERVANT BREAKS IN WITH NEWS THAT SEVERAL NATIVES ARE VIOLENTLY ILL... THE SYMPTOMS ARE OF THE MOST DREADED EVIL OF THE TROPICS -PLAGUE!
6-22
FEVER AND DELIRIUM! -THAT MAY BE PLAGUE!
OHH! -ALL DIE! -WHAT WE DO, MIST' WINGATE?
DON'T GET EXCITED, MOLA!—WHY DIDN'T YOU TELL ME THIS BEFORE?
NO SEEM MUCH AT FIRST!—BESIDES YOU BUSY SAIL ON OCEAN WITH YELLOW HAIRED LADY!—I NO WANT MAKE BOTHER!
I'M GETTING REWARDED QUICKLY FOR MY BAD JUDGMENT! TOO LATE FOR WHINING, THOUGH!—RYAN, DO YOU KNOW ANYTHING ABOUT THIS PLAGUE BUSINESS?
ENOUGH THAT WE'D BETTER GET THOSE NATIVES SEGREGATED OR WE'LL ALL BE CATCHING IT SOON!
COME ON, -WE'LL NEED LUCK AS WELL AS SERUM TO PULL OUT OF THIS!
MILTON CANIFF

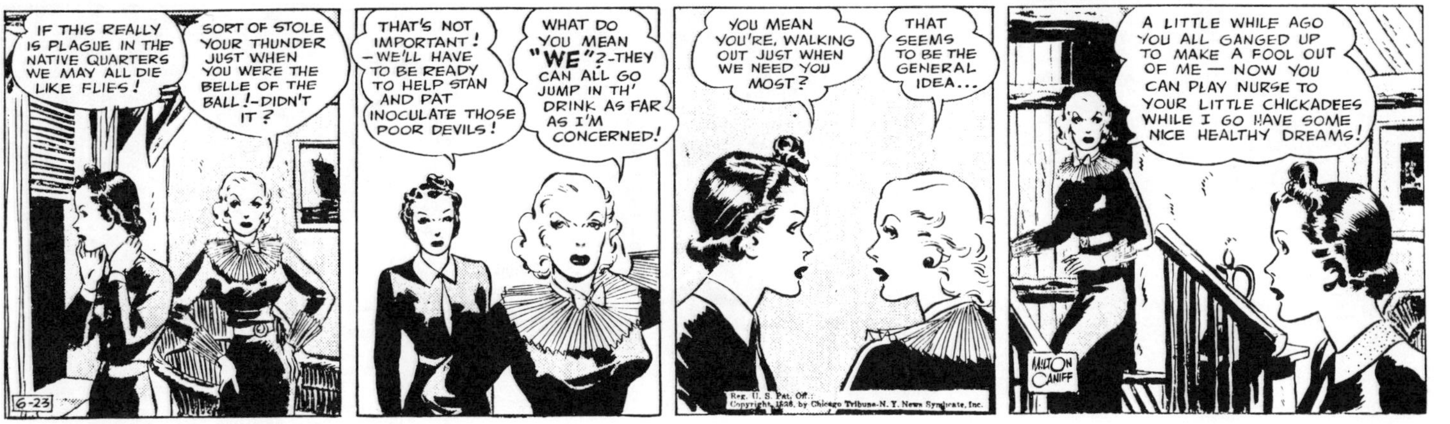
IF THIS REALLY IS PLAGUE IN THE NATIVE QUARTERS WE MAY ALL DIE LIKE FLIES!
SORT OF STOLE YOUR THUNDER JUST WHEN YOU WERE THE BELLE OF THE BALL!-DIDN'T IT?
6-23
THAT'S NOT IMPORTANT! -WE'LL HAVE TO BE READY TO HELP STAN AND PAT INOCULATE THOSE POOR DEVILS!
WHAT DO YOU MEAN "WE"?-THEY CAN ALL GO JUMP IN TH' DRINK AS FAR AS I'M CONCERNED!
YOU MEAN YOU'RE, WALKING OUT JUST WHEN WE NEED YOU MOST?
THAT SEEMS TO BE THE GENERAL IDEA...
Reg. U. S. Pat. Off.: Copyright, 1936, by Chicago Tribune-N. Y. News Syndicate, Inc.
A LITTLE WHILE AGO YOU ALL GANGED UP TO MAKE A FOOL OUT OF ME — NOW YOU CAN PLAY NURSE TO YOUR LITTLE CHICKADEES WHILE I GO HAVE SOME NICE HEALTHY DREAMS!
MILTON CANIFF

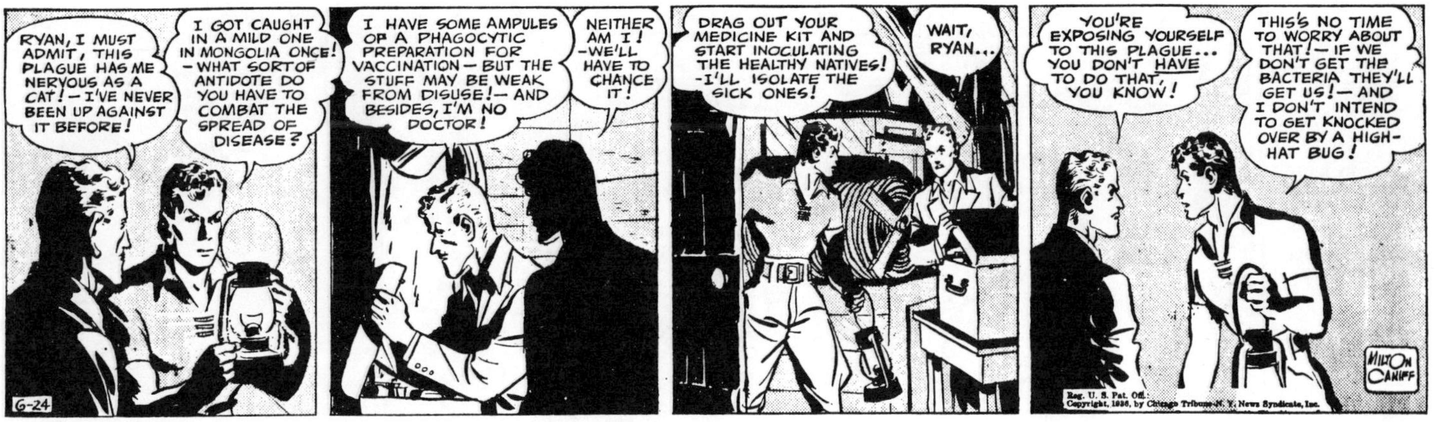
RYAN, I MUST ADMIT, THIS PLAGUE HAS ME NERVOUS AS A CAT! — I'VE NEVER BEEN UP AGAINST IT BEFORE!
I GOT CAUGHT IN A MILD ONE IN MONGOLIA ONCE! -WHAT SORT OF ANTIDOTE DO YOU HAVE TO COMBAT THE SPREAD OF DISEASE?
6-24
I HAVE SOME AMPULES OF A PHAGOCYTIC PREPARATION FOR VACCINATION — BUT THE STUFF MAY BE WEAK FROM DISUSE!— AND BESIDES, I'M NO DOCTOR!
NEITHER AM I! -WE'LL HAVE TO CHANCE IT!
DRAG OUT YOUR MEDICINE KIT AND START INOCULATING THE HEALTHY NATIVES! -I'LL ISOLATE THE SICK ONES!
WAIT, RYAN...
YOU'RE EXPOSING YOURSELF TO THIS PLAGUE... YOU DON'T HAVE TO DO THAT, YOU KNOW!
THIS'S NO TIME TO WORRY ABOUT THAT!— IF WE DON'T GET THE BACTERIA THEY'LL GET US!— AND I DON'T INTEND TO GET KNOCKED OVER BY A HIGH-HAT BUG!
MILTON CANIFF
Reg. U. S. Pat. Off.: Copyright, 1936, by Chicago Tribune-N. Y. News Syndicate, Inc.

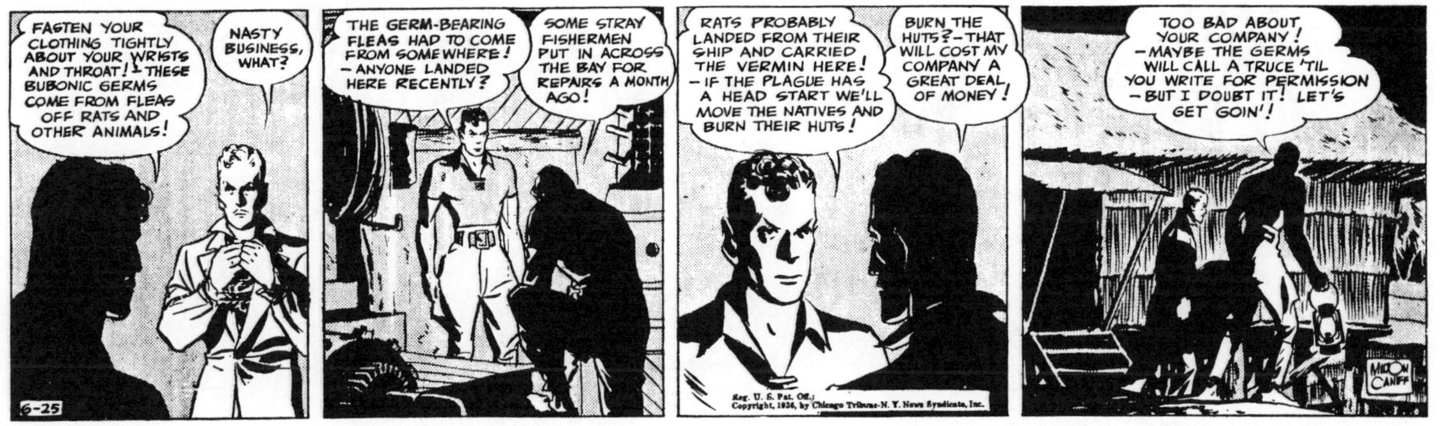
FASTEN YOUR CLOTHING TIGHTLY ABOUT YOUR WRISTS AND THROAT!-THESE BUBONIC GERMS COME FROM FLEAS OFF RATS AND OTHER ANIMALS!
NASTY BUSINESS, WHAT?
6-25
THE GERM-BEARING FLEAS HAD TO COME FROM SOMEWHERE! -ANYONE LANDED HERE RECENTLY?
SOME STRAY FISHERMEN PUT IN ACROSS THE BAY FOR REPAIRS A MONTH AGO!
RATS PROBABLY LANDED FROM THEIR SHIP AND CARRIED THE VERMIN HERE! -IF THE PLAGUE HAS A HEAD START WE'LL MOVE THE NATIVES AND BURN THEIR HUTS!
BURN THE HUTS?-THAT WILL COST MY COMPANY A GREAT DEAL OF MONEY!
Reg. U. S. Pat. Off.: Copyright, 1936, by Chicago Tribune-N. Y. News Syndicate, Inc.
TOO BAD ABOUT YOUR COMPANY! -MAYBE THE GERMS WILL CALL A TRUCE 'TIL YOU WRITE FOR PERMISSION -BUT I DOUBT IT! LET'S GET GOIN'!
MILTON CANIFF

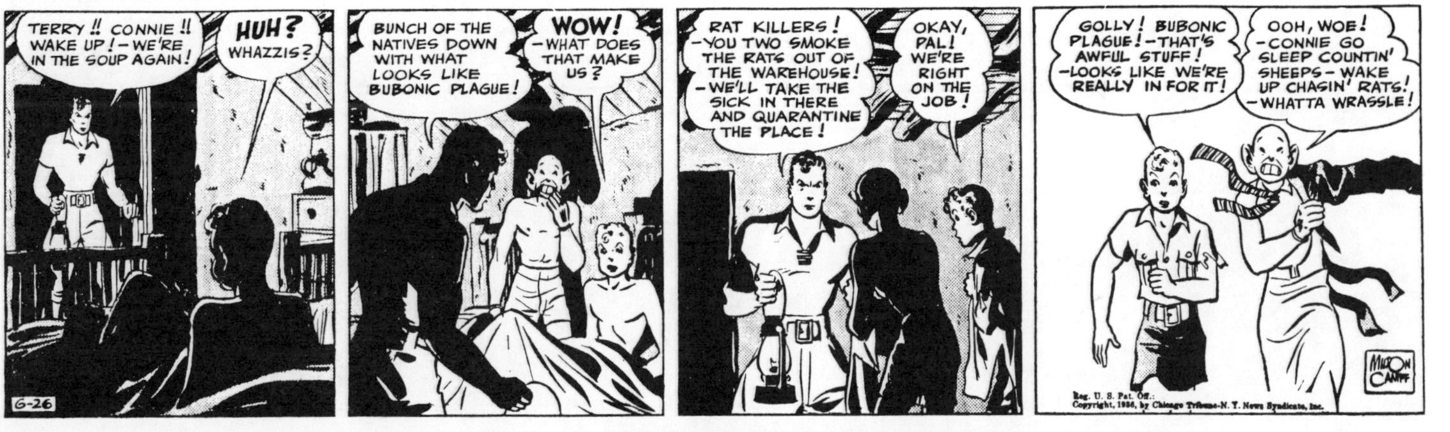
TERRY!! CONNIE!! WAKE UP! - WE'RE IN THE SOUP AGAIN!
HUH? WHAZZIS?
6-26
BUNCH OF THE NATIVES DOWN WITH WHAT LOOKS LIKE BUBONIC PLAGUE!
WOW! -WHAT DOES THAT MAKE US?
RAT KILLERS! -YOU TWO SMOKE THE RATS OUT OF THE WAREHOUSE! -WE'LL TAKE THE SICK IN THERE AND QUARANTINE THE PLACE!
OKAY, PAL! WE'RE RIGHT ON THE JOB!
GOLLY! BUBONIC PLAGUE!-THAT'S AWFUL STUFF! -LOOKS LIKE WE'RE REALLY IN FOR IT!
OOH, WOE! -CONNIE GO SLEEP COUNTIN' SHEEPS-WAKE UP CHASIN' RATS! -WHATTA WRASSLE!
MILTON CANIFF
Reg. U. S. Pat. Off.: Copyright, 1936, by Chicago Tribune-N. Y. News Syndicate, Inc.

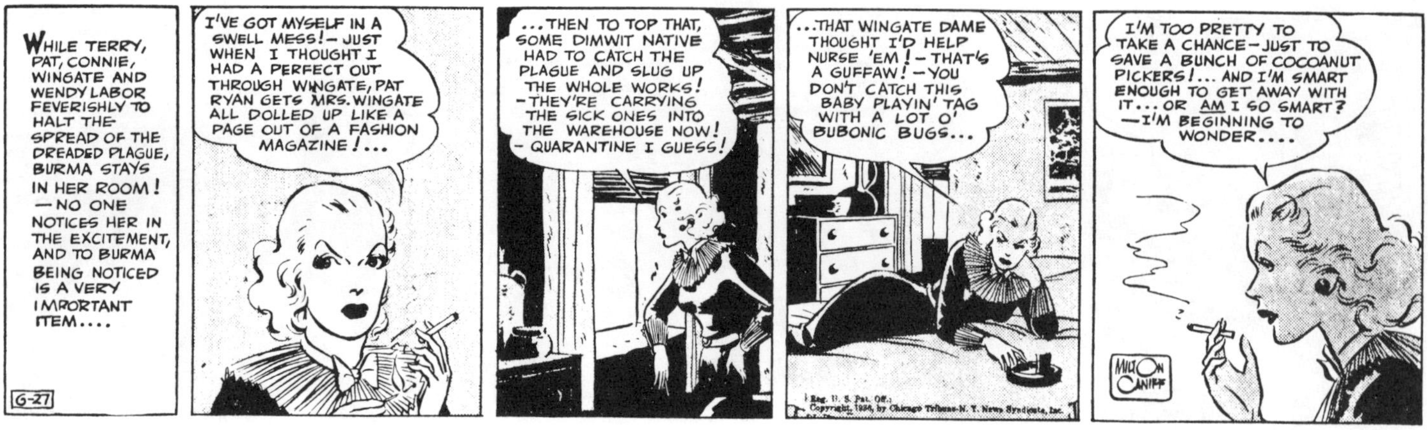
WHILE TERRY, PAT, CONNIE, WINGATE AND WENDY LABOR FEVERISHLY TO HALT THE SPREAD OF THE DREADED PLAGUE, BURMA STAYS IN HER ROOM! —NO ONE NOTICES HER IN THE EXCITEMENT, AND TO BURMA BEING NOTICED IS A VERY IMPORTANT ITEM....
6-27
I'VE GOT MYSELF IN A SWELL MESS! — JUST WHEN I THOUGHT I HAD A PERFECT OUT THROUGH WINGATE, PAT RYAN GETS MRS. WINGATE ALL DOLLED UP LIKE A PAGE OUT OF A FASHION MAGAZINE!...
...THEN TO TOP THAT, SOME DIMWIT NATIVE HAD TO CATCH THE PLAGUE AND SLUG UP THE WHOLE WORKS! -THEY'RE CARRYING THE SICK ONES INTO THE WAREHOUSE NOW! - QUARANTINE I GUESS!
...THAT WINGATE DAME THOUGHT I'D HELP NURSE 'EM! — THAT'S A GUFFAW! — YOU DON'T CATCH THIS BABY PLAYIN' TAG WITH A LOT O' BUBONIC BUGS...
Reg. U. S. Pat. Off.; Copyright, 1936, by Chicago Tribune-N. Y. News Syndicate, Inc.
I'M TOO PRETTY TO TAKE A CHANCE—JUST TO SAVE A BUNCH OF COCOANUT PICKERS!... AND I'M SMART ENOUGH TO GET AWAY WITH IT... OR AM I SO SMART? —I'M BEGINNING TO WONDER....
MILTON CANIFF

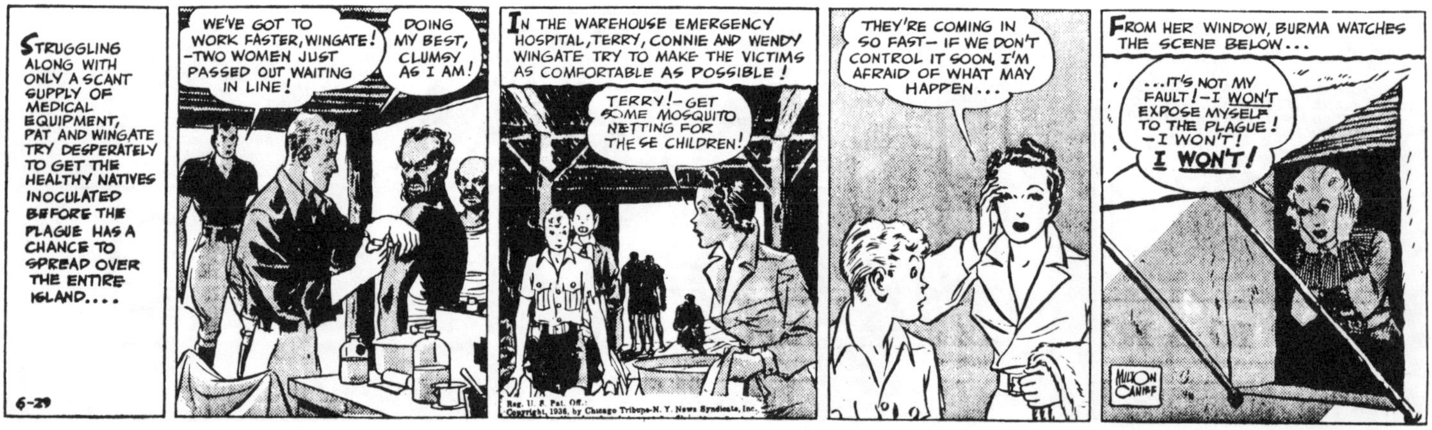
STRUGGLING ALONG WITH ONLY A SCANT SUPPLY OF MEDICAL EQUIPMENT, PAT AND WINGATE TRY DESPERATELY TO GET THE HEALTHY NATIVES INOCULATED BEFORE THE PLAGUE HAS A CHANCE TO SPREAD OVER THE ENTIRE ISLAND....
6-29
WE'VE GOT TO WORK FASTER, WINGATE! -TWO WOMEN JUST PASSED OUT WAITING IN LINE!
DOING MY BEST, CLUMSY AS I AM!
IN THE WAREHOUSE EMERGENCY HOSPITAL, TERRY, CONNIE AND WENDY WINGATE TRY TO MAKE THE VICTIMS AS COMFORTABLE AS POSSIBLE!
TERRY!—GET SOME MOSQUITO NETTING FOR THESE CHILDREN!
Reg. U. S. Pat. Off.; Copyright, 1936, by Chicago Tribune-N. Y. News Syndicate, Inc.
THEY'RE COMING IN SO FAST— IF WE DON'T CONTROL IT SOON, I'M AFRAID OF WHAT MAY HAPPEN...
FROM HER WINDOW, BURMA WATCHES THE SCENE BELOW...
...IT'S NOT MY FAULT! —I WON'T EXPOSE MYSELF TO THE PLAGUE! —I WON'T! I WON'T!
MILTON CANIFF

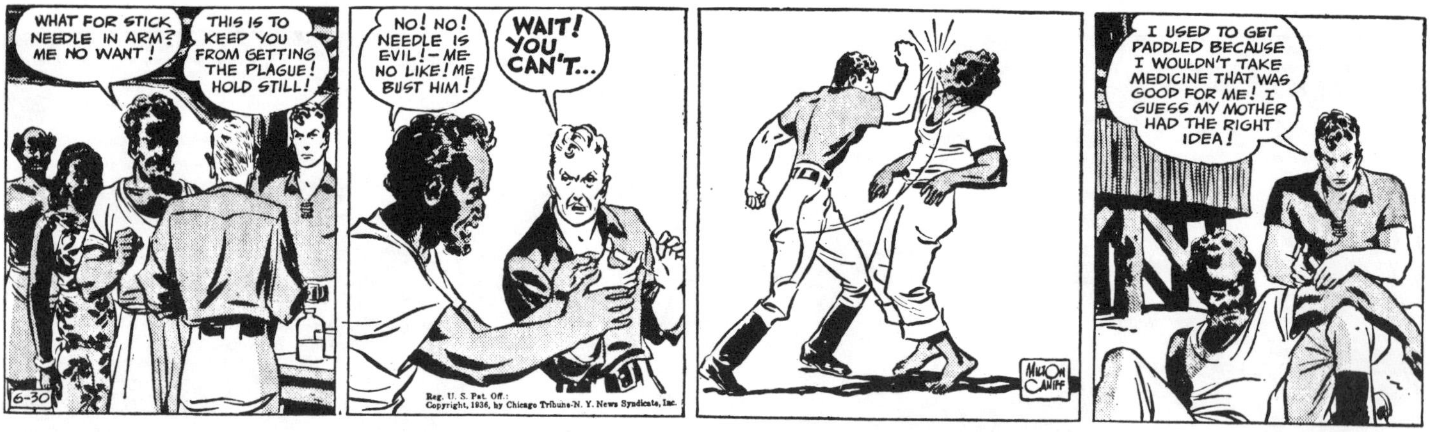
WHAT FOR STICK NEEDLE IN ARM? ME NO WANT!
THIS IS TO KEEP YOU FROM GETTING THE PLAGUE! HOLD STILL!
6-30
NO! NO! NEEDLE IS EVIL!—ME NO LIKE! ME BUST HIM!
WAIT! YOU CAN'T...
Reg. U. S. Pat. Off.; Copyright, 1936, by Chicago Tribune-N. Y. News Syndicate, Inc.
MILTON CANIFF
I USED TO GET PADDLED BECAUSE I WOULDN'T TAKE MEDICINE THAT WAS GOOD FOR ME! I GUESS MY MOTHER HAD THE RIGHT IDEA!

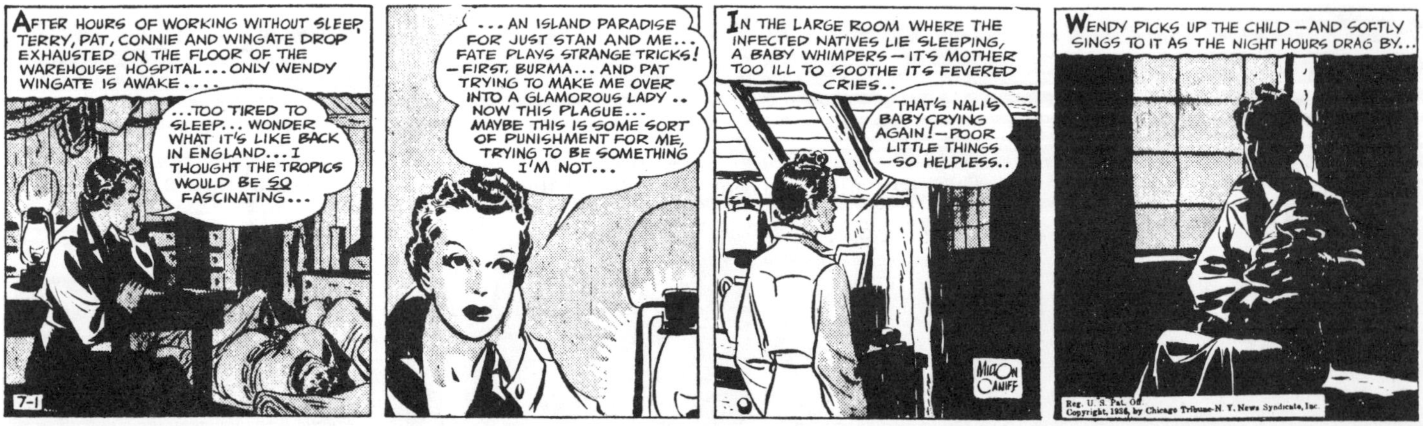
AFTER HOURS OF WORKING WITHOUT SLEEP, TERRY, PAT, CONNIE AND WINGATE DROP EXHAUSTED ON THE FLOOR OF THE WAREHOUSE HOSPITAL... ONLY WENDY WINGATE IS AWAKE....
...TOO TIRED TO SLEEP... WONDER WHAT IT'S LIKE BACK IN ENGLAND... I THOUGHT THE TROPICS WOULD BE SO FASCINATING...
7-1
...AN ISLAND PARADISE FOR JUST STAN AND ME... FATE PLAYS STRANGE TRICKS! -FIRST, BURMA... AND PAT TRYING TO MAKE ME OVER INTO A GLAMOROUS LADY.. NOW THIS PLAGUE... MAYBE THIS IS SOME SORT OF PUNISHMENT FOR ME, TRYING TO BE SOMETHING I'M NOT...
IN THE LARGE ROOM WHERE THE INFECTED NATIVES LIE SLEEPING, A BABY WHIMPERS—IT'S MOTHER TOO ILL TO SOOTHE IT'S FEVERED CRIES..
THAT'S NALI'S BABY CRYING AGAIN!—POOR LITTLE THINGS —SO HELPLESS..
MILTON CANIFF
WENDY PICKS UP THE CHILD—AND SOFTLY SINGS TO IT AS THE NIGHT HOURS DRAG BY...
Reg. U. S. Pat. Off.; Copyright, 1936, by Chicago Tribune-N. Y. News Syndicate, Inc.

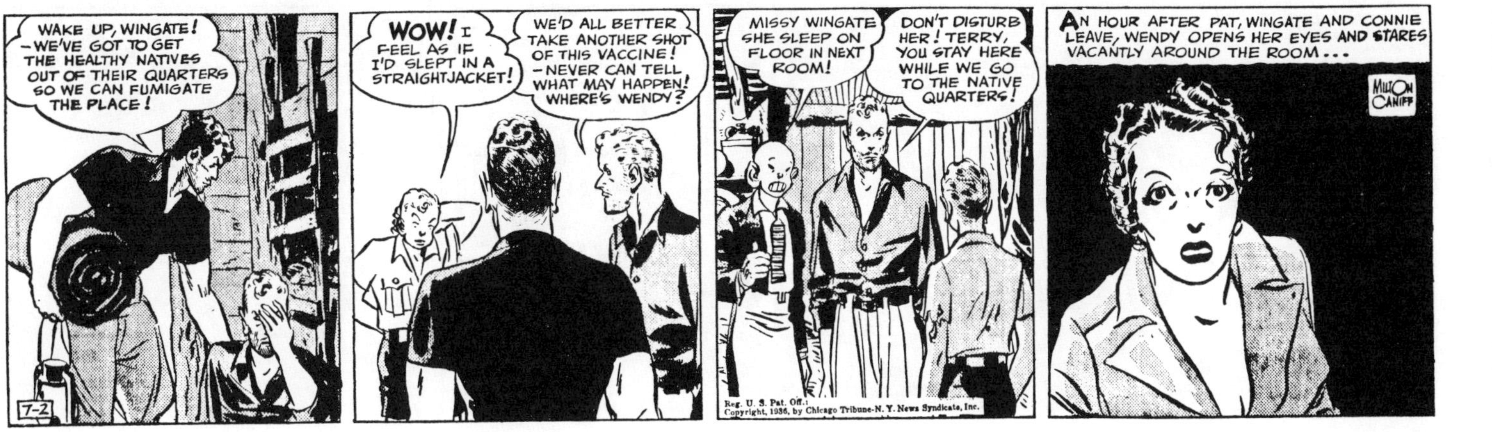
7-2
WAKE UP, WINGATE! -WE'VE GOT TO GET THE HEALTHY NATIVES OUT OF THEIR QUARTERS SO WE CAN FUMIGATE THE PLACE!
WOW! I FEEL AS IF I'D SLEPT IN A STRAIGHTJACKET!
WE'D ALL BETTER TAKE ANOTHER SHOT OF THIS VACCINE! -NEVER CAN TELL WHAT MAY HAPPEN! WHERE'S WENDY?
MISSY WINGATE SHE SLEEP ON FLOOR IN NEXT ROOM!
DON'T DISTURB HER! TERRY, YOU STAY HERE WHILE WE GO TO THE NATIVE QUARTERS!
Reg. U. S. Pat. Off.: Copyright, 1936, by Chicago Tribune-N. Y. News Syndicate, Inc.
AN HOUR AFTER PAT, WINGATE AND CONNIE LEAVE, WENDY OPENS HER EYES AND STARES VACANTLY AROUND THE ROOM...
MILTON CANIFF

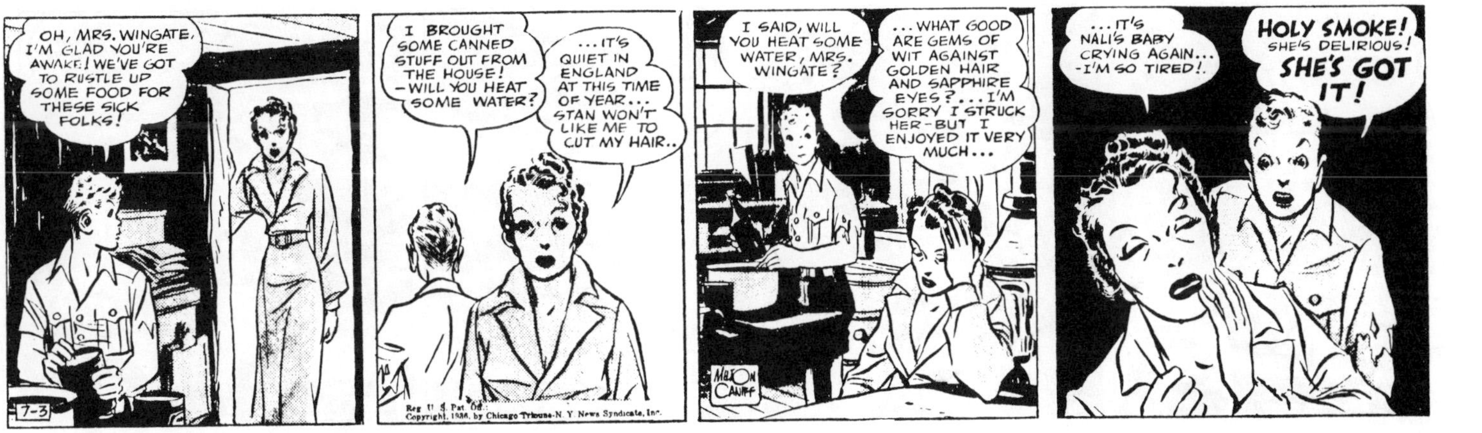
7-3
OH, MRS. WINGATE, I'M GLAD YOU'RE AWAKE! WE'VE GOT TO RUSTLE UP SOME FOOD FOR THESE SICK FOLKS!
I BROUGHT SOME CANNED STUFF OUT FROM THE HOUSE! -WILL YOU HEAT SOME WATER?
...IT'S QUIET IN ENGLAND AT THIS TIME OF YEAR... STAN WON'T LIKE ME TO CUT MY HAIR..
Reg. U. S. Pat. Off.: Copyright, 1936, by Chicago Tribune-N. Y. News Syndicate, Inc.
I SAID, WILL YOU HEAT SOME WATER, MRS. WINGATE?
...WHAT GOOD ARE GEMS OF WIT AGAINST GOLDEN HAIR AND SAPPHIRE EYES?...I'M SORRY I STRUCK HER-BUT I ENJOYED IT VERY MUCH...
MILTON CANIFF
...IT'S NALI'S BABY CRYING AGAIN... -I'M SO TIRED!.
HOLY SMOKE! SHE'S DELIRIOUS! SHE'S GOT IT!

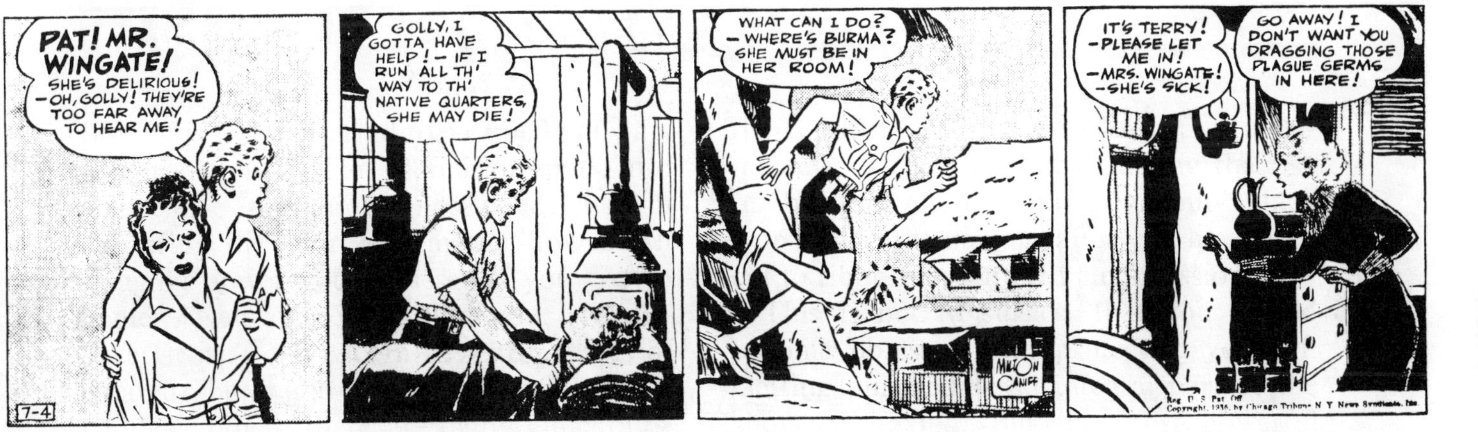
7-4
PAT! MR. WINGATE! SHE'S DELIRIOUS! -OH, GOLLY! THEY'RE TOO FAR AWAY TO HEAR ME!
GOLLY, I GOTTA HAVE HELP! -IF I RUN ALL TH' WAY TO TH' NATIVE QUARTERS, SHE MAY DIE!
WHAT CAN I DO? -WHERE'S BURMA? SHE MUST BE IN HER ROOM!
MILTON CANIFF
IT'S TERRY! -PLEASE LET ME IN! -MRS. WINGATE! -SHE'S SICK!
GO AWAY! I DON'T WANT YOU DRAGGING THOSE PLAGUE GERMS IN HERE!
Reg. U. S. Pat. Off. Copyright, 1936, by Chicago Tribune-N. Y. News Syndicate, Inc.

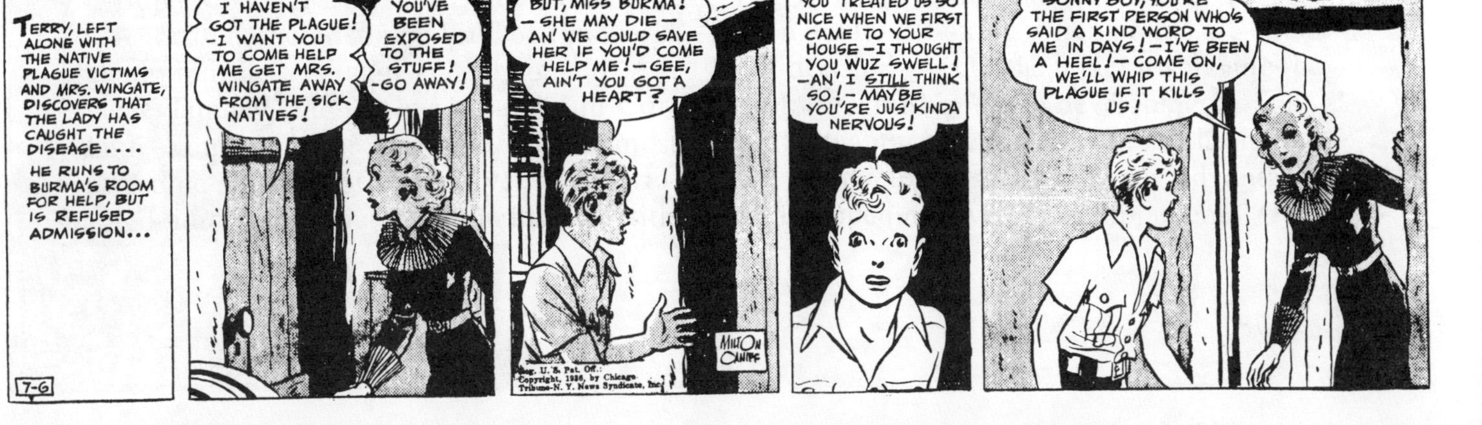
TERRY, LEFT ALONG WITH THE NATIVE PLAGUE VICTIMS AND MRS. WINGATE, DISCOVERS THAT THE LADY HAS CAUGHT THE DISEASE....
HE RUNS TO BURMA'S ROOM FOR HELP, BUT IS REFUSED ADMISSION...
7-6
I HAVEN'T GOT THE PLAGUE! -I WANT YOU TO COME HELP ME GET MRS. WINGATE AWAY FROM THE SICK NATIVES!
YOU'VE BEEN EXPOSED TO THE STUFF! -GO AWAY!
BUT, MISS BURMA! -SHE MAY DIE- AN' WE COULD SAVE HER IF YOU'D COME HELP ME! -GEE, AIN'T YOU GOT A HEART?
Reg. U. S. Pat. Off.: Copyright, 1936, by Chicago Tribune-N. Y. News Syndicate, Inc.
MILTON CANIFF
YOU TREATED US SO NICE WHEN WE FIRST CAME TO YOUR HOUSE -I THOUGHT YOU WUZ SWELL! -AN' I STILL THINK SO! -MAYBE YOU'RE JUS' KINDA NERVOUS!
SONNY BOY, YOU'RE THE FIRST PERSON WHO'S SAID A KIND WORD TO ME IN DAYS! -I'VE BEEN A HEEL! -COME ON, WE'LL WHIP THIS PLAGUE IF IT KILLS US!

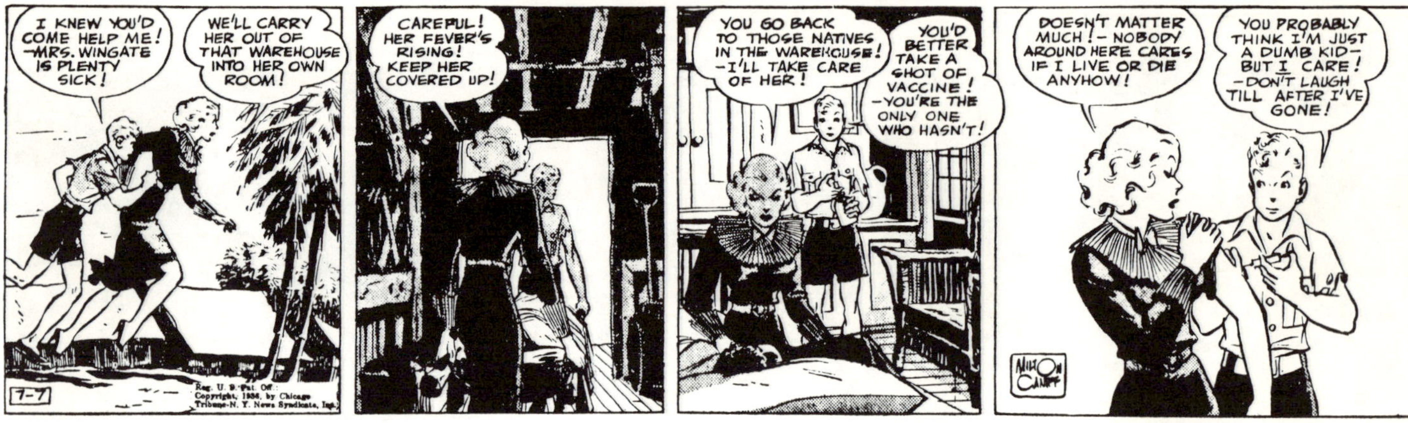
I KNEW YOU'D COME HELP ME! —MRS. WINGATE IS PLENTY SICK!
WE'LL CARRY HER OUT OF THAT WAREHOUSE INTO HER OWN ROOM!
7-7
Reg. U. S. Pat. Off.: Copyright, 1936, by Chicago Tribune-N. Y. News Syndicate, Inc.
CAREFUL! HER FEVER'S RISING! KEEP HER COVERED UP!
YOU GO BACK TO THOSE NATIVES IN THE WAREHOUSE! —I'LL TAKE CARE OF HER!
YOU'D BETTER TAKE A SHOT OF VACCINE! —YOU'RE THE ONLY ONE WHO HASN'T!
DOESN'T MATTER MUCH! —NOBODY AROUND HERE CARES IF I LIVE OR DIE ANYHOW!
YOU PROBABLY THINK I'M JUST A DUMB KID— BUT I CARE! —DON'T LAUGH TILL AFTER I'VE GONE!
MILTON CANIFF

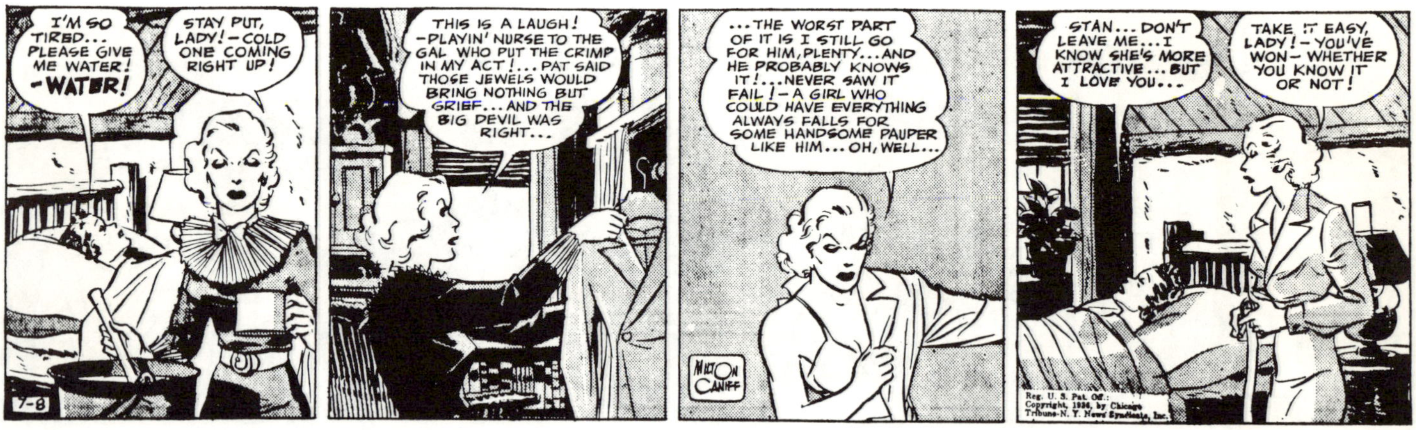
I'M SO TIRED... PLEASE GIVE ME WATER! —WATER!
STAY PUT, LADY! —COLD ONE COMING RIGHT UP!
7-8
THIS IS A LAUGH! —PLAYIN' NURSE TO THE GAL WHO PUT THE CRIMP IN MY ACT!... PAT SAID THOSE JEWELS WOULD BRING NOTHING BUT GRIEF... AND THE BIG DEVIL WAS RIGHT...
...THE WORST PART OF IT IS I STILL GO FOR HIM, PLENTY... AND HE PROBABLY KNOWS IT!... NEVER SAW IT FAIL! —A GIRL WHO COULD HAVE EVERYTHING ALWAYS FALLS FOR SOME HANDSOME PAUPER LIKE HIM... OH, WELL...
MILTON CANIFF
STAN... DON'T LEAVE ME... I KNOW SHE'S MORE ATTRACTIVE... BUT I LOVE YOU...
TAKE IT EASY, LADY! —YOU'VE WON— WHETHER YOU KNOW IT OR NOT!
Reg. U. S. Pat. Off.: Copyright, 1936, by Chicago Tribune-N. Y. News Syndicate, Inc.

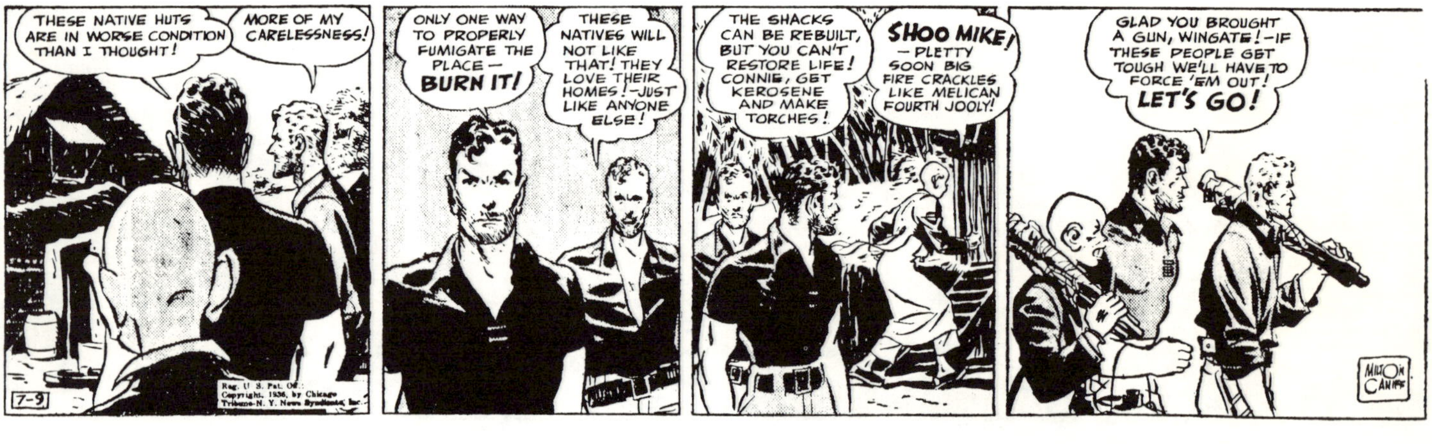
THESE NATIVE HUTS ARE IN WORSE CONDITION THAN I THOUGHT!
MORE OF MY CARELESSNESS!
7-9
Reg. U. S. Pat. Off.: Copyright, 1936, by Chicago Tribune-N. Y. News Syndicate, Inc.
ONLY ONE WAY TO PROPERLY FUMIGATE THE PLACE— BURN IT!
THESE NATIVES WILL NOT LIKE THAT! THEY LOVE THEIR HOMES! —JUST LIKE ANYONE ELSE!
THE SHACKS CAN BE REBUILT, BUT YOU CAN'T RESTORE LIFE! CONNIE, GET KEROSENE AND MAKE TORCHES!
SHOO MIKE! —PLETTY SOON BIG FIRE CRACKLES LIKE MELICAN FOURTH JOOLY!
GLAD YOU BROUGHT A GUN, WINGATE! —IF THESE PEOPLE GET TOUGH WE'LL HAVE TO FORCE 'EM OUT! LET'S GO!
MILTON CANIFF

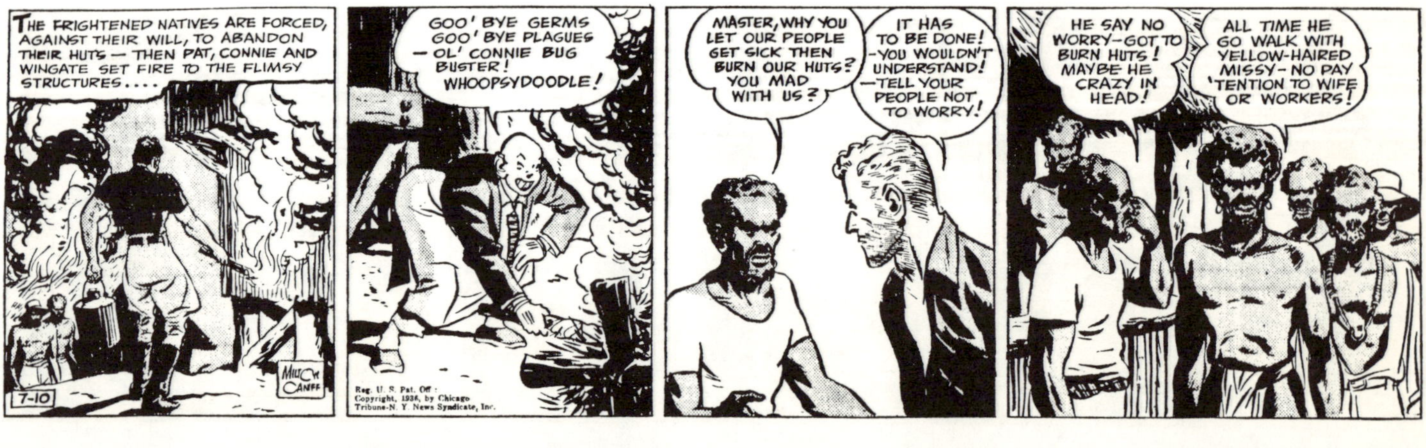
THE FRIGHTENED NATIVES ARE FORCED, AGAINST THEIR WILL, TO ABANDON THEIR HUTS — THEN PAT, CONNIE AND WINGATE SET FIRE TO THE FLIMSY STRUCTURES....
MILTON CANIFF
7-10
GOO' BYE GERMS GOO' BYE PLAGUES —OL' CONNIE BUG BUSTER! WHOOPSYDOODLE!
Reg. U. S. Pat. Off.: Copyright, 1936, by Chicago Tribune-N. Y. News Syndicate, Inc.
MASTER, WHY YOU LET OUR PEOPLE GET SICK THEN BURN OUR HUTS? YOU MAD WITH US?
IT HAS TO BE DONE! —YOU WOULDN'T UNDERSTAND! —TELL YOUR PEOPLE NOT TO WORRY!
HE SAY NO WORRY— GOT TO BURN HUTS! MAYBE HE CRAZY IN HEAD!
ALL TIME HE GO WALK WITH YELLOW-HAIRED MISSY— NO PAY 'TENTION TO WIFE OR WORKERS!

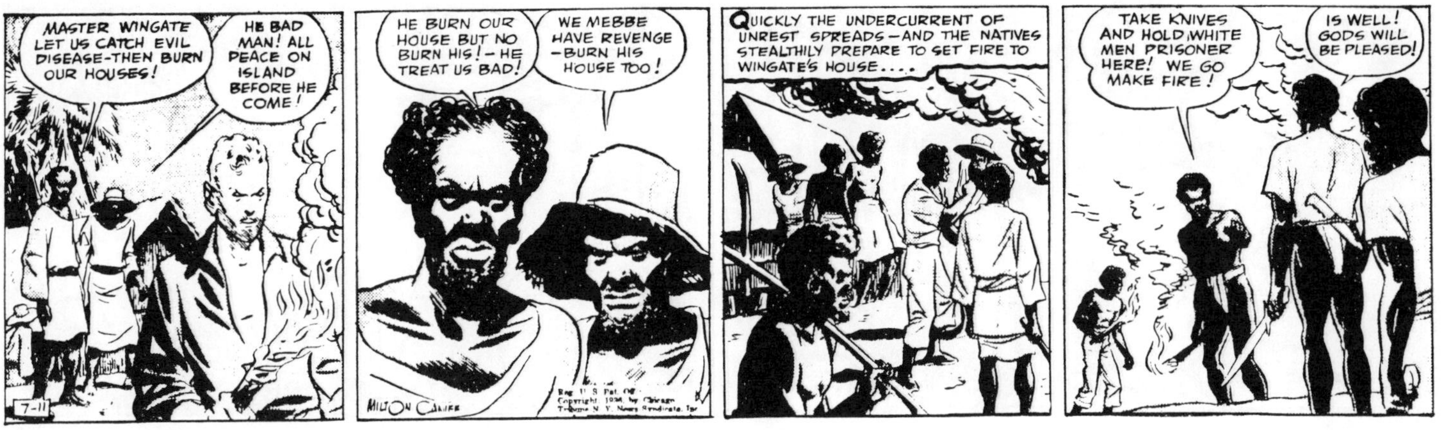
MASTER WINGATE LET US CATCH EVIL DISEASE-THEN BURN OUR HOUSES!
HE BAD MAN! ALL PEACE ON ISLAND BEFORE HE COME!
7-11
HE BURN OUR HOUSE BUT NO BURN HIS!-HE TREAT US BAD!
WE MEBBE HAVE REVENGE -BURN HIS HOUSE TOO!
MILTON CANIFF
Reg. U.S. Pat. Off. Copyright, 1936, by Chicago Tribune-N.Y. News Syndicate, Inc.
QUICKLY THE UNDERCURRENT OF UNREST SPREADS-AND THE NATIVES STEALTHILY PREPARE TO SET FIRE TO WINGATE'S HOUSE....
TAKE KNIVES AND HOLD WHITE MEN PRISONER HERE! WE GO MAKE FIRE!
IS WELL! GODS WILL BE PLEASED!

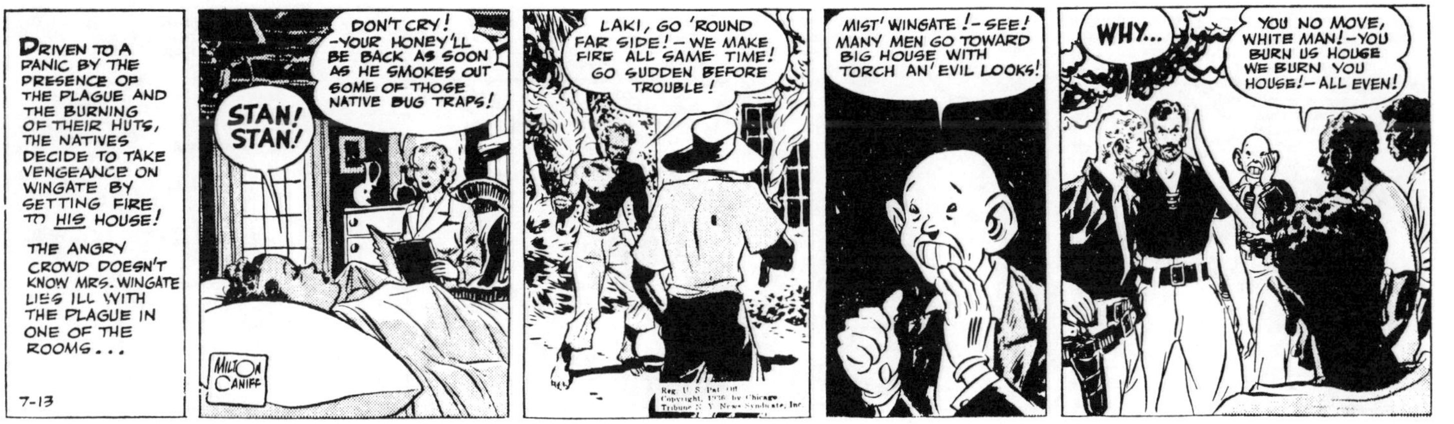
DRIVEN TO A PANIC BY THE PRESENCE OF THE PLAGUE AND THE BURNING OF THEIR HUTS, THE NATIVES DECIDE TO TAKE VENGEANCE ON WINGATE BY SETTING FIRE TO HIS HOUSE!
THE ANGRY CROWD DOESN'T KNOW MRS. WINGATE LIES ILL WITH THE PLAGUE IN ONE OF THE ROOMS...
7-13
STAN! STAN!
DON'T CRY! -YOUR HONEY'LL BE BACK AS SOON AS HE SMOKES OUT SOME OF THOSE NATIVE BUG TRAPS!
MILTON CANIFF
LAKI, GO 'ROUND FAR SIDE!-WE MAKE FIRE ALL SAME TIME! GO SUDDEN BEFORE TROUBLE!
Reg. U.S. Pat. Off. Copyright, 1936, by Chicago Tribune-N.Y. News Syndicate, Inc.
MIST' WINGATE!-SEE! MANY MEN GO TOWARD BIG HOUSE WITH TORCH AN' EVIL LOOKS!
WHY...
YOU NO MOVE, WHITE MAN!-YOU BURN US HOUSE WE BURN YOU HOUSE!-ALL EVEN!

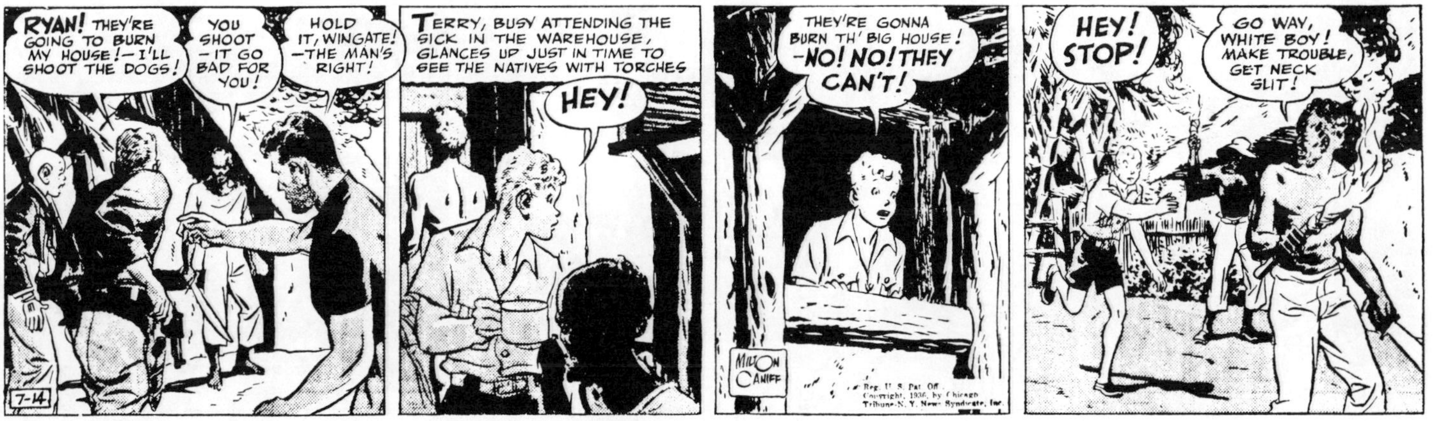
RYAN! THEY'RE GOING TO BURN MY HOUSE!-I'LL SHOOT THE DOGS!
YOU SHOOT -IT GO BAD FOR YOU!
HOLD IT, WINGATE! -THE MAN'S RIGHT!
7-14
TERRY, BUSY ATTENDING THE SICK IN THE WAREHOUSE, GLANCES UP JUST IN TIME TO SEE THE NATIVES WITH TORCHES
HEY!
THEY'RE GONNA BURN TH' BIG HOUSE! -NO! NO! THEY CAN'T!
MILTON CANIFF
Reg. U.S. Pat. Off. Copyright, 1936, by Chicago Tribune-N.Y. News Syndicate, Inc.
HEY! STOP!
GO WAY, WHITE BOY! MAKE TROUBLE, GET NECK SLIT!

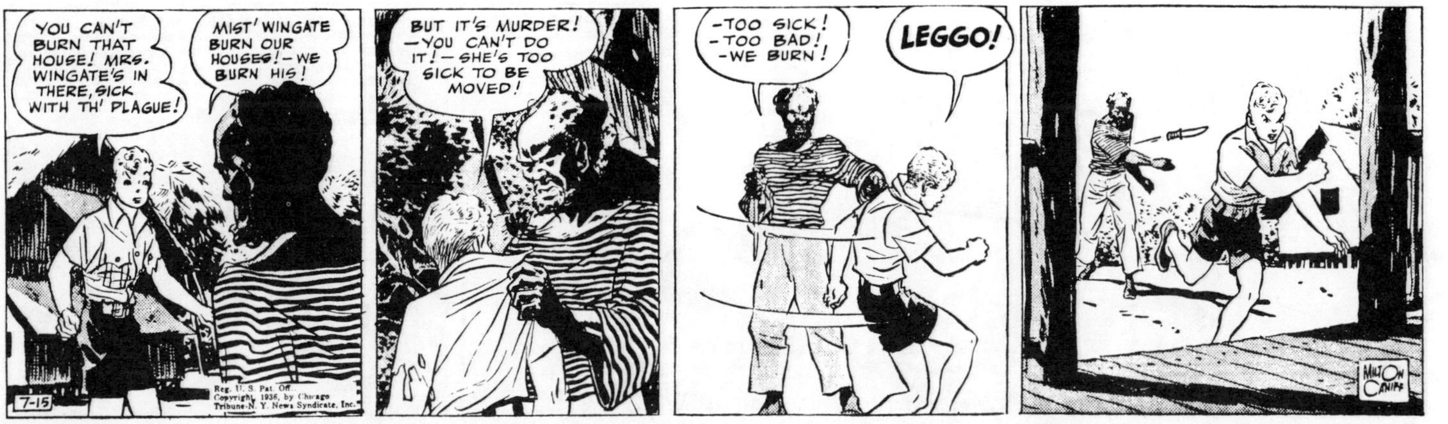
YOU CAN'T BURN THAT HOUSE! MRS. WINGATE'S IN THERE, SICK WITH TH' PLAGUE!
MIST' WINGATE BURN OUR HOUSES!-WE BURN HIS!
7-15
Reg. U.S. Pat. Off. Copyright, 1936, by Chicago Tribune-N.Y. News Syndicate, Inc.
BUT IT'S MURDER! -YOU CAN'T DO IT!-SHE'S TOO SICK TO BE MOVED!
-TOO SICK! -TOO BAD! -WE BURN!
LEGGO!
MILTON CANIFF

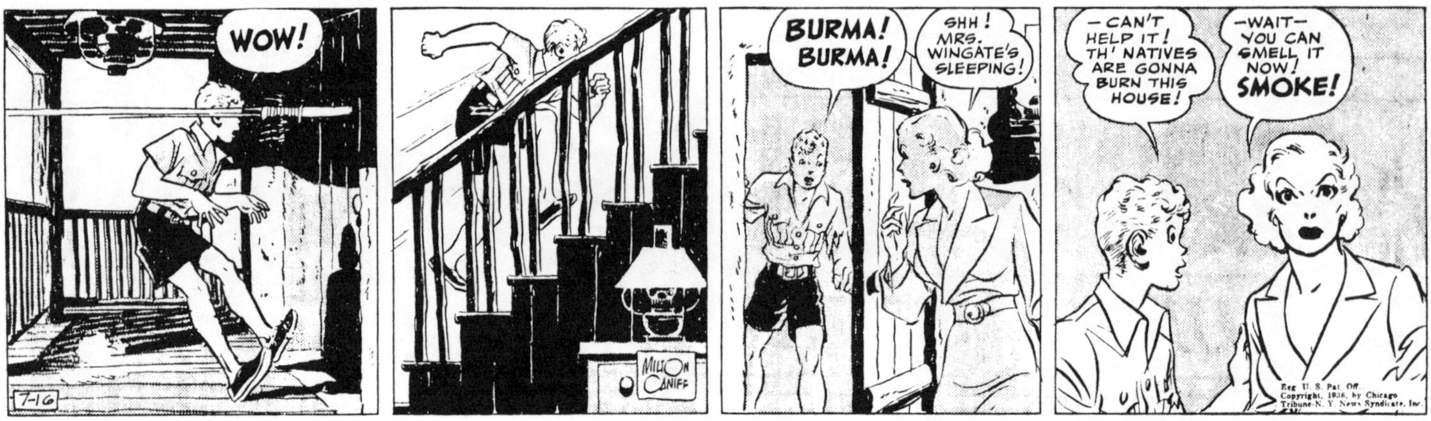
WOW!
7-16
MILTON CANIFF
BURMA! BURMA!
SHH! MRS. WINGATE'S SLEEPING!
—CAN'T HELP IT! TH' NATIVES ARE GONNA BURN THIS HOUSE!
—WAIT— YOU CAN SMELL IT NOW! SMOKE!
Reg. U. S. Pat. Off. Copyright, 1936, by Chicago Tribune-N. Y. News Syndicate, Inc.

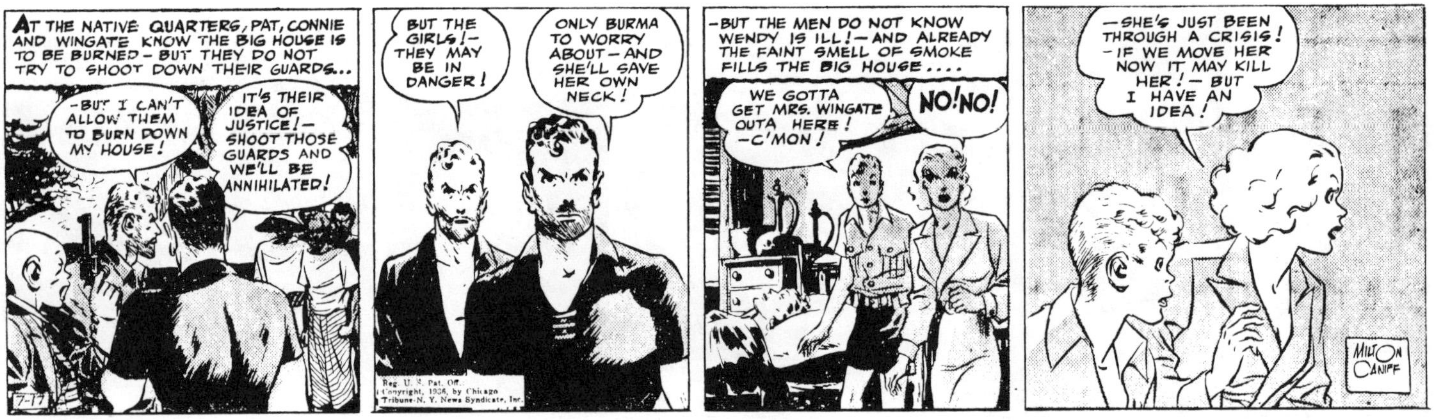
AT THE NATIVE QUARTERS, PAT, CONNIE AND WINGATE KNOW THE BIG HOUSE IS TO BE BURNED — BUT THEY DO NOT TRY TO SHOOT DOWN THEIR GUARDS...
—BUT I CAN'T ALLOW THEM TO BURN DOWN MY HOUSE!
IT'S THEIR IDEA OF JUSTICE! — SHOOT THOSE GUARDS AND WE'LL BE ANNIHILATED!
7-17
BUT THE GIRLS! — THEY MAY BE IN DANGER!
ONLY BURMA TO WORRY ABOUT — AND SHE'LL SAVE HER OWN NECK!
Reg. U. S. Pat. Off. Copyright, 1936, by Chicago Tribune-N. Y. News Syndicate, Inc.
—BUT THE MEN DO NOT KNOW WENDY IS ILL! — AND ALREADY THE FAINT SMELL OF SMOKE FILLS THE BIG HOUSE....
WE GOTTA GET MRS. WINGATE OUTA HERE! —C'MON!
NO! NO!
—SHE'S JUST BEEN THROUGH A CRISIS! —IF WE MOVE HER NOW IT MAY KILL HER! — BUT I HAVE AN IDEA!
MILTON CANIFF

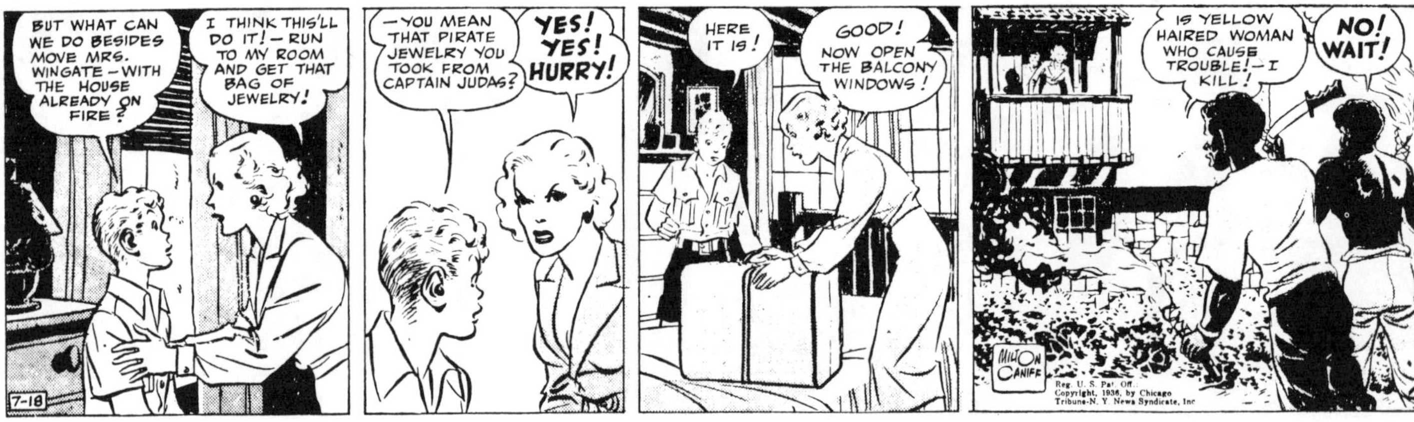
BUT WHAT CAN WE DO BESIDES MOVE MRS. WINGATE — WITH THE HOUSE ALREADY ON FIRE?
I THINK THIS'LL DO IT! — RUN TO MY ROOM AND GET THAT BAG OF JEWELRY!
7-18
—YOU MEAN THAT PIRATE JEWELRY YOU TOOK FROM CAPTAIN JUDAS?
YES! YES! HURRY!
HERE IT IS!
GOOD! NOW OPEN THE BALCONY WINDOWS!
IS YELLOW HAIRED WOMAN WHO CAUSE TROUBLE! — I KILL!
NO! WAIT!
MILTON CANIFF
Reg. U. S. Pat. Off. Copyright, 1936, by Chicago Tribune-N. Y. News Syndicate, Inc

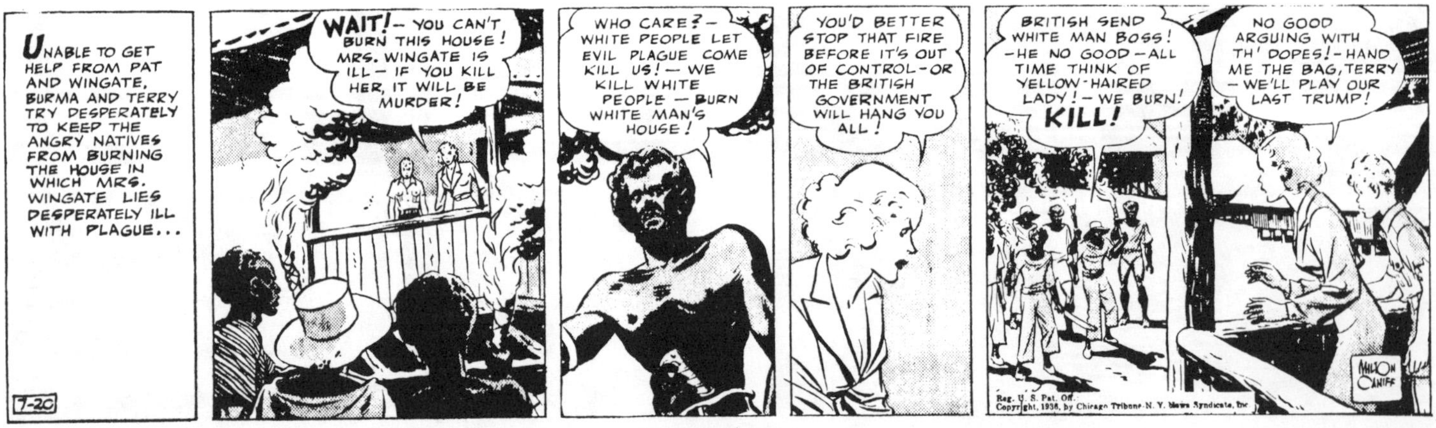
UNABLE TO GET HELP FROM PAT AND WINGATE, BURMA AND TERRY TRY DESPERATELY TO KEEP THE ANGRY NATIVES FROM BURNING THE HOUSE IN WHICH MRS. WINGATE LIES DESPERATELY ILL WITH PLAGUE...
7-20
WAIT! — YOU CAN'T BURN THIS HOUSE! MRS. WINGATE IS ILL — IF YOU KILL HER, IT WILL BE MURDER!
WHO CARE? — WHITE PEOPLE LET EVIL PLAGUE COME KILL US! — WE KILL WHITE PEOPLE — BURN WHITE MAN'S HOUSE!
YOU'D BETTER STOP THAT FIRE BEFORE IT'S OUT OF CONTROL — OR THE BRITISH GOVERNMENT WILL HANG YOU ALL!
BRITISH SEND WHITE MAN BOSS! — HE NO GOOD — ALL TIME THINK OF YELLOW-HAIRED LADY! — WE BURN! KILL!
NO GOOD ARGUING WITH TH' DOPES! — HAND ME THE BAG, TERRY — WE'LL PLAY OUR LAST TRUMP!
MILTON CANIFF
Reg. U. S. Pat. Off. Copyright, 1936, by Chicago Tribune-N. Y. News Syndicate, Inc.

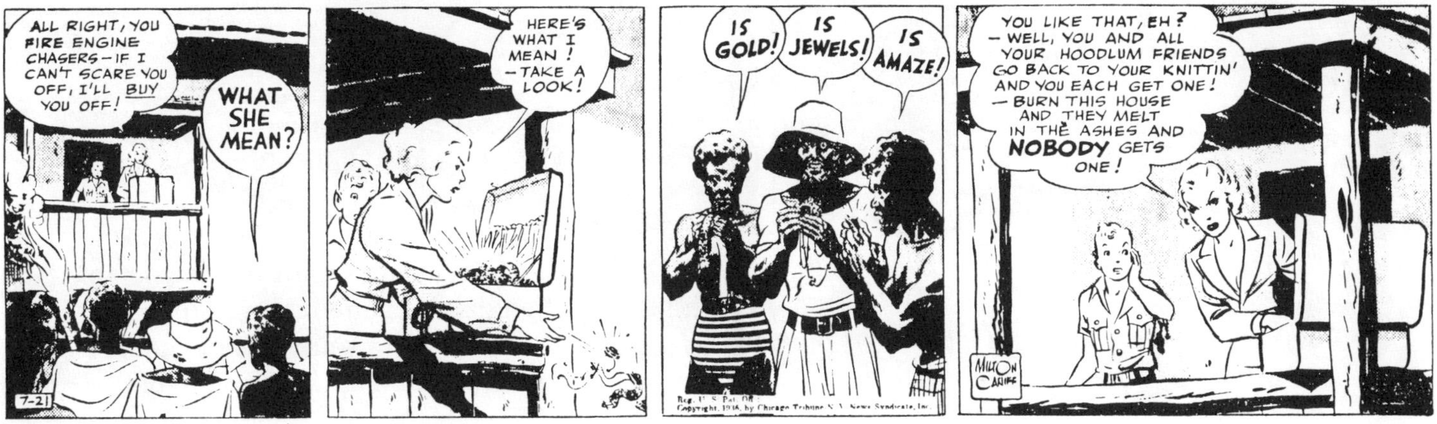
ALL RIGHT, YOU FIRE ENGINE CHASERS—IF I CAN'T SCARE YOU OFF, I'LL BUY YOU OFF!
WHAT SHE MEAN?
HERE'S WHAT I MEAN! —TAKE A LOOK!
IS GOLD!
IS JEWELS!
IS AMAZE!
YOU LIKE THAT, EH? —WELL, YOU AND ALL YOUR HOODLUM FRIENDS GO BACK TO YOUR KNITTIN' AND YOU EACH GET ONE! —BURN THIS HOUSE AND THEY MELT IN THE ASHES AND NOBODY GETS ONE!
MILTON CANIFF
7-21
Reg. U. S. Pat. Off.
Copyright, 1936, by Chicago Tribune N. Y. News Syndicate, Inc.

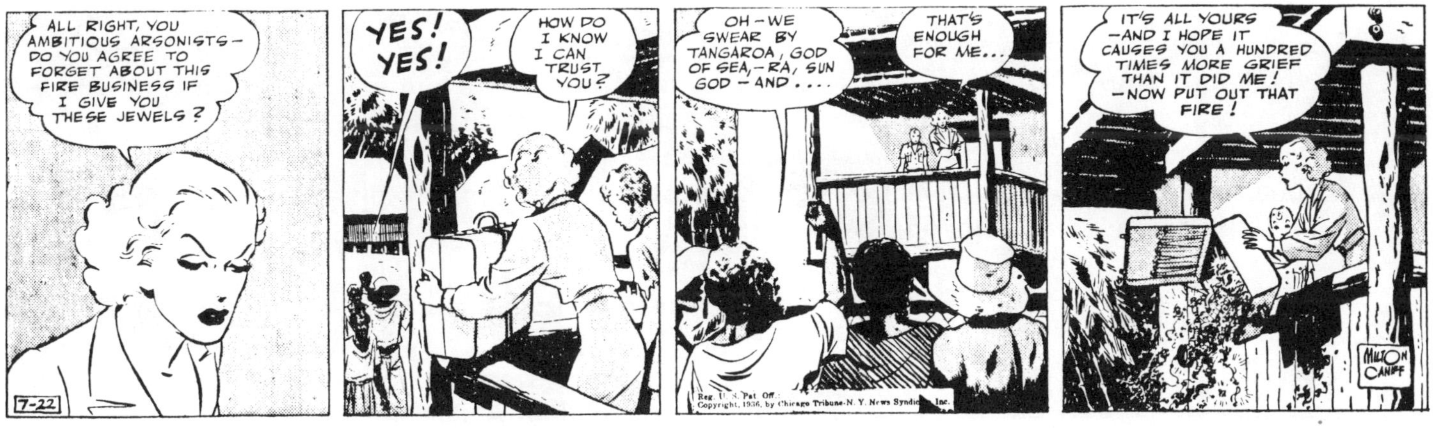
ALL RIGHT, YOU AMBITIOUS ARSONISTS—DO YOU AGREE TO FORGET ABOUT THIS FIRE BUSINESS IF I GIVE YOU THESE JEWELS?
YES! YES!
HOW DO I KNOW I CAN TRUST YOU?
OH—WE SWEAR BY TANGAROA, GOD OF SEA,—RA, SUN GOD—AND....
THAT'S ENOUGH FOR ME...
IT'S ALL YOURS—AND I HOPE IT CAUSES YOU A HUNDRED TIMES MORE GRIEF THAN IT DID ME! —NOW PUT OUT THAT FIRE!
MILTON CANIFF
7-22
Reg. U. S. Pat. Off.
Copyright, 1936, by Chicago Tribune-N. Y. News Syndicate, Inc.

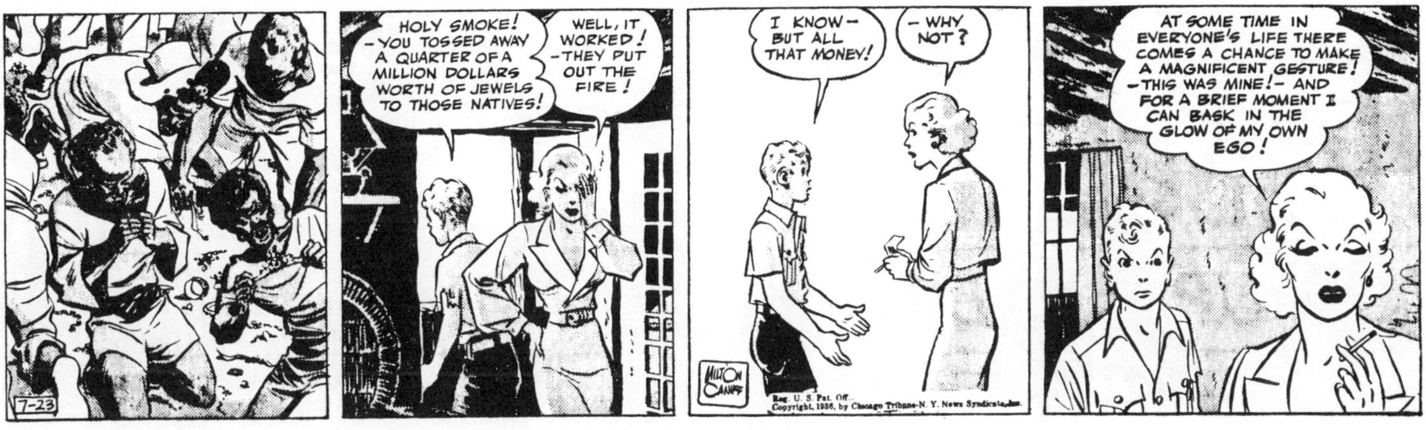
HOLY SMOKE! —YOU TOSSED AWAY A QUARTER OF A MILLION DOLLARS WORTH OF JEWELS TO THOSE NATIVES!
WELL, IT WORKED! —THEY PUT OUT THE FIRE!
I KNOW—BUT ALL THAT MONEY!
—WHY NOT?
AT SOME TIME IN EVERYONE'S LIFE THERE COMES A CHANCE TO MAKE A MAGNIFICENT GESTURE! —THIS WAS MINE!—AND FOR A BRIEF MOMENT I CAN BASK IN THE GLOW OF MY OWN EGO!
MILTON CANIFF
7-23
Reg. U. S. Pat. Off.
Copyright, 1936, by Chicago Tribune-N. Y. News Syndicate, Inc.

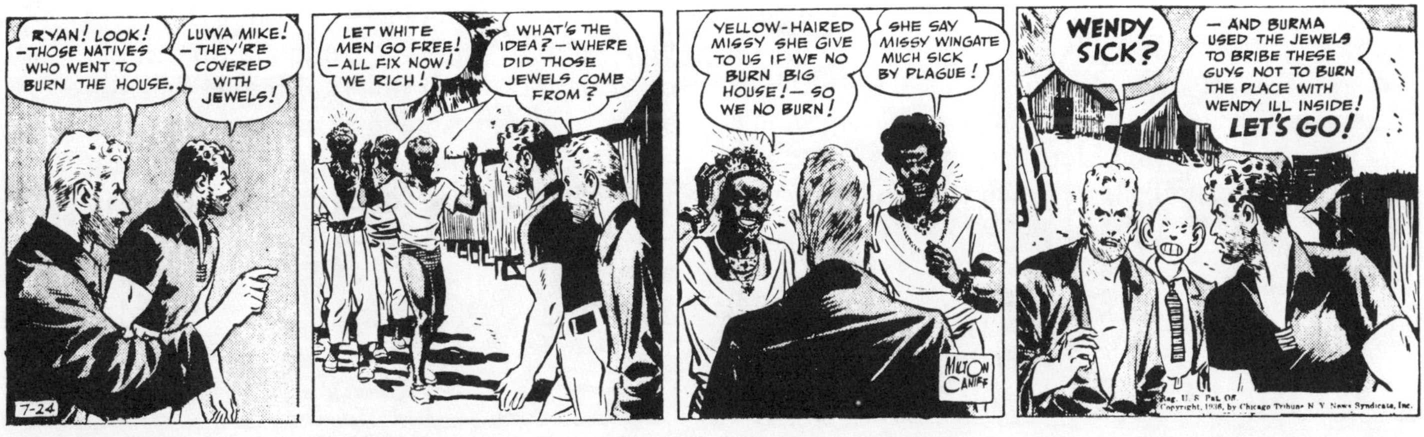
RYAN! LOOK! —THOSE NATIVES WHO WENT TO BURN THE HOUSE.
LUVVA MIKE! —THEY'RE COVERED WITH JEWELS!
LET WHITE MEN GO FREE! —ALL FIX NOW! WE RICH!
WHAT'S THE IDEA? —WHERE DID THOSE JEWELS COME FROM?
YELLOW-HAIRED MISSY SHE GIVE TO US IF WE NO BURN BIG HOUSE!—SO WE NO BURN!
SHE SAY MISSY WINGATE MUCH SICK BY PLAGUE!
WENDY SICK?
—AND BURMA USED THE JEWELS TO BRIBE THESE GUYS NOT TO BURN THE PLACE WITH WENDY ILL INSIDE! LET'S GO!
MILTON CANIFF
7-24
Reg. U. S. Pat. Off.
Copyright, 1936, by Chicago Tribune N. Y. News Syndicate, Inc.

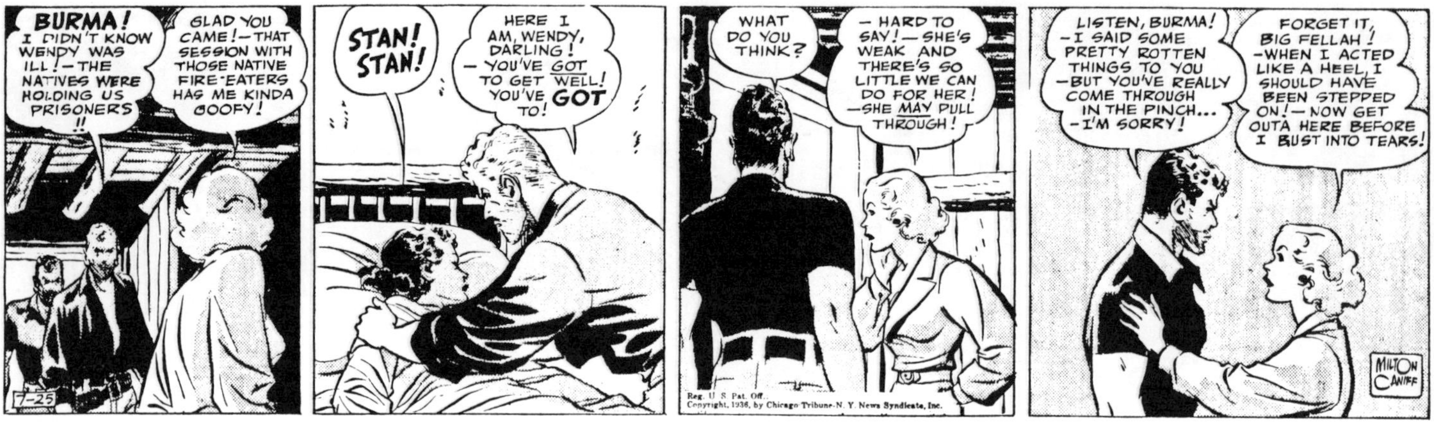
BURMA! I DIDN'T KNOW WENDY WAS ILL! – THE NATIVES WERE HOLDING US PRISONERS !!
GLAD YOU CAME! – THAT SESSION WITH THOSE NATIVE FIRE-EATERS HAS ME KINDA GOOFY!
7-25
STAN! STAN!
HERE I AM, WENDY, DARLING! – YOU'VE GOT TO GET WELL! YOU'VE GOT TO!
WHAT DO YOU THINK?
– HARD TO SAY! – SHE'S WEAK AND THERE'S SO LITTLE WE CAN DO FOR HER! – SHE MAY PULL THROUGH!
Reg. U. S. Pat. Off. Copyright, 1936, by Chicago Tribune-N. Y. News Syndicate, Inc.
LISTEN, BURMA! – I SAID SOME PRETTY ROTTEN THINGS TO YOU – BUT YOU'VE REALLY COME THROUGH IN THE PINCH... – I'M SORRY!
FORGET IT, BIG FELLAH! – WHEN I ACTED LIKE A HEEL, I SHOULD HAVE BEEN STEPPED ON! – NOW GET OUTA HERE BEFORE I BUST INTO TEARS!
MILTON CANIFF

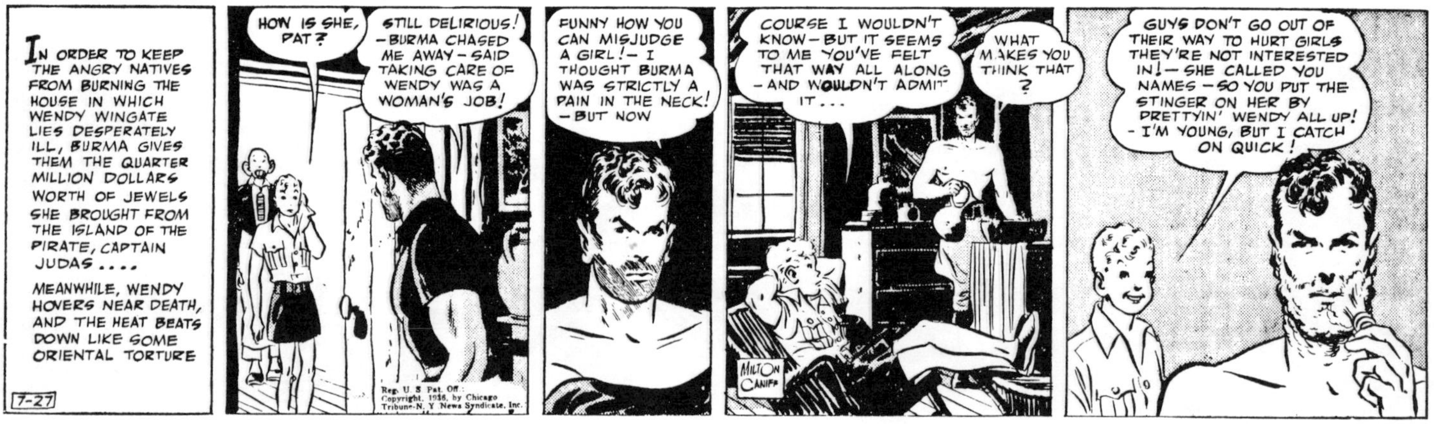
IN ORDER TO KEEP THE ANGRY NATIVES FROM BURNING THE HOUSE IN WHICH WENDY WINGATE LIES DESPERATELY ILL, BURMA GIVES THEM THE QUARTER MILLION DOLLARS WORTH OF JEWELS SHE BROUGHT FROM THE ISLAND OF THE PIRATE, CAPTAIN JUDAS....
MEANWHILE, WENDY HOVERS NEAR DEATH, AND THE HEAT BEATS DOWN LIKE SOME ORIENTAL TORTURE
7-27
HOW IS SHE, PAT?
STILL DELIRIOUS! – BURMA CHASED ME AWAY – SAID TAKING CARE OF WENDY WAS A WOMAN'S JOB!
Reg. U. S. Pat. Off.: Copyright, 1936, by Chicago Tribune-N. Y. News Syndicate, Inc.
FUNNY HOW YOU CAN MISJUDGE A GIRL! – I THOUGHT BURMA WAS STRICTLY A PAIN IN THE NECK! – BUT NOW
COURSE I WOULDN'T KNOW – BUT IT SEEMS TO ME YOU'VE FELT THAT WAY ALL ALONG – AND WOULDN'T ADMIT IT...
WHAT MAKES YOU THINK THAT?
MILTON CANIFF
GUYS DON'T GO OUT OF THEIR WAY TO HURT GIRLS THEY'RE NOT INTERESTED IN! – SHE CALLED YOU NAMES – SO YOU PUT THE STINGER ON HER BY PRETTYIN' WENDY ALL UP! – I'M YOUNG, BUT I CATCH ON QUICK!

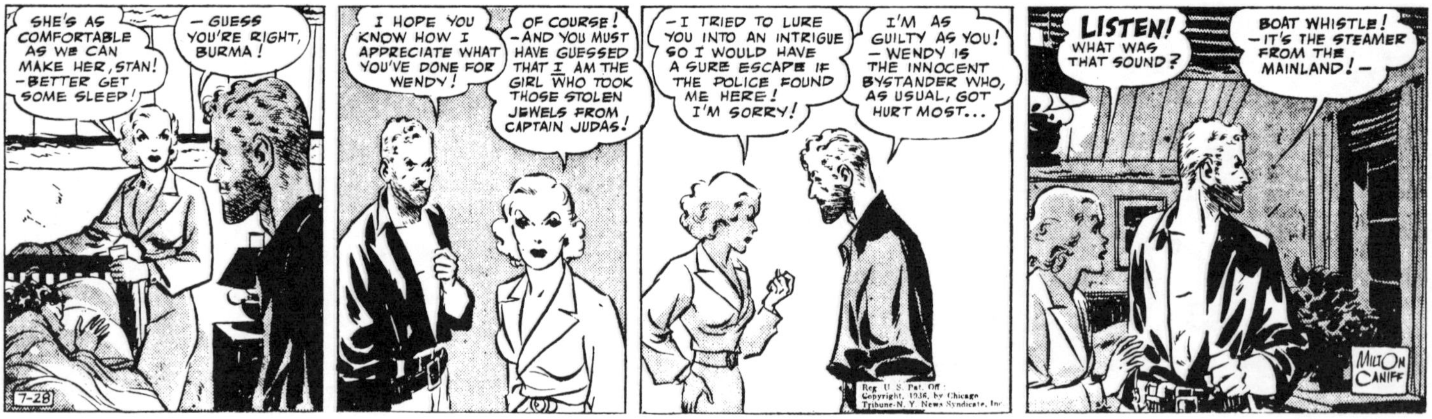
SHE'S AS COMFORTABLE AS WE CAN MAKE HER, STAN! – BETTER GET SOME SLEEP!
– GUESS YOU'RE RIGHT, BURMA!
7-28
I HOPE YOU KNOW HOW I APPRECIATE WHAT YOU'VE DONE FOR WENDY!
OF COURSE! – AND YOU MUST HAVE GUESSED THAT I AM THE GIRL WHO TOOK THOSE STOLEN JEWELS FROM CAPTAIN JUDAS!
– I TRIED TO LURE YOU INTO AN INTRIGUE SO I WOULD HAVE A SURE ESCAPE IF THE POLICE FOUND ME HERE! I'M SORRY!
I'M AS GUILTY AS YOU! – WENDY IS THE INNOCENT BYSTANDER WHO, AS USUAL, GOT HURT MOST...
Reg. U. S. Pat. Off.: Copyright, 1936, by Chicago Tribune-N. Y. News Syndicate, Inc.
LISTEN! WHAT WAS THAT SOUND?
BOAT WHISTLE! – IT'S THE STEAMER FROM THE MAINLAND! –
MILTON CANIFF

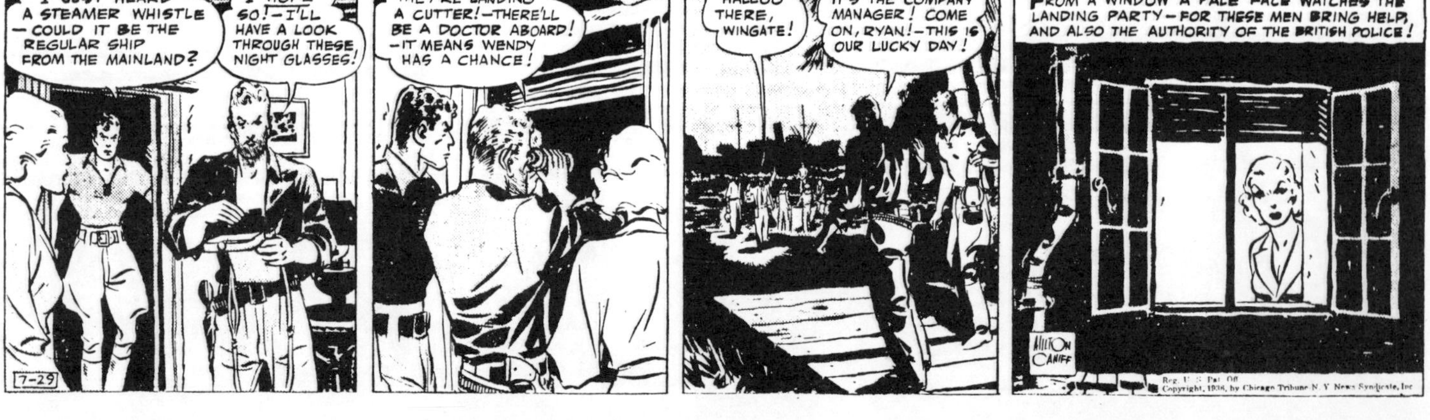
I JUST HEARD A STEAMER WHISTLE – COULD IT BE THE REGULAR SHIP FROM THE MAINLAND?
I HOPE SO! – I'LL HAVE A LOOK THROUGH THESE NIGHT GLASSES!
7-29
THEY'RE LANDING A CUTTER! – THERE'LL BE A DOCTOR ABOARD! – IT MEANS WENDY HAS A CHANCE!
HALLOO THERE, WINGATE!
IT'S THE COMPANY MANAGER! COME ON, RYAN! – THIS IS OUR LUCKY DAY!
FROM A WINDOW A PALE FACE WATCHES THE LANDING PARTY – FOR THESE MEN BRING HELP, AND ALSO THE AUTHORITY OF THE BRITISH POLICE!
MILTON CANIFF
Reg. U. S. Pat. Off. Copyright, 1936, by Chicago Tribune-N. Y. News Syndicate, Inc.

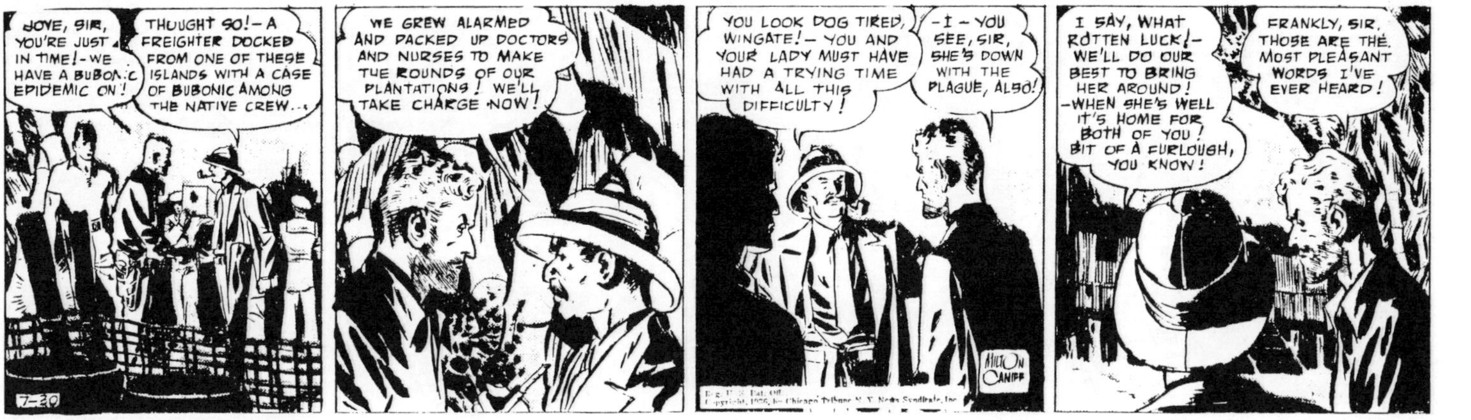
JOVE, SIR, YOU'RE JUST IN TIME! - WE HAVE A BUBONIC EPIDEMIC ON!
THOUGHT SO! - A FREIGHTER DOCKED FROM ONE OF THESE ISLANDS WITH A CASE OF BUBONIC AMONG THE NATIVE CREW...
WE GREW ALARMED AND PACKED UP DOCTORS AND NURSES TO MAKE THE ROUNDS OF OUR PLANTATIONS! WE'LL TAKE CHARGE NOW!
YOU LOOK DOG TIRED, WINGATE! - YOU AND YOUR LADY MUST HAVE HAD A TRYING TIME WITH ALL THIS DIFFICULTY!
- I - YOU SEE, SIR, SHE'S DOWN WITH THE PLAGUE, ALSO!
I SAY, WHAT ROTTEN LUCK! - WE'LL DO OUR BEST TO BRING HER AROUND! - WHEN SHE'S WELL IT'S HOME FOR BOTH OF YOU! BIT OF A FURLOUGH, YOU KNOW!
FRANKLY, SIR, THOSE ARE THE MOST PLEASANT WORDS I'VE EVER HEARD!
MILTON CANIFF
Reg. U. S. Pat. Off. Copyright, 1936, by Chicago Tribune-N. Y. News Syndicate, Inc.
7-30

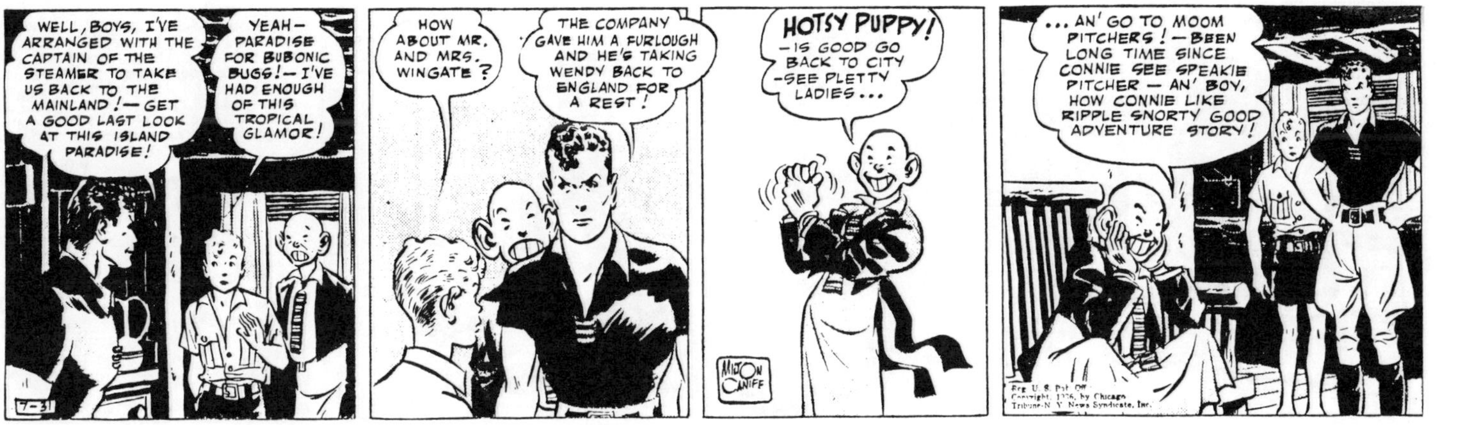
WELL, BOYS, I'VE ARRANGED WITH THE CAPTAIN OF THE STEAMER TO TAKE US BACK TO THE MAINLAND! - GET A GOOD LAST LOOK AT THIS ISLAND PARADISE!
YEAH - PARADISE FOR BUBONIC BUGS! - I'VE HAD ENOUGH OF THIS TROPICAL GLAMOR!
HOW ABOUT MR. AND MRS. WINGATE?
THE COMPANY GAVE HIM A FURLOUGH AND HE'S TAKING WENDY BACK TO ENGLAND FOR A REST!
HOTSY PUPPY! - IS GOOD GO BACK TO CITY - SEE PLETTY LADIES...
... AN' GO TO MOOM PITCHERS! - BEEN LONG TIME SINCE CONNIE SEE SPEAKIE PITCHER - AN' BOY, HOW CONNIE LIKE RIPPLE SNORTY GOOD ADVENTURE STORY!
MILTON CANIFF
Reg. U. S. Pat. Off. Copyright, 1936, by Chicago Tribune-N. Y. News Syndicate, Inc.
7-31

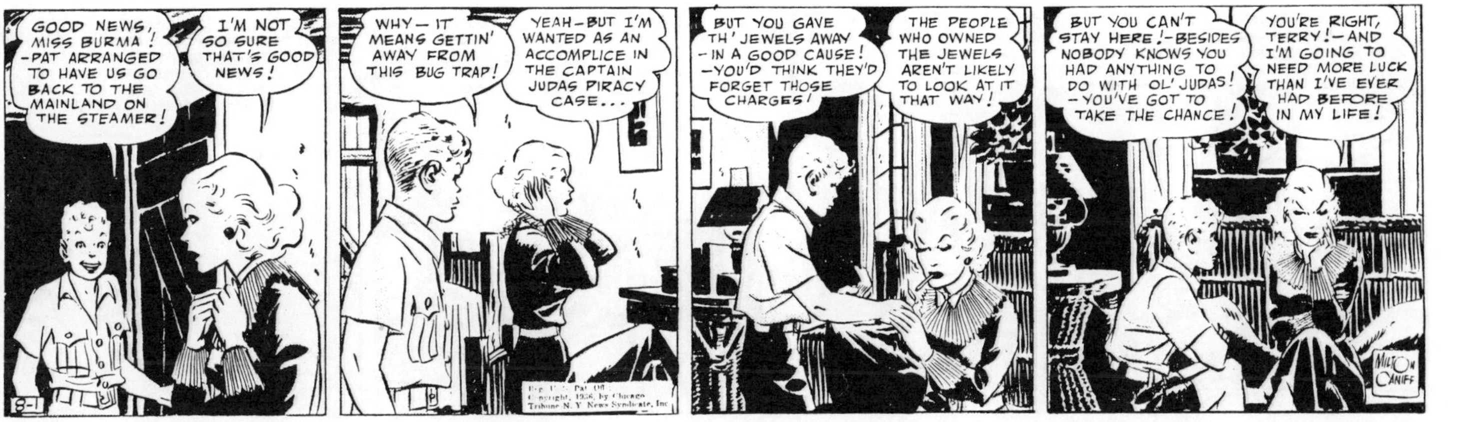
GOOD NEWS, MISS BURMA! - PAT ARRANGED TO HAVE US GO BACK TO THE MAINLAND ON THE STEAMER!
I'M NOT SO SURE THAT'S GOOD NEWS!
WHY - IT MEANS GETTIN' AWAY FROM THIS BUG TRAP!
YEAH - BUT I'M WANTED AS AN ACCOMPLICE IN THE CAPTAIN JUDAS PIRACY CASE...
BUT YOU GAVE TH' JEWELS AWAY - IN A GOOD CAUSE! - YOU'D THINK THEY'D FORGET THOSE CHARGES!
THE PEOPLE WHO OWNED THE JEWELS AREN'T LIKELY TO LOOK AT IT THAT WAY!
BUT YOU CAN'T STAY HERE! - BESIDES NOBODY KNOWS YOU HAD ANYTHING TO DO WITH OL' JUDAS! - YOU'VE GOT TO TAKE THE CHANCE!
YOU'RE RIGHT, TERRY! - AND I'M GOING TO NEED MORE LUCK THAN I'VE EVER HAD BEFORE IN MY LIFE!
MILTON CANIFF
Reg. U. S. Pat. Off. Copyright, 1936, by Chicago Tribune-N. Y. News Syndicate, Inc.
8-1

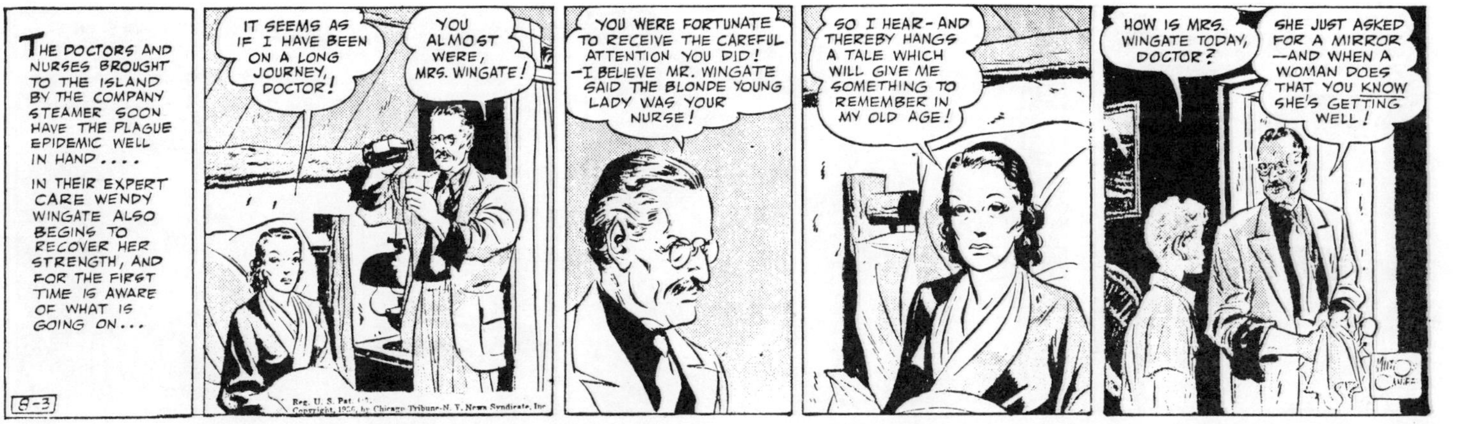
THE DOCTORS AND NURSES BROUGHT TO THE ISLAND BY THE COMPANY STEAMER SOON HAVE THE PLAGUE EPIDEMIC WELL IN HAND....
IN THEIR EXPERT CARE WENDY WINGATE ALSO BEGINS TO RECOVER HER STRENGTH, AND FOR THE FIRST TIME IS AWARE OF WHAT IS GOING ON...
IT SEEMS AS IF I HAVE BEEN ON A LONG JOURNEY, DOCTOR!
YOU ALMOST WERE, MRS. WINGATE!
YOU WERE FORTUNATE TO RECEIVE THE CAREFUL ATTENTION YOU DID! - I BELIEVE MR. WINGATE SAID THE BLONDE YOUNG LADY WAS YOUR NURSE!
SO I HEAR - AND THEREBY HANGS A TALE WHICH WILL GIVE ME SOMETHING TO REMEMBER IN MY OLD AGE!
HOW IS MRS. WINGATE TODAY, DOCTOR?
SHE JUST ASKED FOR A MIRROR - AND WHEN A WOMAN DOES THAT YOU KNOW SHE'S GETTING WELL!
MILTON CANIFF
Reg. U. S. Pat. Off. Copyright, 1936, by Chicago Tribune-N. Y. News Syndicate, Inc.
8-3

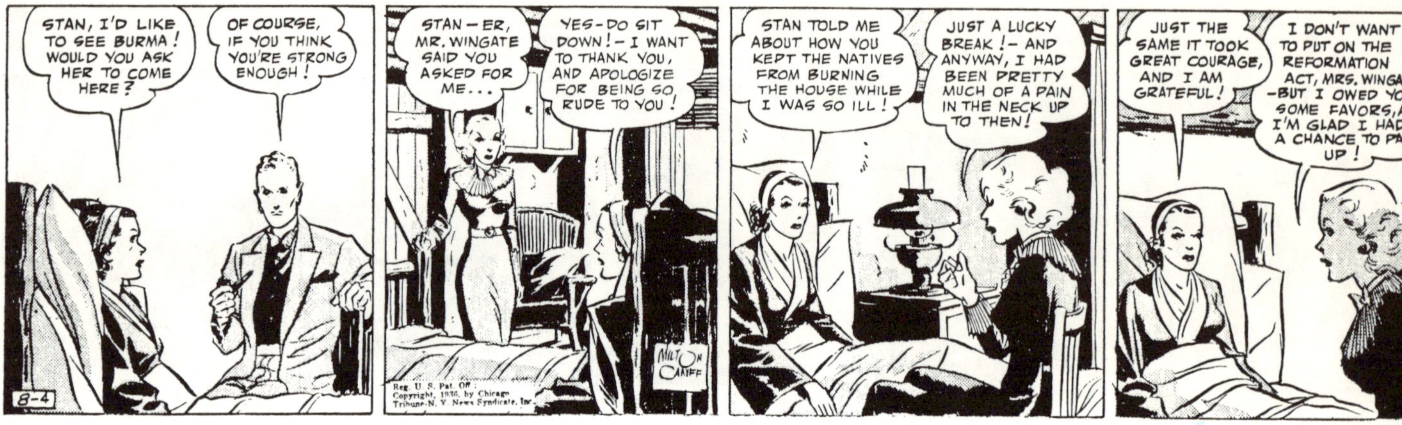
STAN, I'D LIKE TO SEE BURMA! WOULD YOU ASK HER TO COME HERE?
OF COURSE, IF YOU THINK YOU'RE STRONG ENOUGH!
8-4
STAN—ER, MR. WINGATE SAID YOU ASKED FOR ME...
YES-DO SIT DOWN!—I WANT TO THANK YOU, AND APOLOGIZE FOR BEING SO RUDE TO YOU!
Reg. U. S. Pat. Off. Copyright, 1936, by Chicago Tribune-N. Y. News Syndicate, Inc.
MILTON CANIFF
STAN TOLD ME ABOUT HOW YOU KEPT THE NATIVES FROM BURNING THE HOUSE WHILE I WAS SO ILL!
JUST A LUCKY BREAK!—AND ANYWAY, I HAD BEEN PRETTY MUCH OF A PAIN IN THE NECK UP TO THEN!
JUST THE SAME IT TOOK GREAT COURAGE, AND I AM GRATEFUL!
I DON'T WANT TO PUT ON THE REFORMATION ACT, MRS. WINGATE, —BUT I OWED YOU SOME FAVORS, AND I'M GLAD I HAD A CHANCE TO PAY UP!

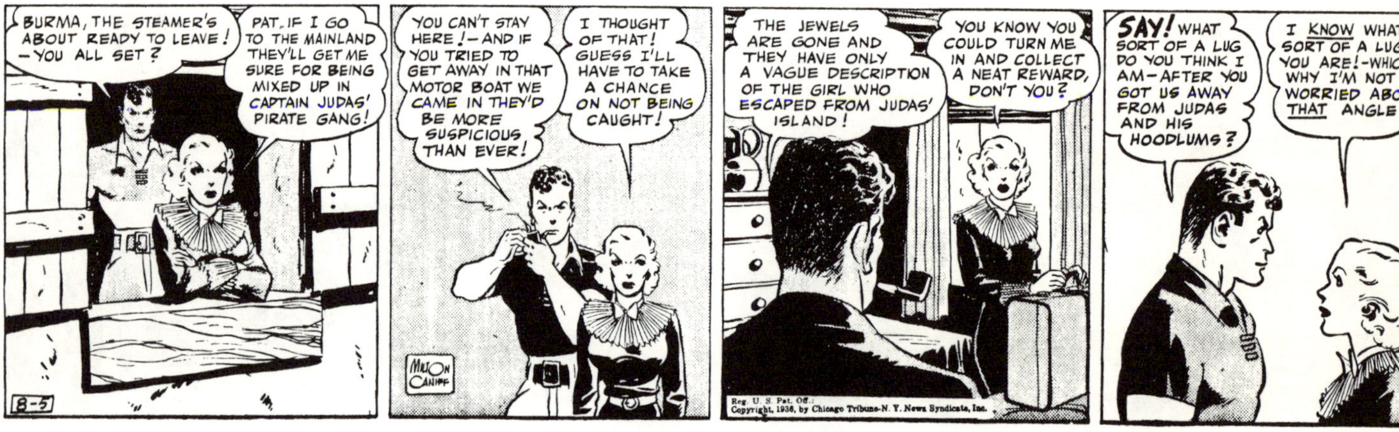
BURMA, THE STEAMER'S ABOUT READY TO LEAVE! —YOU ALL SET?
PAT, IF I GO TO THE MAINLAND THEY'LL GET ME SURE FOR BEING MIXED UP IN CAPTAIN JUDAS' PIRATE GANG!
8-5
YOU CAN'T STAY HERE!—AND IF YOU TRIED TO GET AWAY IN THAT MOTOR BOAT WE CAME IN THEY'D BE MORE SUSPICIOUS THAN EVER!
I THOUGHT OF THAT! GUESS I'LL HAVE TO TAKE A CHANCE ON NOT BEING CAUGHT!
MILTON CANIFF
THE JEWELS ARE GONE AND THEY HAVE ONLY A VAGUE DESCRIPTION OF THE GIRL WHO ESCAPED FROM JUDAS' ISLAND!
YOU KNOW YOU COULD TURN ME IN AND COLLECT A NEAT REWARD, DON'T YOU?
Reg. U. S. Pat. Off. Copyright, 1936, by Chicago Tribune-N. Y. News Syndicate, Inc.
SAY! WHAT SORT OF A LUG DO YOU THINK I AM—AFTER YOU GOT US AWAY FROM JUDAS AND HIS HOODLUMS?
I KNOW WHAT SORT OF A LUG YOU ARE!—WHICH IS WHY I'M NOT WORRIED ABOUT THAT ANGLE!

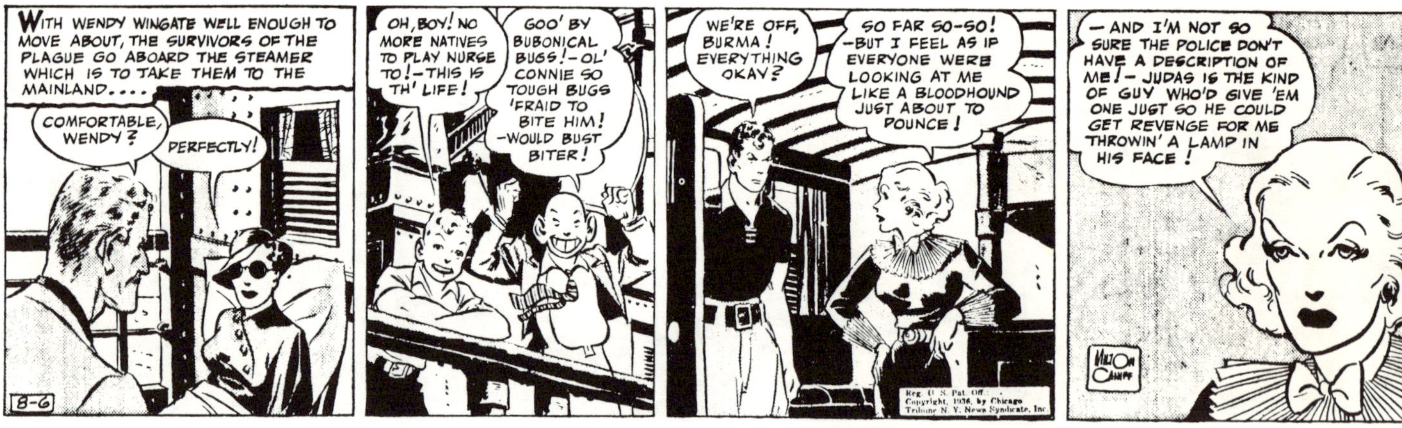
WITH WENDY WINGATE WELL ENOUGH TO MOVE ABOUT, THE SURVIVORS OF THE PLAGUE GO ABOARD THE STEAMER WHICH IS TO TAKE THEM TO THE MAINLAND...
COMFORTABLE, WENDY?
PERFECTLY!
8-6
OH, BOY! NO MORE NATIVES TO PLAY NURSE TO!—THIS IS TH' LIFE!
GOO' BY BUBONICAL BUGS!—OL' CONNIE SO TOUGH BUGS 'FRAID TO BITE HIM! —WOULD BUST BITER!
WE'RE OFF, BURMA! EVERYTHING OKAY?
SO FAR SO-SO! —BUT I FEEL AS IF EVERYONE WERE LOOKING AT ME LIKE A BLOODHOUND JUST ABOUT TO POUNCE!
Reg. U. S. Pat. Off. Copyright, 1936, by Chicago Tribune-N. Y. News Syndicate, Inc.
MILTON CANIFF
—AND I'M NOT SO SURE THE POLICE DON'T HAVE A DESCRIPTION OF ME!—JUDAS IS THE KIND OF GUY WHO'D GIVE 'EM ONE JUST SO HE COULD GET REVENGE FOR ME THROWIN' A LAMP IN HIS FACE!

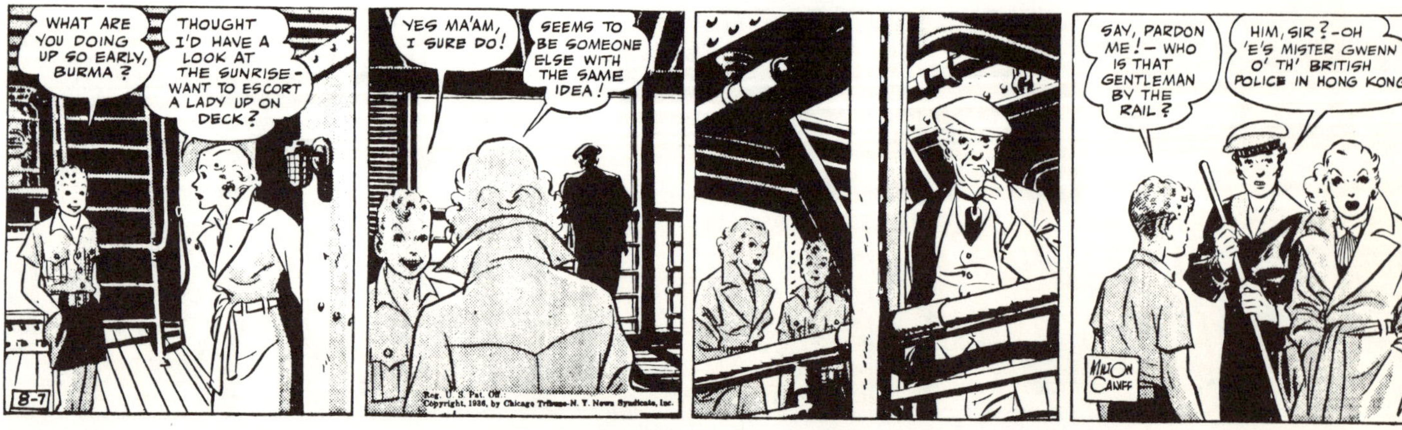
WHAT ARE YOU DOING UP SO EARLY, BURMA?
THOUGHT I'D HAVE A LOOK AT THE SUNRISE- WANT TO ESCORT A LADY UP ON DECK?
8-7
YES MA'AM, I SURE DO!
SEEMS TO BE SOMEONE ELSE WITH THE SAME IDEA!
Reg. U. S. Pat. Off. Copyright, 1936, by Chicago Tribune-N. Y. News Syndicate, Inc.
SAY, PARDON ME!—WHO IS THAT GENTLEMAN BY THE RAIL?
HIM, SIR?—OH 'E'S MISTER GWENN O' TH' BRITISH POLICE IN HONG KONG!
MILTON CANIFF

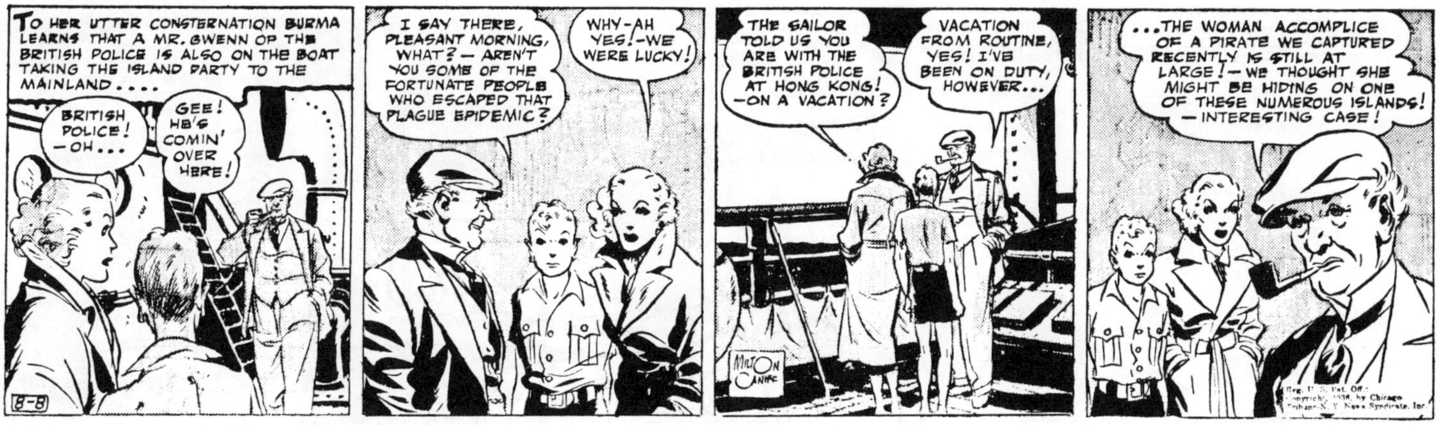
TO HER UTTER CONSTERNATION BURMA LEARNS THAT A MR. GWENN OF THE BRITISH POLICE IS ALSO ON THE BOAT TAKING THE ISLAND PARTY TO THE MAINLAND....
BRITISH POLICE! –OH...
GEE! HE'S COMIN' OVER HERE!
I SAY THERE, PLEASANT MORNING, WHAT? – AREN'T YOU SOME OF THE FORTUNATE PEOPLE WHO ESCAPED THAT PLAGUE EPIDEMIC?
WHY-AH YES! –WE WERE LUCKY!
THE SAILOR TOLD US YOU ARE WITH THE BRITISH POLICE AT HONG KONG! –ON A VACATION?
VACATION FROM ROUTINE, YES! I'VE BEEN ON DUTY, HOWEVER...
MILTON CANIFF
...THE WOMAN ACCOMPLICE OF A PIRATE WE CAPTURED RECENTLY IS STILL AT LARGE! – WE THOUGHT SHE MIGHT BE HIDING ON ONE OF THESE NUMEROUS ISLANDS! – INTERESTING CASE!
Reg. U. S. Pat. Off. Copyright, 1938, by Chicago Tribune-N. Y. News Syndicate, Inc.
8-8

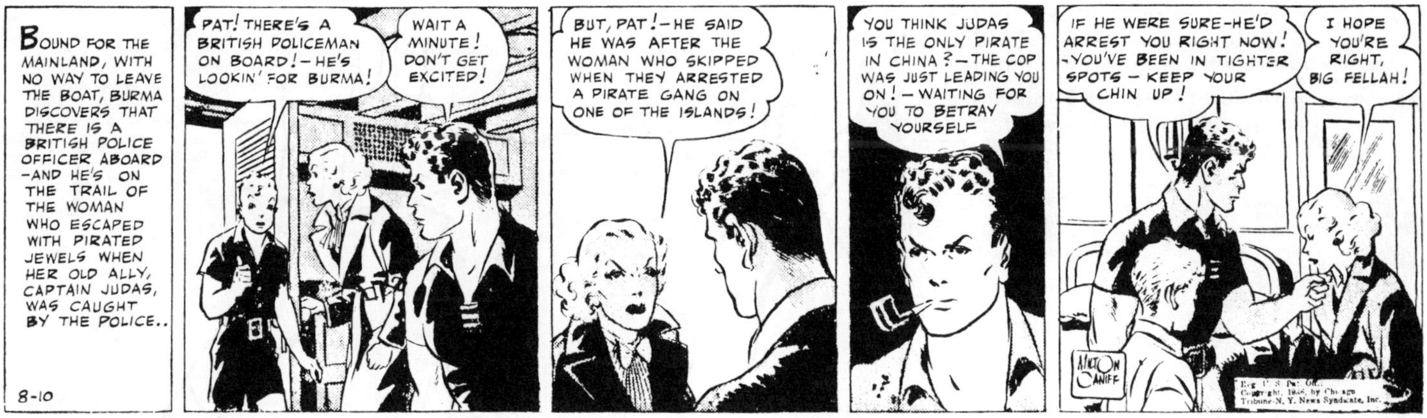
BOUND FOR THE MAINLAND, WITH NO WAY TO LEAVE THE BOAT, BURMA DISCOVERS THAT THERE IS A BRITISH POLICE OFFICER ABOARD –AND HE'S ON THE TRAIL OF THE WOMAN WHO ESCAPED WITH PIRATED JEWELS WHEN HER OLD ALLY, CAPTAIN JUDAS, WAS CAUGHT BY THE POLICE..
8-10
PAT! THERE'S A BRITISH POLICEMAN ON BOARD! – HE'S LOOKIN' FOR BURMA!
WAIT A MINUTE! DON'T GET EXCITED!
BUT, PAT! – HE SAID HE WAS AFTER THE WOMAN WHO SKIPPED WHEN THEY ARRESTED A PIRATE GANG ON ONE OF THE ISLANDS!
YOU THINK JUDAS IS THE ONLY PIRATE IN CHINA? – THE COP WAS JUST LEADING YOU ON! – WAITING FOR YOU TO BETRAY YOURSELF
IF HE WERE SURE-HE'D ARREST YOU RIGHT NOW! -YOU'VE BEEN IN TIGHTER SPOTS – KEEP YOUR CHIN UP!
I HOPE YOU'RE RIGHT, BIG FELLAH!
MILTON CANIFF
Reg. U. S. Pat. Off. Copyright, 1938, by Chicago Tribune-N. Y. News Syndicate, Inc.

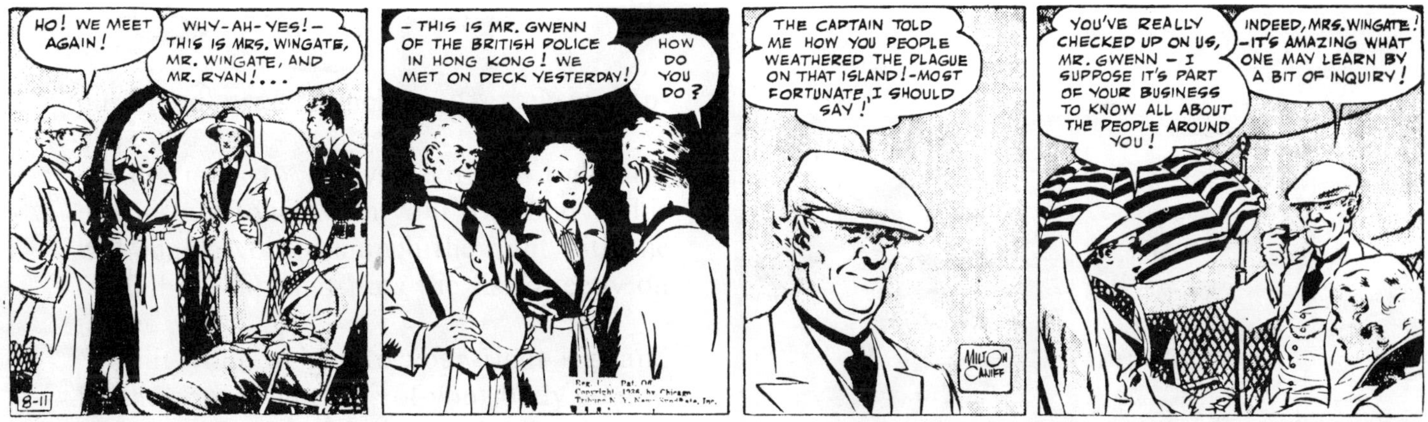
HO! WE MEET AGAIN!
WHY-AH-YES! – THIS IS MRS. WINGATE, MR. WINGATE, AND MR. RYAN!...
8-11
– THIS IS MR. GWENN OF THE BRITISH POLICE IN HONG KONG! WE MET ON DECK YESTERDAY!
HOW DO YOU DO?
Reg. U. S. Pat. Off. Copyright, 1938, by Chicago Tribune-N. Y. News Syndicate, Inc.
THE CAPTAIN TOLD ME HOW YOU PEOPLE WEATHERED THE PLAGUE ON THAT ISLAND! – MOST FORTUNATE, I SHOULD SAY!
MILTON CANIFF
YOU'VE REALLY CHECKED UP ON US, MR. GWENN – I SUPPOSE IT'S PART OF YOUR BUSINESS TO KNOW ALL ABOUT THE PEOPLE AROUND YOU!
INDEED, MRS. WINGATE! – IT'S AMAZING WHAT ONE MAY LEARN BY A BIT OF INQUIRY!

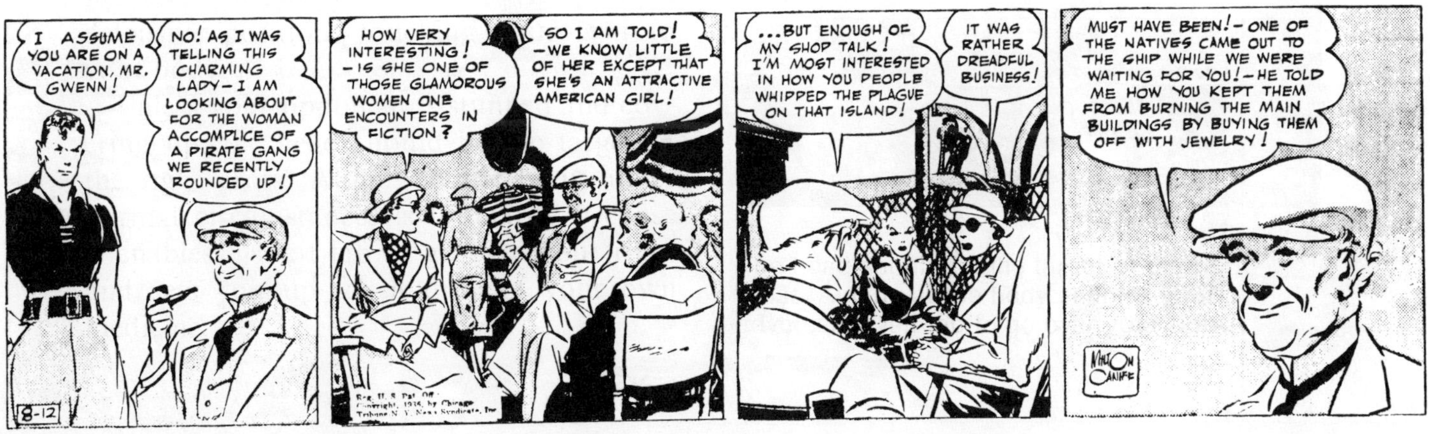
I ASSUME YOU ARE ON A VACATION, MR. GWENN!
NO! AS I WAS TELLING THIS CHARMING LADY – I AM LOOKING ABOUT FOR THE WOMAN ACCOMPLICE OF A PIRATE GANG WE RECENTLY ROUNDED UP!
8-12
HOW VERY INTERESTING! – IS SHE ONE OF THOSE GLAMOROUS WOMEN ONE ENCOUNTERS IN FICTION?
SO I AM TOLD! – WE KNOW LITTLE OF HER EXCEPT THAT SHE'S AN ATTRACTIVE AMERICAN GIRL!
Reg. U. S. Pat. Off. Copyright, 1938, by Chicago Tribune-N. Y. News Syndicate, Inc.
...BUT ENOUGH OF MY SHOP TALK! I'M MOST INTERESTED IN HOW YOU PEOPLE WHIPPED THE PLAGUE ON THAT ISLAND!
IT WAS RATHER DREADFUL BUSINESS!
MUST HAVE BEEN! – ONE OF THE NATIVES CAME OUT TO THE SHIP WHILE WE WERE WAITING FOR YOU! – HE TOLD ME HOW YOU KEPT THEM FROM BURNING THE MAIN BUILDINGS BY BUYING THEM OFF WITH JEWELRY!
MILTON CANIFF

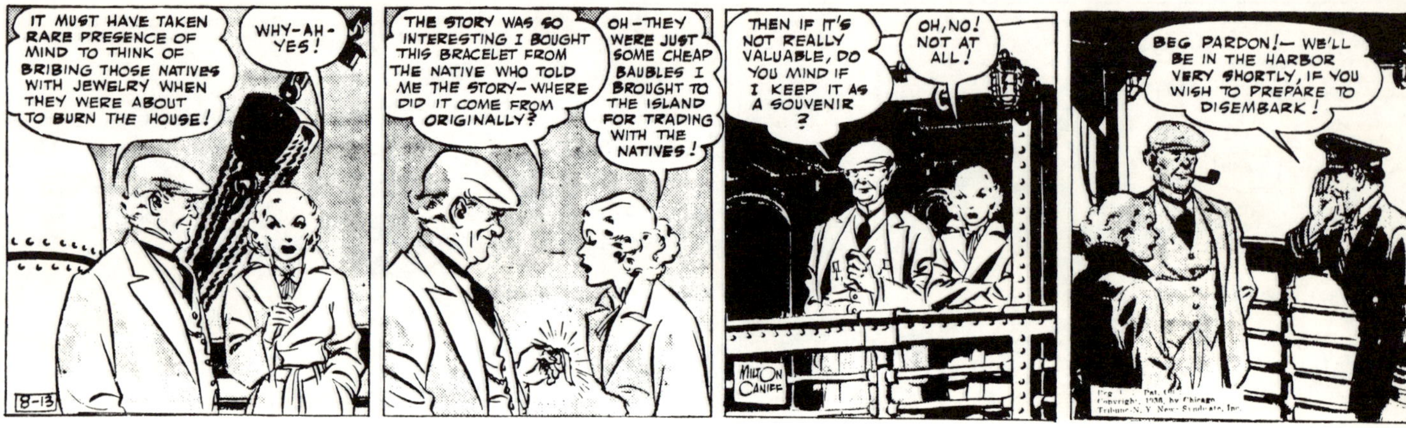
IT MUST HAVE TAKEN RARE PRESENCE OF MIND TO THINK OF BRIBING THOSE NATIVES WITH JEWELRY WHEN THEY WERE ABOUT TO BURN THE HOUSE!
WHY-AH-YES!
8-13
THE STORY WAS SO INTERESTING I BOUGHT THIS BRACELET FROM THE NATIVE WHO TOLD ME THE STORY-WHERE DID IT COME FROM ORIGINALLY?
OH-THEY WERE JUST SOME CHEAP BAUBLES I BROUGHT TO THE ISLAND FOR TRADING WITH THE NATIVES!
THEN IF IT'S NOT REALLY VALUABLE, DO YOU MIND IF I KEEP IT AS A SOUVENIR?
OH, NO! NOT AT ALL!
MILTON CANIFF
BEG PARDON!-WE'LL BE IN THE HARBOR VERY SHORTLY, IF YOU WISH TO PREPARE TO DISEMBARK!

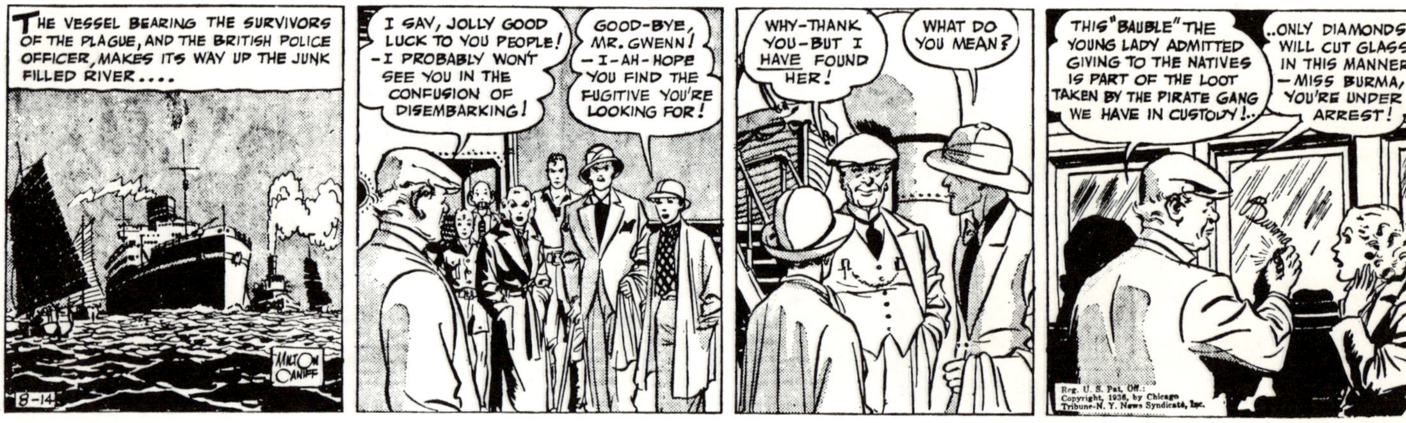
THE VESSEL BEARING THE SURVIVORS OF THE PLAGUE, AND THE BRITISH POLICE OFFICER, MAKES ITS WAY UP THE JUNK FILLED RIVER....
MILTON CANIFF
8-14
I SAY, JOLLY GOOD LUCK TO YOU PEOPLE! -I PROBABLY WON'T SEE YOU IN THE CONFUSION OF DISEMBARKING!
GOOD-BYE, MR. GWENN! -I-AH-HOPE YOU FIND THE FUGITIVE YOU'RE LOOKING FOR!
WHY-THANK YOU-BUT I HAVE FOUND HER!
WHAT DO YOU MEAN?
THIS "BAUBLE" THE YOUNG LADY ADMITTED GIVING TO THE NATIVES IS PART OF THE LOOT TAKEN BY THE PIRATE GANG WE HAVE IN CUSTODY!..
..ONLY DIAMONDS WILL CUT GLASS IN THIS MANNER! -MISS BURMA, YOU'RE UNDER ARREST!
Reg. U. S. Pat. Off. Copyright, 1936, by Chicago Tribune-N. Y. News Syndicate, Inc.

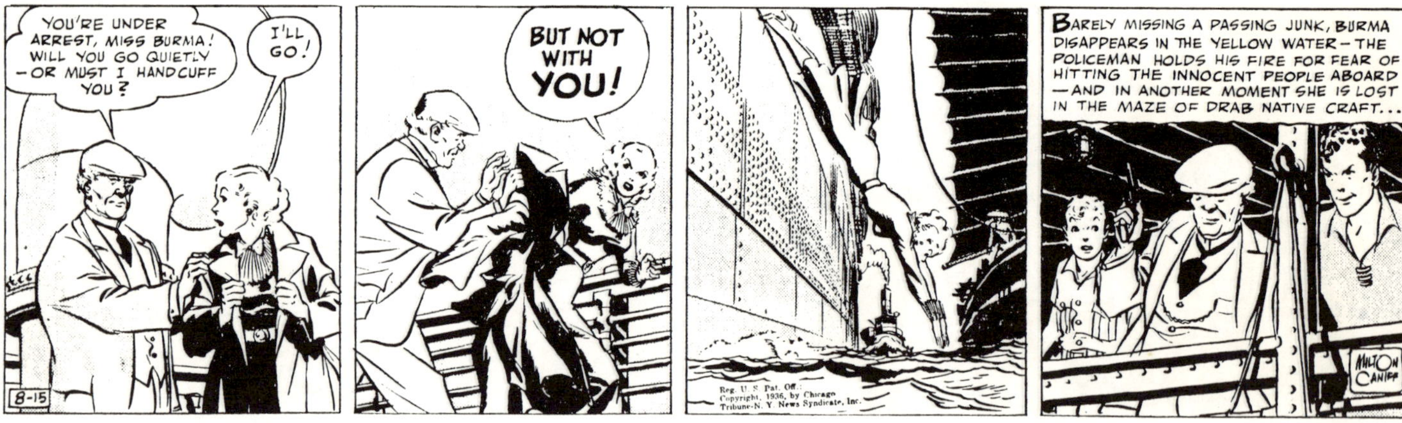
YOU'RE UNDER ARREST, MISS BURMA! WILL YOU GO QUIETLY -OR MUST I HANDCUFF YOU?
I'LL GO!
8-15
BUT NOT WITH YOU!
Reg. U. S. Pat. Off. Copyright, 1936, by Chicago Tribune-N. Y. News Syndicate, Inc.
BARELY MISSING A PASSING JUNK, BURMA DISAPPEARS IN THE YELLOW WATER-THE POLICEMAN HOLDS HIS FIRE FOR FEAR OF HITTING THE INNOCENT PEOPLE ABOARD -AND IN ANOTHER MOMENT SHE IS LOST IN THE MAZE OF DRAB NATIVE CRAFT...
MILTON CANIFF

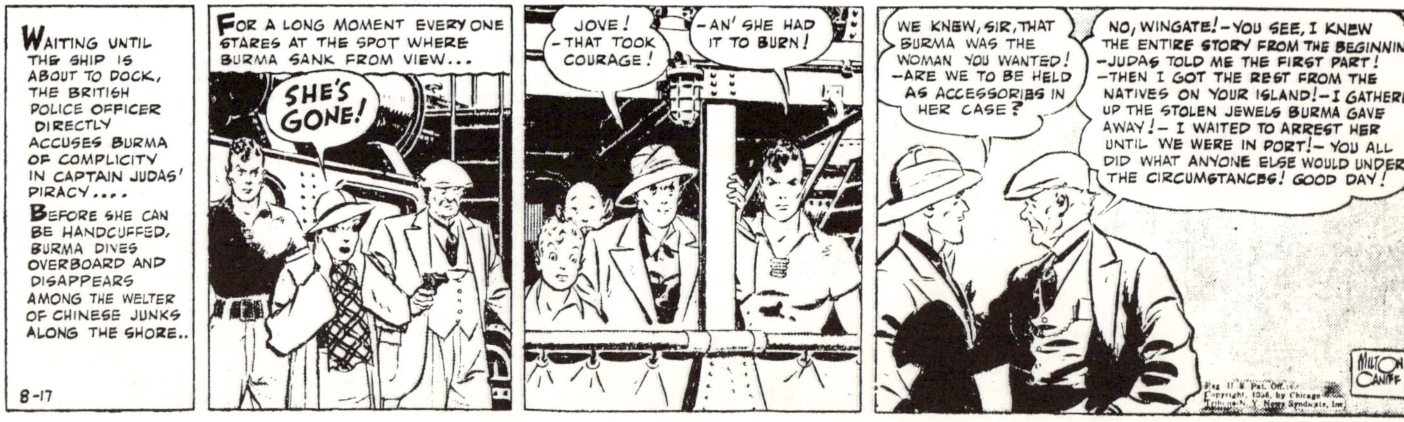
WAITING UNTIL THE SHIP IS ABOUT TO DOCK, THE BRITISH POLICE OFFICER DIRECTLY ACCUSES BURMA OF COMPLICITY IN CAPTAIN JUDAS' PIRACY....
BEFORE SHE CAN BE HANDCUFFED, BURMA DIVES OVERBOARD AND DISAPPEARS AMONG THE WELTER OF CHINESE JUNKS ALONG THE SHORE..
8-17
FOR A LONG MOMENT EVERY ONE STARES AT THE SPOT WHERE BURMA SANK FROM VIEW...
SHE'S GONE!
JOVE! -THAT TOOK COURAGE!
-AN' SHE HAD IT TO BURN!
WE KNEW, SIR, THAT BURMA WAS THE WOMAN YOU WANTED! -ARE WE TO BE HELD AS ACCESSORIES IN HER CASE?
NO, WINGATE! -YOU SEE, I KNEW THE ENTIRE STORY FROM THE BEGINNING! -JUDAS TOLD ME THE FIRST PART! -THEN I GOT THE REST FROM THE NATIVES ON YOUR ISLAND! -I GATHERED UP THE STOLEN JEWELS BURMA GAVE AWAY! -I WAITED TO ARREST HER UNTIL WE WERE IN PORT! -YOU ALL DID WHAT ANYONE ELSE WOULD UNDER THE CIRCUMSTANCES! GOOD DAY!
MILTON CANIFF

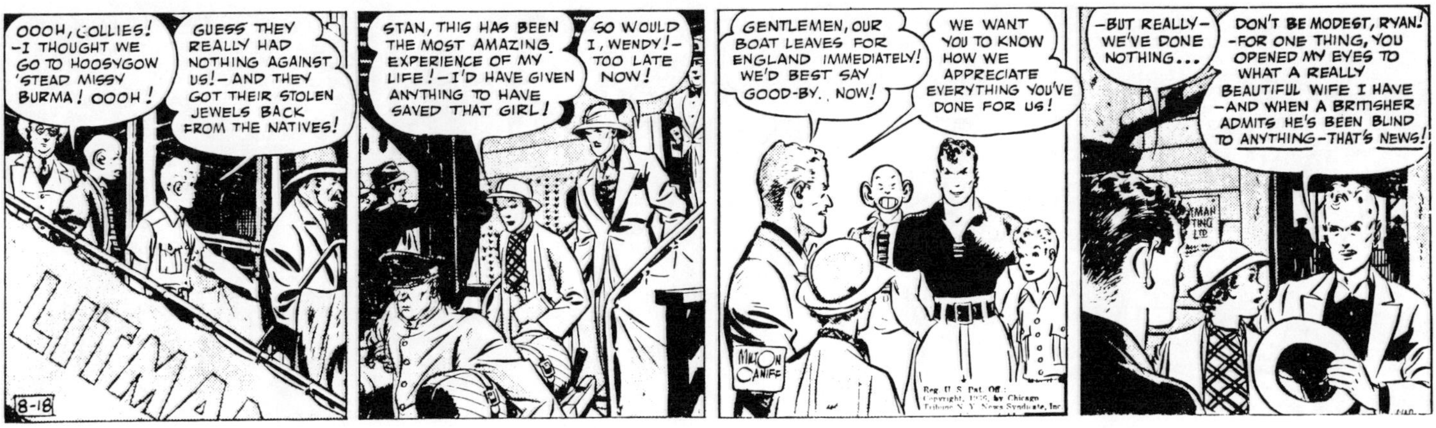
OOOH, GOLLIES! -I THOUGHT WE GO TO HOOSGOW 'STEAD MISSY BURMA! OOOH!
GUESS THEY REALLY HAD NOTHING AGAINST US! -AND THEY GOT THEIR STOLEN JEWELS BACK FROM THE NATIVES!
LITMA
8-18
STAN, THIS HAS BEEN THE MOST AMAZING EXPERIENCE OF MY LIFE! -I'D HAVE GIVEN ANYTHING TO HAVE SAVED THAT GIRL!
SO WOULD I, WENDY! -TOO LATE NOW!
GENTLEMEN, OUR BOAT LEAVES FOR ENGLAND IMMEDIATELY! WE'D BEST SAY GOOD-BY.. NOW!
WE WANT YOU TO KNOW HOW WE APPRECIATE EVERYTHING YOU'VE DONE FOR US!
MILTON CANIFF
Reg. U. S. Pat. Off.: Copyright, 1936, by Chicago Tribune-N. Y. News Syndicate, Inc.
-BUT REALLY- WE'VE DONE NOTHING...
DON'T BE MODEST, RYAN! -FOR ONE THING, YOU OPENED MY EYES TO WHAT A REALLY BEAUTIFUL WIFE I HAVE -AND WHEN A BRITISHER ADMITS HE'S BEEN BLIND TO ANYTHING-THAT'S NEWS!

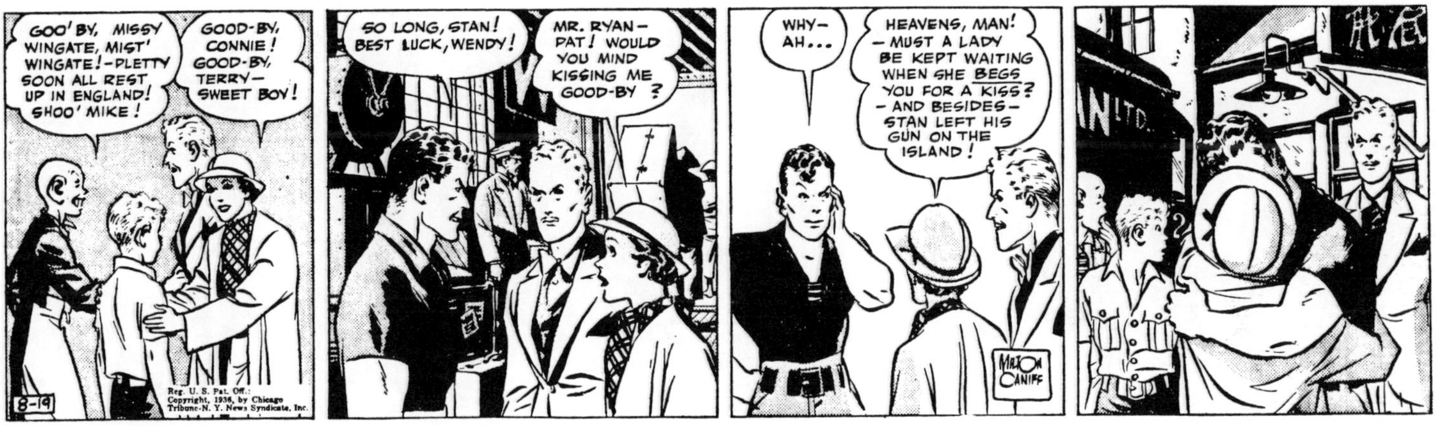
GOO' BY, MISSY WINGATE, MIST' WINGATE! -PLETTY SOON ALL REST UP IN ENGLAND! SHOO' MIKE!
GOOD-BY, CONNIE! GOOD-BY, TERRY- SWEET BOY!
8-19
Reg. U. S. Pat. Off.: Copyright, 1936, by Chicago Tribune-N. Y. News Syndicate, Inc.
SO LONG, STAN! BEST LUCK, WENDY!
MR. RYAN- PAT! WOULD YOU MIND KISSING ME GOOD-BY?
WHY- AH...
HEAVENS, MAN! -MUST A LADY BE KEPT WAITING WHEN SHE BEGS YOU FOR A KISS? -AND BESIDES- STAN LEFT HIS GUN ON THE ISLAND!
MILTON CANIFF

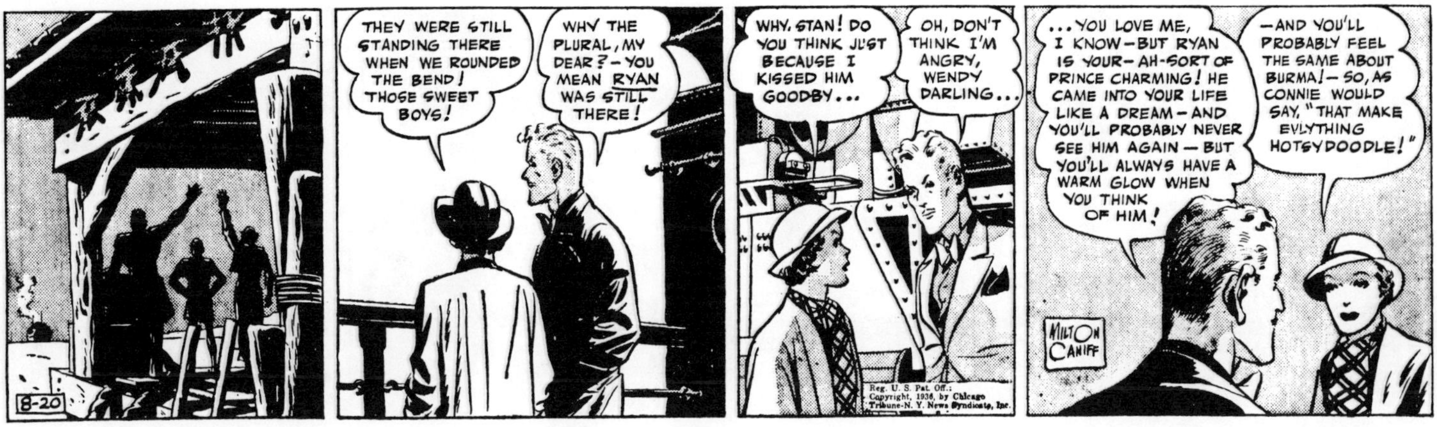
8-20
THEY WERE STILL STANDING THERE WHEN WE ROUNDED THE BEND! THOSE SWEET BOYS!
WHY THE PLURAL, MY DEAR? -YOU MEAN RYAN WAS STILL THERE!
WHY, STAN! DO YOU THINK JUST BECAUSE I KISSED HIM GOODBY...
OH, DON'T THINK I'M ANGRY, WENDY DARLING...
Reg. U. S. Pat. Off.: Copyright, 1936, by Chicago Tribune-N. Y. News Syndicate, Inc.
...YOU LOVE ME, I KNOW-BUT RYAN IS YOUR-AH-SORT OF PRINCE CHARMING! HE CAME INTO YOUR LIFE LIKE A DREAM-AND YOU'LL PROBABLY NEVER SEE HIM AGAIN-BUT YOU'LL ALWAYS HAVE A WARM GLOW WHEN YOU THINK OF HIM!
-AND YOU'LL PROBABLY FEEL THE SAME ABOUT BURMA! -SO, AS CONNIE WOULD SAY, "THAT MAKE EVLYTHING HOTSYDOODLE!"
MILTON CANIFF

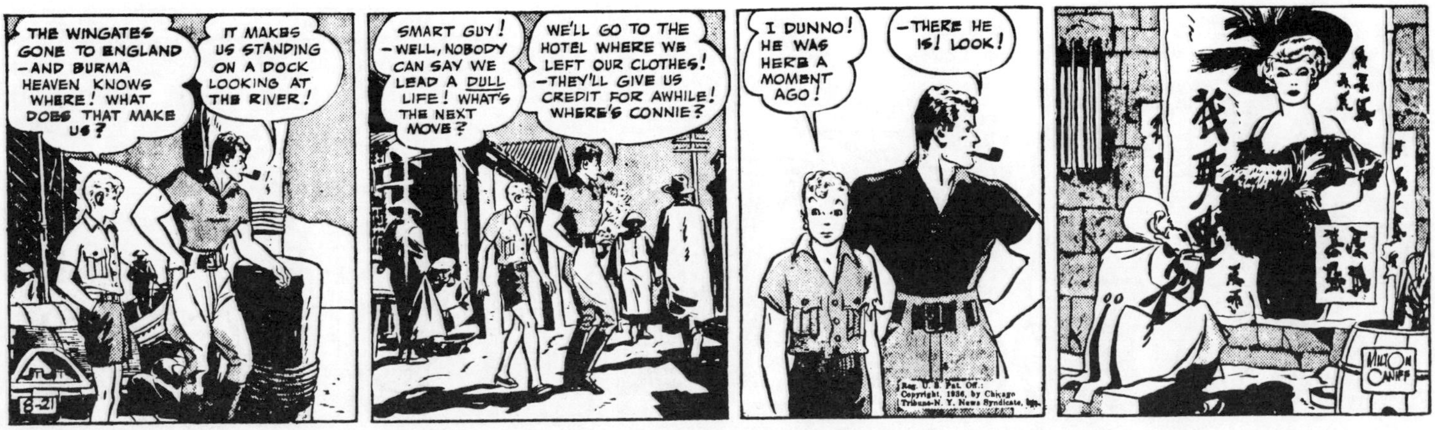
THE WINGATES GONE TO ENGLAND -AND BURMA HEAVEN KNOWS WHERE! WHAT DOES THAT MAKE US?
IT MAKES US STANDING ON A DOCK LOOKING AT THE RIVER!
8-21
SMART GUY! -WELL, NOBODY CAN SAY WE LEAD A DULL LIFE! WHAT'S THE NEXT MOVE?
WE'LL GO TO THE HOTEL WHERE WE LEFT OUR CLOTHES! -THEY'LL GIVE US CREDIT FOR AWHILE! WHERE'S CONNIE?
I DUNNO! HE WAS HERE A MOMENT AGO!
-THERE HE IS! LOOK!
Reg. U. S. Pat. Off.: Copyright, 1936, by Chicago Tribune-N. Y. News Syndicate, Inc.
MILTON CANIFF

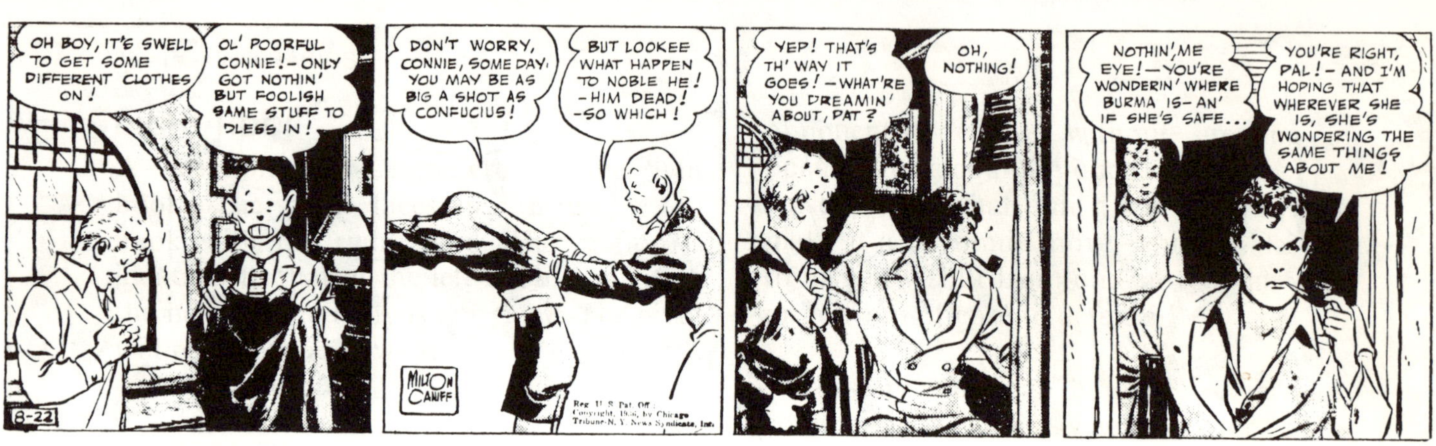
OH BOY, IT'S SWELL TO GET SOME DIFFERENT CLOTHES ON!
OL' POORFUL CONNIE!—ONLY GOT NOTHIN' BUT FOOLISH SAME STUFF TO DLESS IN!
8-22
DON'T WORRY, CONNIE, SOME DAY YOU MAY BE AS BIG A SHOT AS CONFUCIUS!
BUT LOOKEE WHAT HAPPEN TO NOBLE HE!—HIM DEAD!—SO WHICH!
MILTON CANIFF
Reg. U. S. Pat. Off. Copyright, 1936, by Chicago Tribune-N. Y. News Syndicate, Inc.
YEP! THAT'S TH' WAY IT GOES!—WHAT'RE YOU DREAMIN' ABOUT, PAT?
OH, NOTHING!
NOTHIN', ME EYE!—YOU'RE WONDERIN' WHERE BURMA IS—AN' IF SHE'S SAFE...
YOU'RE RIGHT, PAL!—AND I'M HOPING THAT WHEREVER SHE IS, SHE'S WONDERING THE SAME THINGS ABOUT ME!

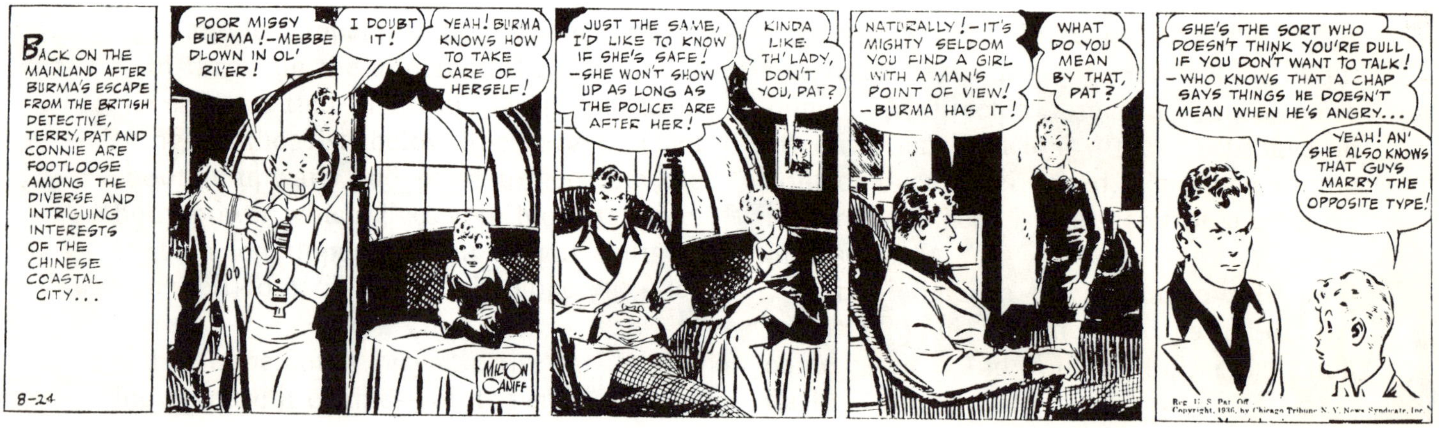
BACK ON THE MAINLAND AFTER BURMA'S ESCAPE FROM THE BRITISH DETECTIVE, TERRY, PAT AND CONNIE ARE FOOTLOOSE AMONG THE DIVERSE AND INTRIGUING INTERESTS OF THE CHINESE COASTAL CITY...
8-24
POOR MISSY BURMA!—MEBBE DLOWN IN OL' RIVER!
I DOUBT IT!
YEAH! BURMA KNOWS HOW TO TAKE CARE OF HERSELF!
JUST THE SAME, I'D LIKE TO KNOW IF SHE'S SAFE!—SHE WON'T SHOW UP AS LONG AS THE POLICE ARE AFTER HER!
KINDA LIKE TH' LADY, DON'T YOU, PAT?
MILTON CANIFF
NATURALLY!—IT'S MIGHTY SELDOM YOU FIND A GIRL WITH A MAN'S POINT OF VIEW!—BURMA HAS IT!
WHAT DO YOU MEAN BY THAT, PAT?
SHE'S THE SORT WHO DOESN'T THINK YOU'RE DULL IF YOU DON'T WANT TO TALK!—WHO KNOWS THAT A CHAP SAYS THINGS HE DOESN'T MEAN WHEN HE'S ANGRY...
YEAH! AN' SHE ALSO KNOWS THAT GUYS MARRY THE OPPOSITE TYPE!
Reg. U. S. Pat. Off. Copyright, 1936, by Chicago Tribune-N. Y. News Syndicate, Inc.

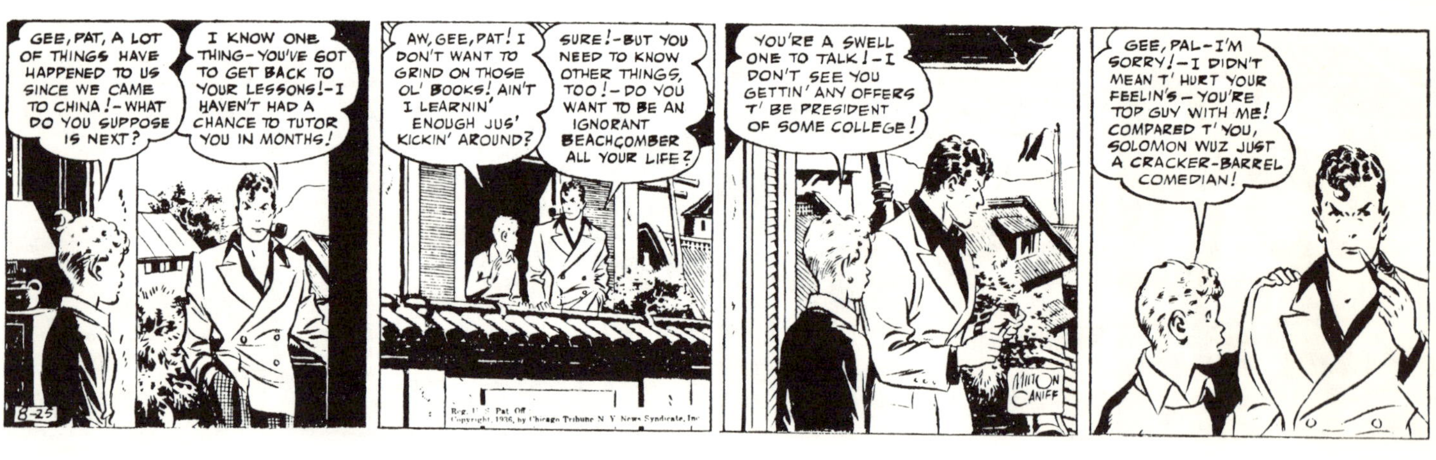
GEE, PAT, A LOT OF THINGS HAVE HAPPENED TO US SINCE WE CAME TO CHINA!—WHAT DO YOU SUPPOSE IS NEXT?
I KNOW ONE THING—YOU'VE GOT TO GET BACK TO YOUR LESSONS!—I HAVEN'T HAD A CHANCE TO TUTOR YOU IN MONTHS!
8-25
AW, GEE, PAT! I DON'T WANT TO GRIND ON THOSE OL' BOOKS! AIN'T I LEARNIN' ENOUGH JUS' KICKIN' AROUND?
SURE!—BUT YOU NEED TO KNOW OTHER THINGS, TOO!—DO YOU WANT TO BE AN IGNORANT BEACHCOMBER ALL YOUR LIFE?
Reg. U. S. Pat. Off. Copyright, 1936, by Chicago Tribune-N. Y. News Syndicate, Inc.
YOU'RE A SWELL ONE TO TALK!—I DON'T SEE YOU GETTIN' ANY OFFERS T' BE PRESIDENT OF SOME COLLEGE!
MILTON CANIFF
GEE, PAL—I'M SORRY!—I DIDN'T MEAN T' HURT YOUR FEELIN'S—YOU'RE TOP GUY WITH ME! COMPARED T' YOU, SOLOMON WUZ JUST A CRACKER-BARREL COMEDIAN!

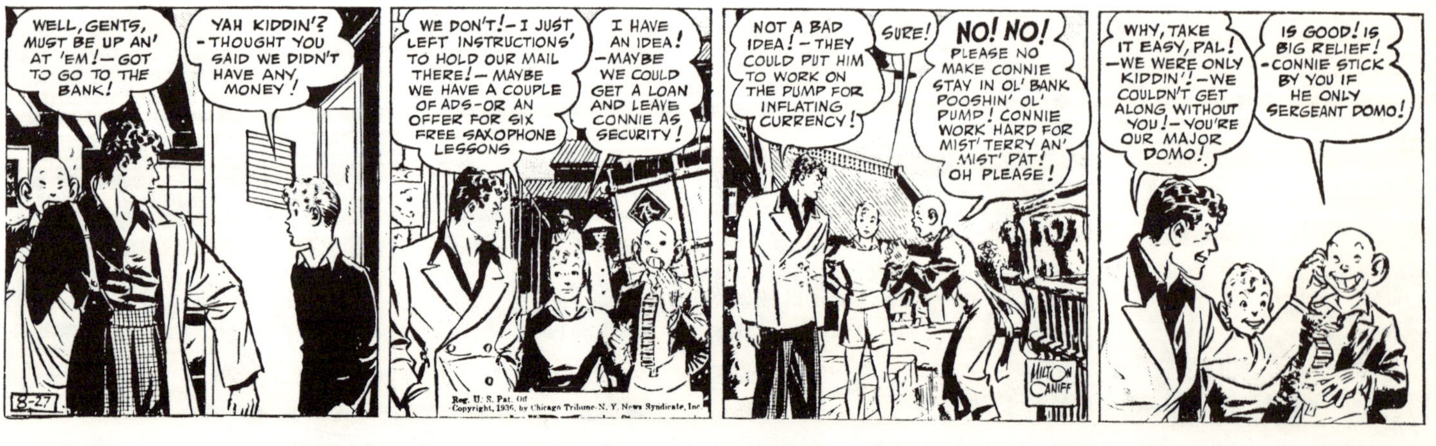
WELL, GENTS, MUST BE UP AN' AT 'EM!—GOT TO GO TO THE BANK!
YAH KIDDIN'?—THOUGHT YOU SAID WE DIDN'T HAVE ANY MONEY!
8-27
WE DON'T!—I JUST LEFT INSTRUCTIONS TO HOLD OUR MAIL THERE!—MAYBE WE HAVE A COUPLE OF ADS—OR AN OFFER FOR SIX FREE SAXOPHONE LESSONS
I HAVE AN IDEA!—MAYBE WE COULD GET A LOAN AND LEAVE CONNIE AS SECURITY!
Reg. U. S. Pat. Off. Copyright, 1936, by Chicago Tribune-N. Y. News Syndicate, Inc.
NOT A BAD IDEA!—THEY COULD PUT HIM TO WORK ON THE PUMP FOR INFLATING CURRENCY!
SURE!
NO! NO! PLEASE NO MAKE CONNIE STAY IN OL' BANK POOSHIN' OL' PUMP! CONNIE WORK HARD FOR MIST' TERRY AN' MIST' PAT! OH PLEASE!
MILTON CANIFF
WHY, TAKE IT EASY, PAL!—WE WERE ONLY KIDDIN'!—WE COULDN'T GET ALONG WITHOUT YOU!—YOU'RE OUR MAJOR DOMO!
IS GOOD! IS BIG RELIEF!—CONNIE STICK BY YOU IF HE ONLY SERGEANT DOMO!

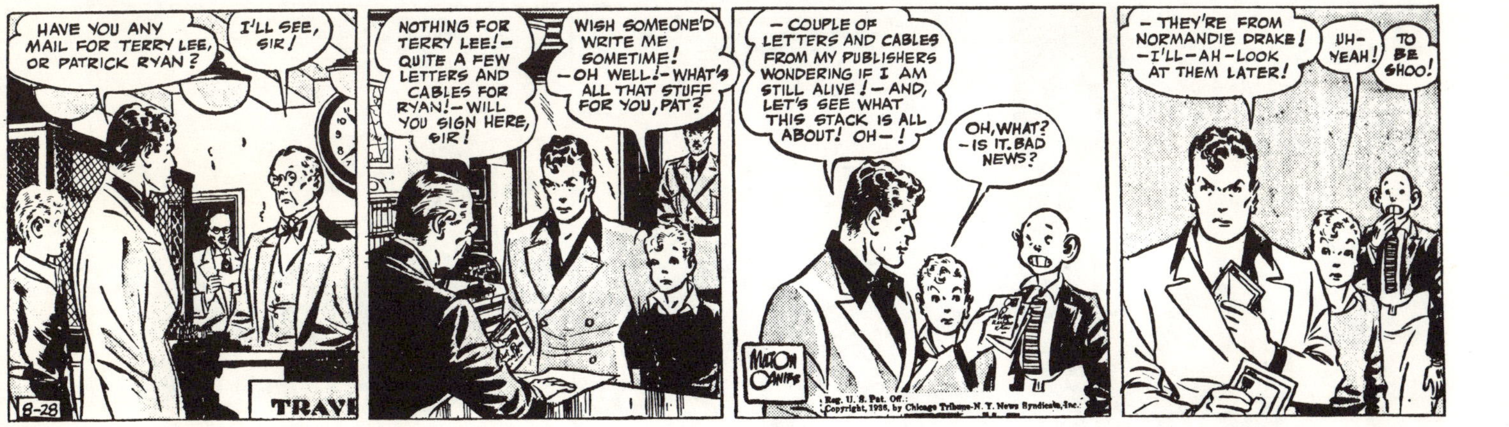
8-28
HAVE YOU ANY MAIL FOR TERRY LEE, OR PATRICK RYAN?
I'LL SEE, SIR!
TRAVE
NOTHING FOR TERRY LEE! — QUITE A FEW LETTERS AND CABLES FOR RYAN! — WILL YOU SIGN HERE, SIR!
WISH SOMEONE'D WRITE ME SOMETIME! — OH WELL! — WHAT'S ALL THAT STUFF FOR YOU, PAT?
— COUPLE OF LETTERS AND CABLES FROM MY PUBLISHERS WONDERING IF I AM STILL ALIVE! — AND, LET'S SEE WHAT THIS STACK IS ALL ABOUT! OH — !
OH, WHAT? — IS IT BAD NEWS?
MILTON CANIFF
Reg. U. S. Pat. Off.: Copyright, 1936, by Chicago Tribune-N. Y. News Syndicate, Inc.
— THEY'RE FROM NORMANDIE DRAKE! — I'LL — AH — LOOK AT THEM LATER!
UH-YEAH!
TO BE SHOO!

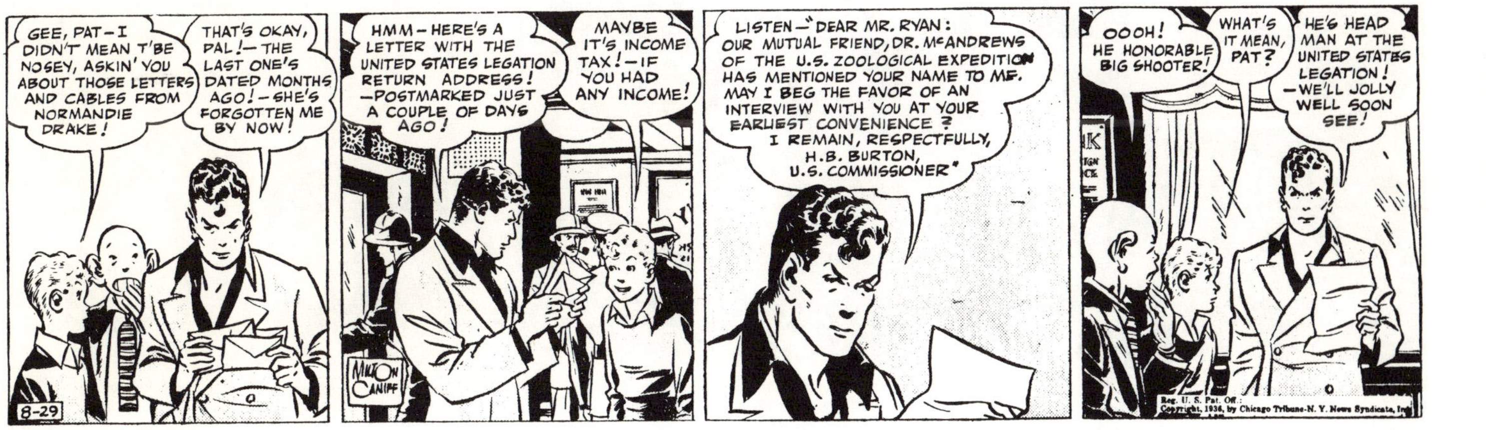
8-29
GEE, PAT — I DIDN'T MEAN T'BE NOSEY, ASKIN' YOU ABOUT THOSE LETTERS AND CABLES FROM NORMANDIE DRAKE!
THAT'S OKAY, PAL! — THE LAST ONE'S DATED MONTHS AGO! — SHE'S FORGOTTEN ME BY NOW!
HMM — HERE'S A LETTER WITH THE UNITED STATES LEGATION RETURN ADDRESS! — POSTMARKED JUST A COUPLE OF DAYS AGO!
MAYBE IT'S INCOME TAX! — IF YOU HAD ANY INCOME!
MILTON CANIFF
LISTEN — "DEAR MR. RYAN: OUR MUTUAL FRIEND, DR. McANDREWS OF THE U.S. ZOOLOGICAL EXPEDITION HAS MENTIONED YOUR NAME TO ME. MAY I BEG THE FAVOR OF AN INTERVIEW WITH YOU AT YOUR EARLIEST CONVENIENCE? I REMAIN, RESPECTFULLY, H.B. BURTON, U.S. COMMISSIONER"
OOOH! HE HONORABLE BIG SHOOTER!
WHAT'S IT MEAN, PAT?
HE'S HEAD MAN AT THE UNITED STATES LEGATION! — WE'LL JOLLY WELL SOON SEE!
Reg. U. S. Pat. Off.: Copyright, 1936, by Chicago Tribune-N. Y. News Syndicate, Inc.

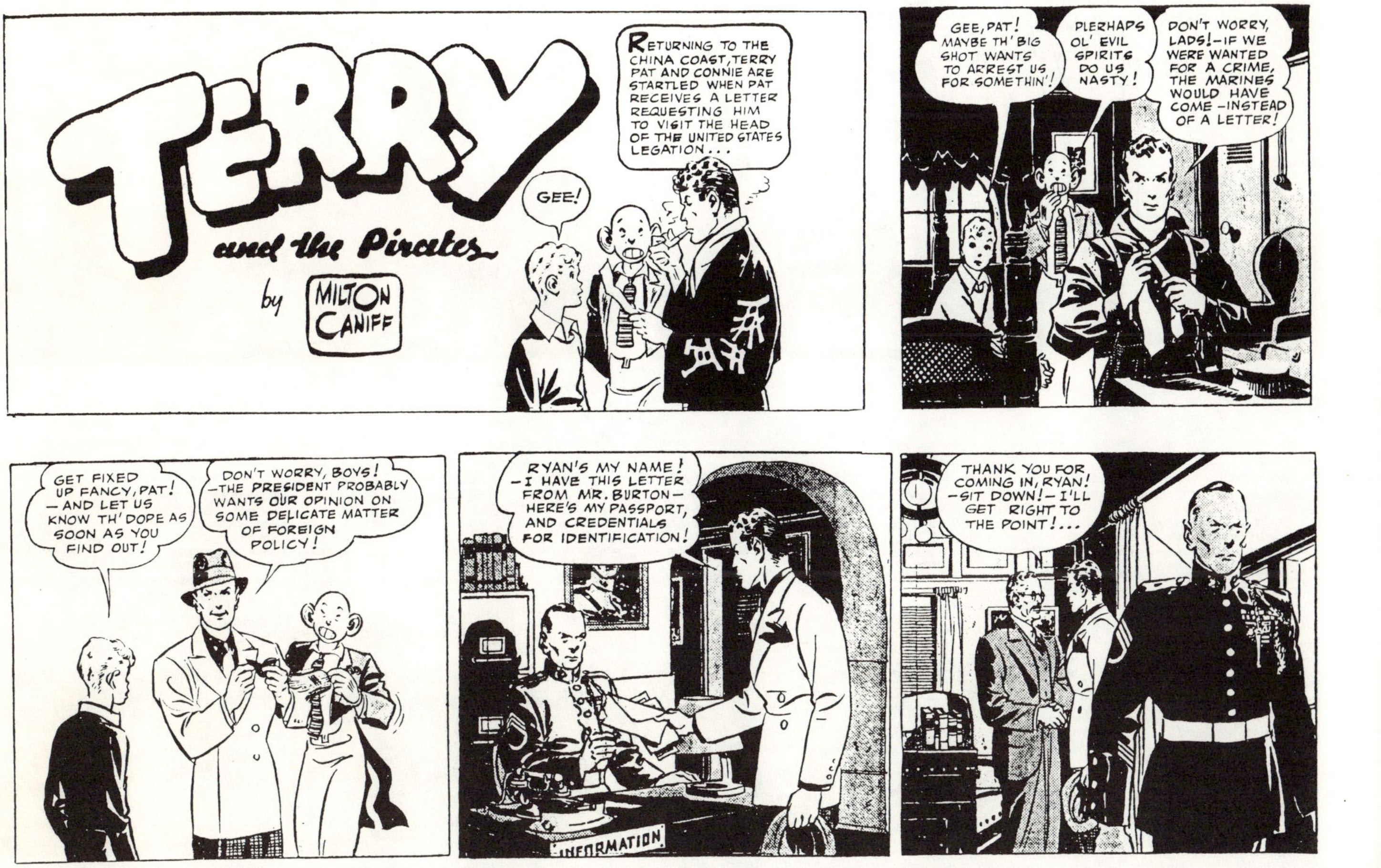
TERRY and the Pirates
by MILTON CANIFF
RETURNING TO THE CHINA COAST, TERRY PAT AND CONNIE ARE STARTLED WHEN PAT RECEIVES A LETTER REQUESTING HIM TO VISIT THE HEAD OF THE UNITED STATES LEGATION...
GEE!
GEE, PAT! MAYBE TH' BIG SHOT WANTS TO ARREST US FOR SOMETHIN'!
PLERHAPS OL' EVIL SPIRITS DO US NASTY!
DON'T WORRY, LADS! — IF WE WERE WANTED FOR A CRIME, THE MARINES WOULD HAVE COME — INSTEAD OF A LETTER!
GET FIXED UP FANCY, PAT! — AND LET US KNOW TH' DOPE AS SOON AS YOU FIND OUT!
DON'T WORRY, BOYS! — THE PRESIDENT PROBABLY WANTS OUR OPINION ON SOME DELICATE MATTER OF FOREIGN POLICY!
RYAN'S MY NAME! — I HAVE THIS LETTER FROM MR. BURTON — HERE'S MY PASSPORT, AND CREDENTIALS FOR IDENTIFICATION!
INFORMATION
THANK YOU FOR COMING IN, RYAN! — SIT DOWN! — I'LL GET RIGHT TO THE POINT!...

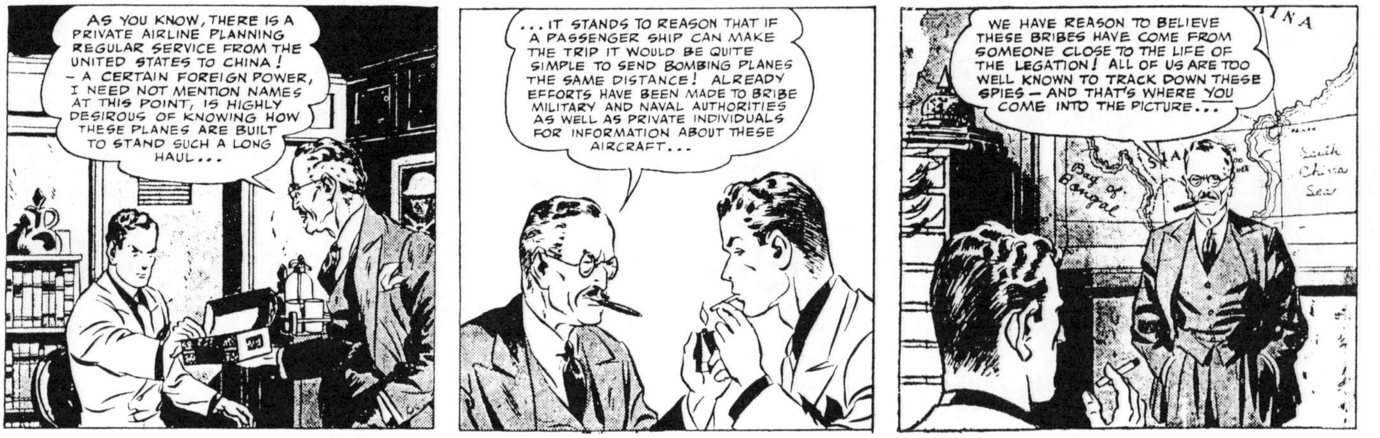

AS YOU KNOW, THERE IS A PRIVATE AIRLINE PLANNING REGULAR SERVICE FROM THE UNITED STATES TO CHINA! – A CERTAIN FOREIGN POWER, I NEED NOT MENTION NAMES AT THIS POINT, IS HIGHLY DESIROUS OF KNOWING HOW THESE PLANES ARE BUILT TO STAND SUCH A LONG HAUL...
... IT STANDS TO REASON THAT IF A PASSENGER SHIP CAN MAKE THE TRIP IT WOULD BE QUITE SIMPLE TO SEND BOMBING PLANES THE SAME DISTANCE! ALREADY EFFORTS HAVE BEEN MADE TO BRIBE MILITARY AND NAVAL AUTHORITIES AS WELL AS PRIVATE INDIVIDUALS FOR INFORMATION ABOUT THESE AIRCRAFT...
WE HAVE REASON TO BELIEVE THESE BRIBES HAVE COME FROM SOMEONE CLOSE TO THE LIFE OF THE LEGATION! ALL OF US ARE TOO WELL KNOWN TO TRACK DOWN THESE SPIES — AND THAT'S WHERE YOU COME INTO THE PICTURE...
Bay of Bengal
South China Sea

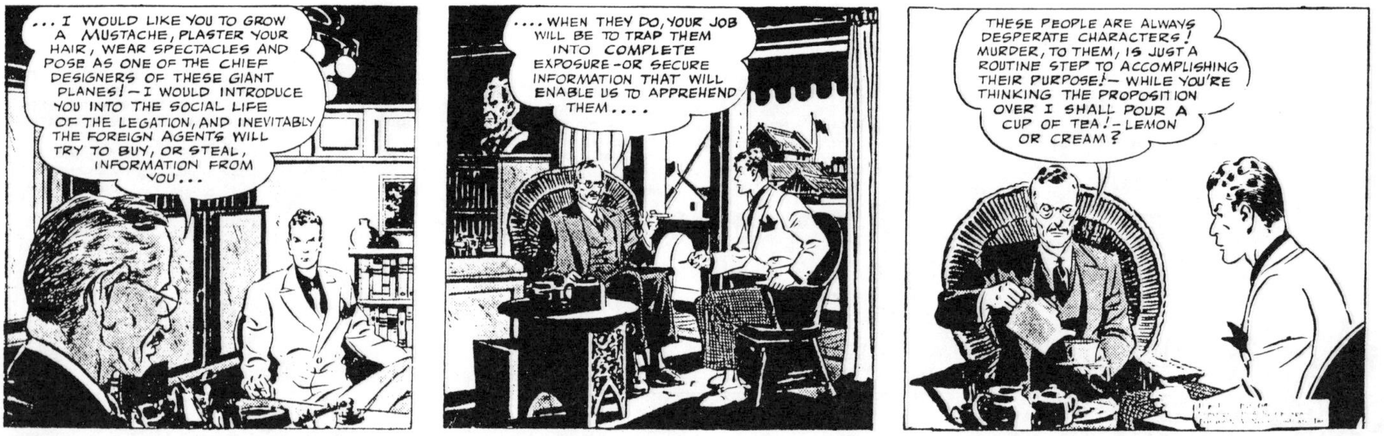

... I WOULD LIKE YOU TO GROW A MUSTACHE, PLASTER YOUR HAIR, WEAR SPECTACLES AND POSE AS ONE OF THE CHIEF DESIGNERS OF THESE GIANT PLANES! – I WOULD INTRODUCE YOU INTO THE SOCIAL LIFE OF THE LEGATION, AND INEVITABLY THE FOREIGN AGENTS WILL TRY TO BUY, OR STEAL, INFORMATION FROM YOU...
.... WHEN THEY DO, YOUR JOB WILL BE TO TRAP THEM INTO COMPLETE EXPOSURE – OR SECURE INFORMATION THAT WILL ENABLE US TO APPREHEND THEM....
THESE PEOPLE ARE ALWAYS DESPERATE CHARACTERS! MURDER, TO THEM, IS JUST A ROUTINE STEP TO ACCOMPLISHING THEIR PURPOSE! – WHILE YOU'RE THINKING THE PROPOSITION OVER I SHALL POUR A CUP OF TEA! – LEMON OR CREAM?

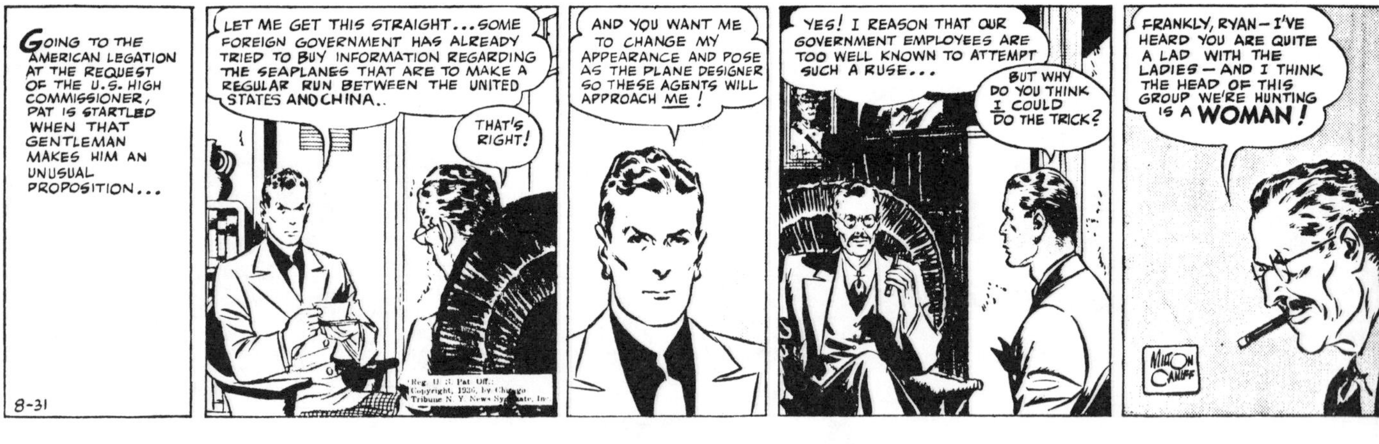

GOING TO THE AMERICAN LEGATION AT THE REQUEST OF THE U.S. HIGH COMMISSIONER, PAT IS STARTLED WHEN THAT GENTLEMAN MAKES HIM AN UNUSUAL PROPOSITION...
8-31
LET ME GET THIS STRAIGHT... SOME FOREIGN GOVERNMENT HAS ALREADY TRIED TO BUY INFORMATION REGARDING THE SEAPLANES THAT ARE TO MAKE A REGULAR RUN BETWEEN THE UNITED STATES AND CHINA..
THAT'S RIGHT!
Reg. U. S. Pat. Off. Copyright, 1936, by Chicago Tribune N. Y. News Syndicate, Inc.
AND YOU WANT ME TO CHANGE MY APPEARANCE AND POSE AS THE PLANE DESIGNER SO THESE AGENTS WILL APPROACH ME!
YES! I REASON THAT OUR GOVERNMENT EMPLOYEES ARE TOO WELL KNOWN TO ATTEMPT SUCH A RUSE...
BUT WHY DO YOU THINK I COULD DO THE TRICK?
FRANKLY, RYAN – I'VE HEARD YOU ARE QUITE A LAD WITH THE LADIES — AND I THINK THE HEAD OF THIS GROUP WE'RE HUNTING IS A WOMAN!
MILTON CANIFF

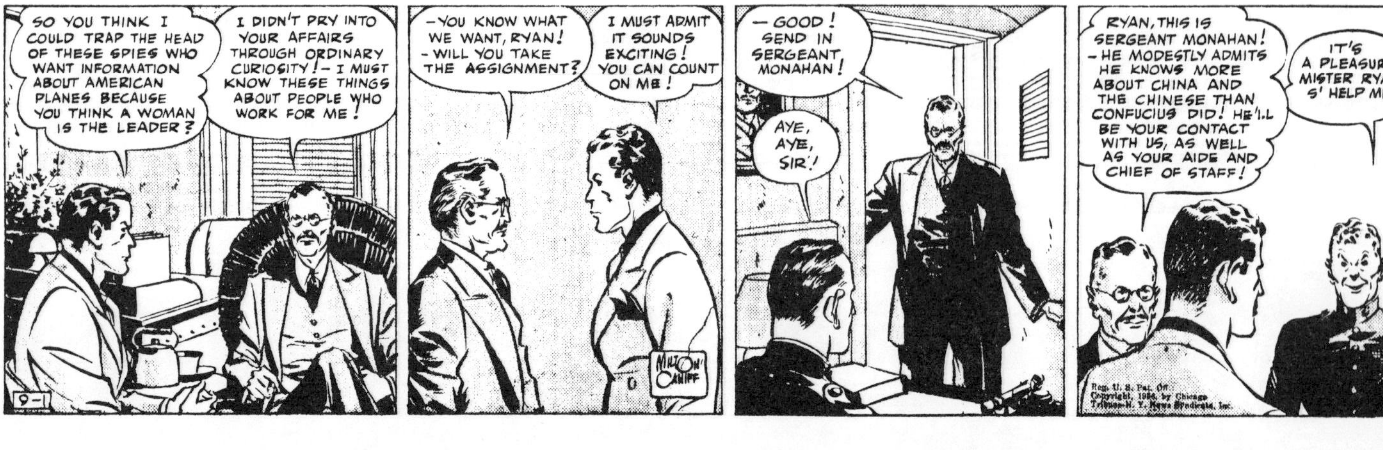

SO YOU THINK I COULD TRAP THE HEAD OF THESE SPIES WHO WANT INFORMATION ABOUT AMERICAN PLANES BECAUSE YOU THINK A WOMAN IS THE LEADER?
I DIDN'T PRY INTO YOUR AFFAIRS THROUGH ORDINARY CURIOSITY! – I MUST KNOW THESE THINGS ABOUT PEOPLE WHO WORK FOR ME!
9-1
– YOU KNOW WHAT WE WANT, RYAN! – WILL YOU TAKE THE ASSIGNMENT?
I MUST ADMIT IT SOUNDS EXCITING! YOU CAN COUNT ON ME!
MILTON CANIFF
– GOOD! SEND IN SERGEANT MONAHAN!
AYE, AYE, SIR!
RYAN, THIS IS SERGEANT MONAHAN! – HE MODESTLY ADMITS HE KNOWS MORE ABOUT CHINA AND THE CHINESE THAN CONFUCIUS DID! HE'LL BE YOUR CONTACT WITH US, AS WELL AS YOUR AIDE AND CHIEF OF STAFF!
IT'S A PLEASURE, MISTER RYAN, S' HELP ME!
Reg. U. S. Pat. Off. Copyright, 1936, by Chicago Tribune-N. Y. News Syndicate, Inc.

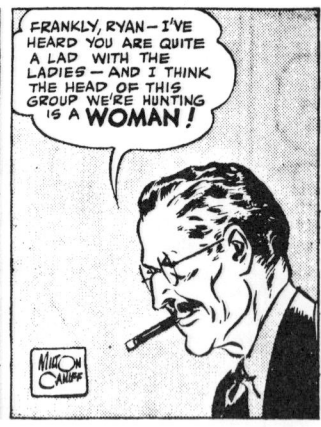

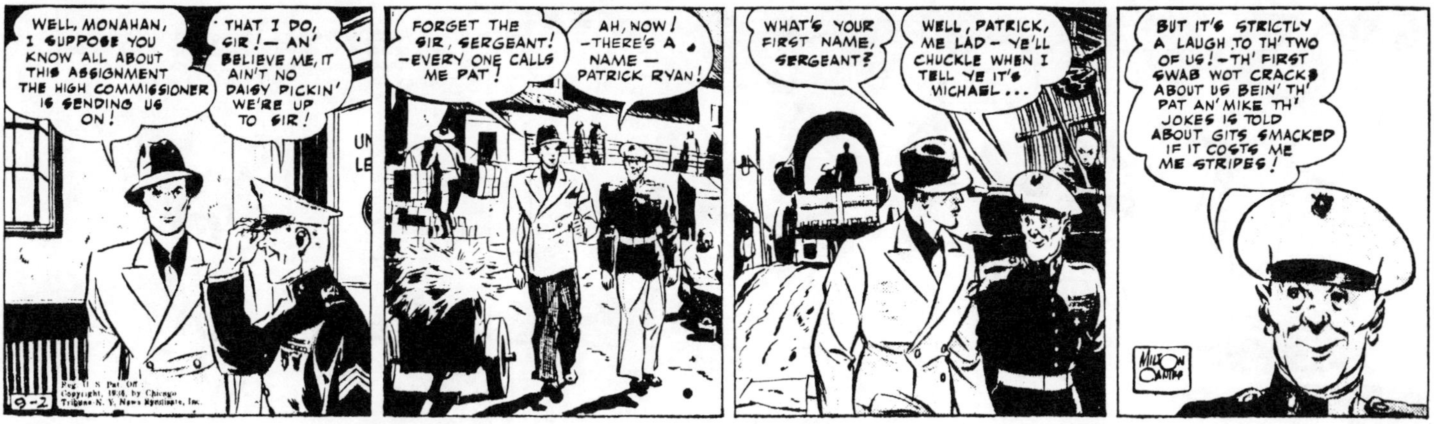
WELL, MONAHAN, I SUPPOSE YOU KNOW ALL ABOUT THIS ASSIGNMENT THE HIGH COMMISSIONER IS SENDING US ON!
THAT I DO, SIR! — AN' BELIEVE ME, IT AIN'T NO DAISY PICKIN' WE'RE UP TO SIR!
9-2
Reg. U. S. Pat. Off.: Copyright, 1936, by Chicago Tribune-N. Y. News Syndicate, Inc.
FORGET THE SIR, SERGEANT! - EVERY ONE CALLS ME PAT!
AH, NOW! - THERE'S A NAME - PATRICK RYAN!
WHAT'S YOUR FIRST NAME, SERGEANT?
WELL, PATRICK, ME LAD - YE'LL CHUCKLE WHEN I TELL YE IT'S MICHAEL...
BUT IT'S STRICTLY A LAUGH TO TH' TWO OF US! - TH' FIRST SWAB WOT CRACKS ABOUT US BEIN' TH' PAT AN' MIKE TH' JOKES IS TOLD ABOUT GITS SMACKED IF IT COSTS ME ME STRIPES!
MILTON CANIFF

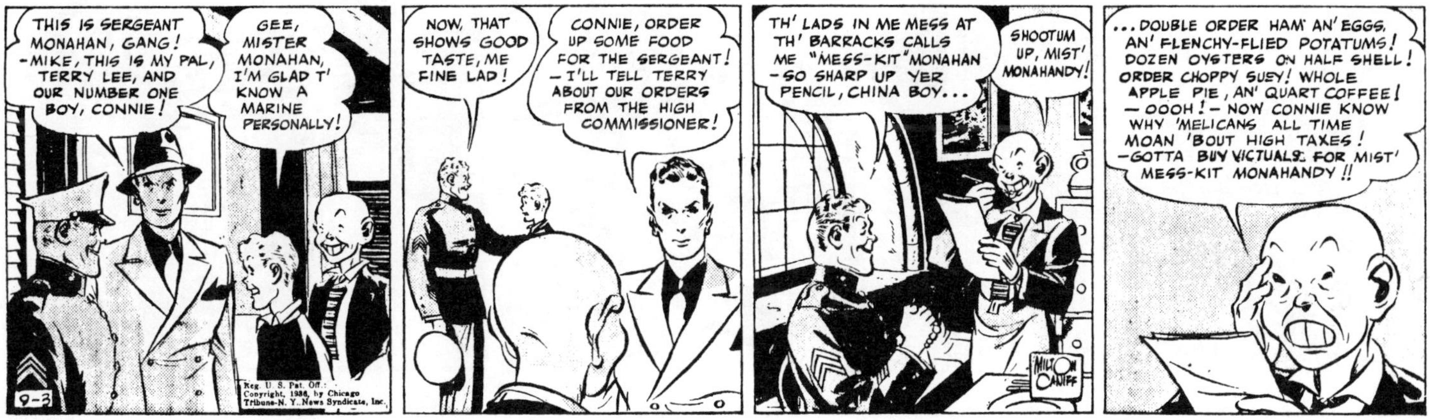
THIS IS SERGEANT MONAHAN, GANG! - MIKE, THIS IS MY PAL, TERRY LEE, AND OUR NUMBER ONE BOY, CONNIE!
GEE, MISTER MONAHAN, I'M GLAD T' KNOW A MARINE PERSONALLY!
9-3
Reg. U. S. Pat. Off.: Copyright, 1936, by Chicago Tribune-N. Y. News Syndicate, Inc.
NOW, THAT SHOWS GOOD TASTE, ME FINE LAD!
CONNIE, ORDER UP SOME FOOD FOR THE SERGEANT! - I'LL TELL TERRY ABOUT OUR ORDERS FROM THE HIGH COMMISSIONER!
TH' LADS IN ME MESS AT TH' BARRACKS CALLS ME "MESS-KIT" MONAHAN - SO SHARP UP YER PENCIL, CHINA BOY...
SHOOTUM UP, MIST' MONAHANDY!
MILTON CANIFF
...DOUBLE ORDER HAM AN' EGGS, AN' FLENCHY-FLIED POTATUMS! DOZEN OYSTERS ON HALF SHELL! ORDER CHOPPY SUEY! WHOLE APPLE PIE, AN' QUART COFFEE! — OOOH! — NOW CONNIE KNOW WHY 'MELICANS ALL TIME MOAN 'BOUT HIGH TAXES! - GOTTA BUY VICTUALS FOR MIST' MESS-KIT MONAHANDY!!

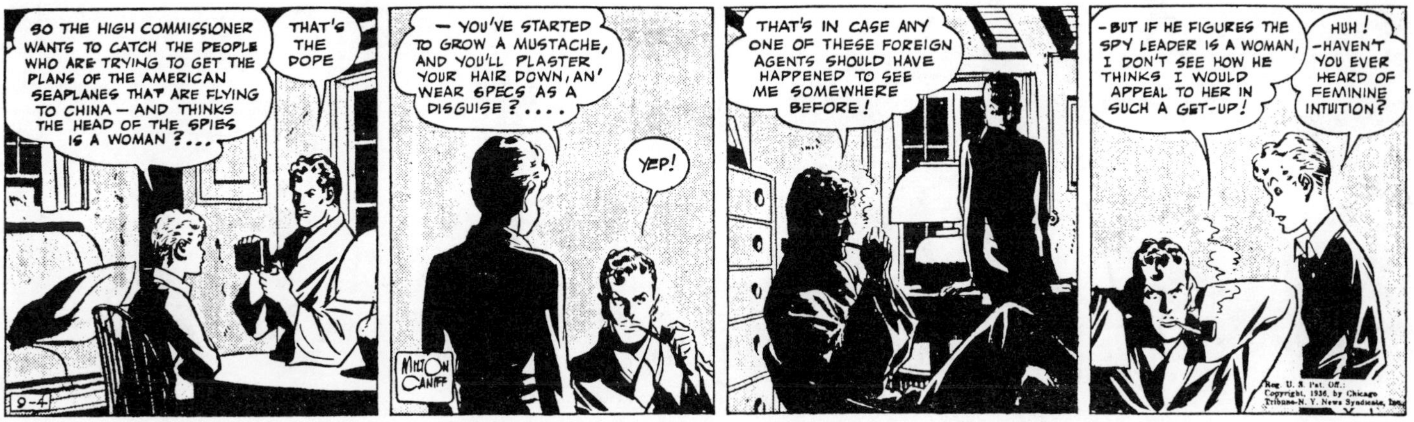
SO THE HIGH COMMISSIONER WANTS TO CATCH THE PEOPLE WHO ARE TRYING TO GET THE PLANS OF THE AMERICAN SEAPLANES THAT ARE FLYING TO CHINA — AND THINKS THE HEAD OF THE SPIES IS A WOMAN?...
THAT'S THE DOPE
MILTON CANIFF
9-4
— YOU'VE STARTED TO GROW A MUSTACHE, AND YOU'LL PLASTER YOUR HAIR DOWN, AN' WEAR SPECS AS A DISGUISE?....
YEP!
THAT'S IN CASE ANY ONE OF THESE FOREIGN AGENTS SHOULD HAVE HAPPENED TO SEE ME SOMEWHERE BEFORE!
— BUT IF HE FIGURES THE SPY LEADER IS A WOMAN, I DON'T SEE HOW HE THINKS I WOULD APPEAL TO HER IN SUCH A GET-UP!
HUH! — HAVEN'T YOU EVER HEARD OF FEMININE INTUITION?
Reg. U. S. Pat. Off.: Copyright, 1936, by Chicago Tribune-N. Y. News Syndicate, Inc.

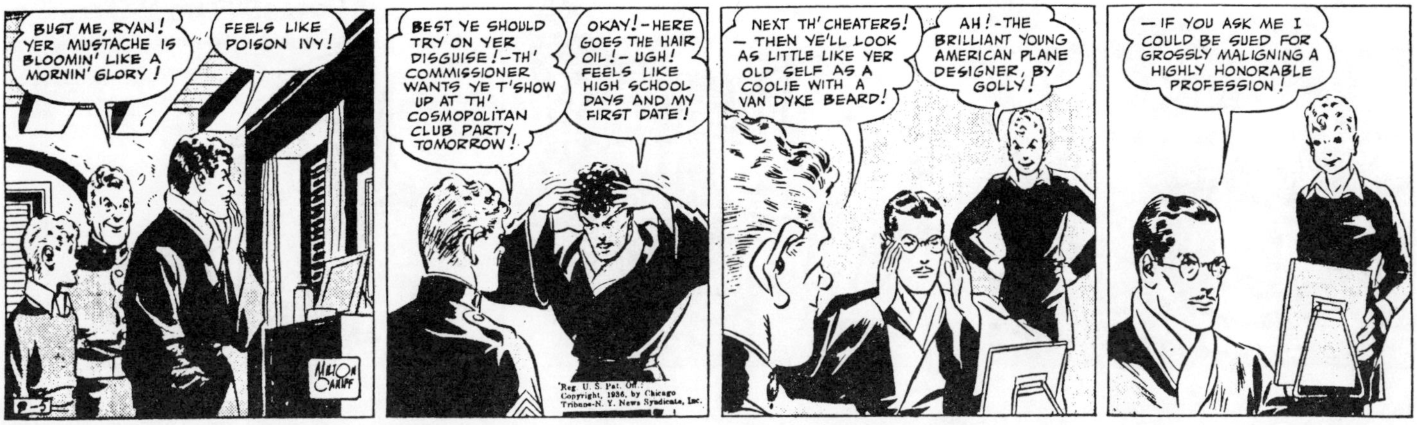
BUST ME, RYAN! YER MUSTACHE IS BLOOMIN' LIKE A MORNIN' GLORY!
FEELS LIKE POISON IVY!
MILTON CANIFF
9-5
BEST YE SHOULD TRY ON YER DISGUISE! — TH' COMMISSIONER WANTS YE T'SHOW UP AT TH' COSMOPOLITAN CLUB PARTY TOMORROW!
OKAY! — HERE GOES THE HAIR OIL! — UGH! FEELS LIKE HIGH SCHOOL DAYS AND MY FIRST DATE!
Reg. U. S. Pat. Off.: Copyright, 1936, by Chicago Tribune-N. Y. News Syndicate, Inc.
NEXT TH' CHEATERS! — THEN YE'LL LOOK AS LITTLE LIKE YER OLD SELF AS A COOLIE WITH A VAN DYKE BEARD!
AH! - THE BRILLIANT YOUNG AMERICAN PLANE DESIGNER, BY GOLLY!
— IF YOU ASK ME I COULD BE SUED FOR GROSSLY MALIGNING A HIGHLY HONORABLE PROFESSION!

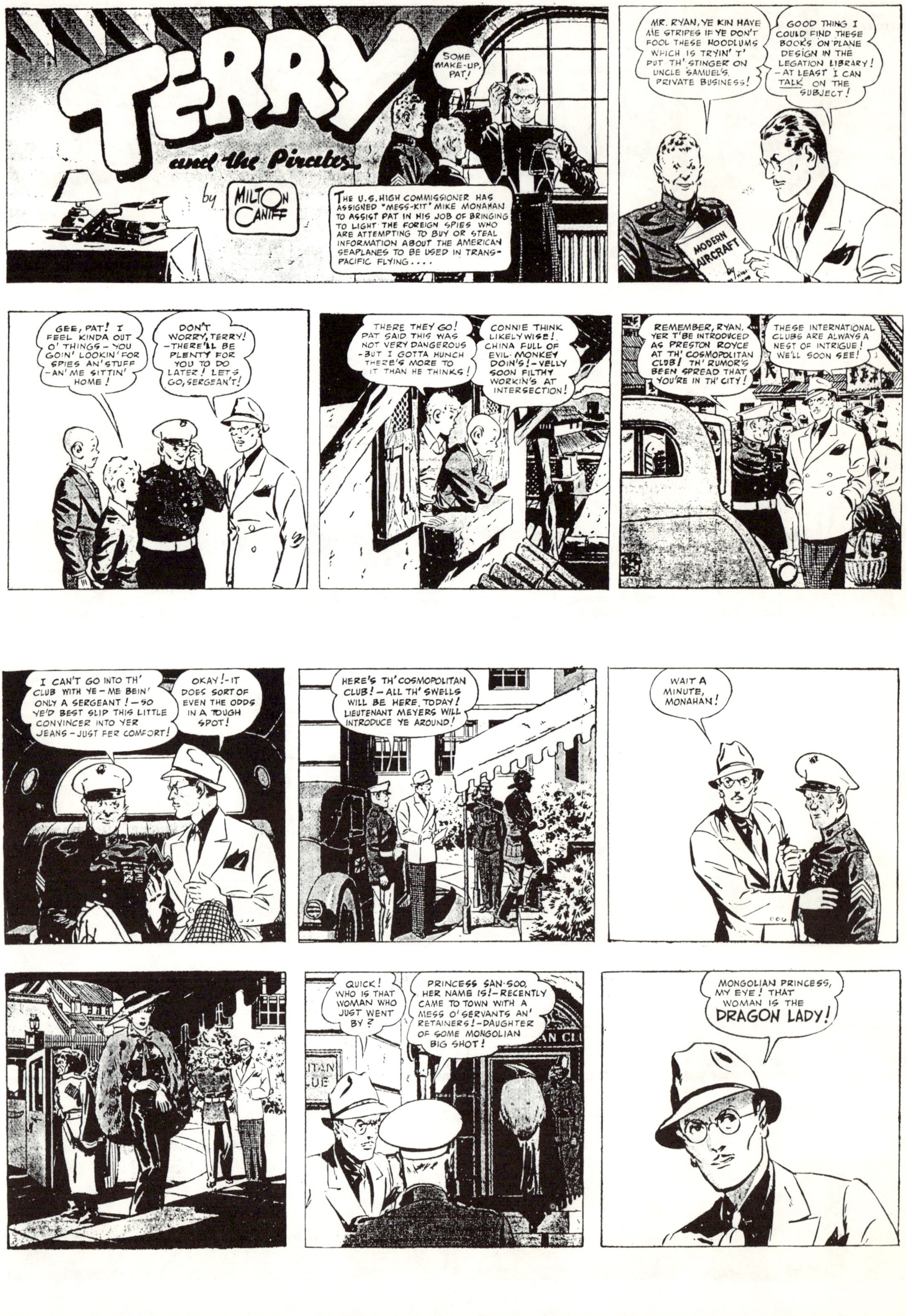
TERRY and the Pirates
by MILTON CANIFF
SOME MAKE-UP, PAT!
THE U.S. HIGH COMMISSIONER HAS ASSIGNED "MESS-KIT" MIKE MONAHAN TO ASSIST PAT IN HIS JOB OF BRINGING TO LIGHT THE FOREIGN SPIES WHO ARE ATTEMPTING TO BUY OR STEAL INFORMATION ABOUT THE AMERICAN SEAPLANES TO BE USED IN TRANS-PACIFIC FLYING....
MR. RYAN, YE KIN HAVE ME STRIPES IF YE DON'T FOOL THESE HOODLUMS WHICH IS TRYIN' T' PUT TH' STINGER ON UNCLE SAMUEL'S PRIVATE BUSINESS!
GOOD THING I COULD FIND THESE BOOKS ON PLANE DESIGN IN THE LEGATION LIBRARY! – AT LEAST I CAN TALK ON THE SUBJECT!
MODERN AIRCRAFT
GEE, PAT! I FEEL KINDA OUT O' THINGS – YOU GOIN' LOOKIN' FOR SPIES AN' STUFF – AN' ME SITTIN' HOME!
DON'T WORRY, TERRY! – THERE'LL BE PLENTY FOR YOU TO DO LATER! LET'S GO, SERGEAN'T!
THERE THEY GO! PAT SAID THIS WAS NOT VERY DANGEROUS – BUT I GOTTA HUNCH THERE'S MORE TO IT THAN HE THINKS!
CONNIE THINK LIKELYWISE! CHINA FULL OF EVIL MONKEY DOIN'S! – VELLY SOON FILTHY WORKIN'S AT INTERSECTION!
REMEMBER, RYAN, YER T'BE INTRODUCED AS PRESTON ROYCE AT TH' COSMOPOLITAN CLUB! TH' RUMOR'S BEEN SPREAD THAT YOU'RE IN TH' CITY!
THESE INTERNATIONAL CLUBS ARE ALWAYS A NEST OF INTRIGUE! WE'LL SOON SEE!
I CAN'T GO INTO TH' CLUB WITH YE – ME BEIN' ONLY A SERGEANT! – SO YE'D BEST SLIP THIS LITTLE CONVINCER INTO YER JEANS – JUST FER COMFORT!
OKAY! – IT DOES SORT OF EVEN THE ODDS IN A TOUGH SPOT!
HERE'S TH' COSMOPOLITAN CLUB! – ALL TH' SWELLS WILL BE HERE TODAY! LIEUTENANT MEYERS WILL INTRODUCE YE AROUND!
WAIT A MINUTE, MONAHAN!
QUICK! WHO IS THAT WOMAN WHO JUST WENT BY?
PRINCESS SAN-SOO, HER NAME IS! – RECENTLY CAME TO TOWN WITH A MESS O' SERVANTS AN' RETAINERS! – DAUGHTER OF SOME MONGOLIAN BIG SHOT!
MONGOLIAN PRINCESS, MY EYE! THAT WOMAN IS THE DRAGON LADY!

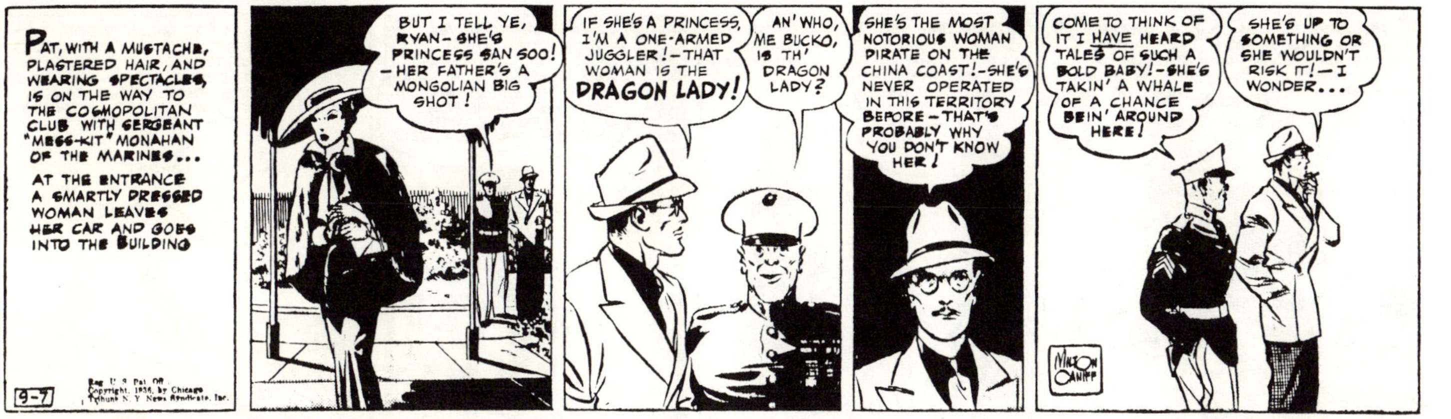
PAT, WITH A MUSTACHE, PLASTERED HAIR, AND WEARING SPECTACLES, IS ON THE WAY TO THE COSMOPOLITAN CLUB WITH SERGEANT "MESS-KIT" MONAHAN OF THE MARINES...
AT THE ENTRANCE A SMARTLY DRESSED WOMAN LEAVES HER CAR AND GOES INTO THE BUILDING
Reg. U. S. Pat. Off. Copyright, 1936, by Chicago Tribune-N. Y. News Syndicate, Inc.
9-7
BUT I TELL YE, RYAN - SHE'S PRINCESS SAN SOO! - HER FATHER'S A MONGOLIAN BIG SHOT!
IF SHE'S A PRINCESS, I'M A ONE-ARMED JUGGLER! - THAT WOMAN IS THE DRAGON LADY!
AN' WHO, ME BUCKO, IS TH' DRAGON LADY?
SHE'S THE MOST NOTORIOUS WOMAN PIRATE ON THE CHINA COAST! - SHE'S NEVER OPERATED IN THIS TERRITORY BEFORE - THAT'S PROBABLY WHY YOU DON'T KNOW HER!
COME TO THINK OF IT I HAVE HEARD TALES OF SUCH A BOLD BABY! - SHE'S TAKIN' A WHALE OF A CHANCE BEIN' AROUND HERE!
SHE'S UP TO SOMETHING OR SHE WOULDN'T RISK IT! - I WONDER...
MILTON CANIFF

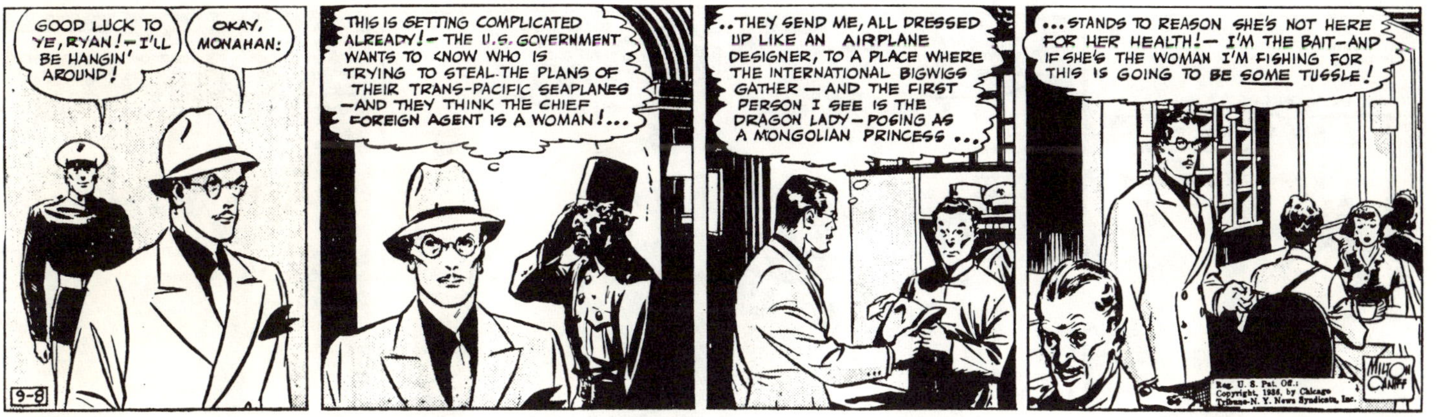
GOOD LUCK TO YE, RYAN! - I'LL BE HANGIN' AROUND!
OKAY, MONAHAN:
9-8
THIS IS GETTING COMPLICATED ALREADY! - THE U.S. GOVERNMENT WANTS TO KNOW WHO IS TRYING TO STEAL THE PLANS OF THEIR TRANS-PACIFIC SEAPLANES - AND THEY THINK THE CHIEF FOREIGN AGENT IS A WOMAN!...
..THEY SEND ME, ALL DRESSED UP LIKE AN AIRPLANE DESIGNER, TO A PLACE WHERE THE INTERNATIONAL BIGWIGS GATHER - AND THE FIRST PERSON I SEE IS THE DRAGON LADY - POSING AS A MONGOLIAN PRINCESS...
...STANDS TO REASON SHE'S NOT HERE FOR HER HEALTH! - I'M THE BAIT - AND IF SHE'S THE WOMAN I'M FISHING FOR THIS IS GOING TO BE SOME TUSSLE!
MILTON CANIFF
Reg. U. S. Pat. Off.: Copyright, 1936, by Chicago Tribune-N. Y. News Syndicate, Inc.

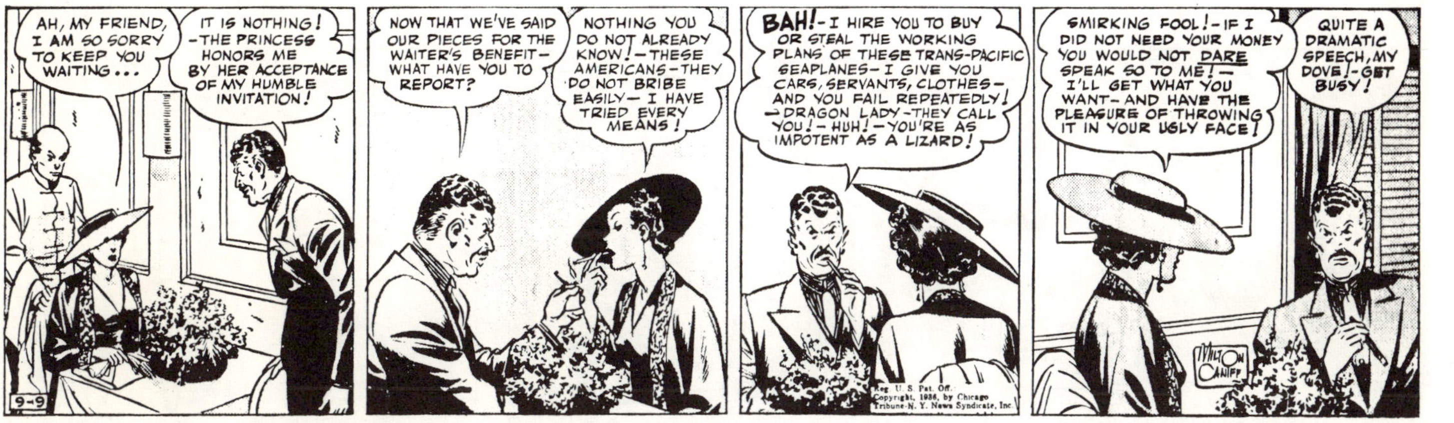
AH, MY FRIEND, I AM SO SORRY TO KEEP YOU WAITING...
IT IS NOTHING! - THE PRINCESS HONORS ME BY HER ACCEPTANCE OF MY HUMBLE INVITATION!
9-9
NOW THAT WE'VE SAID OUR PIECES FOR THE WAITER'S BENEFIT - WHAT HAVE YOU TO REPORT?
NOTHING YOU DO NOT ALREADY KNOW! - THESE AMERICANS - THEY DO NOT BRIBE EASILY - I HAVE TRIED EVERY MEANS!
BAH! - I HIRE YOU TO BUY OR STEAL THE WORKING PLANS OF THESE TRANS-PACIFIC SEAPLANES - I GIVE YOU CARS, SERVANTS, CLOTHES - AND YOU FAIL REPEATEDLY! - DRAGON LADY - THEY CALL YOU! - HUH! - YOU'RE AS IMPOTENT AS A LIZARD!
Reg. U. S. Pat. Off. Copyright, 1936, by Chicago Tribune-N. Y. News Syndicate, Inc.
SMIRKING FOOL! - IF I DID NOT NEED YOUR MONEY YOU WOULD NOT DARE SPEAK SO TO ME! - I'LL GET WHAT YOU WANT - AND HAVE THE PLEASURE OF THROWING IT IN YOUR UGLY FACE!
QUITE A DRAMATIC SPEECH, MY DOVE! - GET BUSY!
MILTON CANIFF

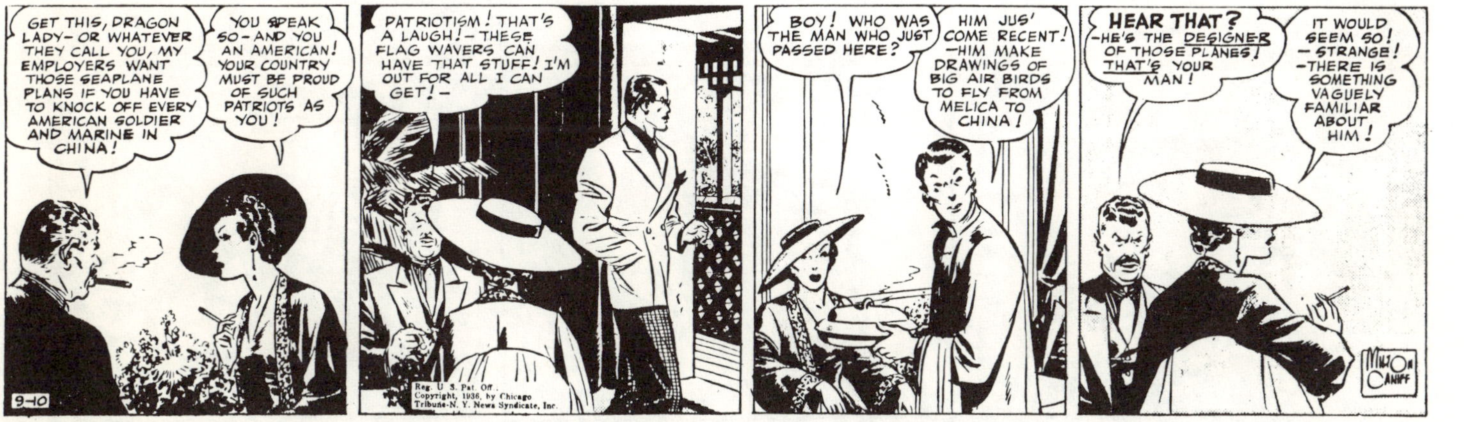
GET THIS, DRAGON LADY - OR WHATEVER THEY CALL YOU, MY EMPLOYERS WANT THOSE SEAPLANE PLANS IF YOU HAVE TO KNOCK OFF EVERY AMERICAN SOLDIER AND MARINE IN CHINA!
YOU SPEAK SO - AND YOU AN AMERICAN! YOUR COUNTRY MUST BE PROUD OF SUCH PATRIOTS AS YOU!
9-10
PATRIOTISM! THAT'S A LAUGH! - THESE FLAG WAVERS CAN HAVE THAT STUFF! I'M OUT FOR ALL I CAN GET! -
Reg. U. S. Pat. Off. Copyright, 1936, by Chicago Tribune-N. Y. News Syndicate, Inc.
BOY! WHO WAS THE MAN WHO JUST PASSED HERE?
HIM JUS' COME RECENT! - HIM MAKE DRAWINGS OF BIG AIR BIRDS TO FLY FROM MELICA TO CHINA!
HEAR THAT? - HE'S THE DESIGNER OF THOSE PLANES! THAT'S YOUR MAN!
IT WOULD SEEM SO! - STRANGE! - THERE IS SOMETHING VAGUELY FAMILIAR ABOUT HIM!
MILTON CANIFF

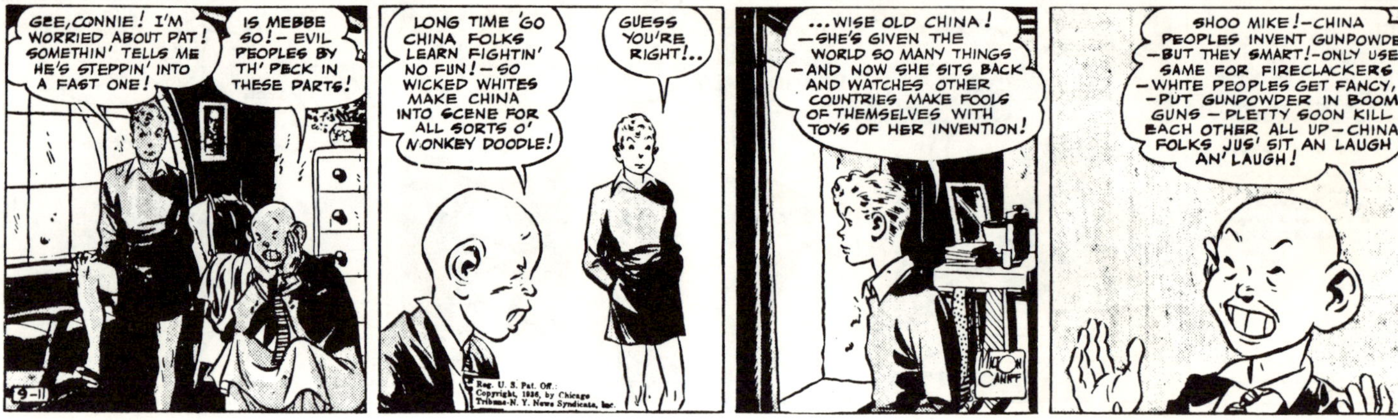

GEE, CONNIE! I'M WORRIED ABOUT PAT! SOMETHIN' TELLS ME HE'S STEPPIN' INTO A FAST ONE!
IS MEBBE SO! — EVIL PEOPLES BY TH' PECK IN THESE PARTS!
9-11
LONG TIME 'GO CHINA FOLKS LEARN FIGHTIN' NO FUN! — SO WICKED WHITES MAKE CHINA INTO SCENE FOR ALL SORTS O' MONKEY DOODLE!
GUESS YOU'RE RIGHT!..
Reg. U. S. Pat. Off. Copyright, 1936, by Chicago Tribune-N. Y. News Syndicate, Inc.
...WISE OLD CHINA! — SHE'S GIVEN THE WORLD SO MANY THINGS — AND NOW SHE SITS BACK AND WATCHES OTHER COUNTRIES MAKE FOOLS OF THEMSELVES WITH TOYS OF HER INVENTION!
MILTON CANIFF
SHOO MIKE! — CHINA PEOPLES INVENT GUNPOWDER — BUT THEY SMART! — ONLY USE SAME FOR FIRECLACKERS! — WHITE PEOPLES GET FANCY, — PUT GUNPOWDER IN BOOM GUNS — PLETTY SOON KILL EACH OTHER ALL UP — CHINA FOLKS JUS' SIT AN LAUGH AN' LAUGH!

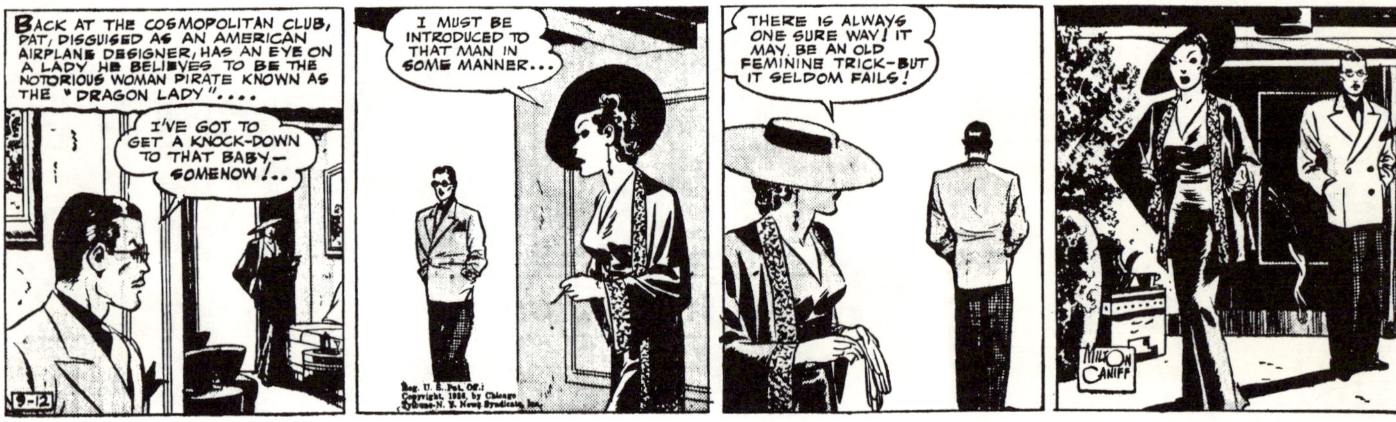

BACK AT THE COSMOPOLITAN CLUB, PAT, DISGUISED AS AN AMERICAN AIRPLANE DESIGNER, HAS AN EYE ON A LADY HE BELIEVES TO BE THE NOTORIOUS WOMAN PIRATE KNOWN AS THE "DRAGON LADY"....
I'VE GOT TO GET A KNOCK-DOWN TO THAT BABY — SOMENOW!..
9-12
I MUST BE INTRODUCED TO THAT MAN IN SOME MANNER...
Reg. U. S. Pat. Off.: Copyright, 1936, by Chicago Tribune-N. Y. News Syndicate, Inc.
THERE IS ALWAYS ONE SURE WAY! IT MAY BE AN OLD FEMININE TRICK — BUT IT SELDOM FAILS!
MILTON CANIFF

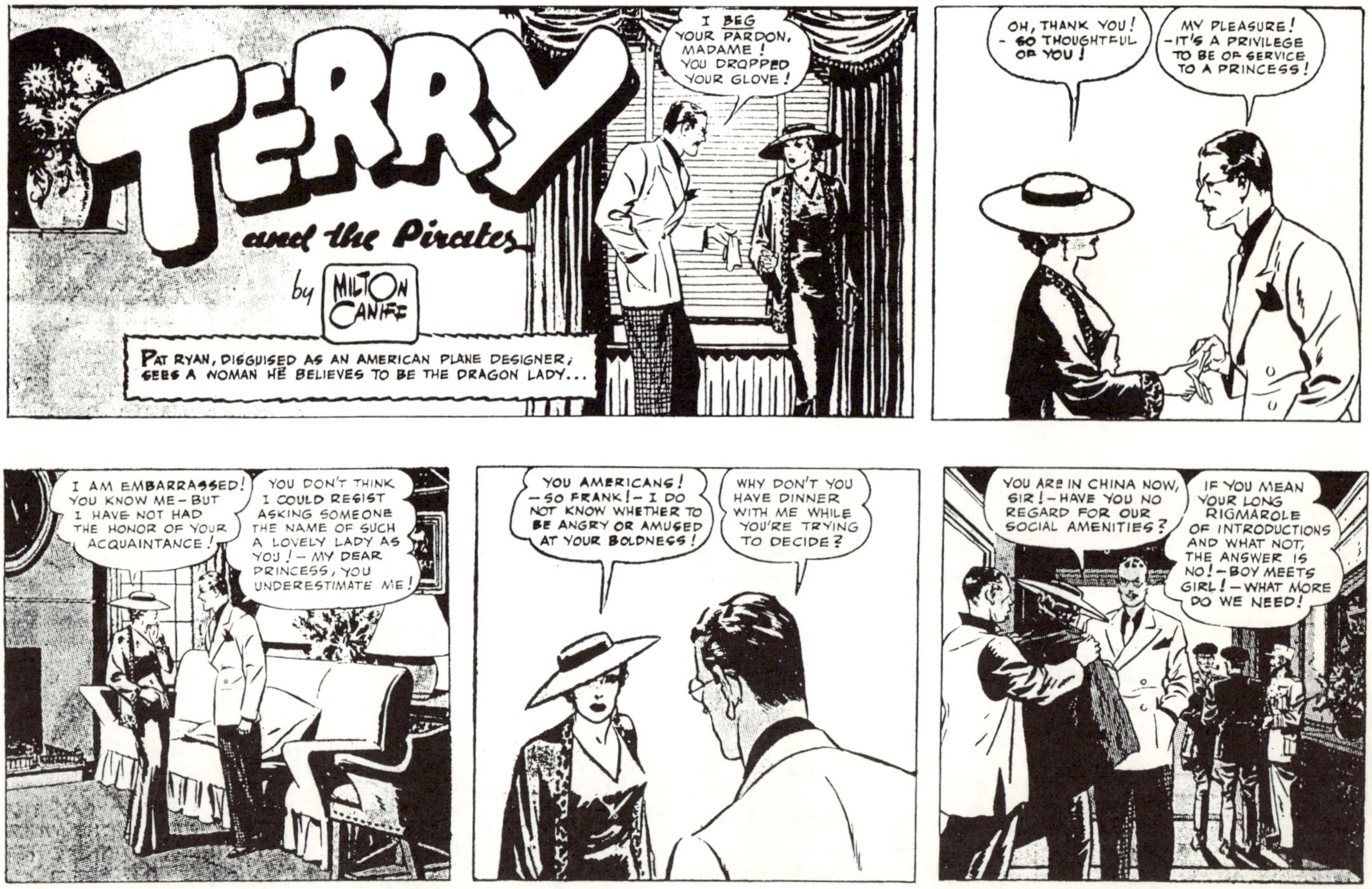

TERRY and the Pirates
by MILTON CANIFF
PAT RYAN, DISGUISED AS AN AMERICAN PLANE DESIGNER, SEES A WOMAN HE BELIEVES TO BE THE DRAGON LADY...
I BEG YOUR PARDON, MADAME! YOU DROPPED YOUR GLOVE!
OH, THANK YOU! — SO THOUGHTFUL OF YOU!
MY PLEASURE! — IT'S A PRIVILEGE TO BE OF SERVICE TO A PRINCESS!
I AM EMBARRASSED! YOU KNOW ME — BUT I HAVE NOT HAD THE HONOR OF YOUR ACQUAINTANCE!
YOU DON'T THINK I COULD RESIST ASKING SOMEONE THE NAME OF SUCH A LOVELY LADY AS YOU! — MY DEAR PRINCESS, YOU UNDERESTIMATE ME!
YOU AMERICANS! — SO FRANK! — I DO NOT KNOW WHETHER TO BE ANGRY OR AMUSED AT YOUR BOLDNESS!
WHY DON'T YOU HAVE DINNER WITH ME WHILE YOU'RE TRYING TO DECIDE?
YOU ARE IN CHINA NOW, SIR! — HAVE YOU NO REGARD FOR OUR SOCIAL AMENITIES?
IF YOU MEAN YOUR LONG RIGMAROLE OF INTRODUCTIONS AND WHAT NOT, THE ANSWER IS NO! — BOY MEETS GIRL! — WHAT MORE DO WE NEED!

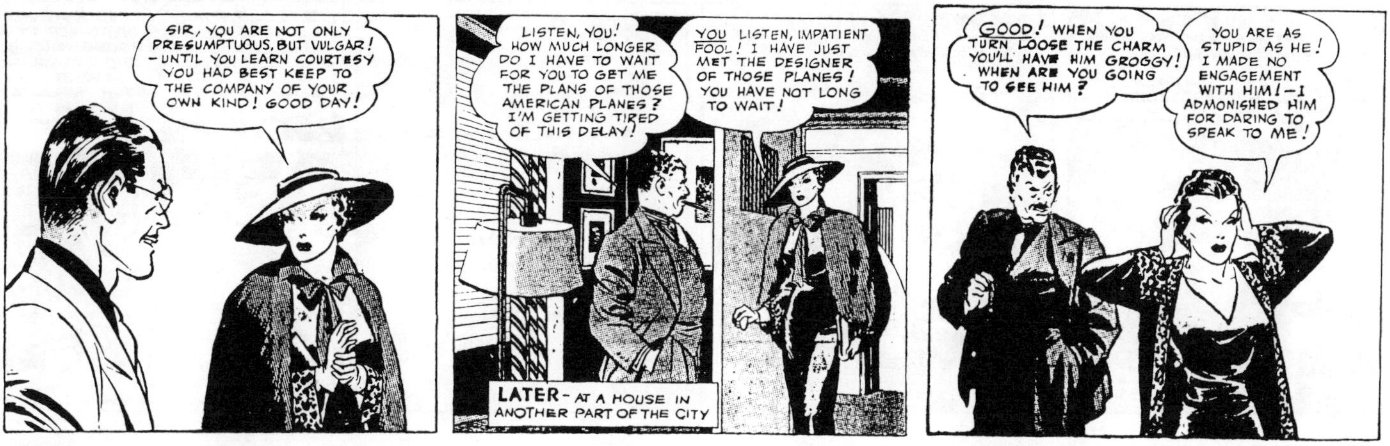
SIR, YOU ARE NOT ONLY PRESUMPTUOUS, BUT VULGAR! –UNTIL YOU LEARN COURTESY YOU HAD BEST KEEP TO THE COMPANY OF YOUR OWN KIND! GOOD DAY!
LISTEN, YOU! HOW MUCH LONGER DO I HAVE TO WAIT FOR YOU TO GET ME THE PLANS OF THOSE AMERICAN PLANES? I'M GETTING TIRED OF THIS DELAY!
YOU LISTEN, IMPATIENT FOOL! I HAVE JUST MET THE DESIGNER OF THOSE PLANES! YOU HAVE NOT LONG TO WAIT!
LATER – AT A HOUSE IN ANOTHER PART OF THE CITY
GOOD! WHEN YOU TURN LOOSE THE CHARM YOU'LL HAVE HIM GROGGY! WHEN ARE YOU GOING TO SEE HIM?
YOU ARE AS STUPID AS HE! I MADE NO ENGAGEMENT WITH HIM! –I ADMONISHED HIM FOR DARING TO SPEAK TO ME!

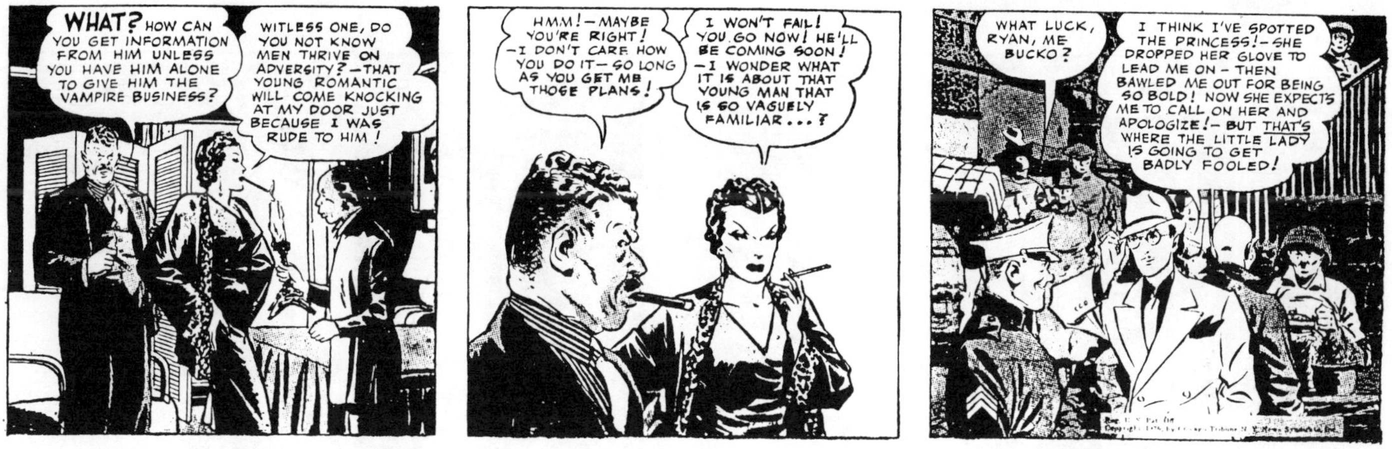
WHAT? HOW CAN YOU GET INFORMATION FROM HIM UNLESS YOU HAVE HIM ALONE TO GIVE HIM THE VAMPIRE BUSINESS?
WITLESS ONE, DO YOU NOT KNOW MEN THRIVE ON ADVERSITY? –THAT YOUNG ROMANTIC WILL COME KNOCKING AT MY DOOR JUST BECAUSE I WAS RUDE TO HIM!
HMM! –MAYBE YOU'RE RIGHT! –I DON'T CARE HOW YOU DO IT – SO LONG AS YOU GET ME THOSE PLANS!
I WON'T FAIL! YOU GO NOW! HE'LL BE COMING SOON! –I WONDER WHAT IT IS ABOUT THAT YOUNG MAN THAT IS SO VAGUELY FAMILIAR...?
WHAT LUCK, RYAN, ME BUCKO?
I THINK I'VE SPOTTED THE PRINCESS! –SHE DROPPED HER GLOVE TO LEAD ME ON – THEN BAWLED ME OUT FOR BEING SO BOLD! NOW SHE EXPECTS ME TO CALL ON HER AND APOLOGIZE! – BUT THAT'S WHERE THE LITTLE LADY IS GOING TO GET BADLY FOOLED!

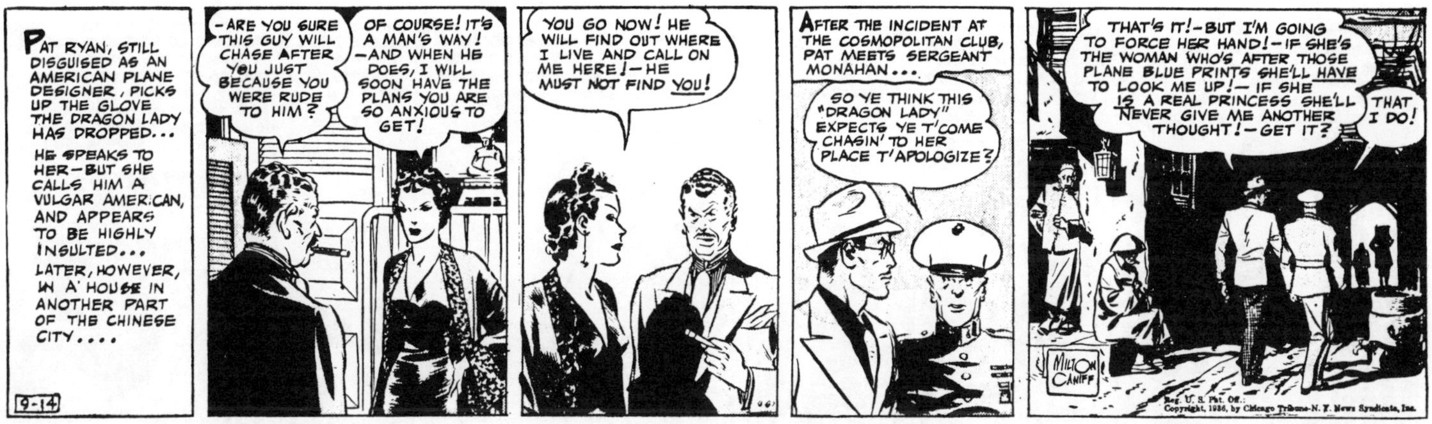
PAT RYAN, STILL DISGUISED AS AN AMERICAN PLANE DESIGNER, PICKS UP THE GLOVE THE DRAGON LADY HAS DROPPED...
HE SPEAKS TO HER – BUT SHE CALLS HIM A VULGAR AMERICAN, AND APPEARS TO BE HIGHLY INSULTED...
LATER, HOWEVER, IN A HOUSE IN ANOTHER PART OF THE CHINESE CITY....
9-14
–ARE YOU SURE THIS GUY WILL CHASE AFTER YOU JUST BECAUSE YOU WERE RUDE TO HIM?
OF COURSE! IT'S A MAN'S WAY! –AND WHEN HE DOES, I WILL SOON HAVE THE PLANS YOU ARE SO ANXIOUS TO GET!
YOU GO NOW! HE WILL FIND OUT WHERE I LIVE AND CALL ON ME HERE! –HE MUST NOT FIND YOU!
AFTER THE INCIDENT AT THE COSMOPOLITAN CLUB, PAT MEETS SERGEANT MONAHAN...
SO YE THINK THIS "DRAGON LADY" EXPECTS YE T'COME CHASIN' TO HER PLACE T'APOLOGIZE?
THAT'S IT! –BUT I'M GOING TO FORCE HER HAND! –IF SHE'S THE WOMAN WHO'S AFTER THOSE PLANE BLUE PRINTS SHE'LL HAVE TO LOOK ME UP! –IF SHE IS A REAL PRINCESS SHE'LL NEVER GIVE ME ANOTHER THOUGHT! –GET IT?
THAT I DO!
MILTON CANIFF
Reg. U. S. Pat. Off.: Copyright, 1936, by Chicago Tribune-N. Y. News Syndicate, Inc.

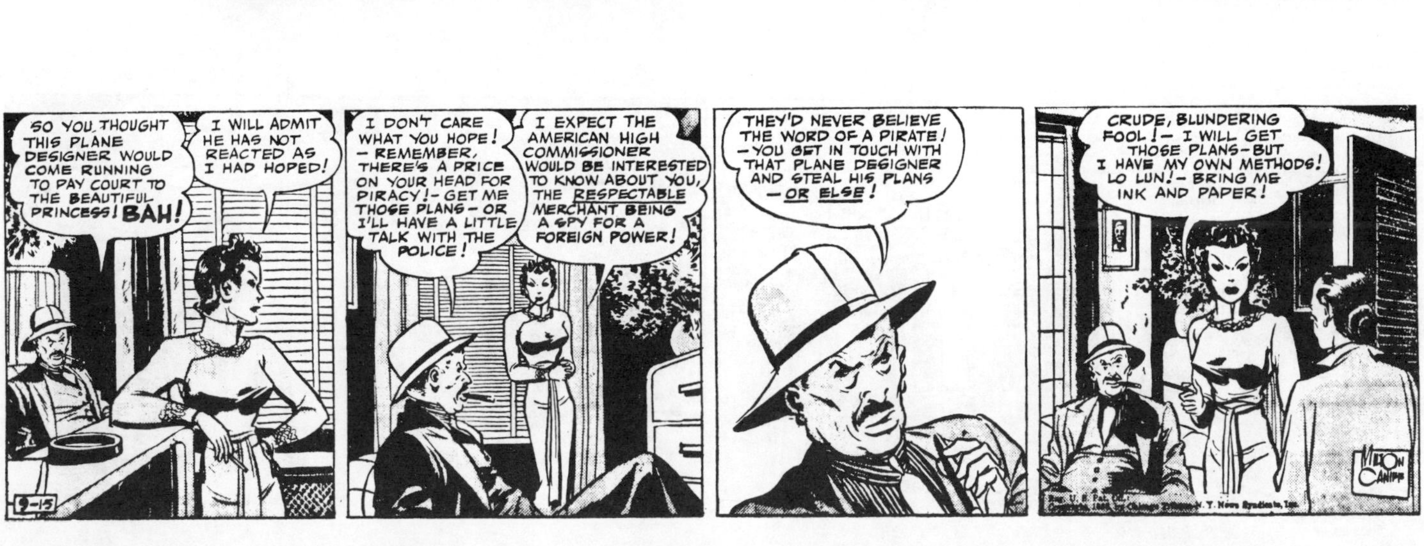
SO YOU THOUGHT THIS PLANE DESIGNER WOULD COME RUNNING TO PAY COURT TO THE BEAUTIFUL PRINCESS! BAH!
I WILL ADMIT HE HAS NOT REACTED AS I HAD HOPED!
9-15
I DON'T CARE WHAT YOU HOPE! –REMEMBER, THERE'S A PRICE ON YOUR HEAD FOR PIRACY! –GET ME THOSE PLANS – OR I'LL HAVE A LITTLE TALK WITH THE POLICE!
I EXPECT THE AMERICAN HIGH COMMISSIONER WOULD BE INTERESTED TO KNOW ABOUT YOU, THE RESPECTABLE MERCHANT BEING A SPY FOR A FOREIGN POWER!
THEY'D NEVER BELIEVE THE WORD OF A PIRATE! –YOU GET IN TOUCH WITH THAT PLANE DESIGNER AND STEAL HIS PLANS –OR ELSE!
CRUDE, BLUNDERING FOOL! – I WILL GET THOSE PLANS – BUT I HAVE MY OWN METHODS! LO LUN! – BRING ME INK AND PAPER!
MILTON CANIFF

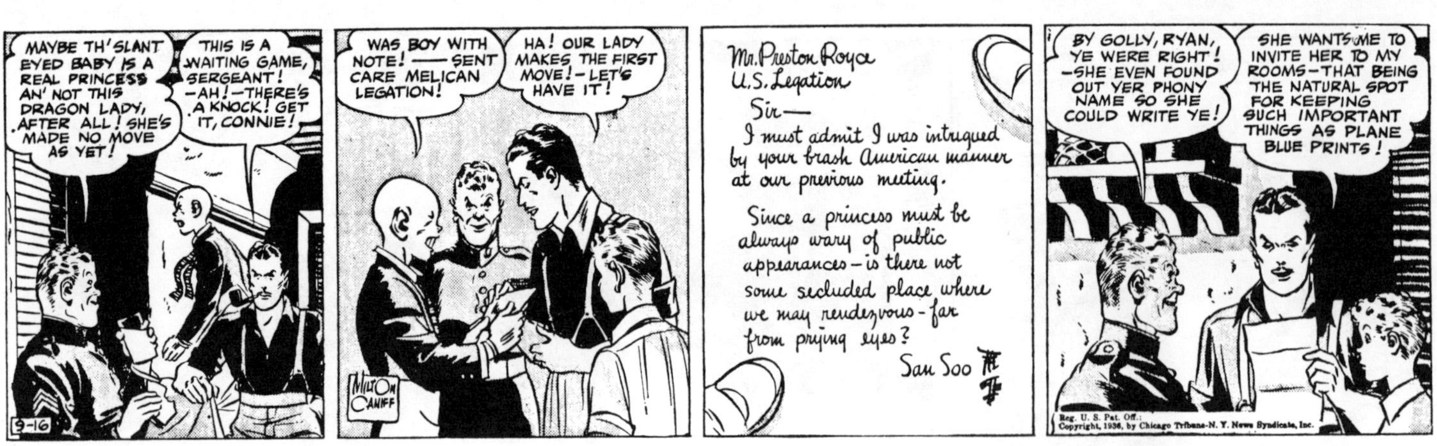
MAYBE TH' SLANT EYED BABY IS A REAL PRINCESS AN' NOT THIS DRAGON LADY, AFTER ALL! SHE'S MADE NO MOVE AS YET!
THIS IS A WAITING GAME, SERGEANT! —AH!—THERE'S A KNOCK! GET IT, CONNIE!
9-16
WAS BOY WITH NOTE! ——SENT CARE MELICAN LEGATION!
HA! OUR LADY MAKES THE FIRST MOVE!—LET'S HAVE IT!
MILTON CANIFF
Mr. Preston Royce
U.S. Legation
Sir—
I must admit I was intrigued by your brash American manner at our previous meeting.
Since a princess must be always wary of public appearances—is there not some secluded place where we may rendezvous—far from prying eyes?
San Soo
BY GOLLY, RYAN, YE WERE RIGHT! —SHE EVEN FOUND OUT YER PHONY NAME SO SHE COULD WRITE YE!
SHE WANTS ME TO INVITE HER TO MY ROOMS—THAT BEING THE NATURAL SPOT FOR KEEPING SUCH IMPORTANT THINGS AS PLANE BLUE PRINTS!
Reg. U. S. Pat. Off.: Copyright, 1936, by Chicago Tribune-N. Y. News Syndicate, Inc.

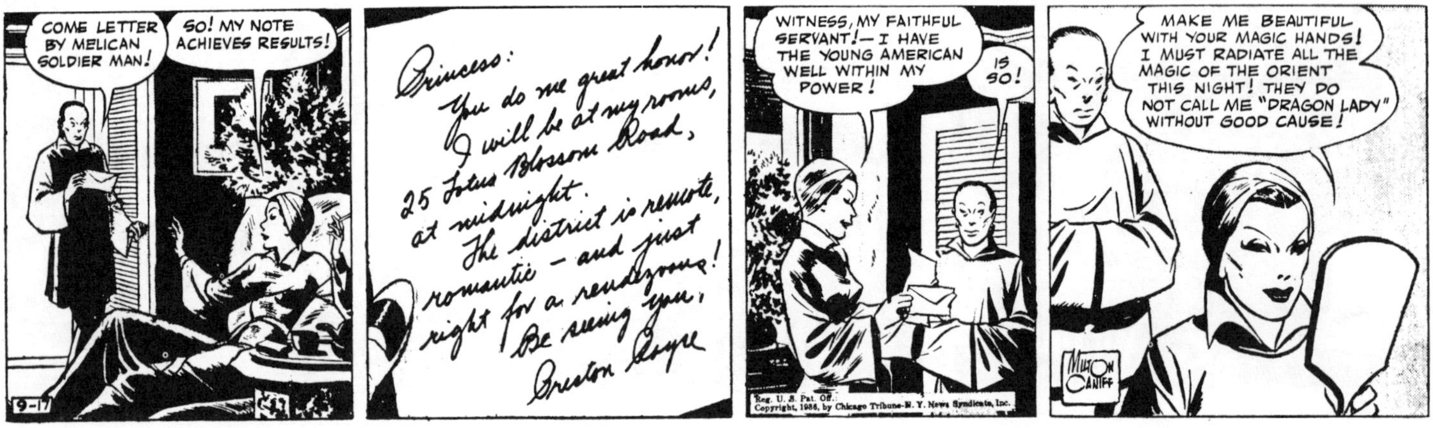
COME LETTER BY MELICAN SOLDIER MAN!
SO! MY NOTE ACHIEVES RESULTS!
9-17
Princess:
You do me great honor!
I will be at my rooms, 25 Lotus Blossom Road, at midnight.
The district is remote, romantic—and just right for a rendezvous!
Be seeing you,
Preston Royce
WITNESS, MY FAITHFUL SERVANT!—I HAVE THE YOUNG AMERICAN WELL WITHIN MY POWER!
IS SO!
Reg. U. S. Pat. Off.: Copyright, 1936, by Chicago Tribune-N. Y. News Syndicate, Inc.
MAKE ME BEAUTIFUL WITH YOUR MAGIC HANDS! I MUST RADIATE ALL THE MAGIC OF THE ORIENT THIS NIGHT! THEY DO NOT CALL ME "DRAGON LADY" WITHOUT GOOD CAUSE!
MILTON CANIFF

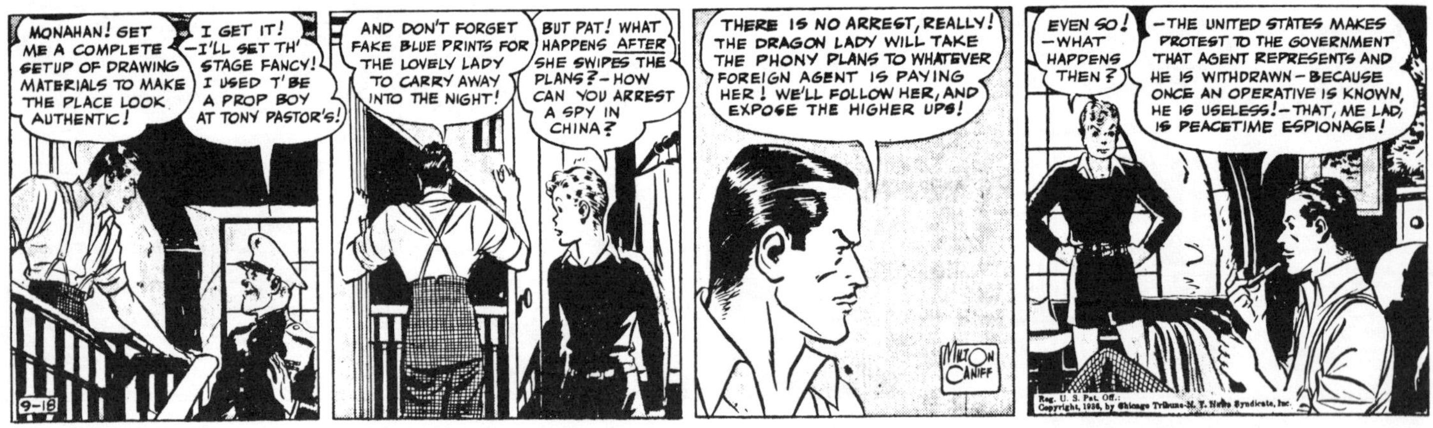
MONAHAN! GET ME A COMPLETE SETUP OF DRAWING MATERIALS TO MAKE THE PLACE LOOK AUTHENTIC!
I GET IT! —I'LL SET TH' STAGE FANCY! I USED T' BE A PROP BOY AT TONY PASTOR'S!
9-18
AND DON'T FORGET FAKE BLUE PRINTS FOR THE LOVELY LADY TO CARRY AWAY INTO THE NIGHT!
BUT PAT! WHAT HAPPENS AFTER SHE SWIPES THE PLANS?—HOW CAN YOU ARREST A SPY IN CHINA?
THERE IS NO ARREST, REALLY! THE DRAGON LADY WILL TAKE THE PHONY PLANS TO WHATEVER FOREIGN AGENT IS PAYING HER! WE'LL FOLLOW HER, AND EXPOSE THE HIGHER UPS!
MILTON CANIFF
EVEN SO! —WHAT HAPPENS THEN?
—THE UNITED STATES MAKES PROTEST TO THE GOVERNMENT THAT AGENT REPRESENTS AND HE IS WITHDRAWN—BECAUSE ONCE AN OPERATIVE IS KNOWN, HE IS USELESS!—THAT, ME LAD, IS PEACETIME ESPIONAGE!
Reg. U. S. Pat. Off.: Copyright, 1936, by Chicago Tribune-N. Y. News Syndicate, Inc.

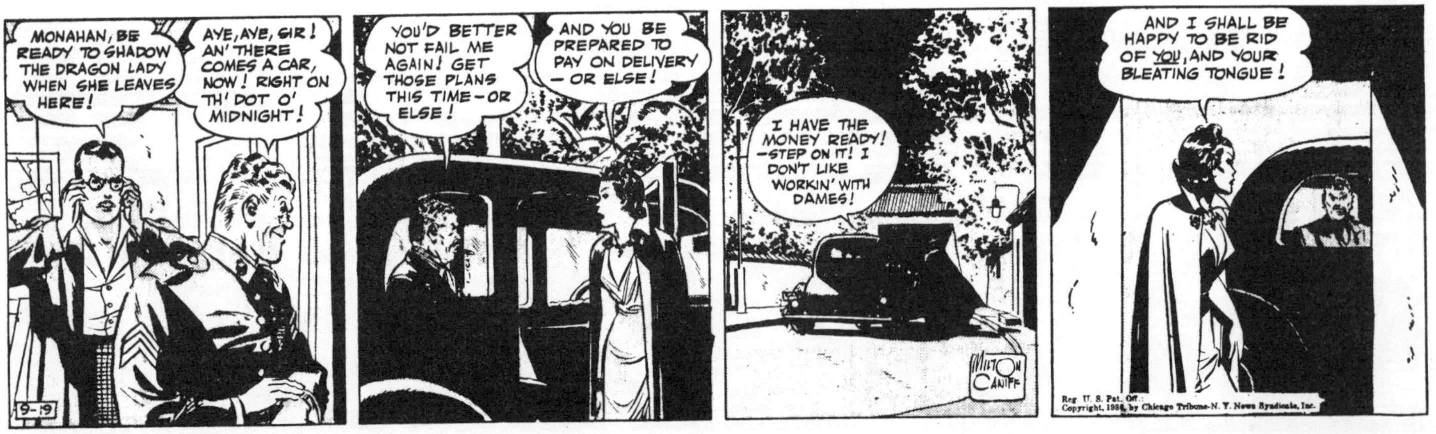
MONAHAN, BE READY TO SHADOW THE DRAGON LADY WHEN SHE LEAVES HERE!
AYE, AYE, SIR! AN' THERE COMES A CAR, NOW! RIGHT ON TH' DOT O' MIDNIGHT!
9-19
YOU'D BETTER NOT FAIL ME AGAIN! GET THOSE PLANS THIS TIME—OR ELSE!
AND YOU BE PREPARED TO PAY ON DELIVERY —OR ELSE!
I HAVE THE MONEY READY! —STEP ON IT! I DON'T LIKE WORKIN' WITH DAMES!
MILTON CANIFF
AND I SHALL BE HAPPY TO BE RID OF YOU, AND YOUR BLEATING TONGUE!
Reg. U. S. Pat. Off.: Copyright, 1936, by Chicago Tribune-N. Y. News Syndicate, Inc.

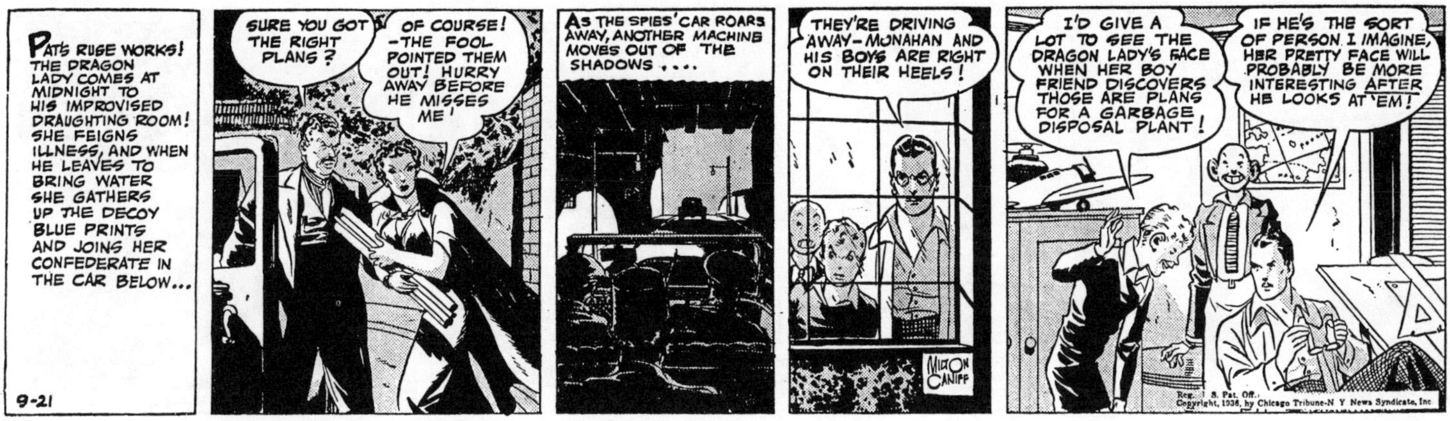
PAT'S RUSE WORKS! THE DRAGON LADY COMES AT MIDNIGHT TO HIS IMPROVISED DRAUGHTING ROOM! SHE FEIGNS ILLNESS, AND WHEN HE LEAVES TO BRING WATER SHE GATHERS UP THE DECOY BLUE PRINTS AND JOINS HER CONFEDERATE IN THE CAR BELOW...
9-21
SURE YOU GOT THE RIGHT PLANS?
OF COURSE! —THE FOOL POINTED THEM OUT! HURRY AWAY BEFORE HE MISSES ME!
AS THE SPIES' CAR ROARS AWAY, ANOTHER MACHINE MOVES OUT OF THE SHADOWS....
THEY'RE DRIVING AWAY—MONAHAN AND HIS BOYS ARE RIGHT ON THEIR HEELS!
MILTON CANIFF
I'D GIVE A LOT TO SEE THE DRAGON LADY'S FACE WHEN HER BOY FRIEND DISCOVERS THOSE ARE PLANS FOR A GARBAGE DISPOSAL PLANT!
IF HE'S THE SORT OF PERSON I IMAGINE, HER PRETTY FACE WILL PROBABLY BE MORE INTERESTING AFTER HE LOOKS AT 'EM!
Reg. U. S. Pat. Off.: Copyright, 1936, by Chicago Tribune-N. Y. News Syndicate, Inc.

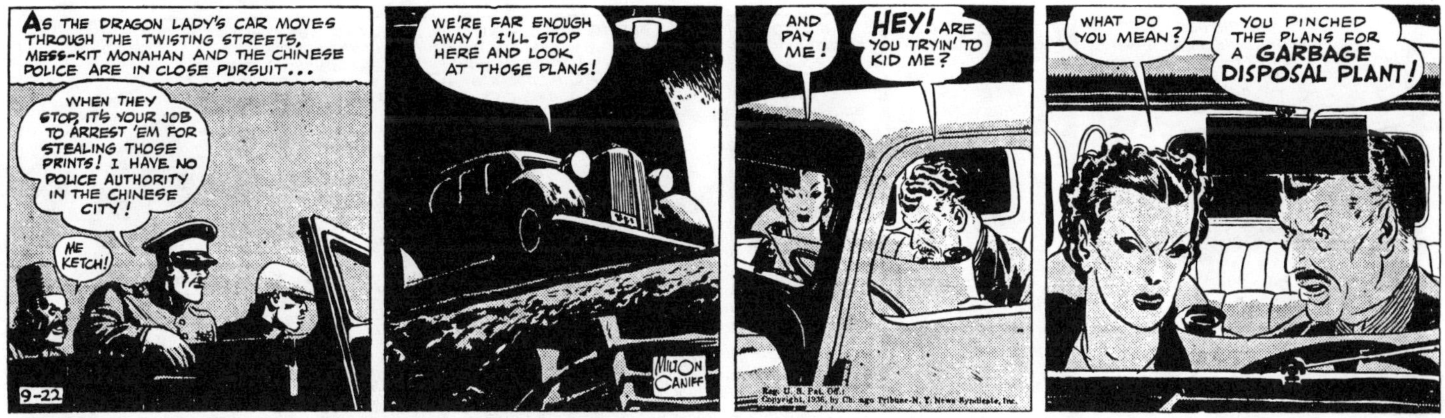
AS THE DRAGON LADY'S CAR MOVES THROUGH THE TWISTING STREETS, MESS-KIT MONAHAN AND THE CHINESE POLICE ARE IN CLOSE PURSUIT...
WHEN THEY STOP, IT'S YOUR JOB TO ARREST 'EM FOR STEALING THOSE PRINTS! I HAVE NO POLICE AUTHORITY IN THE CHINESE CITY!
ME KETCH!
9-22
WE'RE FAR ENOUGH AWAY! I'LL STOP HERE AND LOOK AT THOSE PLANS!
MILTON CANIFF
AND PAY ME!
HEY! ARE YOU TRYIN' TO KID ME?
Reg. U. S. Pat. Off.: Copyright, 1936, by Chicago Tribune-N. Y. News Syndicate, Inc.
WHAT DO YOU MEAN?
YOU PINCHED THE PLANS FOR A GARBAGE DISPOSAL PLANT!

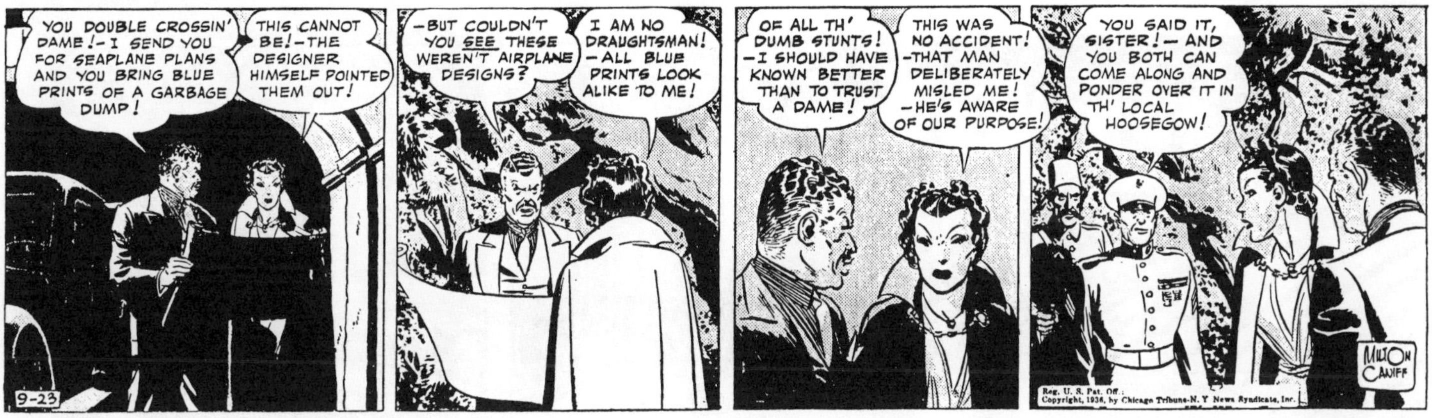
YOU DOUBLE CROSSIN' DAME!—I SEND YOU FOR SEAPLANE PLANS AND YOU BRING BLUE PRINTS OF A GARBAGE DUMP!
THIS CANNOT BE!—THE DESIGNER HIMSELF POINTED THEM OUT!
9-23
—BUT COULDN'T YOU SEE THESE WEREN'T AIRPLANE DESIGNS?
I AM NO DRAUGHTSMAN! —ALL BLUE PRINTS LOOK ALIKE TO ME!
OF ALL TH' DUMB STUNTS! —I SHOULD HAVE KNOWN BETTER THAN TO TRUST A DAME!
THIS WAS NO ACCIDENT! —THAT MAN DELIBERATELY MISLED ME! —HE'S AWARE OF OUR PURPOSE!
YOU SAID IT, SISTER!—AND YOU BOTH CAN COME ALONG AND PONDER OVER IT IN TH' LOCAL HOOSEGOW!
MILTON CANIFF
Reg. U. S. Pat. Off.: Copyright, 1936, by Chicago Tribune-N. Y. News Syndicate, Inc.

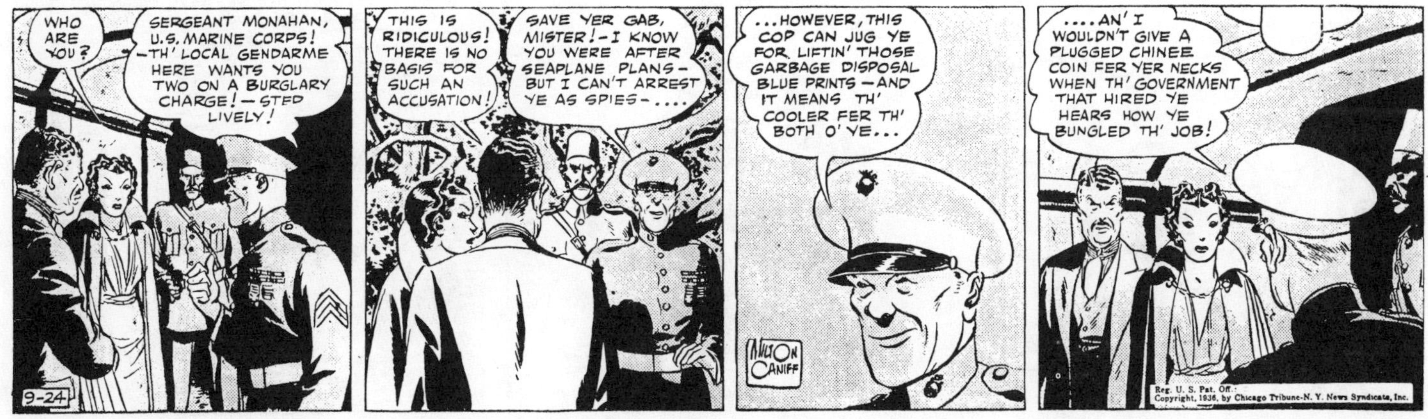
WHO ARE YOU?
SERGEANT MONAHAN, U.S. MARINE CORPS! —TH' LOCAL GENDARME HERE WANTS YOU TWO ON A BURGLARY CHARGE!—STEP LIVELY!
9-24
THIS IS RIDICULOUS! THERE IS NO BASIS FOR SUCH AN ACCUSATION!
SAVE YER GAB, MISTER!—I KNOW YOU WERE AFTER SEAPLANE PLANS—BUT I CAN'T ARREST YE AS SPIES—....
...HOWEVER, THIS COP CAN JUG YE FOR LIFTIN' THOSE GARBAGE DISPOSAL BLUE PRINTS—AND IT MEANS TH' COOLER FER TH' BOTH O' YE...
MILTON CANIFF
....AN' I WOULDN'T GIVE A PLUGGED CHINEE COIN FER YER NECKS WHEN TH' GOVERNMENT THAT HIRED YE HEARS HOW YE BUNGLED TH' JOB!
Reg. U. S. Pat. Off.: Copyright, 1936, by Chicago Tribune-N. Y. News Syndicate, Inc.

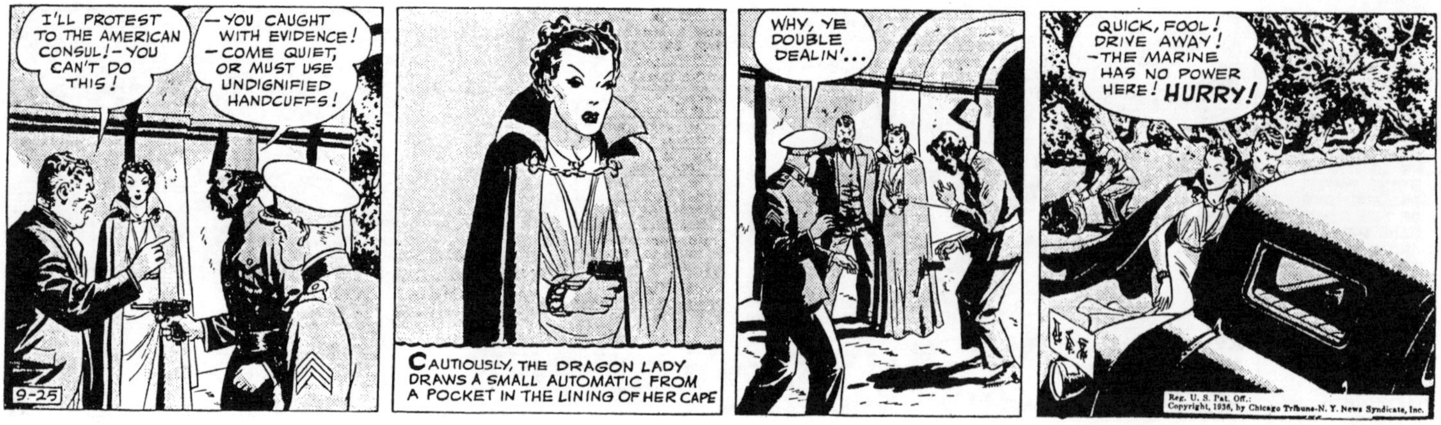

I'LL PROTEST TO THE AMERICAN CONSUL! —YOU CAN'T DO THIS!
—YOU CAUGHT WITH EVIDENCE! —COME QUIET, OR MUST USE UNDIGNIFIED HANDCUFFS!
9-25
CAUTIOUSLY, THE DRAGON LADY DRAWS A SMALL AUTOMATIC FROM A POCKET IN THE LINING OF HER CAPE
WHY, YE DOUBLE DEALIN'...
QUICK, FOOL! DRIVE AWAY! —THE MARINE HAS NO POWER HERE! HURRY!
Reg. U. S. Pat. Off.: Copyright, 1936, by Chicago Tribune-N. Y. News Syndicate, Inc.

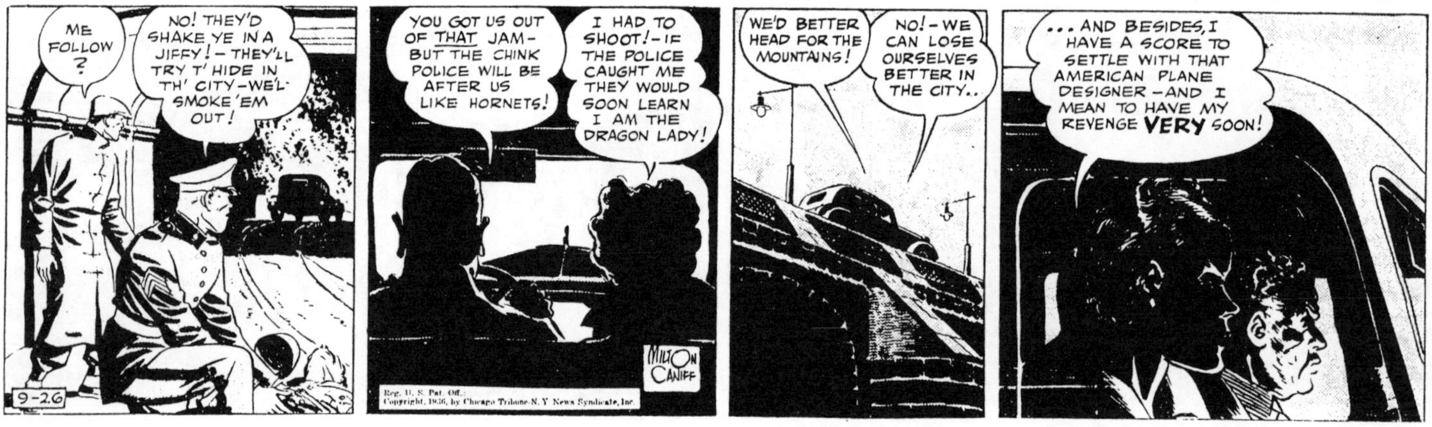

ME FOLLOW ?
NO! THEY'D SHAKE YE IN A JIFFY! —THEY'LL TRY T' HIDE IN TH' CITY—WE'L SMOKE 'EM OUT!
9-26
YOU GOT US OUT OF THAT JAM—BUT THE CHINK POLICE WILL BE AFTER US LIKE HORNETS!
I HAD TO SHOOT! —IF THE POLICE CAUGHT ME THEY WOULD SOON LEARN I AM THE DRAGON LADY!
MILTON CANIFF
Reg. U. S. Pat. Off.: Copyright, 1936, by Chicago Tribune-N. Y. News Syndicate, Inc.
WE'D BETTER HEAD FOR THE MOUNTAINS!
NO! —WE CAN LOSE OURSELVES BETTER IN THE CITY..
... AND BESIDES, I HAVE A SCORE TO SETTLE WITH THAT AMERICAN PLANE DESIGNER—AND I MEAN TO HAVE MY REVENGE VERY SOON!

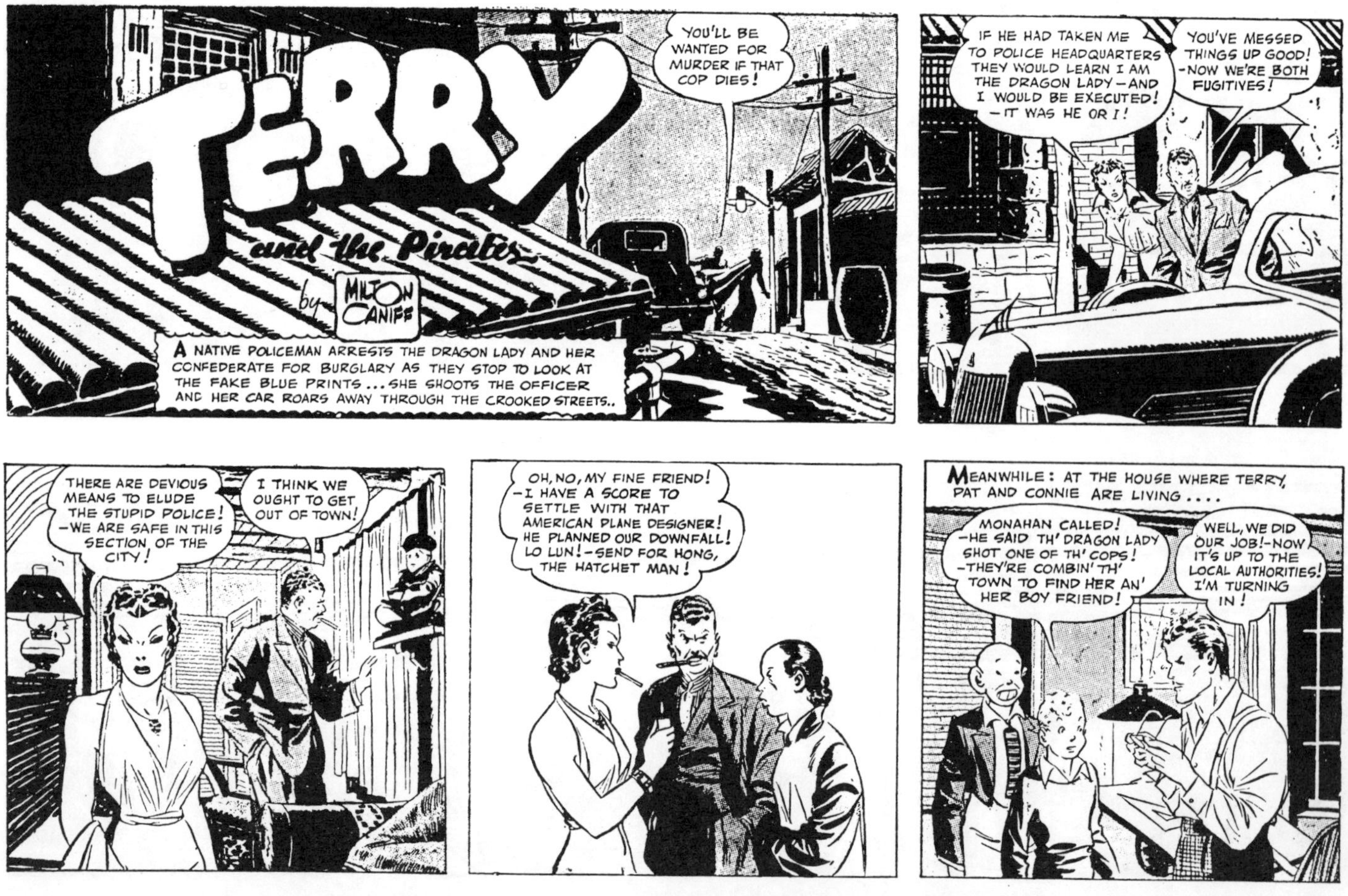

TERRY and the Pirates by MILTON CANIFF
YOU'LL BE WANTED FOR MURDER IF THAT COP DIES!
A NATIVE POLICEMAN ARRESTS THE DRAGON LADY AND HER CONFEDERATE FOR BURGLARY AS THEY STOP TO LOOK AT THE FAKE BLUE PRINTS ... SHE SHOOTS THE OFFICER AND HER CAR ROARS AWAY THROUGH THE CROOKED STREETS..
IF HE HAD TAKEN ME TO POLICE HEADQUARTERS THEY WOULD LEARN I AM THE DRAGON LADY—AND I WOULD BE EXECUTED! —IT WAS HE OR I!
YOU'VE MESSED THINGS UP GOOD! —NOW WE'RE BOTH FUGITIVES!
THERE ARE DEVIOUS MEANS TO ELUDE THE STUPID POLICE! —WE ARE SAFE IN THIS SECTION OF THE CITY!
I THINK WE OUGHT TO GET OUT OF TOWN!
OH, NO, MY FINE FRIEND! —I HAVE A SCORE TO SETTLE WITH THAT AMERICAN PLANE DESIGNER! HE PLANNED OUR DOWNFALL! LO LUN! —SEND FOR HONG, THE HATCHET MAN!
MEANWHILE: AT THE HOUSE WHERE TERRY, PAT AND CONNIE ARE LIVING ....
MONAHAN CALLED! —HE SAID TH' DRAGON LADY SHOT ONE OF TH' COPS! —THEY'RE COMBIN' TH' TOWN TO FIND HER AN' HER BOY FRIEND!
WELL, WE DID OUR JOB! —NOW IT'S UP TO THE LOCAL AUTHORITIES! I'M TURNING IN!

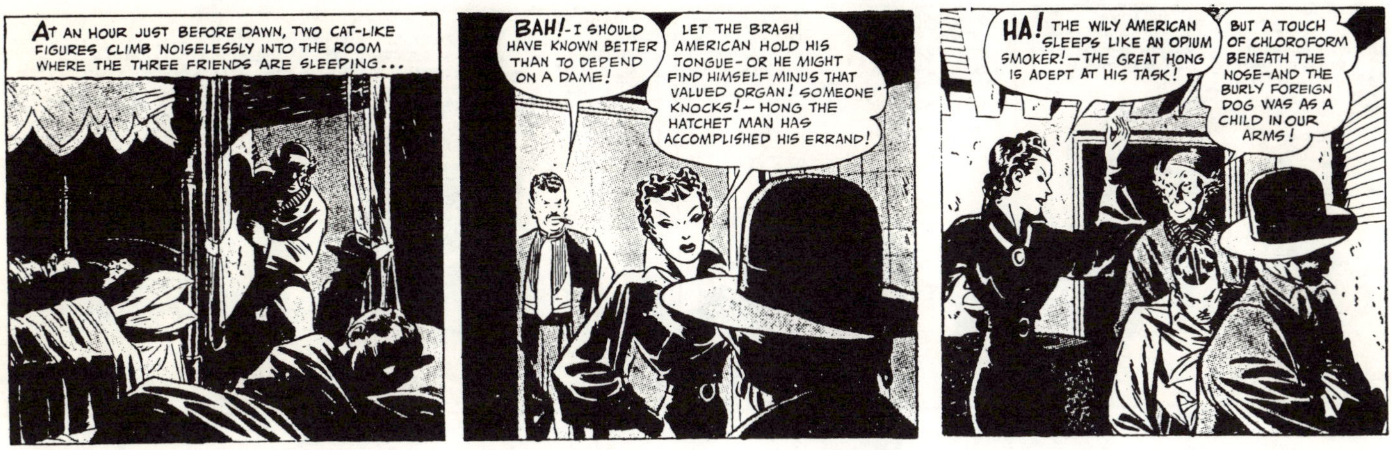
AT AN HOUR JUST BEFORE DAWN, TWO CAT-LIKE FIGURES CLIMB NOISELESSLY INTO THE ROOM WHERE THE THREE FRIENDS ARE SLEEPING...
BAH! - I SHOULD HAVE KNOWN BETTER THAN TO DEPEND ON A DAME!
LET THE BRASH AMERICAN HOLD HIS TONGUE - OR HE MIGHT FIND HIMSELF MINUS THAT VALUED ORGAN! SOMEONE KNOCKS! - HONG THE HATCHET MAN HAS ACCOMPLISHED HIS ERRAND!
HA! THE WILY AMERICAN SLEEPS LIKE AN OPIUM SMOKER! - THE GREAT HONG IS ADEPT AT HIS TASK!
BUT A TOUCH OF CHLOROFORM BENEATH THE NOSE - AND THE BURLY FOREIGN DOG WAS AS A CHILD IN OUR ARMS!

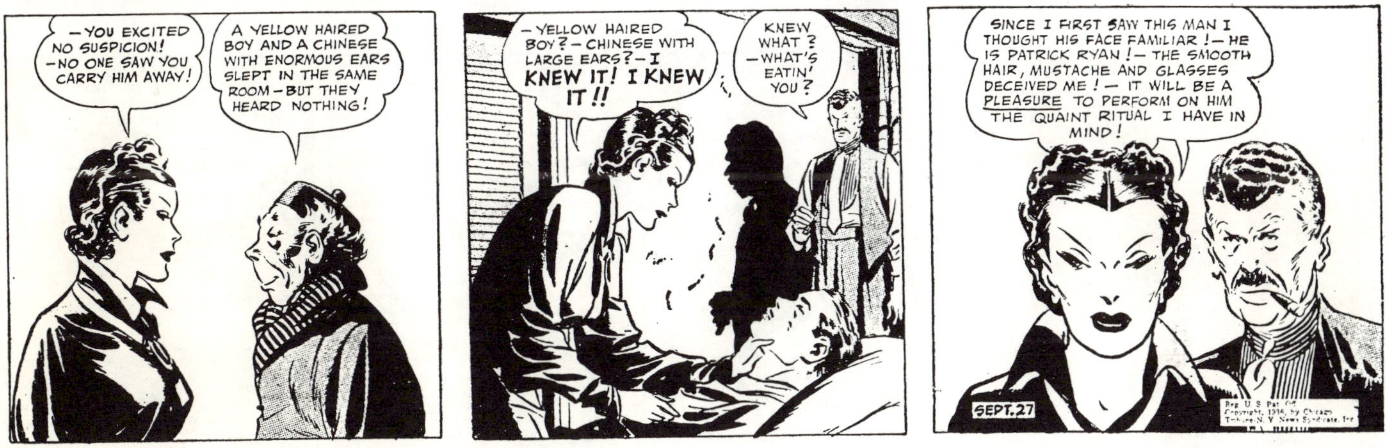
- YOU EXCITED NO SUSPICION! - NO ONE SAW YOU CARRY HIM AWAY!
A YELLOW HAIRED BOY AND A CHINESE WITH ENORMOUS EARS SLEPT IN THE SAME ROOM - BUT THEY HEARD NOTHING!
- YELLOW HAIRED BOY? - CHINESE WITH LARGE EARS? - I KNEW IT! I KNEW IT!!
KNEW WHAT? - WHAT'S EATIN' YOU?
SINCE I FIRST SAW THIS MAN I THOUGHT HIS FACE FAMILIAR! - HE IS PATRICK RYAN! - THE SMOOTH HAIR, MUSTACHE AND GLASSES DECEIVED ME! - IT WILL BE A PLEASURE TO PERFORM ON HIM THE QUAINT RITUAL I HAVE IN MIND!
SEPT. 27

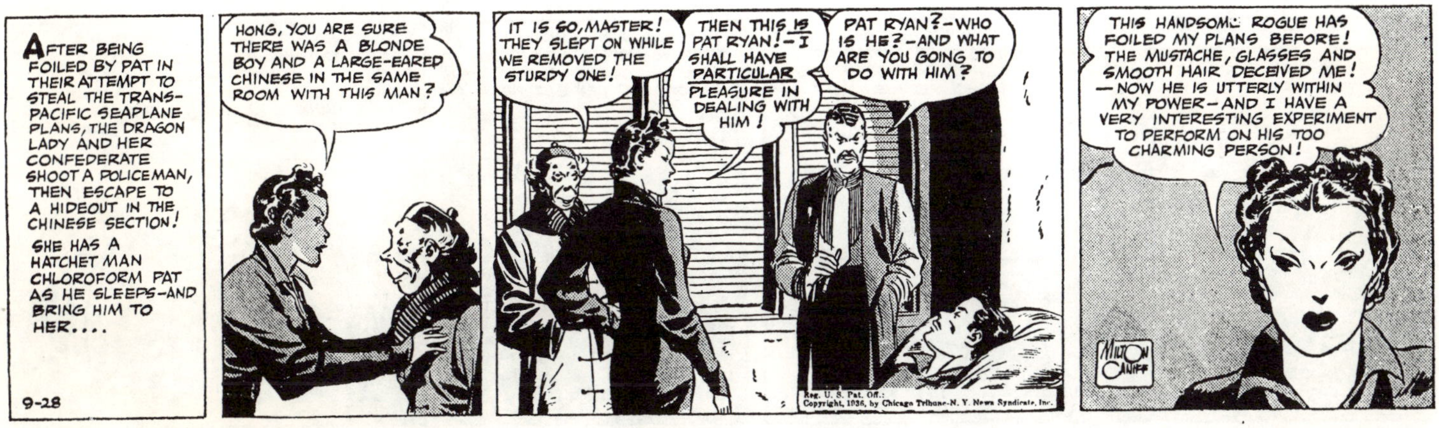
AFTER BEING FOILED BY PAT IN THEIR ATTEMPT TO STEAL THE TRANS-PACIFIC SEAPLANE PLANS, THE DRAGON LADY AND HER CONFEDERATE SHOOT A POLICEMAN, THEN ESCAPE TO A HIDEOUT IN THE CHINESE SECTION! SHE HAS A HATCHET MAN CHLOROFORM PAT AS HE SLEEPS - AND BRING HIM TO HER....
9-28
HONG, YOU ARE SURE THERE WAS A BLONDE BOY AND A LARGE-EARED CHINESE IN THE SAME ROOM WITH THIS MAN?
IT IS SO, MASTER! THEY SLEPT ON WHILE WE REMOVED THE STURDY ONE!
THEN THIS IS PAT RYAN! - I SHALL HAVE PARTICULAR PLEASURE IN DEALING WITH HIM!
PAT RYAN? - WHO IS HE? - AND WHAT ARE YOU GOING TO DO WITH HIM?
Reg. U. S. Pat. Off.: Copyright, 1936, by Chicago Tribune-N. Y. News Syndicate, Inc.
THIS HANDSOME ROGUE HAS FOILED MY PLANS BEFORE! THE MUSTACHE, GLASSES AND SMOOTH HAIR DECEIVED ME! - NOW HE IS UTTERLY WITHIN MY POWER - AND I HAVE A VERY INTERESTING EXPERIMENT TO PERFORM ON HIS TOO CHARMING PERSON!
MILTON CANIFF

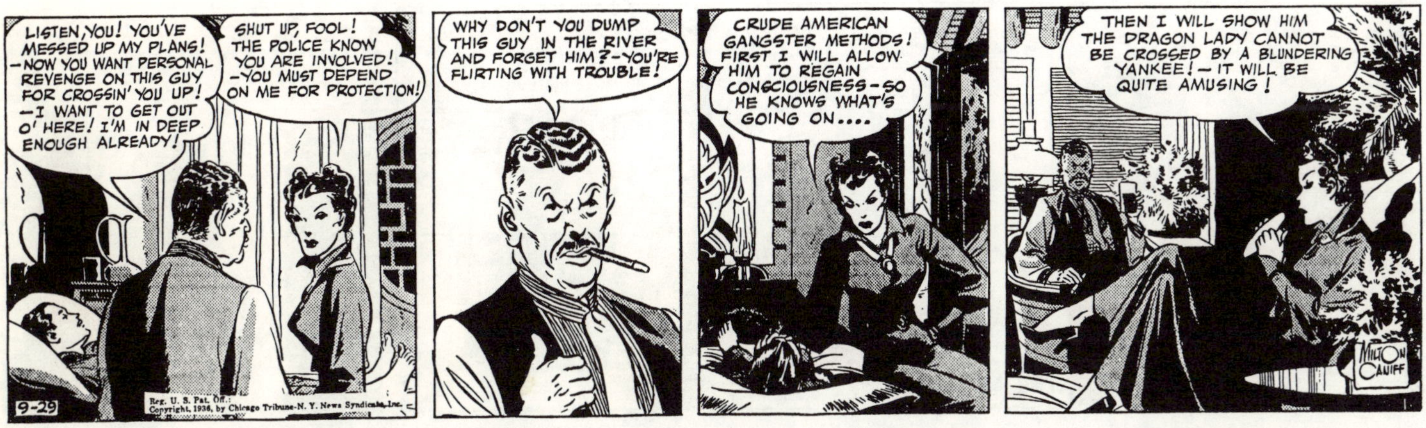
LISTEN, YOU! YOU'VE MESSED UP MY PLANS! - NOW YOU WANT PERSONAL REVENGE ON THIS GUY FOR CROSSIN' YOU UP! - I WANT TO GET OUT O' HERE! I'M IN DEEP ENOUGH ALREADY!
SHUT UP, FOOL! THE POLICE KNOW YOU ARE INVOLVED! - YOU MUST DEPEND ON ME FOR PROTECTION!
9-29
Reg. U. S. Pat. Off.: Copyright, 1936, by Chicago Tribune-N. Y. News Syndicate, Inc.
WHY DON'T YOU DUMP THIS GUY IN THE RIVER AND FORGET HIM? - YOU'RE FLIRTING WITH TROUBLE!
CRUDE AMERICAN GANGSTER METHODS! FIRST I WILL ALLOW HIM TO REGAIN CONSCIOUSNESS - SO HE KNOWS WHAT'S GOING ON....
THEN I WILL SHOW HIM THE DRAGON LADY CANNOT BE CROSSED BY A BLUNDERING YANKEE! - IT WILL BE QUITE AMUSING!
MILTON CANIFF

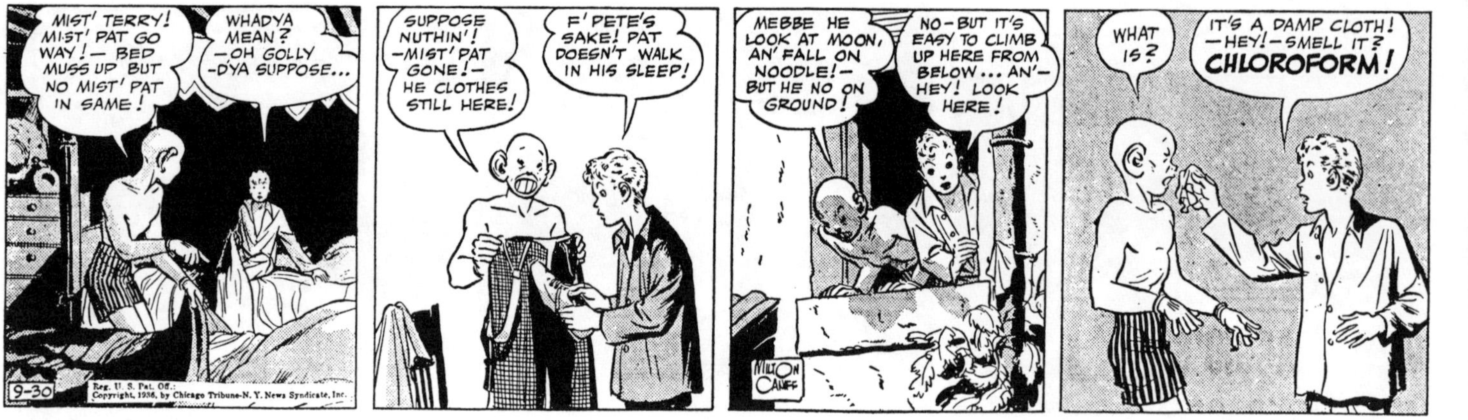
MIST' TERRY! MIST' PAT GO WAY! — BED MUSS UP BUT NO MIST' PAT IN SAME!
WHADYA MEAN? —OH GOLLY -DYA SUPPOSE...
SUPPOSE NUTHIN'! —MIST' PAT GONE! — HE CLOTHES STILL HERE!
F' PETE'S SAKE! PAT DOESN'T WALK IN HIS SLEEP!
MEBBE HE LOOK AT MOON, AN' FALL ON NOODLE! — BUT HE NO ON GROUND!
NO—BUT IT'S EASY TO CLIMB UP HERE FROM BELOW... AN'— HEY! LOOK HERE!
WHAT IS?
IT'S A DAMP CLOTH! —HEY!—SMELL IT? CHLOROFORM!
9-30
Reg. U. S. Pat. Off.: Copyright, 1936, by Chicago Tribune-N. Y. News Syndicate, Inc.
MILTON CANIFF

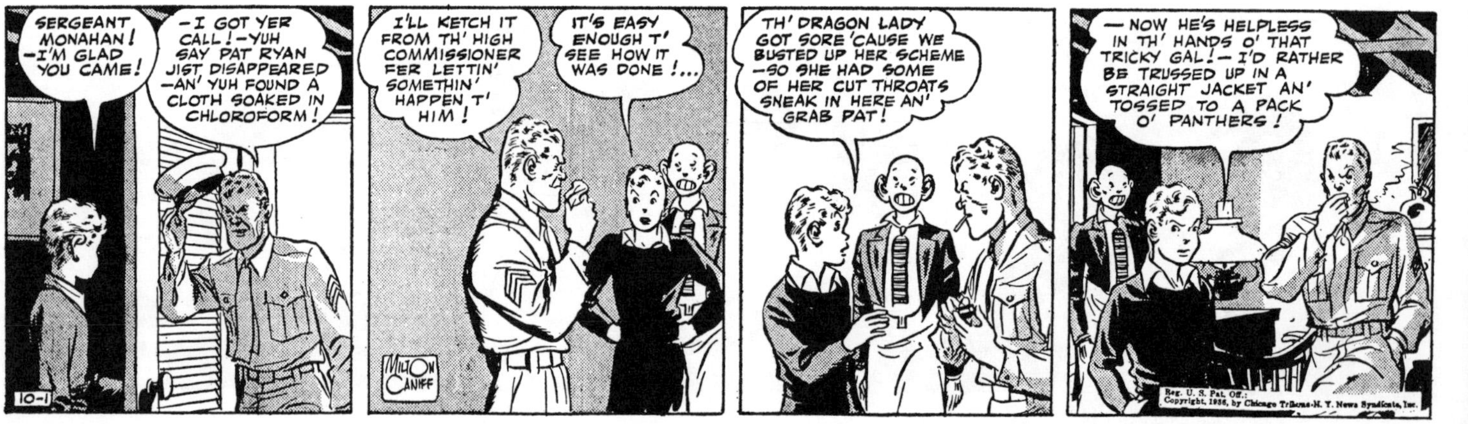
SERGEANT MONAHAN! —I'M GLAD YOU CAME!
—I GOT YER CALL! —YUH SAY PAT RYAN JIST DISAPPEARED —AN' YUH FOUND A CLOTH SOAKED IN CHLOROFORM!
I'LL KETCH IT FROM TH' HIGH COMMISSIONER FER LETTIN' SOMETHIN' HAPPEN T' HIM!
IT'S EASY ENOUGH T' SEE HOW IT WAS DONE!...
TH' DRAGON LADY GOT SORE 'CAUSE WE BUSTED UP HER SCHEME —SO SHE HAD SOME OF HER CUT THROATS SNEAK IN HERE AN' GRAB PAT!
— NOW HE'S HELPLESS IN TH' HANDS O' THAT TRICKY GAL! — I'D RATHER BE TRUSSED UP IN A STRAIGHT JACKET AN' TOSSED TO A PACK O' PANTHERS!
10-1
MILTON CANIFF
Reg. U. S. Pat. Off.: Copyright, 1936, by Chicago Tribune-N. Y. News Syndicate, Inc.

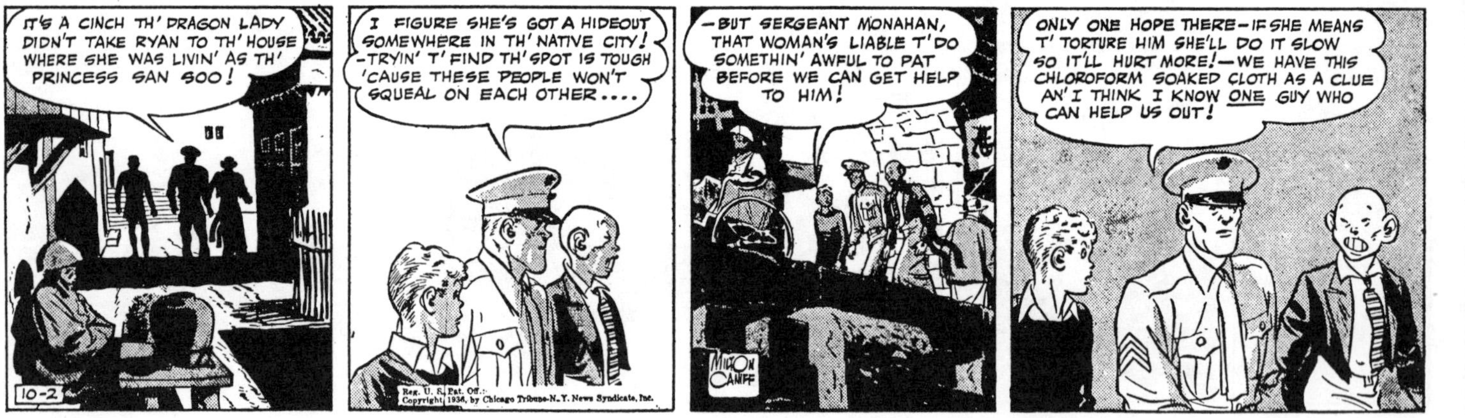
IT'S A CINCH TH' DRAGON LADY DIDN'T TAKE RYAN TO TH' HOUSE WHERE SHE WAS LIVIN' AS TH' PRINCESS SAN SOO!
I FIGURE SHE'S GOT A HIDEOUT SOMEWHERE IN TH' NATIVE CITY! -TRYIN' T' FIND TH' SPOT IS TOUGH 'CAUSE THESE PEOPLE WON'T SQUEAL ON EACH OTHER....
—BUT SERGEANT MONAHAN, THAT WOMAN'S LIABLE T' DO SOMETHIN' AWFUL TO PAT BEFORE WE CAN GET HELP TO HIM!
ONLY ONE HOPE THERE—IF SHE MEANS T' TORTURE HIM SHE'LL DO IT SLOW SO IT'LL HURT MORE!—WE HAVE THIS CHLOROFORM SOAKED CLOTH AS A CLUE AN' I THINK I KNOW ONE GUY WHO CAN HELP US OUT!
10-2
Reg. U. S. Pat. Off.: Copyright, 1936, by Chicago Tribune-N. Y. News Syndicate, Inc.
MILTON CANIFF

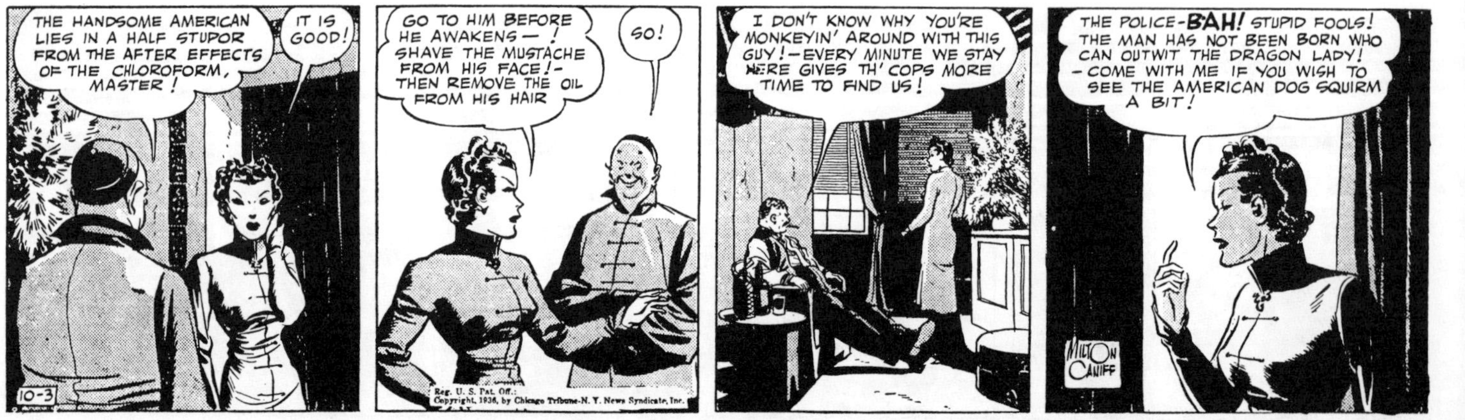
THE HANDSOME AMERICAN LIES IN A HALF STUPOR FROM THE AFTER EFFECTS OF THE CHLOROFORM, MASTER!
IT IS GOOD!
GO TO HIM BEFORE HE AWAKENS — ! SHAVE THE MUSTACHE FROM HIS FACE! — THEN REMOVE THE OIL FROM HIS HAIR
SO!
I DON'T KNOW WHY YOU'RE MONKEYIN' AROUND WITH THIS GUY! — EVERY MINUTE WE STAY HERE GIVES TH' COPS MORE TIME TO FIND US!
THE POLICE-BAH! STUPID FOOLS! THE MAN HAS NOT BEEN BORN WHO CAN OUTWIT THE DRAGON LADY! - COME WITH ME IF YOU WISH TO SEE THE AMERICAN DOG SQUIRM A BIT!
10-3
Reg. U. S. Pat. Off.: Copyright, 1936, by Chicago Tribune-N. Y. News Syndicate, Inc.
MILTON CANIFF

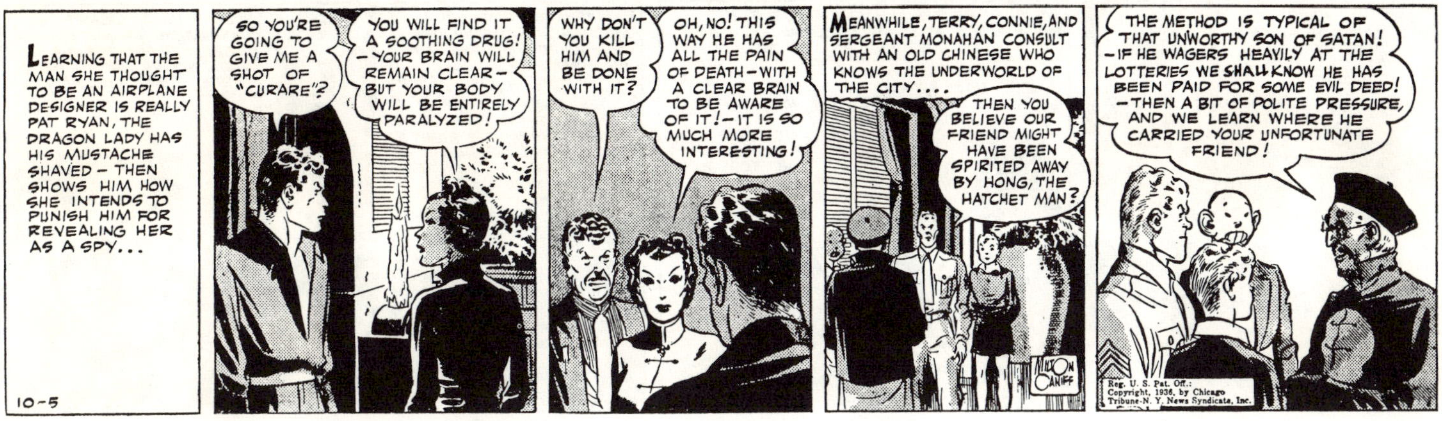
LEARNING THAT THE MAN SHE THOUGHT TO BE AN AIRPLANE DESIGNER IS REALLY PAT RYAN, THE DRAGON LADY HAS HIS MUSTACHE SHAVED – THEN SHOWS HIM HOW SHE INTENDS TO PUNISH HIM FOR REVEALING HER AS A SPY...
10-5
SO YOU'RE GOING TO GIVE ME A SHOT OF "CURARE"?
YOU WILL FIND IT A SOOTHING DRUG! – YOUR BRAIN WILL REMAIN CLEAR – BUT YOUR BODY WILL BE ENTIRELY PARALYZED!
WHY DON'T YOU KILL HIM AND BE DONE WITH IT?
OH, NO! THIS WAY HE HAS ALL THE PAIN OF DEATH – WITH A CLEAR BRAIN TO BE AWARE OF IT! – IT IS SO MUCH MORE INTERESTING!
MEANWHILE, TERRY, CONNIE, AND SERGEANT MONAHAN CONSULT WITH AN OLD CHINESE WHO KNOWS THE UNDERWORLD OF THE CITY....
THEN YOU BELIEVE OUR FRIEND MIGHT HAVE BEEN SPIRITED AWAY BY HONG, THE HATCHET MAN?
MILTON CANIFF
THE METHOD IS TYPICAL OF THAT UNWORTHY SON OF SATAN! – IF HE WAGERS HEAVILY AT THE LOTTERIES WE SHALL KNOW HE HAS BEEN PAID FOR SOME EVIL DEED! – THEN A BIT OF POLITE PRESSURE, AND WE LEARN WHERE HE CARRIED YOUR UNFORTUNATE FRIEND!
Reg. U. S. Pat. Off.: Copyright, 1936, by Chicago Tribune-N. Y. News Syndicate, Inc.

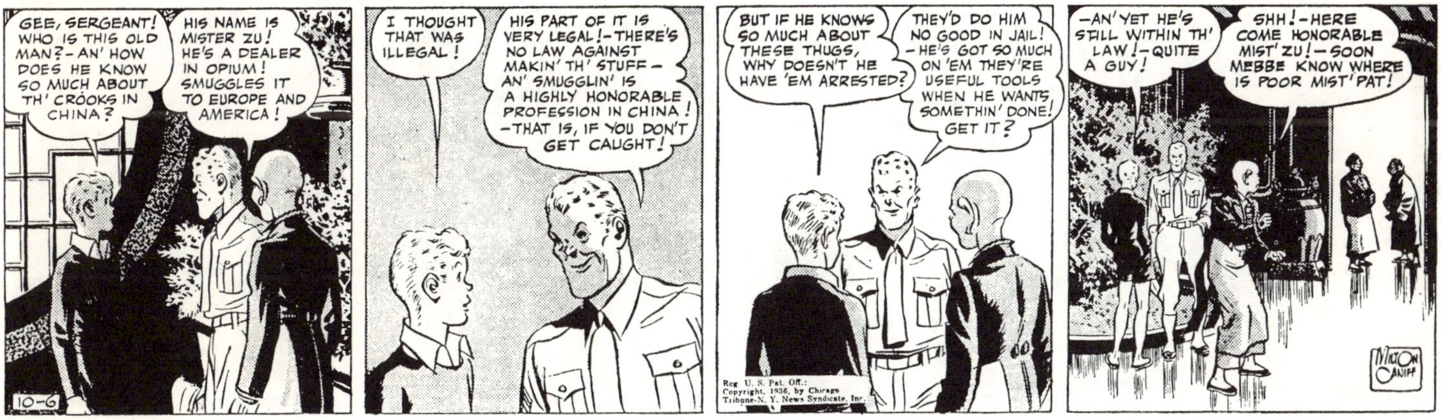
GEE, SERGEANT! WHO IS THIS OLD MAN? – AN' HOW DOES HE KNOW SO MUCH ABOUT TH' CROOKS IN CHINA?
HIS NAME IS MISTER ZU! HE'S A DEALER IN OPIUM! SMUGGLES IT TO EUROPE AND AMERICA!
10-6
I THOUGHT THAT WAS ILLEGAL!
HIS PART OF IT IS VERY LEGAL! – THERE'S NO LAW AGAINST MAKIN' TH' STUFF – AN' SMUGGLIN' IS A HIGHLY HONORABLE PROFESSION IN CHINA! – THAT IS, IF YOU DON'T GET CAUGHT!
BUT IF HE KNOWS SO MUCH ABOUT THESE THUGS, WHY DOESN'T HE HAVE 'EM ARRESTED?
THEY'D DO HIM NO GOOD IN JAIL! – HE'S GOT SO MUCH ON 'EM THEY'RE USEFUL TOOLS WHEN HE WANTS SOMETHIN' DONE! GET IT?
Reg. U. S. Pat. Off.: Copyright, 1936, by Chicago Tribune-N. Y. News Syndicate, Inc.
– AN' YET HE'S STILL WITHIN TH' LAW! – QUITE A GUY!
SHH! – HERE COME HONORABLE MIST' ZU! – SOON MEBBE KNOW WHERE IS POOR MIST' PAT!
MILTON CANIFF

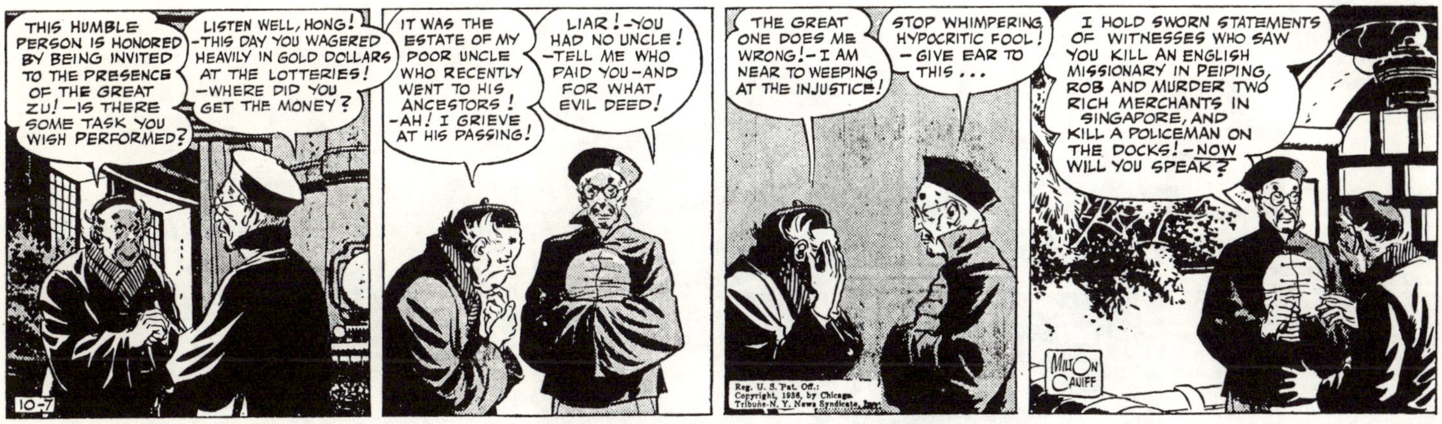
THIS HUMBLE PERSON IS HONORED BY BEING INVITED TO THE PRESENCE OF THE GREAT ZU! – IS THERE SOME TASK YOU WISH PERFORMED?
LISTEN WELL, HONG! – THIS DAY YOU WAGERED HEAVILY IN GOLD DOLLARS AT THE LOTTERIES! – WHERE DID YOU GET THE MONEY?
10-7
IT WAS THE ESTATE OF MY POOR UNCLE WHO RECENTLY WENT TO HIS ANCESTORS! – AH! I GRIEVE AT HIS PASSING!
LIAR! – YOU HAD NO UNCLE! – TELL ME WHO PAID YOU – AND FOR WHAT EVIL DEED!
THE GREAT ONE DOES ME WRONG! – I AM NEAR TO WEEPING AT THE INJUSTICE!
STOP WHIMPERING, HYPOCRITIC FOOL! – GIVE EAR TO THIS...
Reg. U. S. Pat. Off.: Copyright, 1936, by Chicago Tribune-N. Y. News Syndicate, Inc.
MILTON CANIFF
I HOLD SWORN STATEMENTS OF WITNESSES WHO SAW YOU KILL AN ENGLISH MISSIONARY IN PEIPING, ROB AND MURDER TWO RICH MERCHANTS IN SINGAPORE, AND KILL A POLICEMAN ON THE DOCKS! – NOW WILL YOU SPEAK?

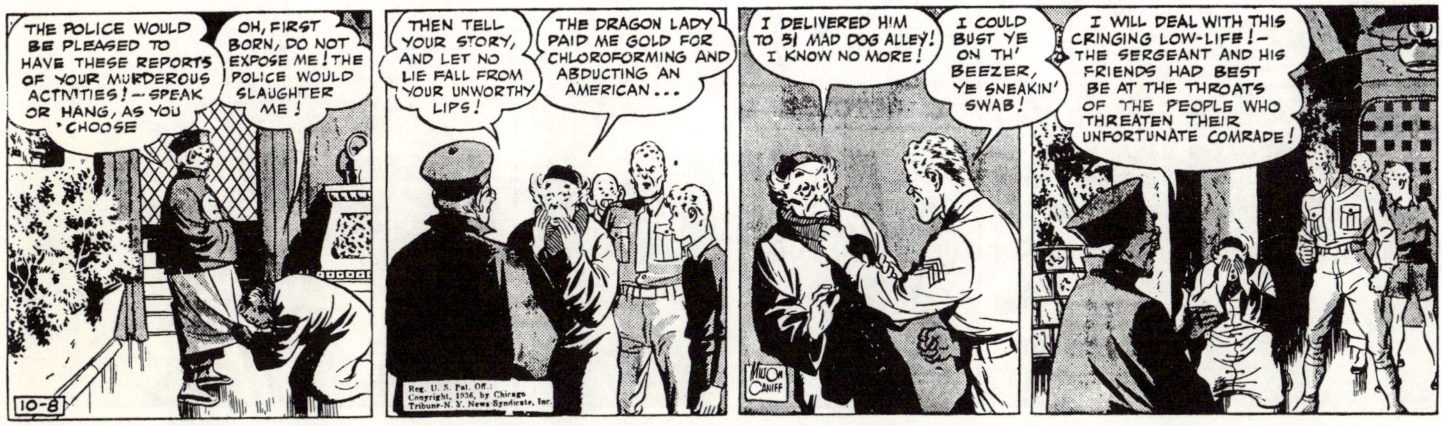
THE POLICE WOULD BE PLEASED TO HAVE THESE REPORTS OF YOUR MURDEROUS ACTIVITIES! – SPEAK OR HANG, AS YOU CHOOSE
OH, FIRST BORN, DO NOT EXPOSE ME! THE POLICE WOULD SLAUGHTER ME!
10-8
THEN TELL YOUR STORY, AND LET NO LIE FALL FROM YOUR UNWORTHY LIPS!
THE DRAGON LADY PAID ME GOLD FOR CHLOROFORMING AND ABDUCTING AN AMERICAN...
Reg. U. S. Pat. Off.: Copyright, 1936, by Chicago Tribune-N. Y. News Syndicate, Inc.
I DELIVERED HIM TO 51 MAD DOG ALLEY! I KNOW NO MORE!
I COULD BUST YE ON TH' BEEZER, YE SNEAKIN' SWAB!
MILTON CANIFF
I WILL DEAL WITH THIS CRINGING LOW-LIFE! – THE SERGEANT AND HIS FRIENDS HAD BEST BE AT THE THROATS OF THE PEOPLE WHO THREATEN THEIR UNFORTUNATE COMRADE!

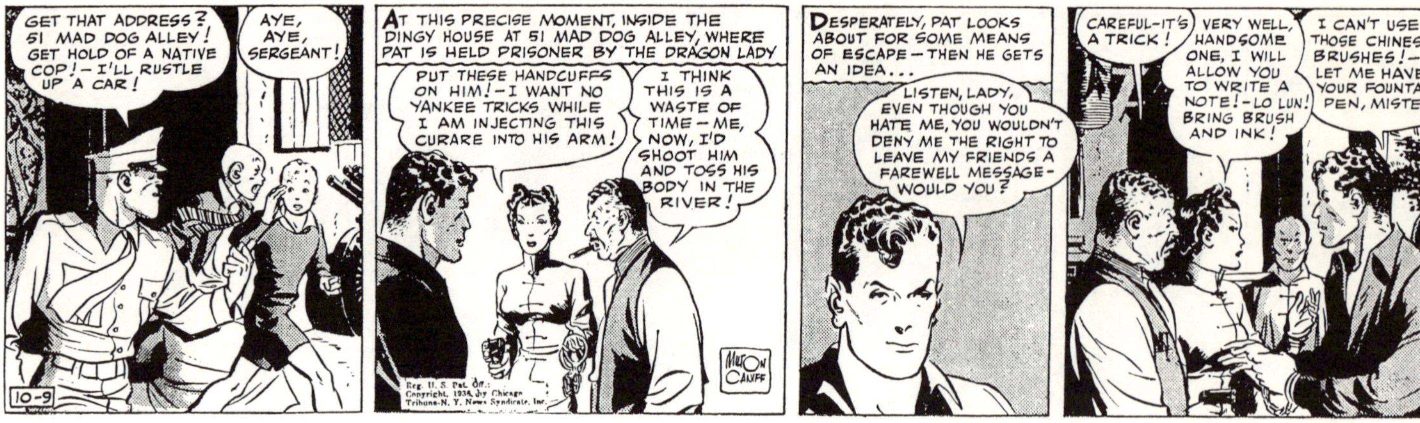
GET THAT ADDRESS? 51 MAD DOG ALLEY! GET HOLD OF A NATIVE COP! — I'LL RUSTLE UP A CAR!
AYE, AYE, SERGEANT!
10-9
AT THIS PRECISE MOMENT, INSIDE THE DINGY HOUSE AT 51 MAD DOG ALLEY, WHERE PAT IS HELD PRISONER BY THE DRAGON LADY
PUT THESE HANDCUFFS ON HIM! — I WANT NO YANKEE TRICKS WHILE I AM INJECTING THIS CURARE INTO HIS ARM!
I THINK THIS IS A WASTE OF TIME — ME, NOW, I'D SHOOT HIM AND TOSS HIS BODY IN THE RIVER!
Reg. U. S. Pat. Off.: Copyright, 1938, by Chicago Tribune-N. Y. News Syndicate, Inc.
MILTON CANIFF
DESPERATELY, PAT LOOKS ABOUT FOR SOME MEANS OF ESCAPE — THEN HE GETS AN IDEA...
LISTEN, LADY, EVEN THOUGH YOU HATE ME, YOU WOULDN'T DENY ME THE RIGHT TO LEAVE MY FRIENDS A FAREWELL MESSAGE — WOULD YOU?
CAREFUL — IT'S A TRICK!
VERY WELL, HANDSOME ONE, I WILL ALLOW YOU TO WRITE A NOTE! — LO LUN! BRING BRUSH AND INK!
I CAN'T USE THOSE CHINESE BRUSHES! — LET ME HAVE YOUR FOUNTAIN PEN, MISTER!

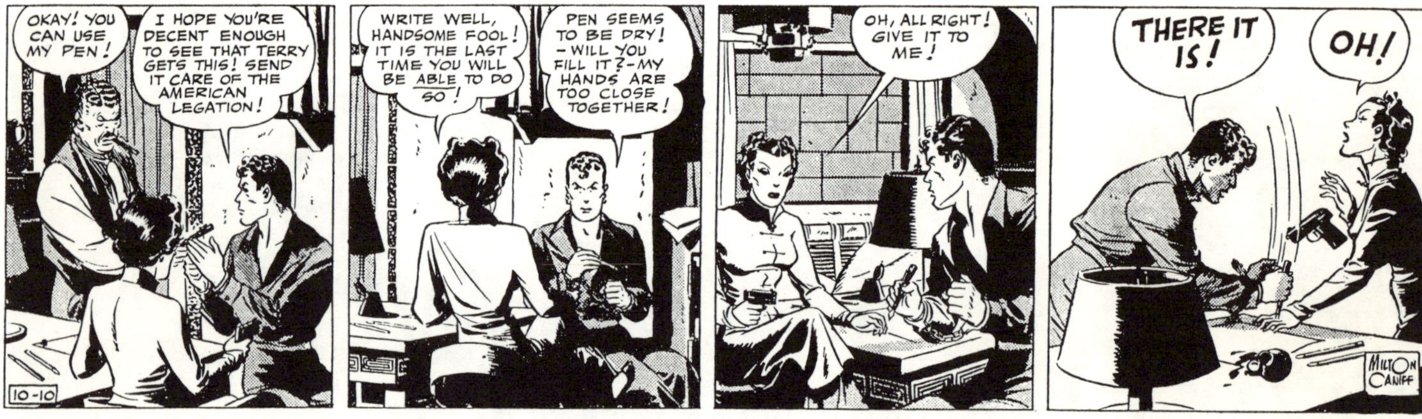
OKAY! YOU CAN USE MY PEN!
I HOPE YOU'RE DECENT ENOUGH TO SEE THAT TERRY GETS THIS! SEND IT CARE OF THE AMERICAN LEGATION!
10-10
WRITE WELL, HANDSOME FOOL! IT IS THE LAST TIME YOU WILL BE ABLE TO DO SO!
PEN SEEMS TO BE DRY! — WILL YOU FILL IT? — MY HANDS ARE TOO CLOSE TOGETHER!
OH, ALL RIGHT! GIVE IT TO ME!
THERE IT IS!
OH!
MILTON CANIFF

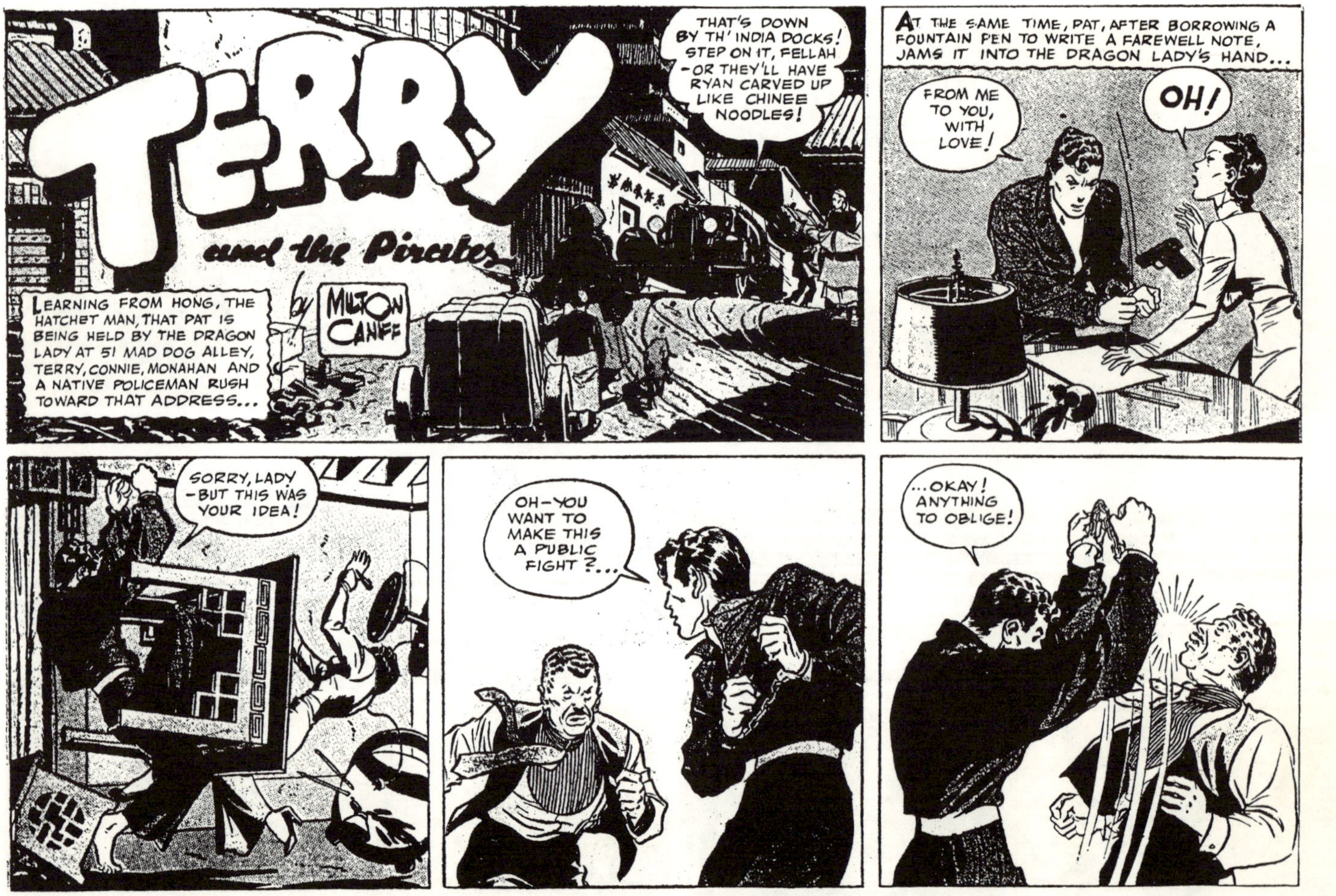
TERRY and the Pirates by MILTON CANIFF
LEARNING FROM HONG, THE HATCHET MAN, THAT PAT IS BEING HELD BY THE DRAGON LADY AT 51 MAD DOG ALLEY, TERRY, CONNIE, MONAHAN AND A NATIVE POLICEMAN RUSH TOWARD THAT ADDRESS...
THAT'S DOWN BY TH' INDIA DOCKS! STEP ON IT, FELLAH — OR THEY'LL HAVE RYAN CARVED UP LIKE CHINEE NOODLES!
AT THE SAME TIME, PAT, AFTER BORROWING A FOUNTAIN PEN TO WRITE A FAREWELL NOTE, JAMS IT INTO THE DRAGON LADY'S HAND...
FROM ME TO YOU, WITH LOVE!
OH!
SORRY, LADY — BUT THIS WAS YOUR IDEA!
OH — YOU WANT TO MAKE THIS A PUBLIC FIGHT?...
...OKAY! ANYTHING TO OBLIGE!

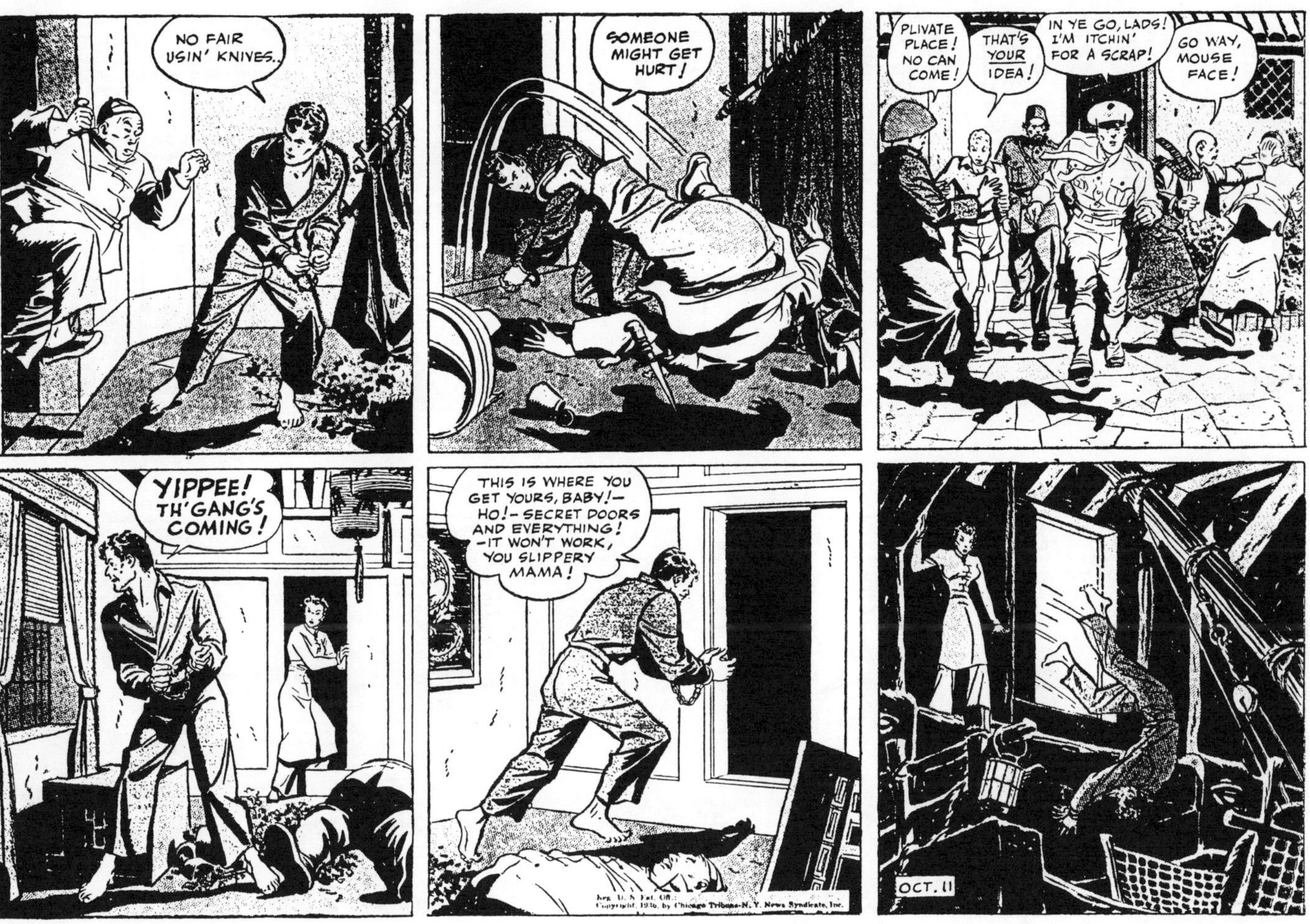
NO FAIR USIN' KNIVES..
SOMEONE MIGHT GET HURT!
PLIVATE PLACE! NO CAN COME!
THAT'S YOUR IDEA!
IN YE GO, LADS! I'M ITCHIN' FOR A SCRAP!
GO WAY, MOUSE FACE!
YIPPEE! TH' GANG'S COMING!
THIS IS WHERE YOU GET YOURS, BABY!—HO!—SECRET DOORS AND EVERYTHING!—IT WON'T WORK, YOU SLIPPERY MAMA!
Reg. U. S. Pat. Off.: Copyright, 1936, by Chicago Tribune-N. Y. News Syndicate, Inc.
OCT. 11

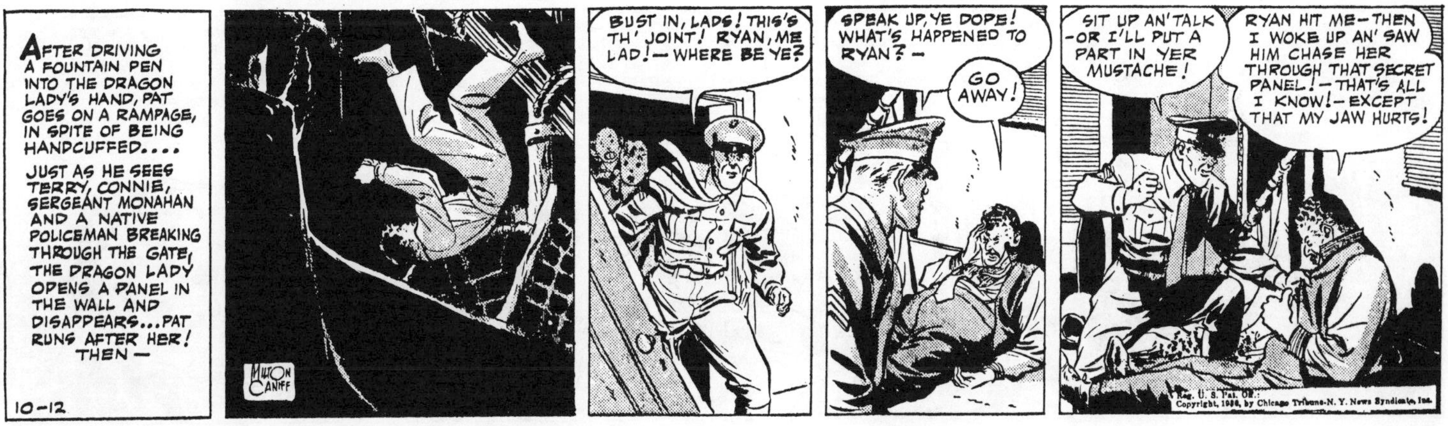
AFTER DRIVING A FOUNTAIN PEN INTO THE DRAGON LADY'S HAND, PAT GOES ON A RAMPAGE, IN SPITE OF BEING HANDCUFFED....
JUST AS HE SEES TERRY, CONNIE, SERGEANT MONAHAN AND A NATIVE POLICEMAN BREAKING THROUGH THE GATE, THE DRAGON LADY OPENS A PANEL IN THE WALL AND DISAPPEARS...PAT RUNS AFTER HER! THEN—
10-12
MILTON CANIFF
BUST IN, LADS! THIS'S TH' JOINT! RYAN, ME LAD!—WHERE BE YE?
SPEAK UP, YE DOPE! WHAT'S HAPPENED TO RYAN?—
GO AWAY!
SIT UP AN' TALK—OR I'LL PUT A PART IN YER MUSTACHE!
RYAN HIT ME—THEN I WOKE UP AN' SAW HIM CHASE HER THROUGH THAT SECRET PANEL!—THAT'S ALL I KNOW!—EXCEPT THAT MY JAW HURTS!
Reg. U. S. Pat. Off.: Copyright, 1936, by Chicago Tribune-N. Y. News Syndicate, Inc.

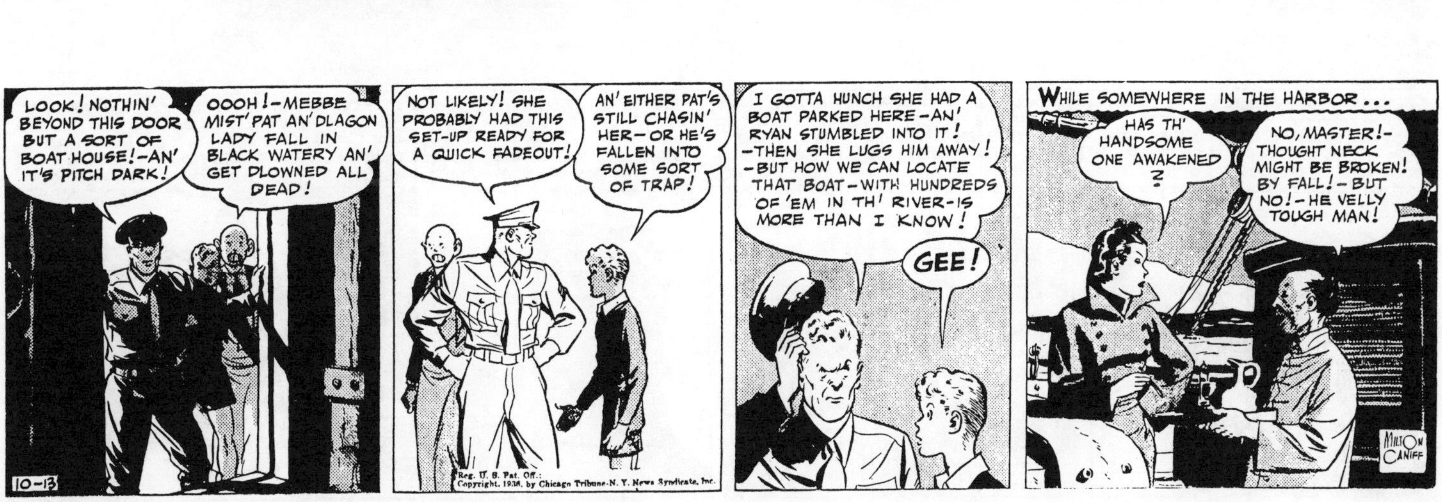
LOOK! NOTHIN' BEYOND THIS DOOR BUT A SORT OF BOAT HOUSE!—AN' IT'S PITCH DARK!
OOOH!—MEBBE MIST' PAT AN' DLAGON LADY FALL IN BLACK WATERY AN' GET DLOWNED ALL DEAD!
10-13
NOT LIKELY! SHE PROBABLY HAD THIS SET-UP READY FOR A QUICK FADEOUT!
AN' EITHER PAT'S STILL CHASIN' HER—OR HE'S FALLEN INTO SOME SORT OF TRAP!
Reg. U. S. Pat. Off.: Copyright, 1936, by Chicago Tribune-N. Y. News Syndicate, Inc.
I GOTTA HUNCH SHE HAD A BOAT PARKED HERE—AN' RYAN STUMBLED INTO IT!—THEN SHE LUGS HIM AWAY!—BUT HOW WE CAN LOCATE THAT BOAT—WITH HUNDREDS OF 'EM IN TH' RIVER—IS MORE THAN I KNOW!
GEE!
WHILE SOMEWHERE IN THE HARBOR...
HAS TH' HANDSOME ONE AWAKENED?
NO, MASTER!—THOUGHT NECK MIGHT BE BROKEN! BY FALL!—BUT NO!—HE VELLY TOUGH MAN!
MILTON CANIFF

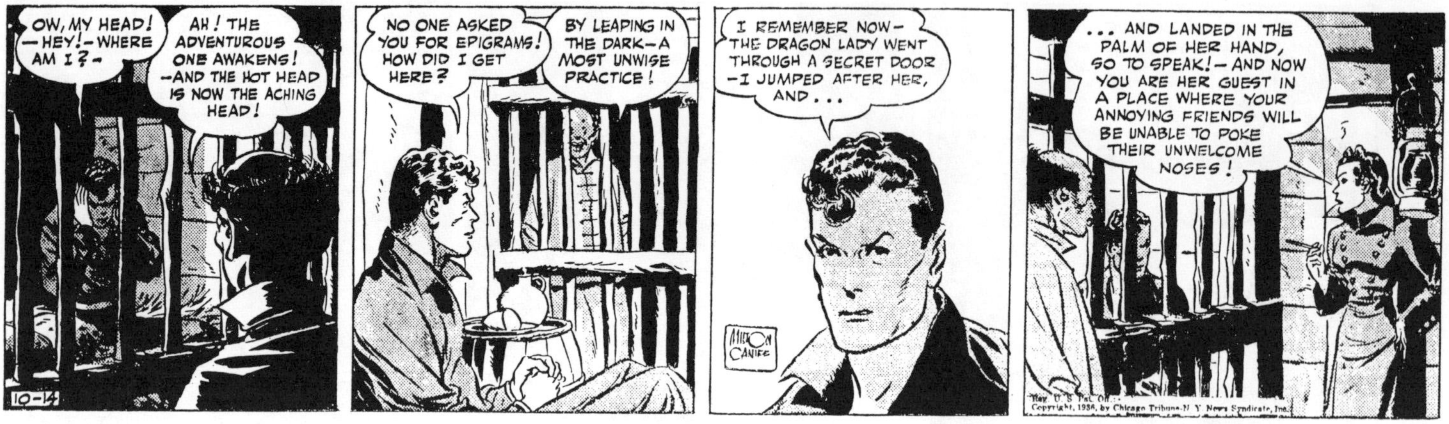
10-14
OW, MY HEAD! —HEY!—WHERE AM I?—
AH! THE ADVENTUROUS ONE AWAKENS! —AND THE HOT HEAD IS NOW THE ACHING HEAD!
NO ONE ASKED YOU FOR EPIGRAMS! HOW DID I GET HERE?
BY LEAPING IN THE DARK—A MOST UNWISE PRACTICE!
I REMEMBER NOW— THE DRAGON LADY WENT THROUGH A SECRET DOOR —I JUMPED AFTER HER, AND...
MILTON CANIFF
... AND LANDED IN THE PALM OF HER HAND, SO TO SPEAK!—AND NOW YOU ARE HER GUEST IN A PLACE WHERE YOUR ANNOYING FRIENDS WILL BE UNABLE TO POKE THEIR UNWELCOME NOSES!
Reg. U. S. Pat. Off.: Copyright, 1936, by Chicago Tribune-N. Y. News Syndicate, Inc.

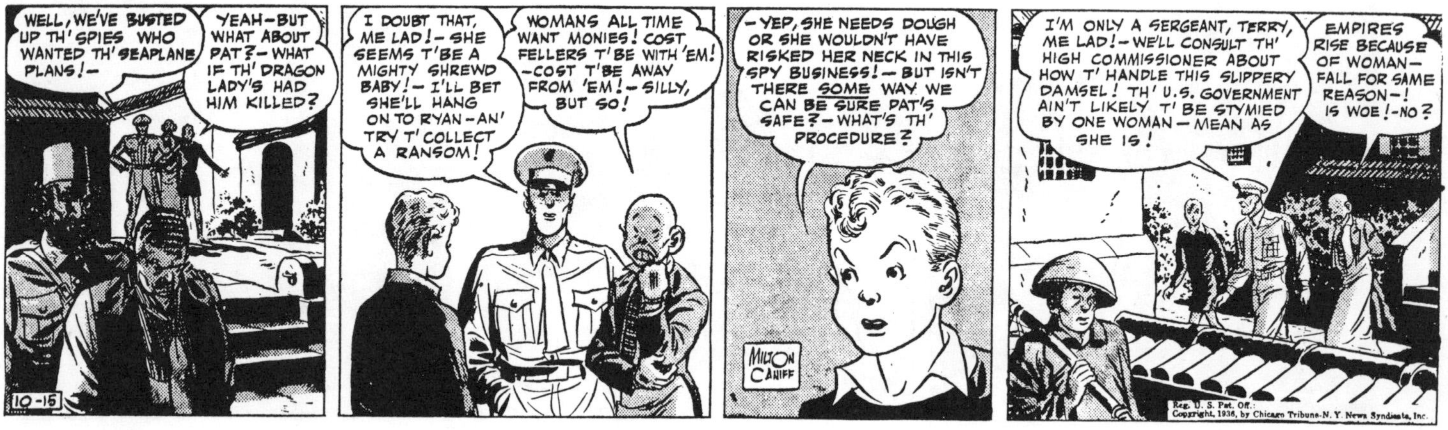
10-15
WELL, WE'VE BUSTED UP TH' SPIES WHO WANTED TH' SEAPLANE PLANS!—
YEAH—BUT WHAT ABOUT PAT?—WHAT IF TH' DRAGON LADY'S HAD HIM KILLED?
I DOUBT THAT, ME LAD!—SHE SEEMS T'BE A MIGHTY SHREWD BABY!—I'LL BET SHE'LL HANG ON TO RYAN—AN' TRY T' COLLECT A RANSOM!
WOMANS ALL TIME WANT MONIES! COST FELLERS T'BE WITH 'EM! —COST T'BE AWAY FROM 'EM!—SILLY, BUT SO!
—YEP, SHE NEEDS DOUGH OR SHE WOULDN'T HAVE RISKED HER NECK IN THIS SPY BUSINESS!—BUT ISN'T THERE SOME WAY WE CAN BE SURE PAT'S SAFE?—WHAT'S TH' PROCEDURE?
MILTON CANIFF
I'M ONLY A SERGEANT, TERRY, ME LAD!—WE'LL CONSULT TH' HIGH COMMISSIONER ABOUT HOW T' HANDLE THIS SLIPPERY DAMSEL! TH' U.S. GOVERNMENT AIN'T LIKELY T' BE STYMIED BY ONE WOMAN—MEAN AS SHE IS!
EMPIRES RISE BECAUSE OF WOMAN—FALL FOR SAME REASON—! IS WOE!—NO?
Reg. U. S. Pat. Off.: Copyright, 1936, by Chicago Tribune-N. Y. News Syndicate, Inc.

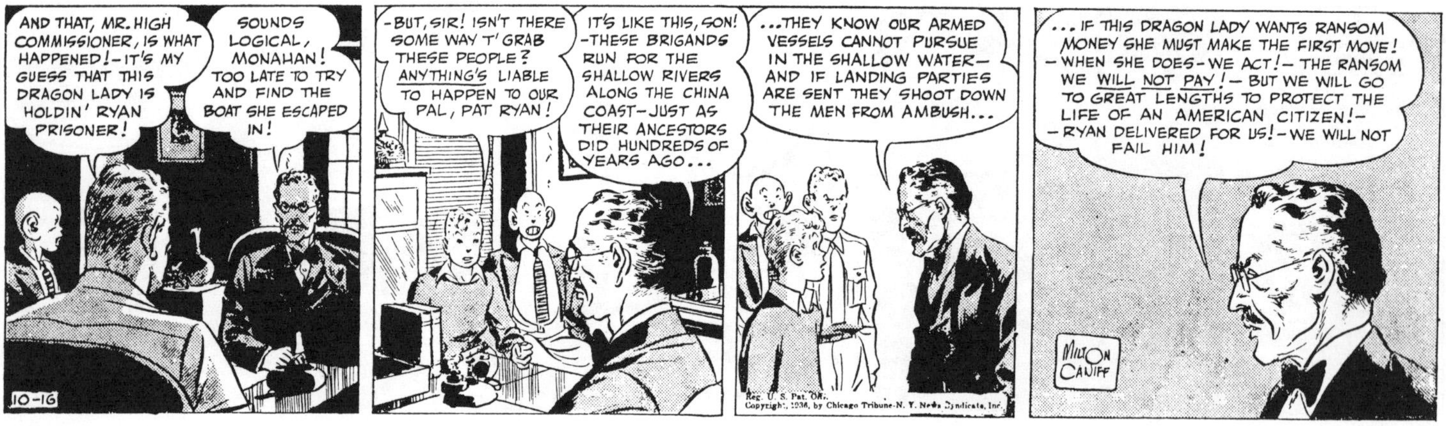
10-16
AND THAT, MR. HIGH COMMISSIONER, IS WHAT HAPPENED!—IT'S MY GUESS THAT THIS DRAGON LADY IS HOLDIN' RYAN PRISONER!
SOUNDS LOGICAL, MONAHAN! TOO LATE TO TRY AND FIND THE BOAT SHE ESCAPED IN!
—BUT, SIR! ISN'T THERE SOME WAY T' GRAB THESE PEOPLE? ANYTHING'S LIABLE TO HAPPEN TO OUR PAL, PAT RYAN!
IT'S LIKE THIS, SON! —THESE BRIGANDS RUN FOR THE SHALLOW RIVERS ALONG THE CHINA COAST—JUST AS THEIR ANCESTORS DID HUNDREDS OF YEARS AGO...
...THEY KNOW OUR ARMED VESSELS CANNOT PURSUE IN THE SHALLOW WATER— AND IF LANDING PARTIES ARE SENT THEY SHOOT DOWN THE MEN FROM AMBUSH...
Reg. U. S. Pat. Off.: Copyright, 1936, by Chicago Tribune-N. Y. News Syndicate, Inc.
...IF THIS DRAGON LADY WANTS RANSOM MONEY SHE MUST MAKE THE FIRST MOVE! —WHEN SHE DOES—WE ACT!—THE RANSOM WE WILL NOT PAY!—BUT WE WILL GO TO GREAT LENGTHS TO PROTECT THE LIFE OF AN AMERICAN CITIZEN!— —RYAN DELIVERED FOR US!—WE WILL NOT FAIL HIM!
MILTON CANIFF

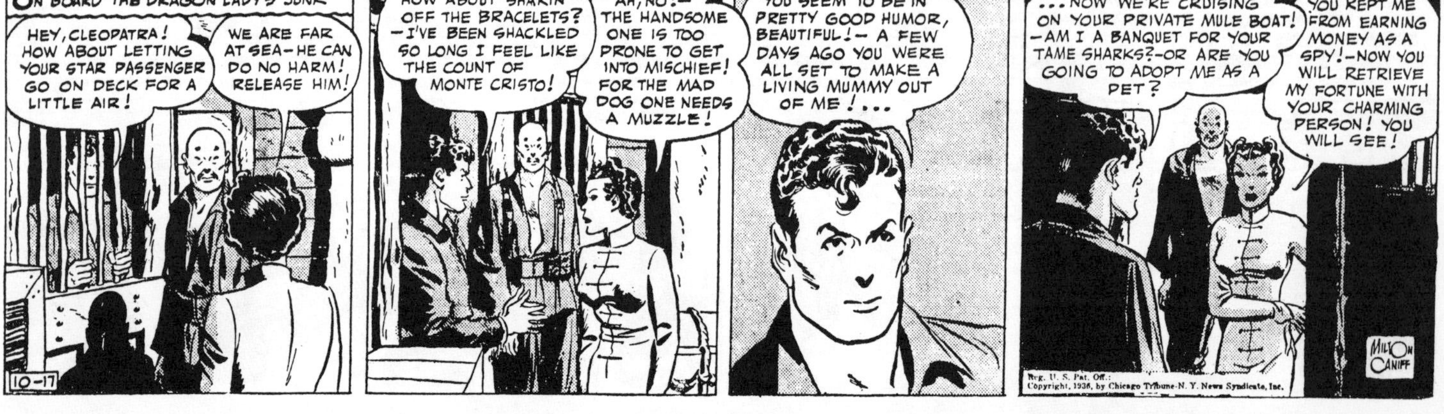
ON BOARD THE DRAGON LADY'S JUNK
HEY, CLEOPATRA! HOW ABOUT LETTING YOUR STAR PASSENGER GO ON DECK FOR A LITTLE AIR!
WE ARE FAR AT SEA—HE CAN DO NO HARM! RELEASE HIM!
10-17
HOW ABOUT SHAKIN' OFF THE BRACELETS? —I'VE BEEN SHACKLED SO LONG I FEEL LIKE THE COUNT OF MONTE CRISTO!
AH, NO!— THE HANDSOME ONE IS TOO PRONE TO GET INTO MISCHIEF! FOR THE MAD DOG ONE NEEDS A MUZZLE!
YOU SEEM TO BE IN PRETTY GOOD HUMOR, BEAUTIFUL!—A FEW DAYS AGO YOU WERE ALL SET TO MAKE A LIVING MUMMY OUT OF ME!...
...NOW WE'RE CRUISING ON YOUR PRIVATE MULE BOAT! —AM I A BANQUET FOR YOUR TAME SHARKS?—OR ARE YOU GOING TO ADOPT ME AS A PET?
YOU KEPT ME FROM EARNING MONEY AS A SPY!—NOW YOU WILL RETRIEVE MY FORTUNE WITH YOUR CHARMING PERSON! YOU WILL SEE!
MILTON CANIFF
Reg. U. S. Pat. Off.: Copyright, 1936, by Chicago Tribune-N. Y. News Syndicate, Inc.

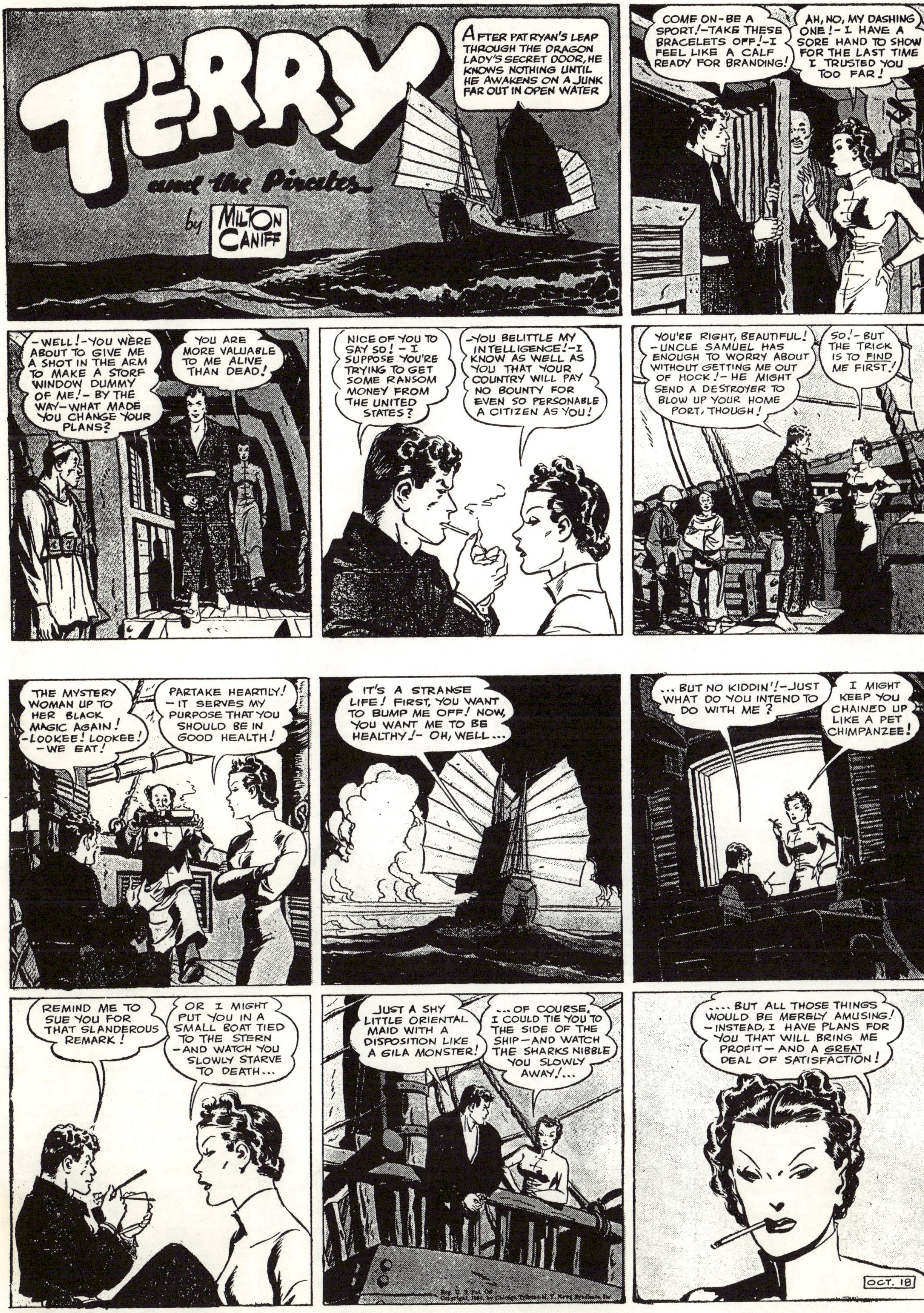
TERRY and the Pirates
by MILTON CANIFF
AFTER PAT RYAN'S LEAP THROUGH THE DRAGON LADY'S SECRET DOOR, HE KNOWS NOTHING UNTIL HE AWAKENS ON A JUNK FAR OUT IN OPEN WATER
COME ON - BE A SPORT! - TAKE THESE BRACELETS OFF! - I FEEL LIKE A CALF READY FOR BRANDING!
AH, NO, MY DASHING ONE! - I HAVE A SORE HAND TO SHOW FOR THE LAST TIME I TRUSTED YOU TOO FAR!
- WELL! - YOU WERE ABOUT TO GIVE ME A SHOT IN THE ARM TO MAKE A STORE WINDOW DUMMY OF ME! - BY THE WAY - WHAT MADE YOU CHANGE YOUR PLANS?
YOU ARE MORE VALUABLE TO ME ALIVE THAN DEAD!
NICE OF YOU TO SAY SO! - I SUPPOSE YOU'RE TRYING TO GET SOME RANSOM MONEY FROM THE UNITED STATES?
- YOU BELITTLE MY INTELLIGENCE! - I KNOW AS WELL AS YOU THAT YOUR COUNTRY WILL PAY NO BOUNTY FOR EVEN SO PERSONABLE A CITIZEN AS YOU!
YOU'RE RIGHT, BEAUTIFUL! - UNCLE SAMUEL HAS ENOUGH TO WORRY ABOUT WITHOUT GETTING ME OUT OF HOCK! - HE MIGHT SEND A DESTROYER TO BLOW UP YOUR HOME PORT, THOUGH!
SO! - BUT THE TRICK IS TO FIND ME FIRST!
THE MYSTERY WOMAN UP TO HER BLACK MAGIC AGAIN! - LOOKEE! LOOKEE! - WE EAT!
PARTAKE HEARTILY! - IT SERVES MY PURPOSE THAT YOU SHOULD BE IN GOOD HEALTH!
IT'S A STRANGE LIFE! FIRST, YOU WANT TO BUMP ME OFF! NOW, YOU WANT ME TO BE HEALTHY! - OH, WELL...
... BUT NO KIDDIN'! - JUST WHAT DO YOU INTEND TO DO WITH ME?
I MIGHT KEEP YOU CHAINED UP LIKE A PET CHIMPANZEE!
REMIND ME TO SUE YOU FOR THAT SLANDEROUS REMARK!
OR I MIGHT PUT YOU IN A SMALL BOAT TIED TO THE STERN - AND WATCH YOU SLOWLY STARVE TO DEATH...
JUST A SHY LITTLE ORIENTAL MAID WITH A DISPOSITION LIKE A GILA MONSTER!
... OF COURSE, I COULD TIE YOU TO THE SIDE OF THE SHIP - AND WATCH THE SHARKS NIBBLE YOU SLOWLY AWAY!...
.... BUT ALL THOSE THINGS WOULD BE MERELY AMUSING! - INSTEAD, I HAVE PLANS FOR YOU THAT WILL BRING ME PROFIT - AND A GREAT DEAL OF SATISFACTION!
OCT. 18

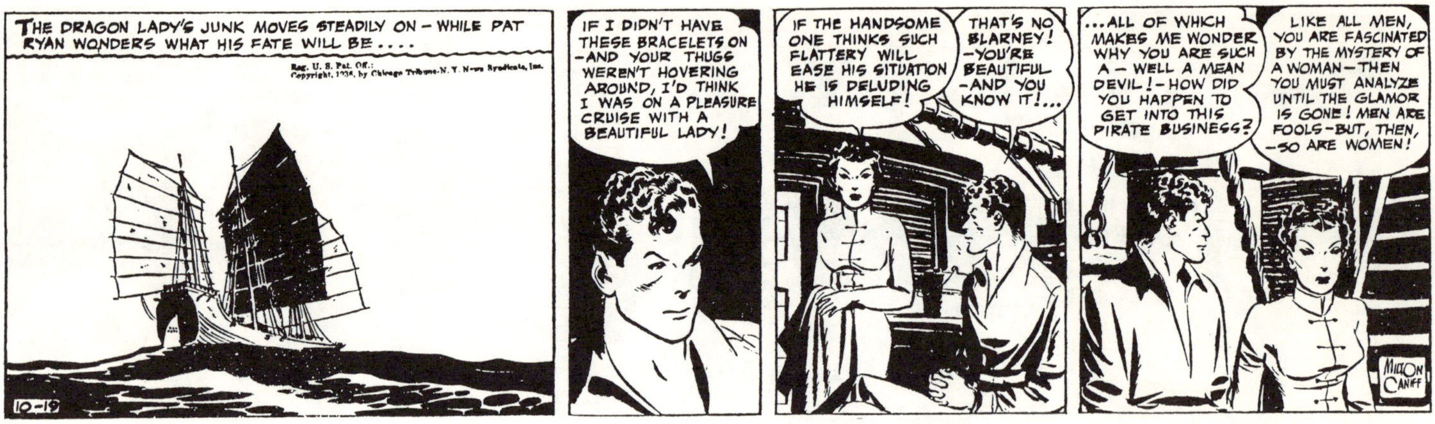
THE DRAGON LADY'S JUNK MOVES STEADILY ON – WHILE PAT RYAN WONDERS WHAT HIS FATE WILL BE....
Reg. U. S. Pat. Off.: Copyright, 1936, by Chicago Tribune-N. Y. News Syndicate, Inc.
10-19
IF I DIDN'T HAVE THESE BRACELETS ON –AND YOUR THUGS WEREN'T HOVERING AROUND, I'D THINK I WAS ON A PLEASURE CRUISE WITH A BEAUTIFUL LADY!
IF THE HANDSOME ONE THINKS SUCH FLATTERY WILL EASE HIS SITUATION HE IS DELUDING HIMSELF!
THAT'S NO BLARNEY! –YOU'RE BEAUTIFUL –AND YOU KNOW IT!...
...ALL OF WHICH MAKES ME WONDER WHY YOU ARE SUCH A – WELL A MEAN DEVIL! – HOW DID YOU HAPPEN TO GET INTO THIS PIRATE BUSINESS?
LIKE ALL MEN, YOU ARE FASCINATED BY THE MYSTERY OF A WOMAN – THEN YOU MUST ANALYZE UNTIL THE GLAMOR IS GONE! MEN ARE FOOLS – BUT, THEN, – SO ARE WOMEN!
MILTON CANIFF

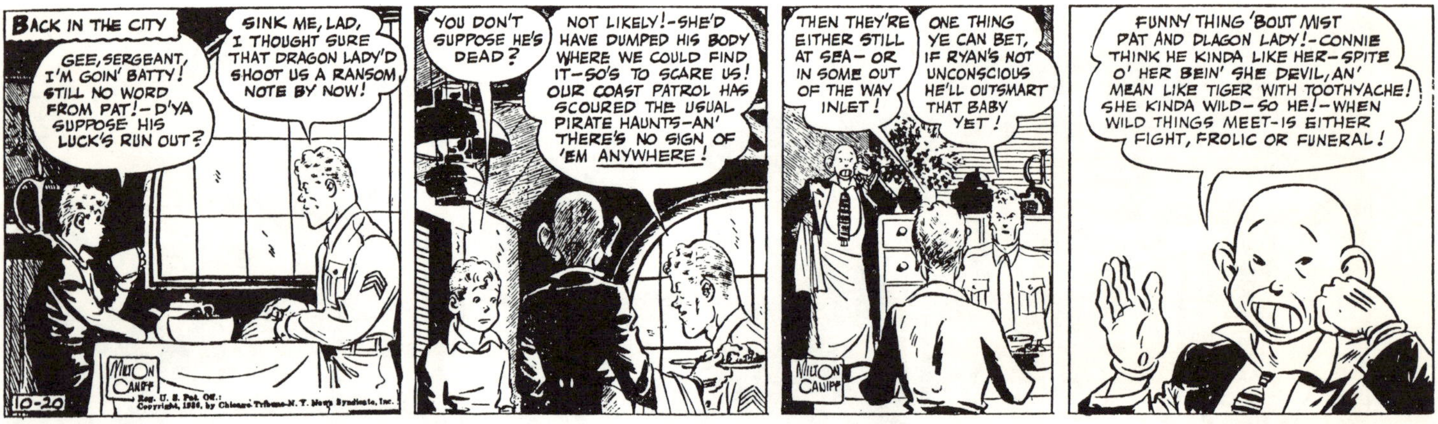
BACK IN THE CITY
GEE, SERGEANT, I'M GOIN' BATTY! STILL NO WORD FROM PAT! – D'YA SUPPOSE HIS LUCK'S RUN OUT?
SINK ME, LAD, I THOUGHT SURE THAT DRAGON LADY'D SHOOT US A RANSOM NOTE BY NOW!
MILTON CANIFF
10-20
Reg. U. S. Pat. Off.: Copyright, 1936, by Chicago Tribune-N. Y. News Syndicate, Inc.
YOU DON'T SUPPOSE HE'S DEAD?
NOT LIKELY! – SHE'D HAVE DUMPED HIS BODY WHERE WE COULD FIND IT – SO'S TO SCARE US! OUR COAST PATROL HAS SCOURED THE USUAL PIRATE HAUNTS – AN' THERE'S NO SIGN OF 'EM ANYWHERE!
THEN THEY'RE EITHER STILL AT SEA – OR IN SOME OUT OF THE WAY INLET!
ONE THING YE CAN BET, IF RYAN'S NOT UNCONSCIOUS HE'LL OUTSMART THAT BABY YET!
MILTON CANIFF
FUNNY THING 'BOUT MIST PAT AND DLAGON LADY! – CONNIE THINK HE KINDA LIKE HER – SPITE O' HER BEIN' SHE DEVIL, AN' MEAN LIKE TIGER WITH TOOTHYACHE! SHE KINDA WILD – SO HE! – WHEN WILD THINGS MEET – IS EITHER FIGHT, FROLIC OR FUNERAL!

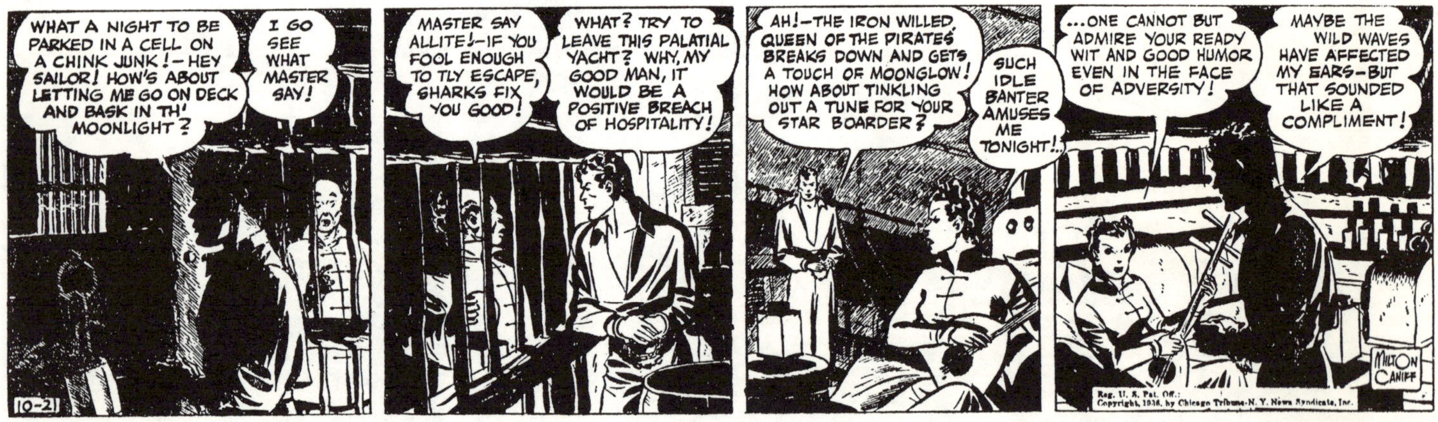
WHAT A NIGHT TO BE PARKED IN A CELL ON A CHINK JUNK! – HEY SAILOR! HOW'S ABOUT LETTING ME GO ON DECK AND BASK IN TH' MOONLIGHT?
I GO SEE WHAT MASTER SAY!
10-21
MASTER SAY ALLITE! – IF YOU FOOL ENOUGH TO TLY ESCAPE, SHARKS FIX YOU GOOD!
WHAT? TRY TO LEAVE THIS PALATIAL YACHT? WHY, MY GOOD MAN, IT WOULD BE A POSITIVE BREACH OF HOSPITALITY!
AH! – THE IRON WILLED QUEEN OF THE PIRATES BREAKS DOWN AND GETS A TOUCH OF MOONGLOW! HOW ABOUT TINKLING OUT A TUNE FOR YOUR STAR BOARDER?
SUCH IDLE BANTER AMUSES ME TONIGHT!
...ONE CANNOT BUT ADMIRE YOUR READY WIT AND GOOD HUMOR EVEN IN THE FACE OF ADVERSITY!
MAYBE THE WILD WAVES HAVE AFFECTED MY EARS – BUT THAT SOUNDED LIKE A COMPLIMENT!
MILTON CANIFF
Reg. U. S. Pat. Off.: Copyright, 1936, by Chicago Tribune-N. Y. News Syndicate, Inc.

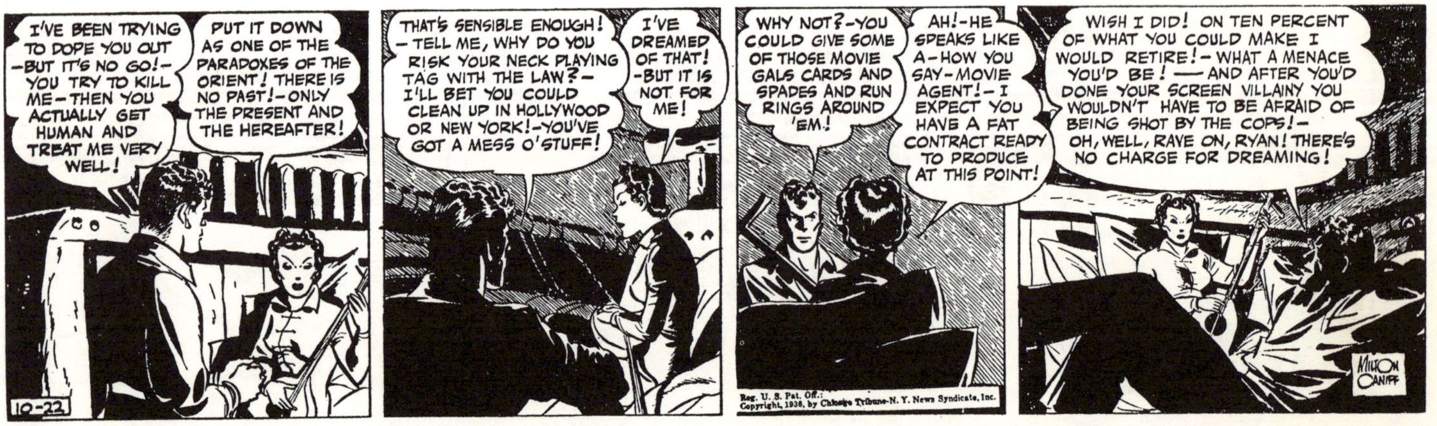
I'VE BEEN TRYING TO DOPE YOU OUT –BUT IT'S NO GO! – YOU TRY TO KILL ME – THEN YOU ACTUALLY GET HUMAN AND TREAT ME VERY WELL!
PUT IT DOWN AS ONE OF THE PARADOXES OF THE ORIENT! THERE IS NO PAST! – ONLY THE PRESENT AND THE HEREAFTER!
10-22
THAT'S SENSIBLE ENOUGH! – TELL ME, WHY DO YOU RISK YOUR NECK PLAYING TAG WITH THE LAW? – I'LL BET YOU COULD CLEAN UP IN HOLLYWOOD OR NEW YORK! – YOU'VE GOT A MESS O' STUFF!
I'VE DREAMED OF THAT! –BUT IT IS NOT FOR ME!
WHY NOT? – YOU COULD GIVE SOME OF THOSE MOVIE GALS CARDS AND SPADES AND RUN RINGS AROUND 'EM!
AH! – HE SPEAKS LIKE A – HOW YOU SAY – MOVIE AGENT! – I EXPECT YOU HAVE A FAT CONTRACT READY TO PRODUCE AT THIS POINT!
Reg. U. S. Pat. Off.: Copyright, 1936, by Chicago Tribune-N. Y. News Syndicate, Inc.
WISH I DID! ON TEN PERCENT OF WHAT YOU COULD MAKE I WOULD RETIRE! – WHAT A MENACE YOU'D BE! — AND AFTER YOU'D DONE YOUR SCREEN VILLAINY YOU WOULDN'T HAVE TO BE AFRAID OF BEING SHOT BY THE COPS! – OH, WELL, RAVE ON, RYAN! THERE'S NO CHARGE FOR DREAMING!
MILTON CANIFF

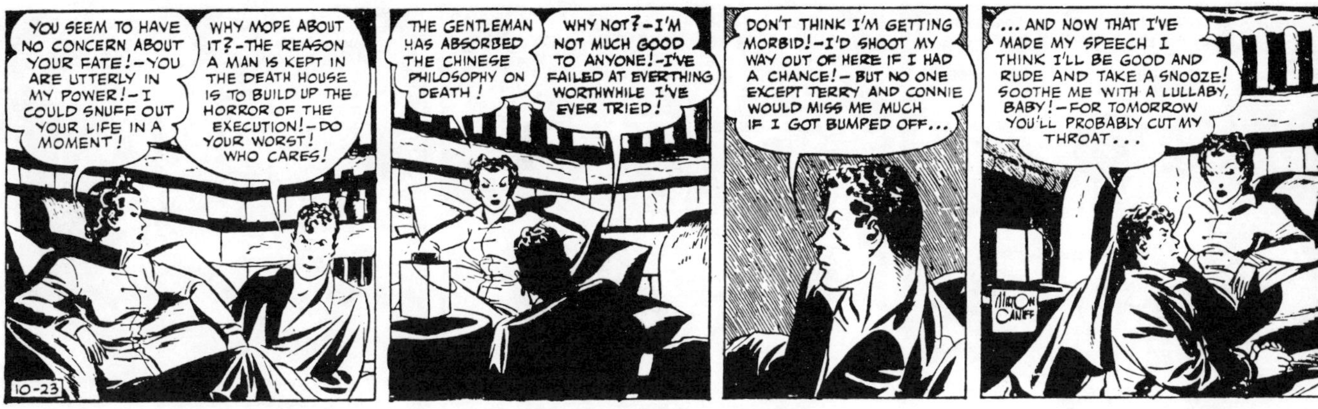
YOU SEEM TO HAVE NO CONCERN ABOUT YOUR FATE! -YOU ARE UTTERLY IN MY POWER! -I COULD SNUFF OUT YOUR LIFE IN A MOMENT!
WHY MOPE ABOUT IT? -THE REASON A MAN IS KEPT IN THE DEATH HOUSE IS TO BUILD UP THE HORROR OF THE EXECUTION! -DO YOUR WORST! WHO CARES!
THE GENTLEMAN HAS ABSORBED THE CHINESE PHILOSOPHY ON DEATH!
WHY NOT? -I'M NOT MUCH GOOD TO ANYONE! -I'VE FAILED AT EVERTHING WORTHWHILE I'VE EVER TRIED!
DON'T THINK I'M GETTING MORBID! -I'D SHOOT MY WAY OUT OF HERE IF I HAD A CHANCE! -BUT NO ONE EXCEPT TERRY AND CONNIE WOULD MISS ME MUCH IF I GOT BUMPED OFF...
... AND NOW THAT I'VE MADE MY SPEECH I THINK I'LL BE GOOD AND RUDE AND TAKE A SNOOZE! SOOTHE ME WITH A LULLABY, BABY! -FOR TOMORROW YOU'LL PROBABLY CUT MY THROAT...
MILTON CANIFF
10-23

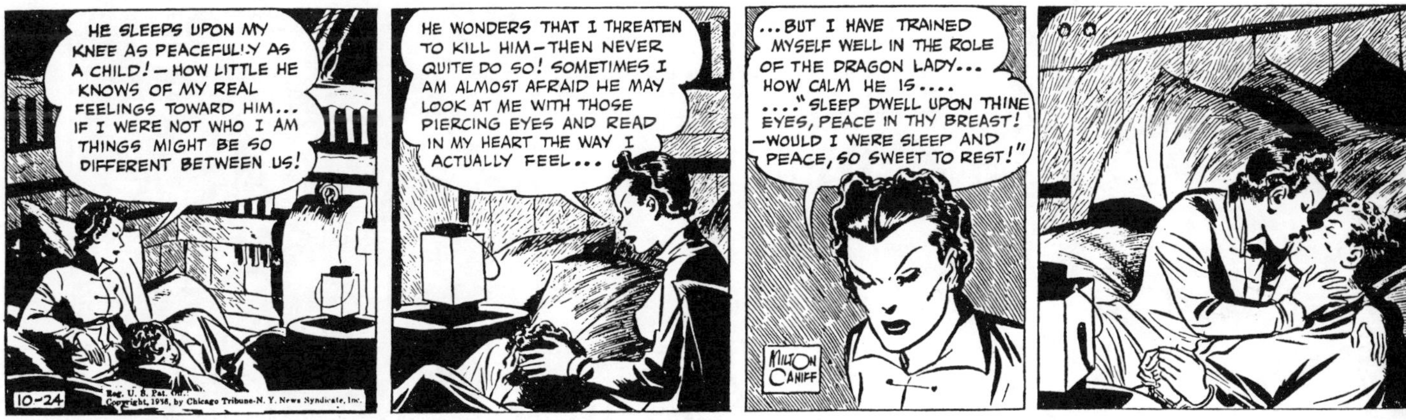
HE SLEEPS UPON MY KNEE AS PEACEFULLY AS A CHILD! -HOW LITTLE HE KNOWS OF MY REAL FEELINGS TOWARD HIM... IF I WERE NOT WHO I AM THINGS MIGHT BE SO DIFFERENT BETWEEN US!
HE WONDERS THAT I THREATEN TO KILL HIM-THEN NEVER QUITE DO SO! SOMETIMES I AM ALMOST AFRAID HE MAY LOOK AT ME WITH THOSE PIERCING EYES AND READ IN MY HEART THE WAY I ACTUALLY FEEL...
... BUT I HAVE TRAINED MYSELF WELL IN THE ROLE OF THE DRAGON LADY... HOW CALM HE IS.... ...."SLEEP DWELL UPON THINE EYES, PEACE IN THY BREAST! -WOULD I WERE SLEEP AND PEACE, SO SWEET TO REST!"
MILTON CANIFF
10-24
Reg. U. S. Pat. Off. Copyright, 1938, by Chicago Tribune-N. Y. News Syndicate, Inc.

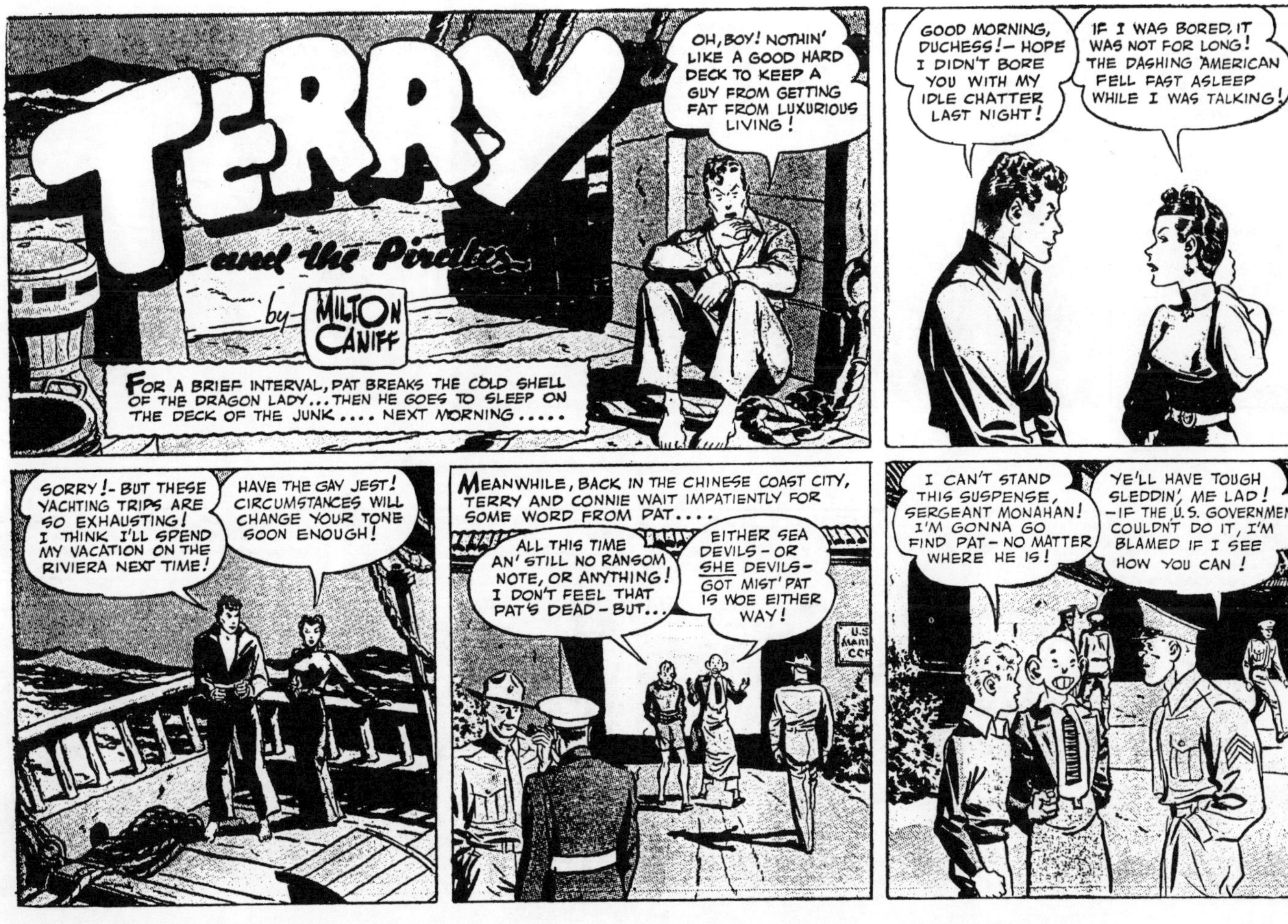
TERRY and the Pirates by MILTON CANIFF
FOR A BRIEF INTERVAL, PAT BREAKS THE COLD SHELL OF THE DRAGON LADY... THEN HE GOES TO SLEEP ON THE DECK OF THE JUNK.... NEXT MORNING.....
OH, BOY! NOTHIN' LIKE A GOOD HARD DECK TO KEEP A GUY FROM GETTING FAT FROM LUXURIOUS LIVING!
GOOD MORNING, DUCHESS! -HOPE I DIDN'T BORE YOU WITH MY IDLE CHATTER LAST NIGHT!
IF I WAS BORED, IT WAS NOT FOR LONG! THE DASHING AMERICAN FELL FAST ASLEEP WHILE I WAS TALKING!
SORRY! -BUT THESE YACHTING TRIPS ARE SO EXHAUSTING! I THINK I'LL SPEND MY VACATION ON THE RIVIERA NEXT TIME!
HAVE THE GAY JEST! CIRCUMSTANCES WILL CHANGE YOUR TONE SOON ENOUGH!
MEANWHILE, BACK IN THE CHINESE COAST CITY, TERRY AND CONNIE WAIT IMPATIENTLY FOR SOME WORD FROM PAT....
ALL THIS TIME AN' STILL NO RANSOM NOTE, OR ANYTHING! I DON'T FEEL THAT PAT'S DEAD-BUT...
EITHER SEA DEVILS-OR SHE DEVILS-GOT MIST' PAT IS WOE EITHER WAY!
I CAN'T STAND THIS SUSPENSE, SERGEANT MONAHAN! I'M GONNA GO FIND PAT-NO MATTER WHERE HE IS!
YE'LL HAVE TOUGH SLEDDIN', ME LAD! -IF THE U.S. GOVERNMENT COULDN'T DO IT, I'M BLAMED IF I SEE HOW YOU CAN!

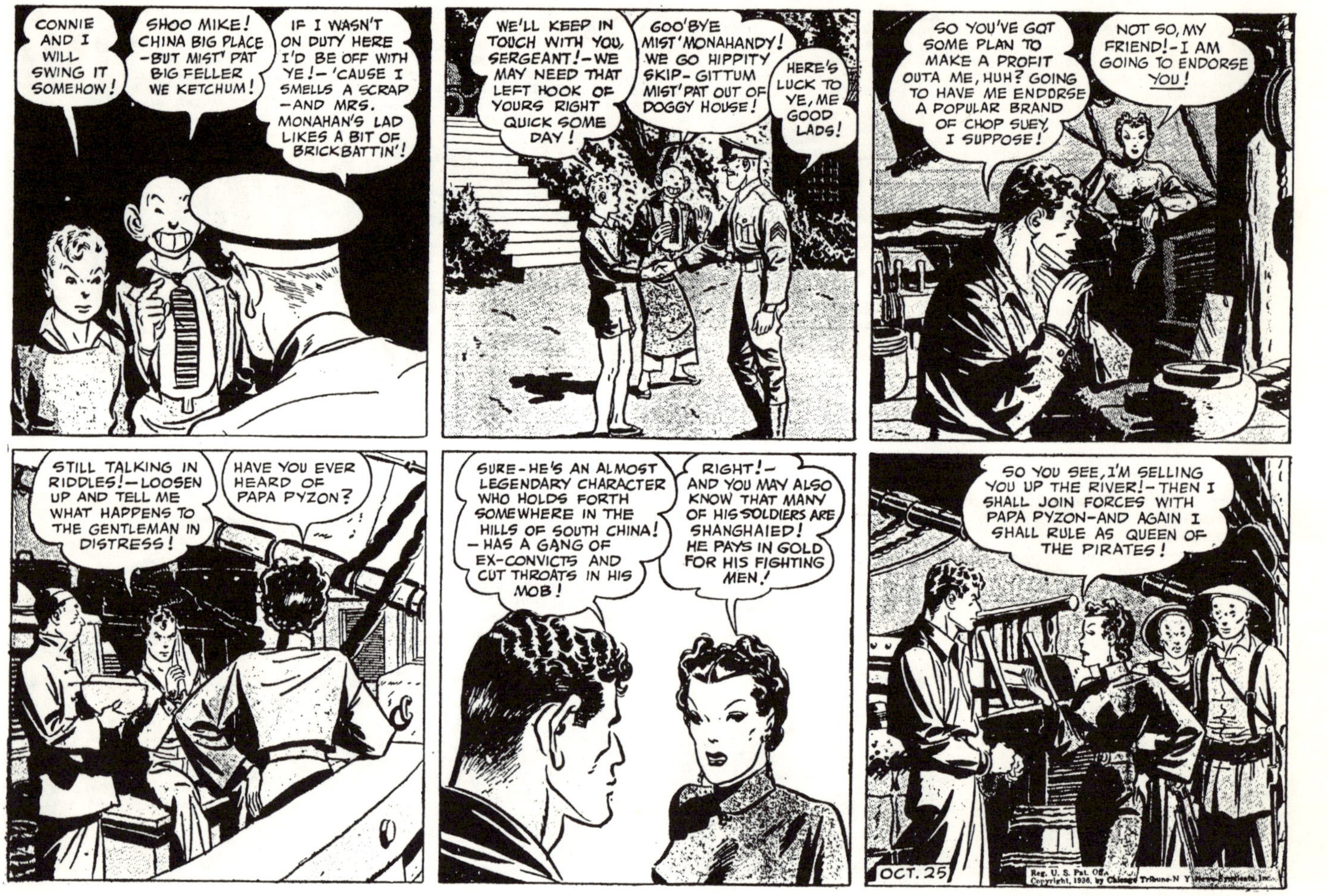
CONNIE AND I WILL SWING IT SOMEHOW!
SHOO MIKE! CHINA BIG PLACE -BUT MIST' PAT BIG FELLER WE KETCHUM!
IF I WASN'T ON DUTY HERE I'D BE OFF WITH YE! -'CAUSE I SMELLS A SCRAP -AND MRS. MONAHAN'S LAD LIKES A BIT OF BRICKBATTIN'!
WE'LL KEEP IN TOUCH WITH YOU, SERGEANT! -WE MAY NEED THAT LEFT HOOK OF YOURS RIGHT QUICK SOME DAY!
GOO'BYE MIST' MONAHANDY! WE GO HIPPITY SKIP-GITTUM MIST' PAT OUT OF DOGGY HOUSE!
HERE'S LUCK TO YE, ME GOOD LADS!
SO YOU'VE GOT SOME PLAN TO MAKE A PROFIT OUTA ME, HUH? GOING TO HAVE ME ENDORSE A POPULAR BRAND OF CHOP SUEY, I SUPPOSE!
NOT SO, MY FRIEND! -I AM GOING TO ENDORSE YOU!
STILL TALKING IN RIDDLES! -LOOSEN UP AND TELL ME WHAT HAPPENS TO THE GENTLEMAN IN DISTRESS!
HAVE YOU EVER HEARD OF PAPA PYZON?
SURE-HE'S AN ALMOST LEGENDARY CHARACTER WHO HOLDS FORTH SOMEWHERE IN THE HILLS OF SOUTH CHINA! -HAS A GANG OF EX-CONVICTS AND CUT THROATS IN HIS MOB!
RIGHT! -AND YOU MAY ALSO KNOW THAT MANY OF HIS SOLDIERS ARE SHANGHAIED! HE PAYS IN GOLD FOR HIS FIGHTING MEN!
SO YOU SEE, I'M SELLING YOU UP THE RIVER! -THEN I SHALL JOIN FORCES WITH PAPA PYZON-AND AGAIN I SHALL RULE AS QUEEN OF THE PIRATES!
OCT. 25

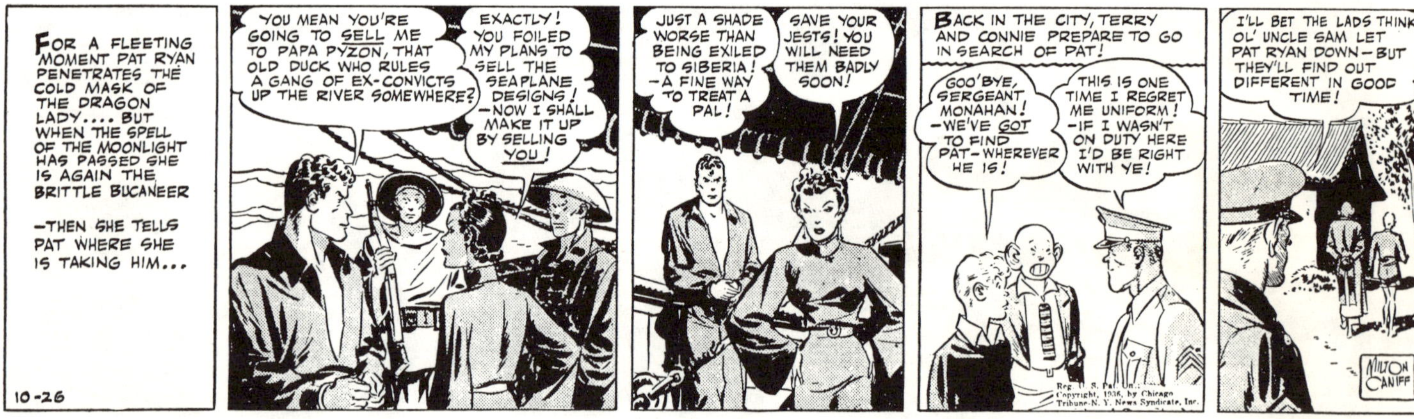
FOR A FLEETING MOMENT PAT RYAN PENETRATES THE COLD MASK OF THE DRAGON LADY.... BUT WHEN THE SPELL OF THE MOONLIGHT HAS PASSED SHE IS AGAIN THE BRITTLE BUCANEER
-THEN SHE TELLS PAT WHERE SHE IS TAKING HIM...
10-26
YOU MEAN YOU'RE GOING TO SELL ME TO PAPA PYZON, THAT OLD DUCK WHO RULES A GANG OF EX-CONVICTS UP THE RIVER SOMEWHERE?
EXACTLY! YOU FOILED MY PLANS TO SELL THE SEAPLANE DESIGNS! -NOW I SHALL MAKE IT UP BY SELLING YOU!
JUST A SHADE WORSE THAN BEING EXILED TO SIBERIA! -A FINE WAY TO TREAT A PAL!
SAVE YOUR JESTS! YOU WILL NEED THEM BADLY SOON!
BACK IN THE CITY, TERRY AND CONNIE PREPARE TO GO IN SEARCH OF PAT!
GOO'BYE, SERGEANT MONAHAN! -WE'VE GOT TO FIND PAT-WHEREVER HE IS!
THIS IS ONE TIME I REGRET ME UNIFORM! -IF I WASN'T ON DUTY HERE I'D BE RIGHT WITH YE!
Copyright, 1936, by Chicago Tribune-N. Y. News Syndicate, Inc.
I'LL BET THE LADS THINK OL' UNCLE SAM LET PAT RYAN DOWN-BUT THEY'LL FIND OUT DIFFERENT IN GOOD TIME!
MILTON CANIFF

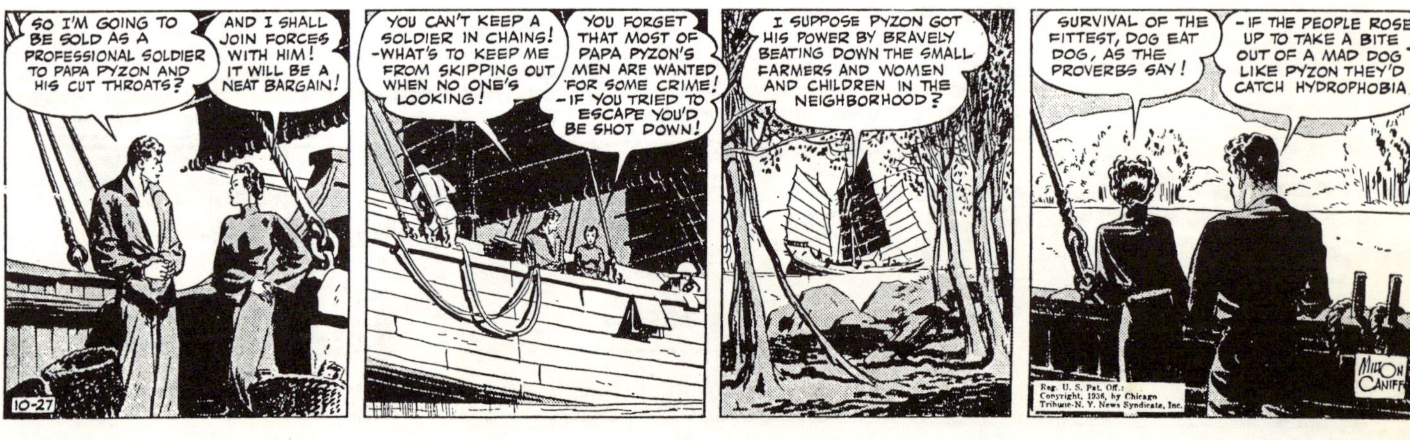
SO I'M GOING TO BE SOLD AS A PROFESSIONAL SOLDIER TO PAPA PYZON AND HIS CUT THROATS?
AND I SHALL JOIN FORCES WITH HIM! IT WILL BE A NEAT BARGAIN!
10-27
YOU CAN'T KEEP A SOLDIER IN CHAINS! -WHAT'S TO KEEP ME FROM SKIPPING OUT WHEN NO ONE'S LOOKING!
YOU FORGET THAT MOST OF PAPA PYZON'S MEN ARE WANTED FOR SOME CRIME! -IF YOU TRIED TO ESCAPE YOU'D BE SHOT DOWN!
I SUPPOSE PYZON GOT HIS POWER BY BRAVELY BEATING DOWN THE SMALL FARMERS AND WOMEN AND CHILDREN IN THE NEIGHBORHOOD?
SURVIVAL OF THE FITTEST, DOG EAT DOG, AS THE PROVERBS SAY!
-IF THE PEOPLE ROSE UP TO TAKE A BITE OUT OF A MAD DOG LIKE PYZON THEY'D CATCH HYDROPHOBIA!
MILTON CANIFF
Reg. U. S. Pat. Off.: Copyright, 1936, by Chicago Tribune-N. Y. News Syndicate, Inc.

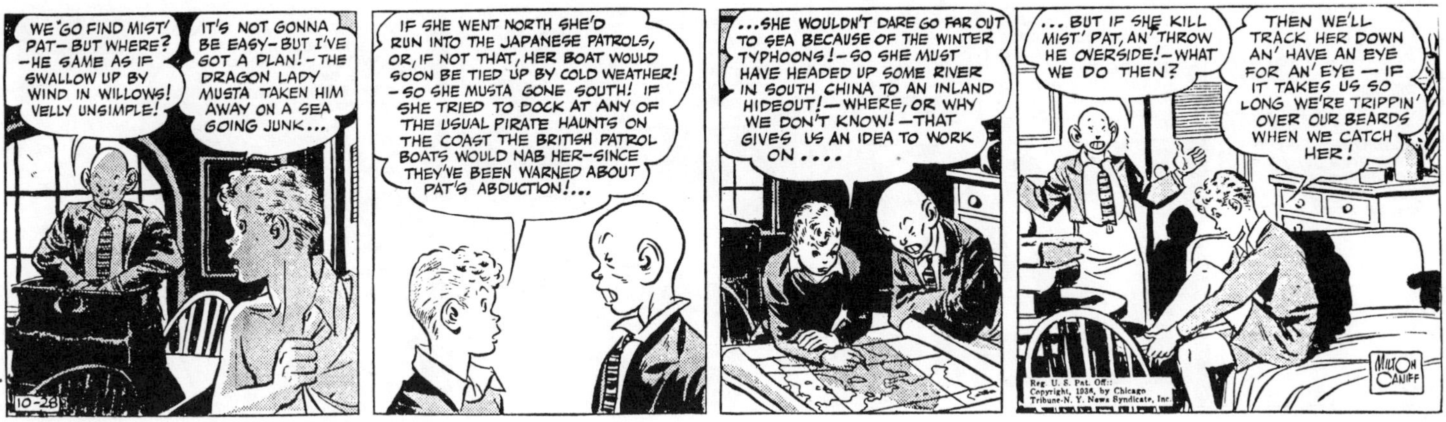
WE GO FIND MIST' PAT—BUT WHERE? —HE SAME AS IF SWALLOW UP BY WIND IN WILLOWS! VELLY UNSIMPLE!
IT'S NOT GONNA BE EASY—BUT I'VE GOT A PLAN!—THE DRAGON LADY MUSTA TAKEN HIM AWAY ON A SEA GOING JUNK...
10-28
IF SHE WENT NORTH SHE'D RUN INTO THE JAPANESE PATROLS, OR, IF NOT THAT, HER BOAT WOULD SOON BE TIED UP BY COLD WEATHER! —SO SHE MUSTA GONE SOUTH! IF SHE TRIED TO DOCK AT ANY OF THE USUAL PIRATE HAUNTS ON THE COAST THE BRITISH PATROL BOATS WOULD NAB HER—SINCE THEY'VE BEEN WARNED ABOUT PAT'S ABDUCTION!...
...SHE WOULDN'T DARE GO FAR OUT TO SEA BECAUSE OF THE WINTER TYPHOONS!—SO SHE MUST HAVE HEADED UP SOME RIVER IN SOUTH CHINA TO AN INLAND HIDEOUT!—WHERE, OR WHY WE DON'T KNOW!—THAT GIVES US AN IDEA TO WORK ON....
Reg. U. S. Pat. Off.: Copyright, 1936, by Chicago Tribune-N. Y. News Syndicate, Inc.
... BUT IF SHE KILL MIST' PAT, AN' THROW HE OVERSIDE!—WHAT WE DO THEN?
THEN WE'LL TRACK HER DOWN AN' HAVE AN EYE FOR AN' EYE—IF IT TAKES US SO LONG WE'RE TRIPPIN' OVER OUR BEARDS WHEN WE CATCH HER!
MILTON CANIFF

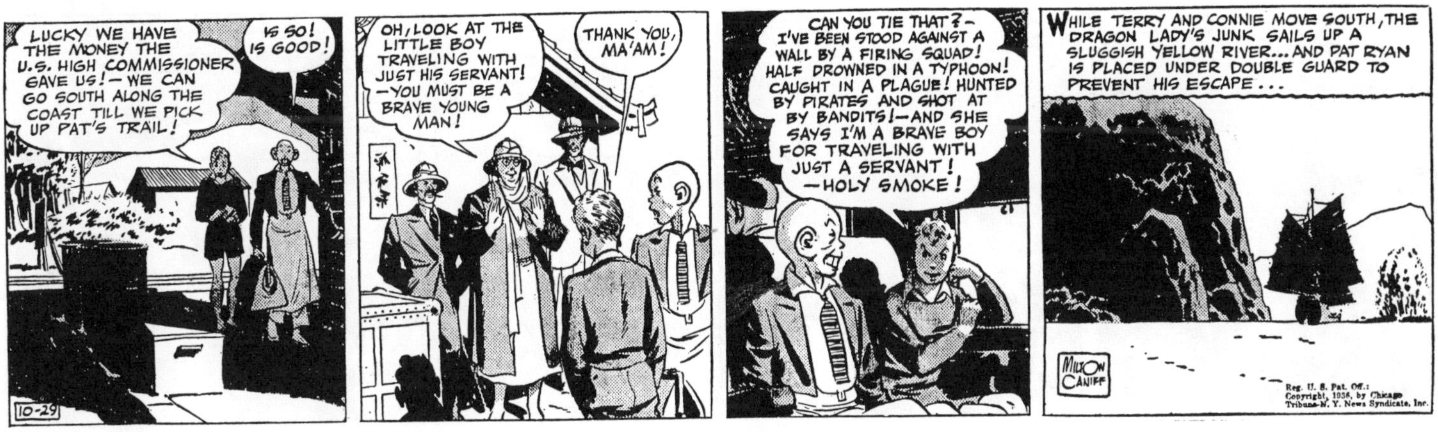
LUCKY WE HAVE THE MONEY THE U.S. HIGH COMMISSIONER GAVE US!—WE CAN GO SOUTH ALONG THE COAST TILL WE PICK UP PAT'S TRAIL!
IS SO! IS GOOD!
10-29
OH, LOOK AT THE LITTLE BOY TRAVELING WITH JUST HIS SERVANT! —YOU MUST BE A BRAVE YOUNG MAN!
THANK YOU, MA'AM!
CAN YOU TIE THAT?— I'VE BEEN STOOD AGAINST A WALL BY A FIRING SQUAD! HALF DROWNED IN A TYPHOON! CAUGHT IN A PLAGUE! HUNTED BY PIRATES AND SHOT AT BY BANDITS!—AND SHE SAYS I'M A BRAVE BOY FOR TRAVELING WITH JUST A SERVANT! —HOLY SMOKE!
WHILE TERRY AND CONNIE MOVE SOUTH, THE DRAGON LADY'S JUNK SAILS UP A SLUGGISH YELLOW RIVER... AND PAT RYAN IS PLACED UNDER DOUBLE GUARD TO PREVENT HIS ESCAPE...
MILTON CANIFF
Reg. U. S. Pat. Off.: Copyright, 1936, by Chicago Tribune-N. Y. News Syndicate, Inc.

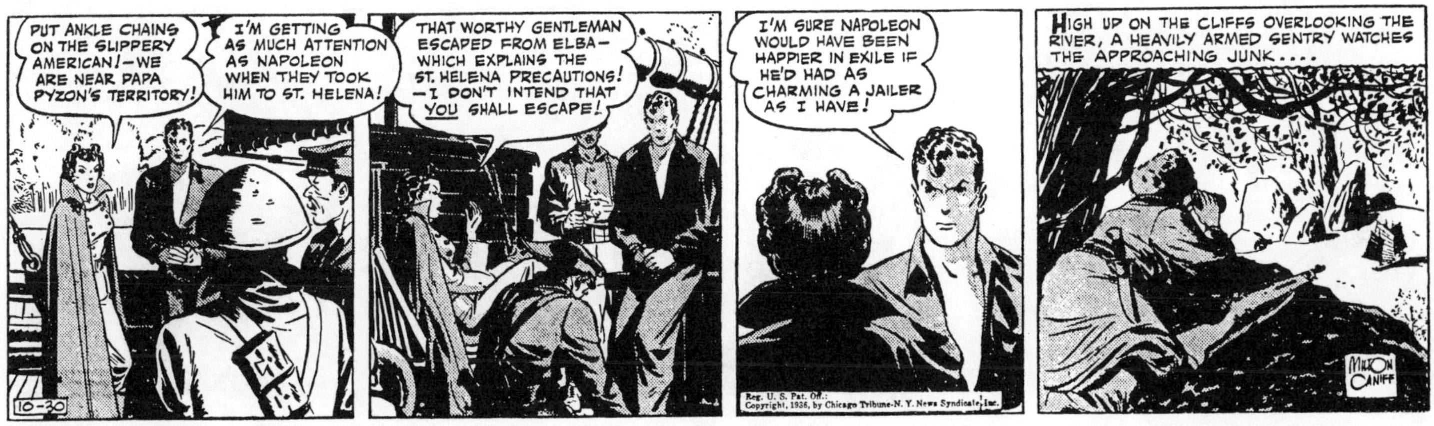
PUT ANKLE CHAINS ON THE SLIPPERY AMERICAN!—WE ARE NEAR PAPA PYZON'S TERRITORY!
I'M GETTING AS MUCH ATTENTION AS NAPOLEON WHEN THEY TOOK HIM TO ST. HELENA!
10-30
THAT WORTHY GENTLEMAN ESCAPED FROM ELBA— WHICH EXPLAINS THE ST. HELENA PRECAUTIONS! —I DON'T INTEND THAT YOU SHALL ESCAPE!
I'M SURE NAPOLEON WOULD HAVE BEEN HAPPIER IN EXILE IF HE'D HAD AS CHARMING A JAILER AS I HAVE!
Reg. U. S. Pat. Off.: Copyright, 1936, by Chicago Tribune-N. Y. News Syndicate, Inc.
HIGH UP ON THE CLIFFS OVERLOOKING THE RIVER, A HEAVILY ARMED SENTRY WATCHES THE APPROACHING JUNK....
MILTON CANIFF

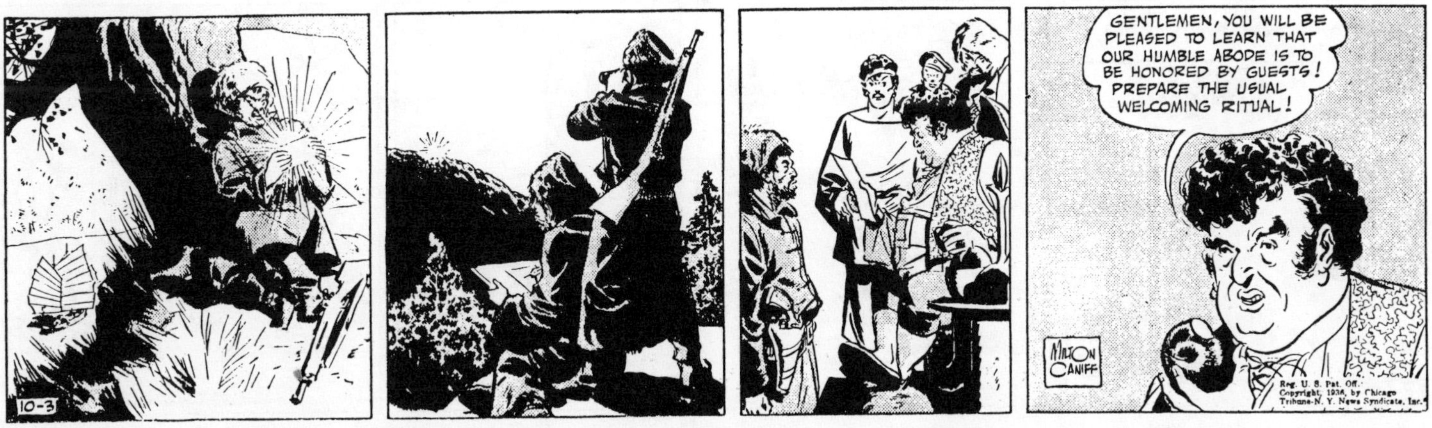
10-3
GENTLEMEN, YOU WILL BE PLEASED TO LEARN THAT OUR HUMBLE ABODE IS TO BE HONORED BY GUESTS! PREPARE THE USUAL WELCOMING RITUAL!
MILTON CANIFF
Reg. U. S. Pat. Off.: Copyright, 1936, by Chicago Tribune-N. Y. News Syndicate, Inc.

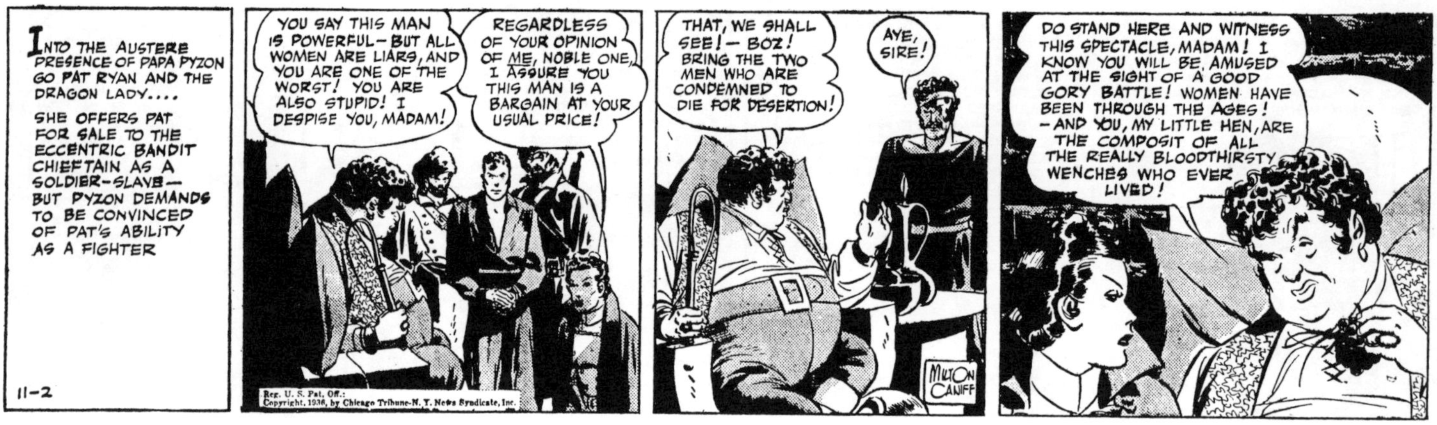
INTO THE AUSTERE PRESENCE OF PAPA PYZON GO PAT RYAN AND THE DRAGON LADY....
SHE OFFERS PAT FOR SALE TO THE ECCENTRIC BANDIT CHIEFTAIN AS A SOLDIER-SLAVE— BUT PYZON DEMANDS TO BE CONVINCED OF PAT'S ABILITY AS A FIGHTER
11-2
YOU SAY THIS MAN IS POWERFUL— BUT ALL WOMEN ARE LIARS, AND YOU ARE ONE OF THE WORST! YOU ARE ALSO STUPID! I DESPISE YOU, MADAM!
REGARDLESS OF YOUR OPINION OF ME, NOBLE ONE, I ASSURE YOU THIS MAN IS A BARGAIN AT YOUR USUAL PRICE!
Reg. U. S. Pat. Off.: Copyright, 1936, by Chicago Tribune-N. Y. News Syndicate, Inc.
THAT, WE SHALL SEE! — BOZ! BRING THE TWO MEN WHO ARE CONDEMNED TO DIE FOR DESERTION!
AYE, SIRE!
MILTON CANIFF
DO STAND HERE AND WITNESS THIS SPECTACLE, MADAM! I KNOW YOU WILL BE AMUSED AT THE SIGHT OF A GOOD GORY BATTLE! WOMEN HAVE BEEN THROUGH THE AGES! — AND YOU, MY LITTLE HEN, ARE THE COMPOSIT OF ALL THE REALLY BLOODTHIRSTY WENCHES WHO EVER LIVED!

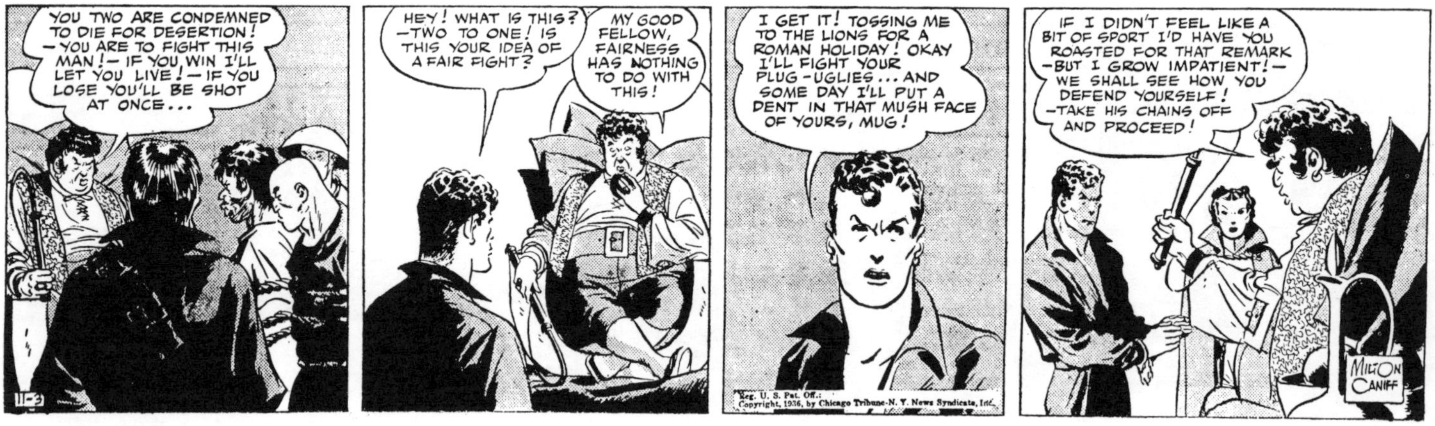
YOU TWO ARE CONDEMNED TO DIE FOR DESERTION! — YOU ARE TO FIGHT THIS MAN! — IF YOU WIN I'LL LET YOU LIVE! — IF YOU LOSE YOU'LL BE SHOT AT ONCE...
11-3
HEY! WHAT IS THIS? — TWO TO ONE! IS THIS YOUR IDEA OF A FAIR FIGHT?
MY GOOD FELLOW, FAIRNESS HAS NOTHING TO DO WITH THIS!
I GET IT! TOSSING ME TO THE LIONS FOR A ROMAN HOLIDAY! OKAY I'LL FIGHT YOUR PLUG-UGLIES... AND SOME DAY I'LL PUT A DENT IN THAT MUSH FACE OF YOURS, MUG!
Reg. U. S. Pat. Off.: Copyright, 1936, by Chicago Tribune-N. Y. News Syndicate, Inc.
IF I DIDN'T FEEL LIKE A BIT OF SPORT I'D HAVE YOU ROASTED FOR THAT REMARK — BUT I GROW IMPATIENT! — WE SHALL SEE HOW YOU DEFEND YOURSELF! — TAKE HIS CHAINS OFF AND PROCEED!
MILTON CANIFF

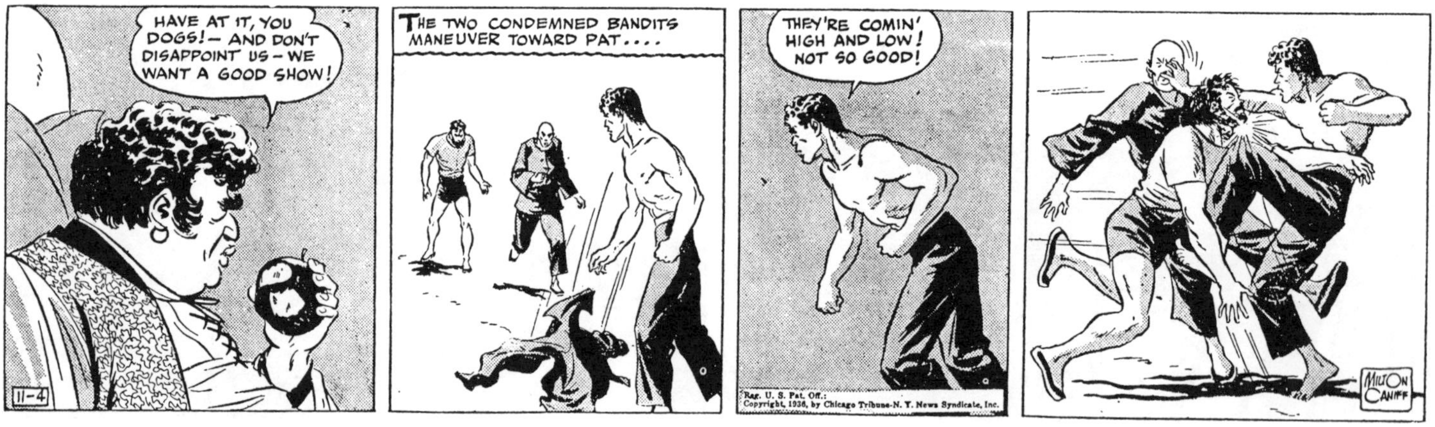
HAVE AT IT, YOU DOGS! — AND DON'T DISAPPOINT US — WE WANT A GOOD SHOW!
11-4
THE TWO CONDEMNED BANDITS MANEUVER TOWARD PAT....
THEY'RE COMIN' HIGH AND LOW! NOT SO GOOD!
Reg. U. S. Pat. Off.: Copyright, 1936, by Chicago Tribune-N. Y. News Syndicate, Inc.
MILTON CANIFF

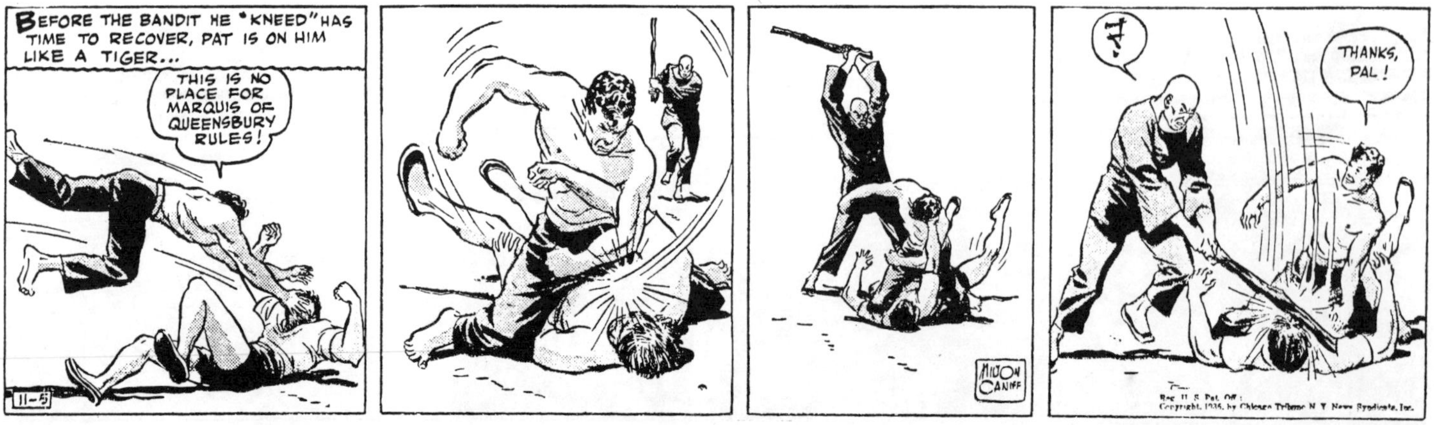
BEFORE THE BANDIT HE "KNEED" HAS TIME TO RECOVER, PAT IS ON HIM LIKE A TIGER...
THIS IS NO PLACE FOR MARQUIS OF QUEENSBURY RULES!
11-5
MILTON CANIFF
THANKS, PAL!
Reg. U. S. Pat. Off.: Copyright, 1936, by Chicago Tribune-N. Y. News Syndicate, Inc.

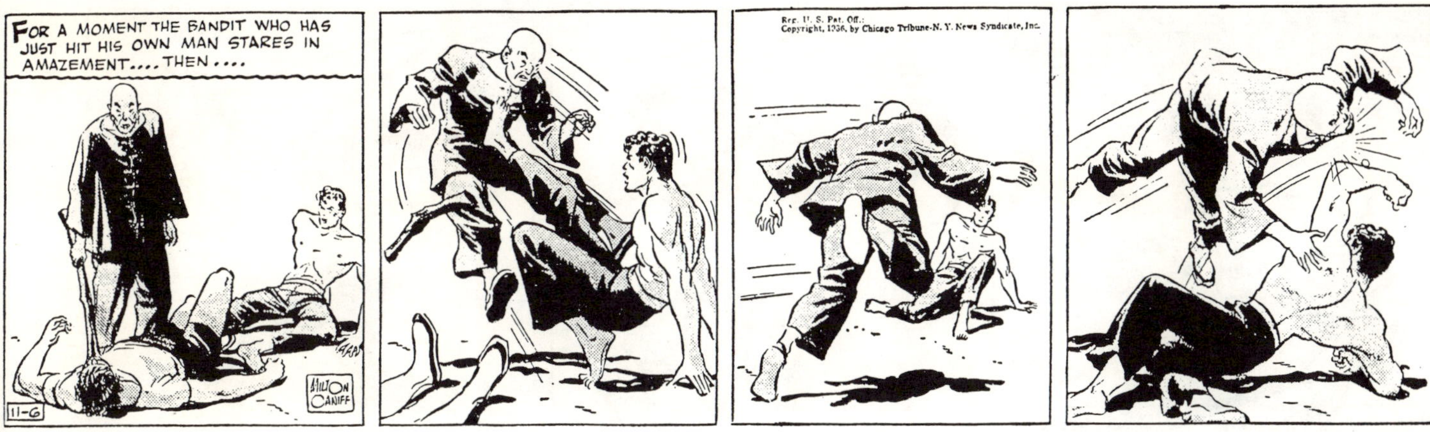
FOR A MOMENT THE BANDIT WHO HAS JUST HIT HIS OWN MAN STARES IN AMAZEMENT.... THEN....
MILTON CANIFF
11-6
Reg. U. S. Pat. Off.:
Copyright, 1936, by Chicago Tribune-N. Y. News Syndicate, Inc.

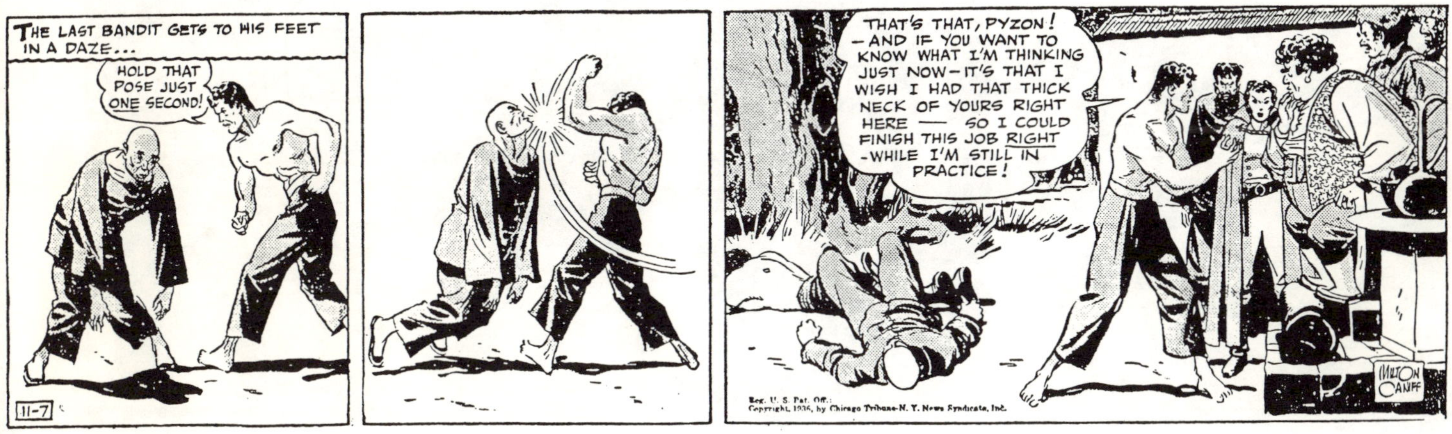
THE LAST BANDIT GETS TO HIS FEET IN A DAZE...
HOLD THAT POSE JUST ONE SECOND!
11-7
THAT'S THAT, PYZON! – AND IF YOU WANT TO KNOW WHAT I'M THINKING JUST NOW – IT'S THAT I WISH I HAD THAT THICK NECK OF YOURS RIGHT HERE — SO I COULD FINISH THIS JOB RIGHT – WHILE I'M STILL IN PRACTICE!
MILTON CANIFF
Reg. U. S. Pat. Off.:
Copyright, 1936, by Chicago Tribune-N. Y. News Syndicate, Inc.

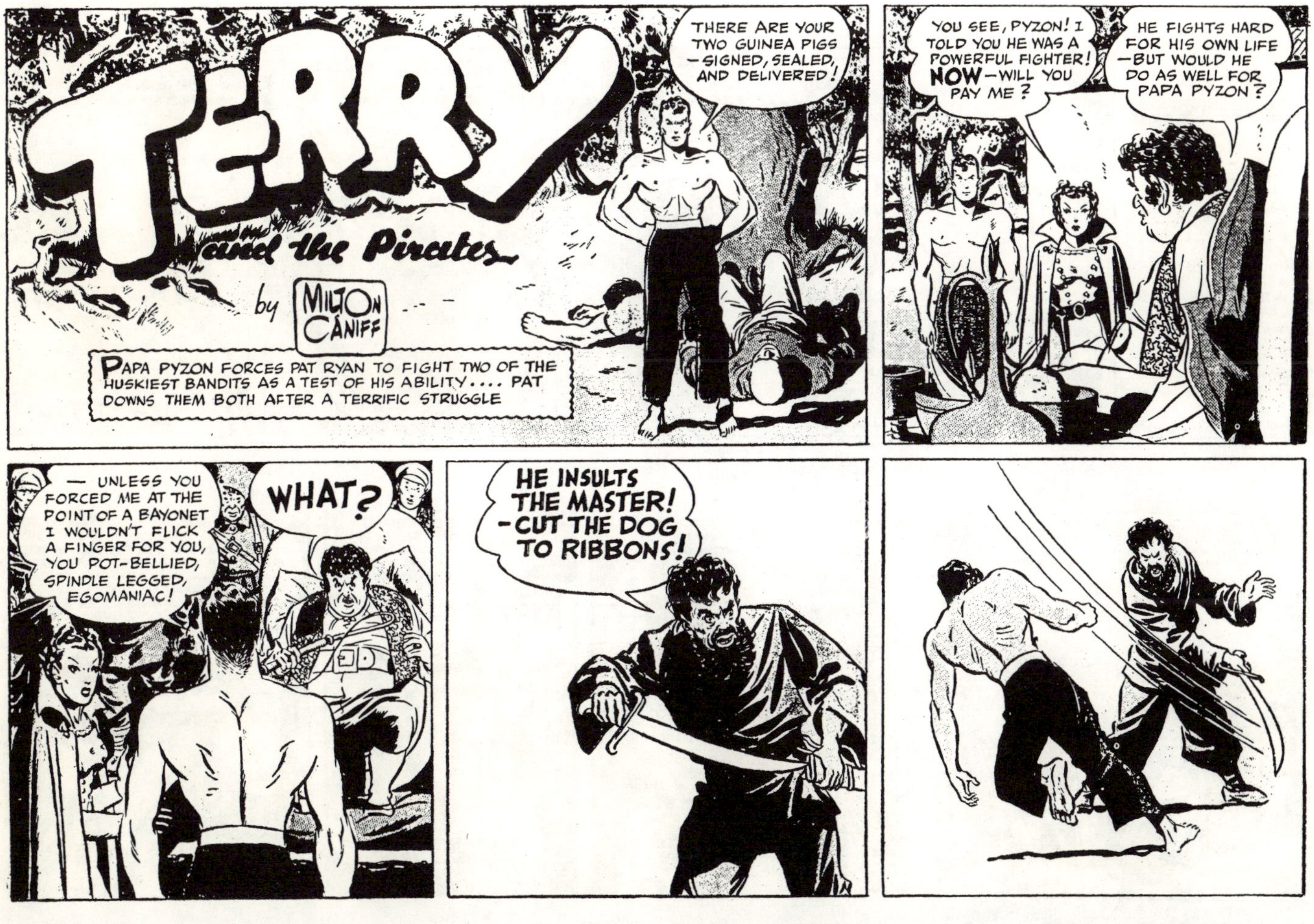
TERRY and the Pirates
by MILTON CANIFF
PAPA PYZON FORCES PAT RYAN TO FIGHT TWO OF THE HUSKIEST BANDITS AS A TEST OF HIS ABILITY.... PAT DOWNS THEM BOTH AFTER A TERRIFIC STRUGGLE
THERE ARE YOUR TWO GUINEA PIGS – SIGNED, SEALED, AND DELIVERED!
YOU SEE, PYZON! I TOLD YOU HE WAS A POWERFUL FIGHTER! NOW – WILL YOU PAY ME?
HE FIGHTS HARD FOR HIS OWN LIFE – BUT WOULD HE DO AS WELL FOR PAPA PYZON?
— UNLESS YOU FORCED ME AT THE POINT OF A BAYONET I WOULDN'T FLICK A FINGER FOR YOU, YOU POT-BELLIED, SPINDLE LEGGED, EGOMANIAC!
WHAT?
HE INSULTS THE MASTER! – CUT THE DOG TO RIBBONS!

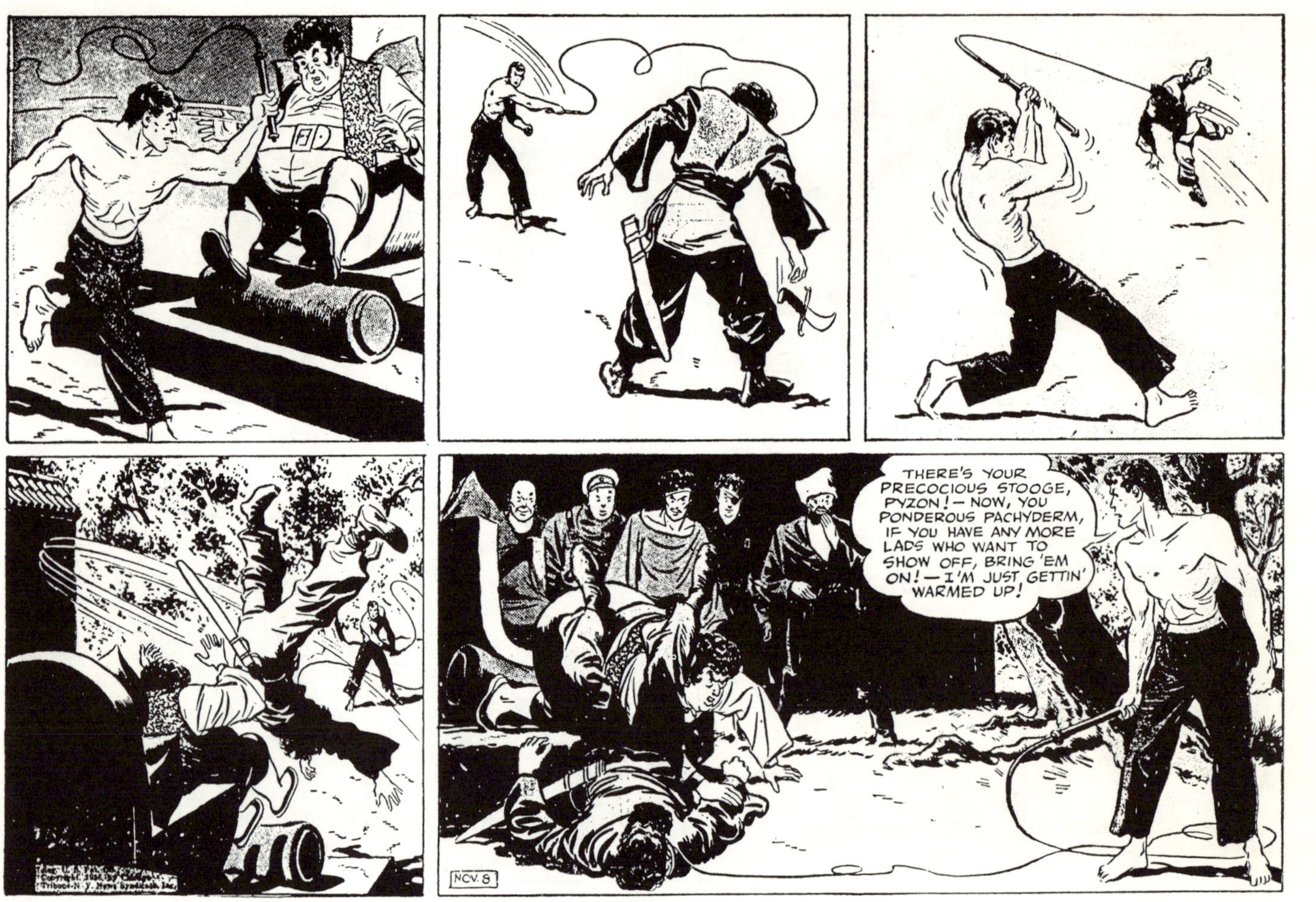
THERE'S YOUR PRECOCIOUS STOOGE, PYZON! — NOW, YOU PONDEROUS PACHYDERM, IF YOU HAVE ANY MORE LADS WHO WANT TO SHOW OFF, BRING 'EM ON! — I'M JUST GETTIN' WARMED UP!
NOV. 8

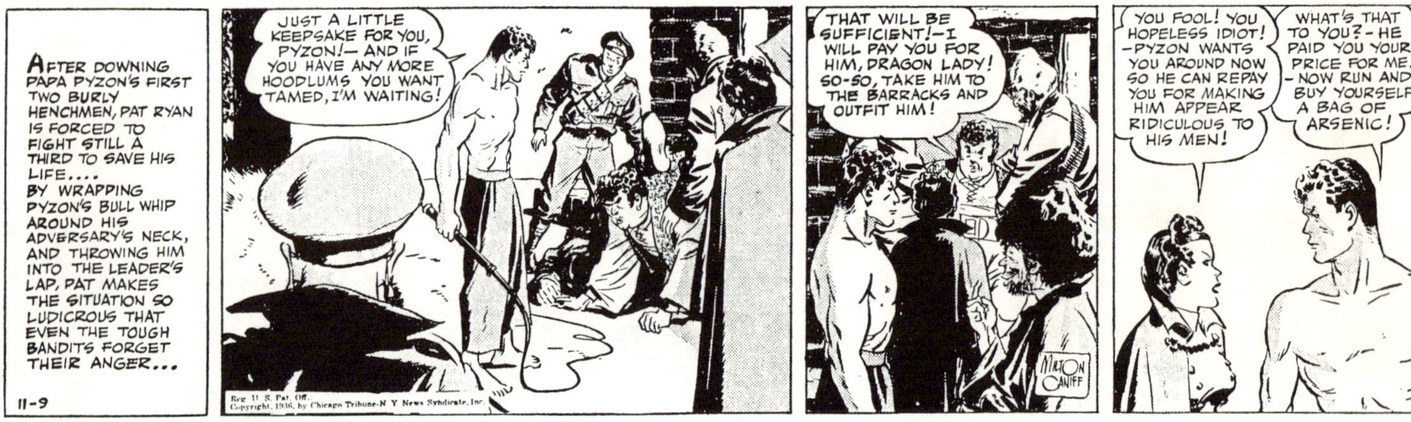
AFTER DOWNING PAPA PYZON'S FIRST TWO BURLY HENCHMEN, PAT RYAN IS FORCED TO FIGHT STILL A THIRD TO SAVE HIS LIFE.... BY WRAPPING PYZON'S BULL WHIP AROUND HIS ADVERSARY'S NECK, AND THROWING HIM INTO THE LEADER'S LAP, PAT MAKES THE SITUATION SO LUDICROUS THAT EVEN THE TOUGH BANDITS FORGET THEIR ANGER...
11-9
JUST A LITTLE KEEPSAKE FOR YOU, PYZON! — AND IF YOU HAVE ANY MORE HOODLUMS YOU WANT TAMED, I'M WAITING!
Reg. U. S. Pat. Off. Copyright, 1936, by Chicago Tribune-N. Y. News Syndicate, Inc.
THAT WILL BE SUFFICIENT! — I WILL PAY YOU FOR HIM, DRAGON LADY! SO-SO, TAKE HIM TO THE BARRACKS AND OUTFIT HIM!
MILTON CANIFF
YOU FOOL! YOU HOPELESS IDIOT! — PYZON WANTS YOU AROUND NOW SO HE CAN REPAY YOU FOR MAKING HIM APPEAR RIDICULOUS TO HIS MEN!
WHAT'S THAT TO YOU? — HE PAID YOU YOUR PRICE FOR ME! — NOW RUN AND BUY YOURSELF A BAG OF ARSENIC!

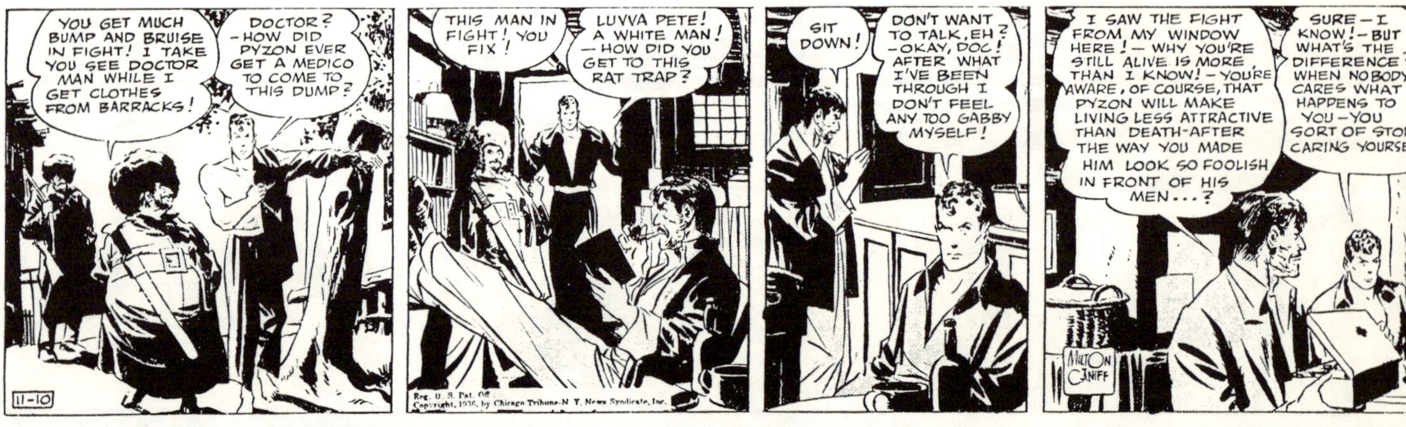
YOU GET MUCH BUMP AND BRUISE IN FIGHT! I TAKE YOU SEE DOCTOR MAN WHILE I GET CLOTHES FROM BARRACKS!
DOCTOR? — HOW DID PYZON EVER GET A MEDICO TO COME TO THIS DUMP?
11-10
THIS MAN IN FIGHT! YOU FIX!
LUVVA PETE! A WHITE MAN! — HOW DID YOU GET TO THIS RAT TRAP?
Reg. U. S. Pat. Off. Copyright, 1936, by Chicago Tribune-N. Y. News Syndicate, Inc.
SIT DOWN!
DON'T WANT TO TALK, EH? — OKAY, DOC! AFTER WHAT I'VE BEEN THROUGH I DON'T FEEL ANY TOO GABBY MYSELF!
I SAW THE FIGHT FROM MY WINDOW HERE! — WHY YOU'RE STILL ALIVE IS MORE THAN I KNOW! — YOU'RE AWARE, OF COURSE, THAT PYZON WILL MAKE LIVING LESS ATTRACTIVE THAN DEATH AFTER THE WAY YOU MADE HIM LOOK SO FOOLISH IN FRONT OF HIS MEN...?
SURE — I KNOW! — BUT WHAT'S THE DIFFERENCE? WHEN NOBODY CARES WHAT HAPPENS TO YOU — YOU SORT OF STOP CARING YOURSELF!
MILTON CANIFF

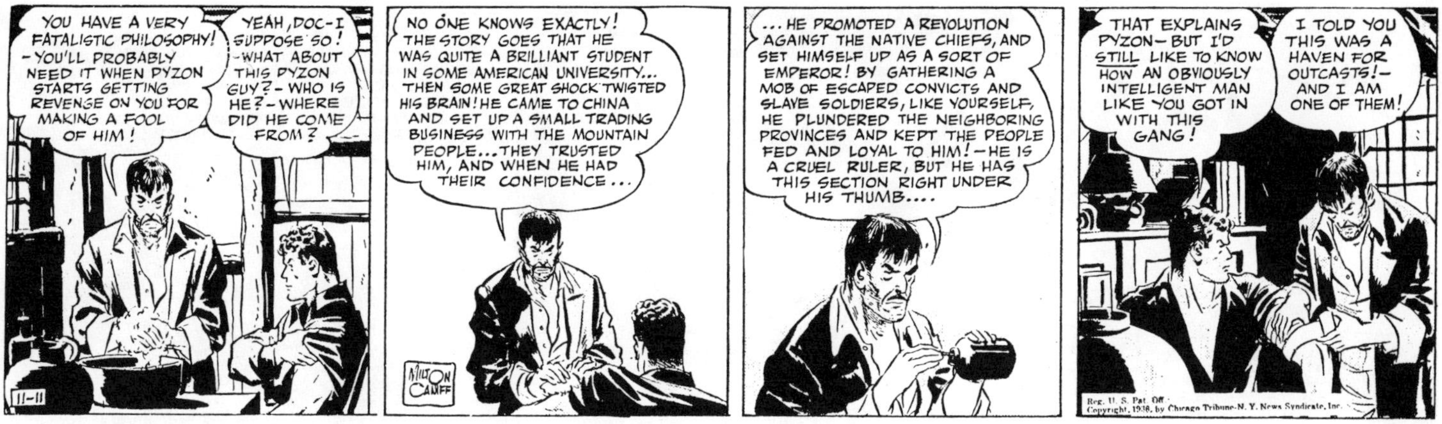
YOU HAVE A VERY FATALISTIC PHILOSOPHY! -YOU'LL PROBABLY NEED IT WHEN PYZON STARTS GETTING REVENGE ON YOU FOR MAKING A FOOL OF HIM!
YEAH, DOC-I SUPPOSE SO! -WHAT ABOUT THIS PYZON GUY?-WHO IS HE?-WHERE DID HE COME FROM?
11-11
NO ONE KNOWS EXACTLY! THE STORY GOES THAT HE WAS QUITE A BRILLIANT STUDENT IN SOME AMERICAN UNIVERSITY... THEN SOME GREAT SHOCK TWISTED HIS BRAIN! HE CAME TO CHINA AND SET UP A SMALL TRADING BUSINESS WITH THE MOUNTAIN PEOPLE... THEY TRUSTED HIM, AND WHEN HE HAD THEIR CONFIDENCE...
MILTON CANIFF
...HE PROMOTED A REVOLUTION AGAINST THE NATIVE CHIEFS, AND SET HIMSELF UP AS A SORT OF EMPEROR! BY GATHERING A MOB OF ESCAPED CONVICTS AND SLAVE SOLDIERS, LIKE YOURSELF, HE PLUNDERED THE NEIGHBORING PROVINCES AND KEPT THE PEOPLE FED AND LOYAL TO HIM!-HE IS A CRUEL RULER, BUT HE HAS THIS SECTION RIGHT UNDER HIS THUMB....
THAT EXPLAINS PYZON-BUT I'D STILL LIKE TO KNOW HOW AN OBVIOUSLY INTELLIGENT MAN LIKE YOU GOT IN WITH THIS GANG!
I TOLD YOU THIS WAS A HAVEN FOR OUTCASTS!- AND I AM ONE OF THEM!
Reg. U. S. Pat. Off.
Copyright, 1938, by Chicago Tribune-N. Y. News Syndicate, Inc.

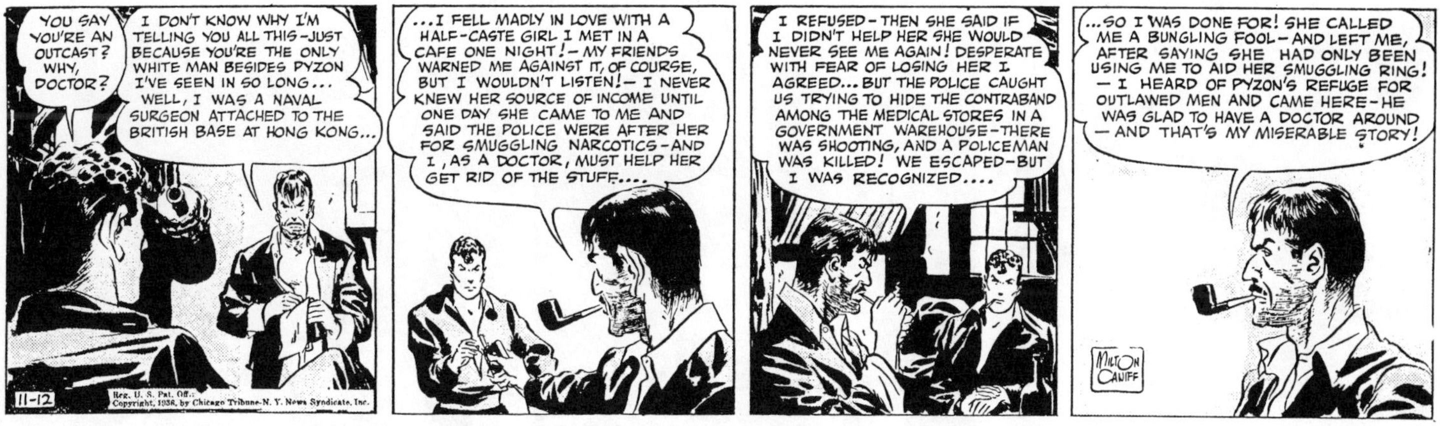
YOU SAY YOU'RE AN OUTCAST? WHY, DOCTOR?
I DON'T KNOW WHY I'M TELLING YOU ALL THIS-JUST BECAUSE YOU'RE THE ONLY WHITE MAN BESIDES PYZON I'VE SEEN IN SO LONG... WELL, I WAS A NAVAL SURGEON ATTACHED TO THE BRITISH BASE AT HONG KONG...
11-12
Reg. U. S. Pat. Off.
Copyright, 1938, by Chicago Tribune-N. Y. News Syndicate, Inc.
...I FELL MADLY IN LOVE WITH A HALF-CASTE GIRL I MET IN A CAFE ONE NIGHT!-MY FRIENDS WARNED ME AGAINST IT, OF COURSE, BUT I WOULDN'T LISTEN!- I NEVER KNEW HER SOURCE OF INCOME UNTIL ONE DAY SHE CAME TO ME AND SAID THE POLICE WERE AFTER HER FOR SMUGGLING NARCOTICS-AND I, AS A DOCTOR, MUST HELP HER GET RID OF THE STUFF....
I REFUSED-THEN SHE SAID IF I DIDN'T HELP HER SHE WOULD NEVER SEE ME AGAIN! DESPERATE WITH FEAR OF LOSING HER I AGREED... BUT THE POLICE CAUGHT US TRYING TO HIDE THE CONTRABAND AMONG THE MEDICAL STORES IN A GOVERNMENT WAREHOUSE-THERE WAS SHOOTING, AND A POLICEMAN WAS KILLED! WE ESCAPED-BUT I WAS RECOGNIZED....
...SO I WAS DONE FOR! SHE CALLED ME A BUNGLING FOOL-AND LEFT ME, AFTER SAYING SHE HAD ONLY BEEN USING ME TO AID HER SMUGGLING RING! - I HEARD OF PYZON'S REFUGE FOR OUTLAWED MEN AND CAME HERE-HE WAS GLAD TO HAVE A DOCTOR AROUND -AND THAT'S MY MISERABLE STORY!
MILTON CANIFF

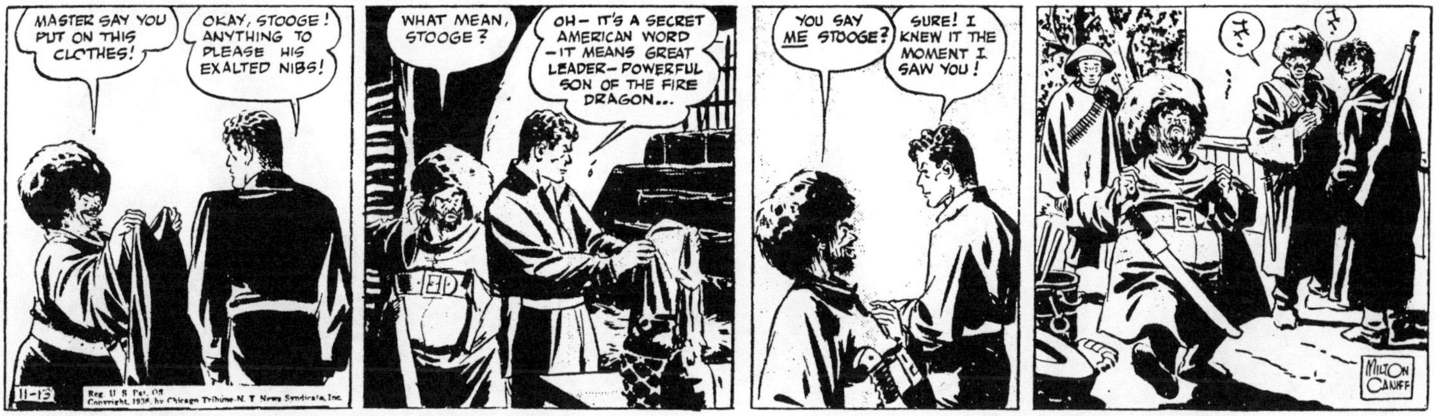
MASTER SAY YOU PUT ON THIS CLOTHES!
OKAY, STOOGE! ANYTHING TO PLEASE HIS EXALTED NIBS!
11-13
Reg. U. S. Pat. Off.
Copyright, 1938, by Chicago Tribune-N. Y. News Syndicate, Inc.
WHAT MEAN, STOOGE?
OH- IT'S A SECRET AMERICAN WORD -IT MEANS GREAT LEADER-POWERFUL SON OF THE FIRE DRAGON...
YOU SAY ME STOOGE?
SURE! I KNEW IT THE MOMENT I SAW YOU!
MILTON CANIFF

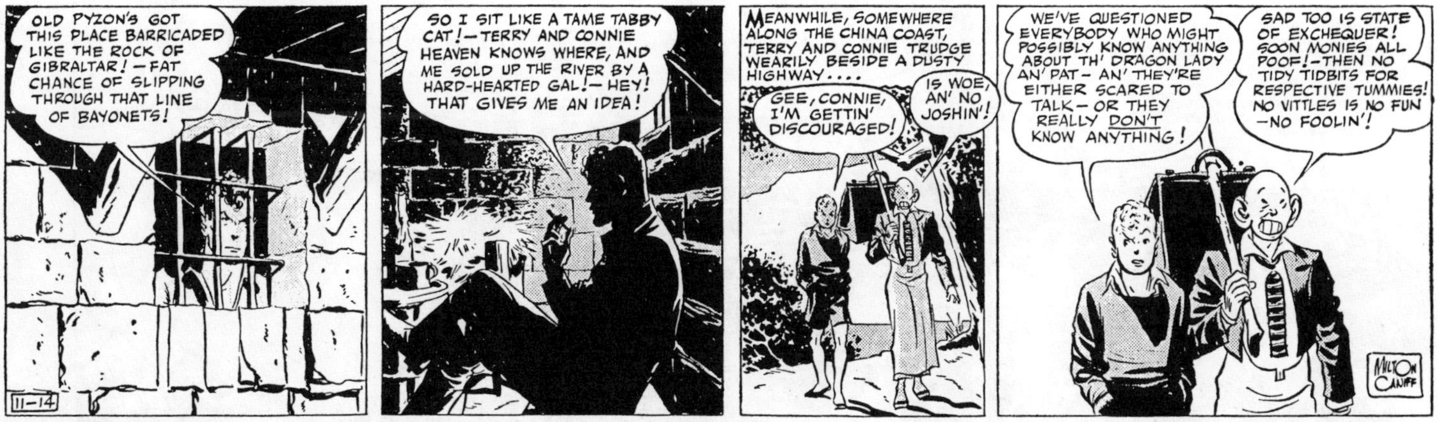
OLD PYZON'S GOT THIS PLACE BARRICADED LIKE THE ROCK OF GIBRALTAR! -FAT CHANCE OF SLIPPING THROUGH THAT LINE OF BAYONETS!
11-14
SO I SIT LIKE A TAME TABBY CAT!-TERRY AND CONNIE HEAVEN KNOWS WHERE, AND ME SOLD UP THE RIVER BY A HARD-HEARTED GAL!-HEY! THAT GIVES ME AN IDEA!
MEANWHILE, SOMEWHERE ALONG THE CHINA COAST, TERRY AND CONNIE TRUDGE WEARILY BESIDE A DUSTY HIGHWAY....
GEE, CONNIE, I'M GETTIN' DISCOURAGED!
IS WOE, AN' NO JOSHIN'!
WE'VE QUESTIONED EVERYBODY WHO MIGHT POSSIBLY KNOW ANYTHING ABOUT TH' DRAGON LADY AN' PAT- AN' THEY'RE EITHER SCARED TO TALK- OR THEY REALLY DON'T KNOW ANYTHING!
SAD TOO IS STATE OF EXCHEQUER! SOON MONIES ALL POOF!-THEN NO TIDY TIDBITS FOR RESPECTIVE TUMMIES! NO VITTLES IS NO FUN -NO FOOLIN'!
MILTON CANIFF

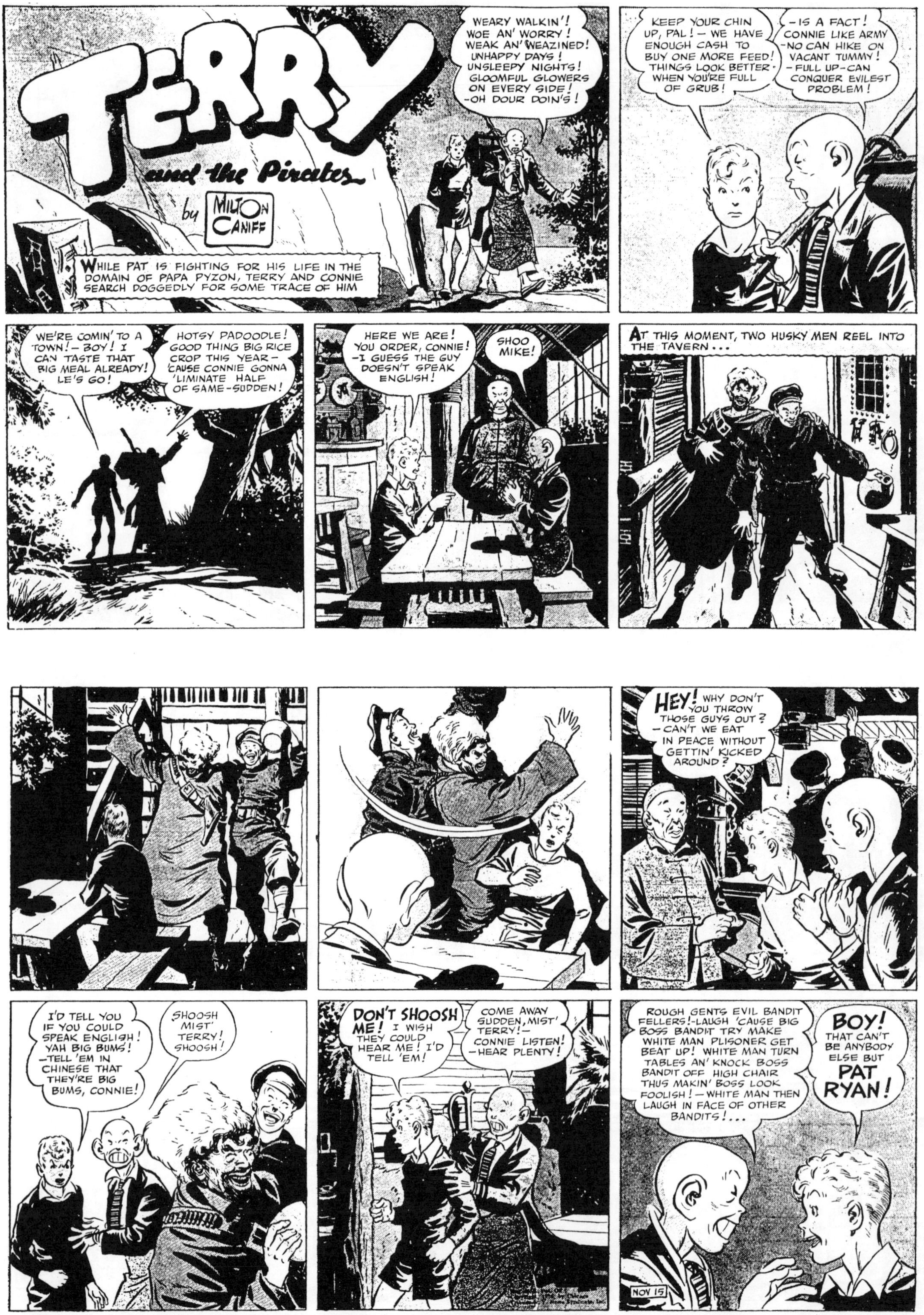
TERRY and the Pirates
by MILTON CANIFF
WHILE PAT IS FIGHTING FOR HIS LIFE IN THE DOMAIN OF PAPA PYZON, TERRY AND CONNIE SEARCH DOGGEDLY FOR SOME TRACE OF HIM
WEARY WALKIN'! WOE AN' WORRY! WEAK AN' WEAZINED! UNHAPPY DAYS! UNSLEEPY NIGHTS! GLOOMFUL GLOWERS ON EVERY SIDE! -OH DOUR DOIN'S!
KEEP YOUR CHIN UP, PAL! — WE HAVE ENOUGH CASH TO BUY ONE MORE FEED! THINGS LOOK BETTER WHEN YOU'RE FULL OF GRUB!
-IS A FACT! CONNIE LIKE ARMY -NO CAN HIKE ON VACANT TUMMY! -FULL UP-CAN CONQUER EVILEST PROBLEM!
WE'RE COMIN' TO A TOWN! — BOY! I CAN TASTE THAT BIG MEAL ALREADY! LE'S GO!
HOTSY PADOODLE! GOOD THING BIG RICE CROP THIS YEAR- 'CAUSE CONNIE GONNA 'LIMINATE HALF OF SAME-SUDDEN!
HERE WE ARE! YOU ORDER, CONNIE! -I GUESS THE GUY DOESN'T SPEAK ENGLISH!
SHOO MIKE!
AT THIS MOMENT, TWO HUSKY MEN REEL INTO THE TAVERN...
HEY! WHY DON'T YOU THROW THOSE GUYS OUT? -CAN'T WE EAT IN PEACE WITHOUT GETTIN' KICKED AROUND?
I'D TELL YOU IF YOU COULD SPEAK ENGLISH! YAH BIG BUMS! -TELL 'EM IN CHINESE THAT THEY'RE BIG BUMS, CONNIE!
SHOOSH MIST' TERRY! SHOOSH!
DON'T SHOOSH ME! I WISH THEY COULD HEAR ME! I'D TELL 'EM!
COME AWAY SUDDEN, MIST' TERRY!- CONNIE LISTEN! -HEAR PLENTY!
ROUGH GENTS EVIL BANDIT FELLERS!-LAUGH 'CAUSE BIG BOSS BANDIT TRY MAKE WHITE MAN PLISONER GET BEAT UP! WHITE MAN TURN TABLES AN' KNOCK BOSS BANDIT OFF HIGH CHAIR THUS MAKIN' BOSS LOOK FOOLISH! — WHITE MAN THEN LAUGH IN FACE OF OTHER BANDITS!...
BOY! THAT CAN'T BE ANYBODY ELSE BUT PAT RYAN!
NOV 15

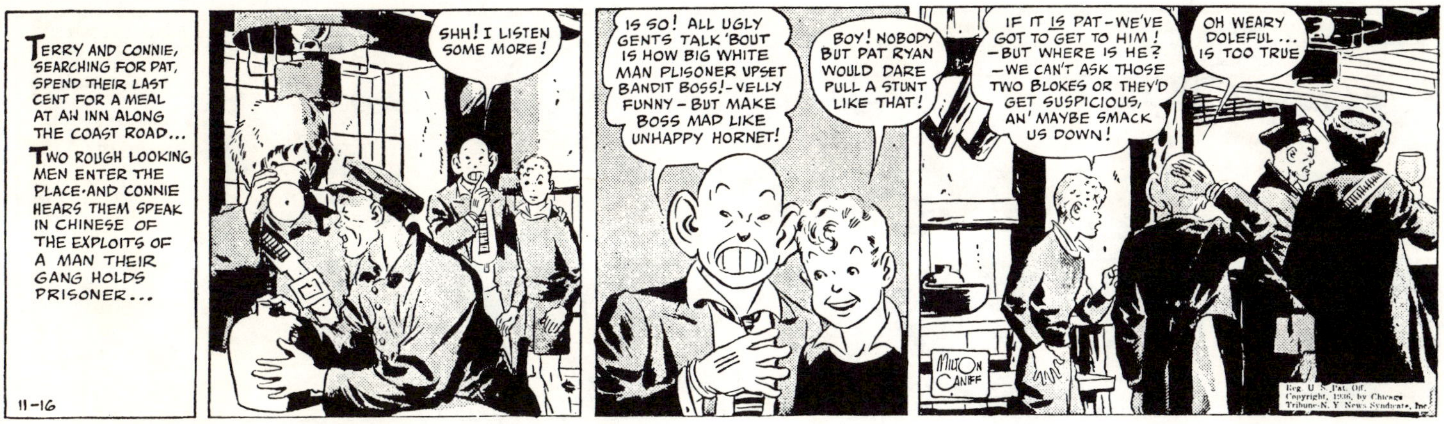
TERRY AND CONNIE, SEARCHING FOR PAT, SPEND THEIR LAST CENT FOR A MEAL AT AN INN ALONG THE COAST ROAD...
TWO ROUGH LOOKING MEN ENTER THE PLACE-AND CONNIE HEARS THEM SPEAK IN CHINESE OF THE EXPLOITS OF A MAN THEIR GANG HOLDS PRISONER...
11-16
SHH! I LISTEN SOME MORE!
IS SO! ALL UGLY GENTS TALK 'BOUT IS HOW BIG WHITE MAN PLISONER UPSET BANDIT BOSS!-VELLY FUNNY-BUT MAKE BOSS MAD LIKE UNHAPPY HORNET!
BOY! NOBODY BUT PAT RYAN WOULD DARE PULL A STUNT LIKE THAT!
IF IT IS PAT-WE'VE GOT TO GET TO HIM! -BUT WHERE IS HE? -WE CAN'T ASK THOSE TWO BLOKES OR THEY'D GET SUSPICIOUS, AN' MAYBE SMACK US DOWN!
OH WEARY DOLEFUL ... IS TOO TRUE
MILTON CANIFF
Reg. U.S. Pat. Off. Copyright, 1936, by Chicago Tribune-N.Y. News Syndicate, Inc.

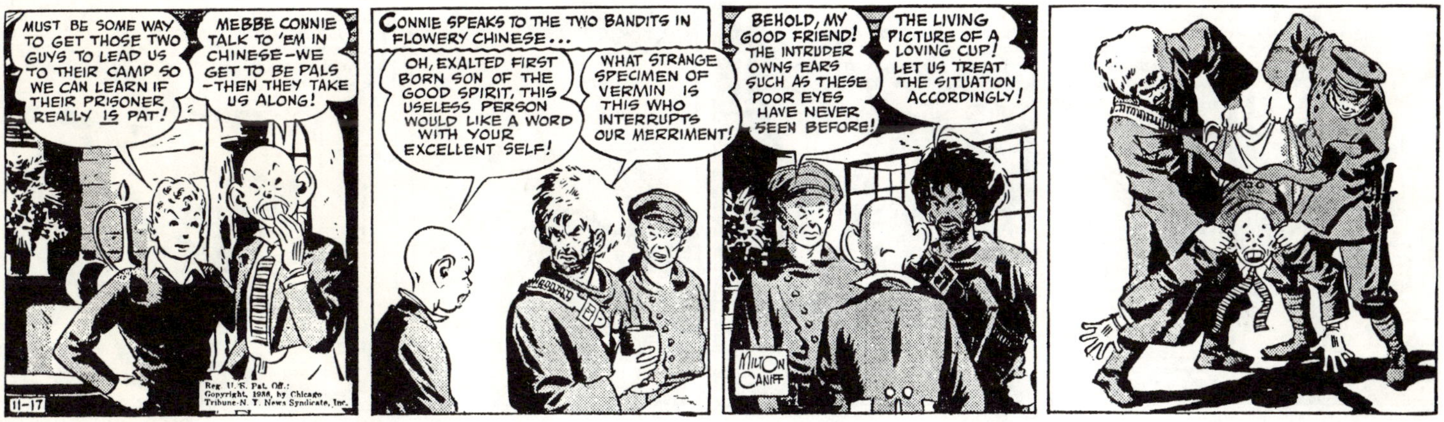
MUST BE SOME WAY TO GET THOSE TWO GUYS TO LEAD US TO THEIR CAMP SO WE CAN LEARN IF THEIR PRISONER REALLY IS PAT!
MEBBE CONNIE TALK TO 'EM IN CHINESE-WE GET TO BE PALS -THEN THEY TAKE US ALONG!
11-17
Reg. U.S. Pat. Off.; Copyright, 1936, by Chicago Tribune-N.Y. News Syndicate, Inc.
CONNIE SPEAKS TO THE TWO BANDITS IN FLOWERY CHINESE...
OH, EXALTED FIRST BORN SON OF THE GOOD SPIRIT, THIS USELESS PERSON WOULD LIKE A WORD WITH YOUR EXCELLENT SELF!
WHAT STRANGE SPECIMEN OF VERMIN IS THIS WHO INTERRUPTS OUR MERRIMENT!
BEHOLD, MY GOOD FRIEND! THE INTRUDER OWNS EARS SUCH AS THESE POOR EYES HAVE NEVER SEEN BEFORE!
THE LIVING PICTURE OF A LOVING CUP! LET US TREAT THE SITUATION ACCORDINGLY!
MILTON CANIFF

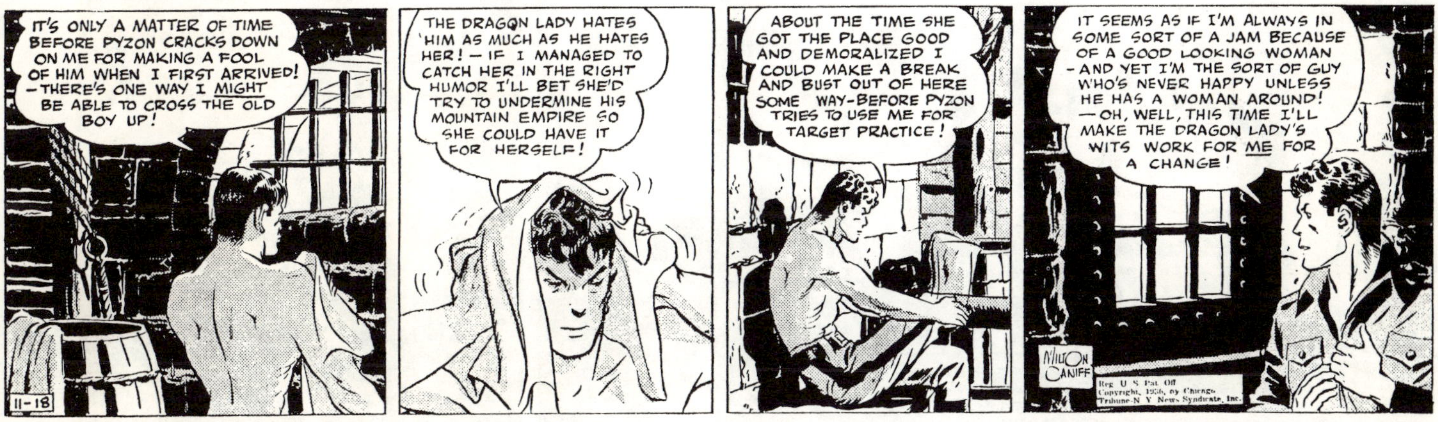
IT'S ONLY A MATTER OF TIME BEFORE PYZON CRACKS DOWN ON ME FOR MAKING A FOOL OF HIM WHEN I FIRST ARRIVED! -THERE'S ONE WAY I MIGHT BE ABLE TO CROSS THE OLD BOY UP!
11-18
THE DRAGON LADY HATES HIM AS MUCH AS HE HATES HER! -IF I MANAGED TO CATCH HER IN THE RIGHT HUMOR I'LL BET SHE'D TRY TO UNDERMINE HIS MOUNTAIN EMPIRE SO SHE COULD HAVE IT FOR HERSELF!
ABOUT THE TIME SHE GOT THE PLACE GOOD AND DEMORALIZED I COULD MAKE A BREAK AND BUST OUT OF HERE SOME WAY-BEFORE PYZON TRIES TO USE ME FOR TARGET PRACTICE!
IT SEEMS AS IF I'M ALWAYS IN SOME SORT OF A JAM BECAUSE OF A GOOD LOOKING WOMAN -AND YET I'M THE SORT OF GUY WHO'S NEVER HAPPY UNLESS HE HAS A WOMAN AROUND! -OH, WELL, THIS TIME I'LL MAKE THE DRAGON LADY'S WITS WORK FOR ME FOR A CHANGE!
MILTON CANIFF
Reg. U.S. Pat. Off. Copyright, 1936, by Chicago Tribune-N.Y. News Syndicate, Inc.

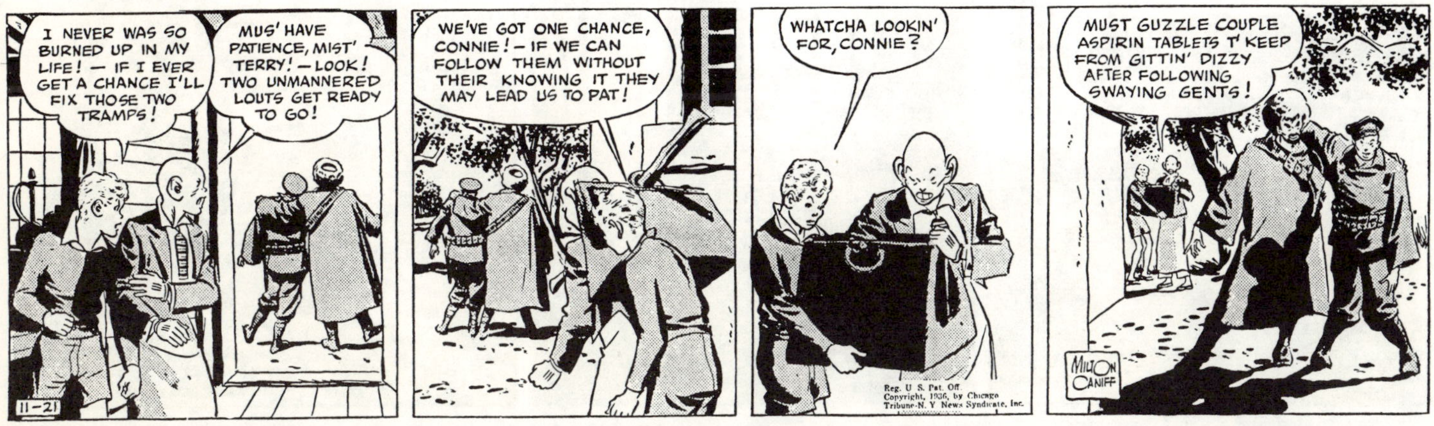
I NEVER WAS SO BURNED UP IN MY LIFE! -IF I EVER GET A CHANCE I'LL FIX THOSE TWO TRAMPS!
MUS' HAVE PATIENCE, MIST' TERRY! -LOOK! TWO UNMANNERED LOUTS GET READY TO GO!
11-21
WE'VE GOT ONE CHANCE, CONNIE! -IF WE CAN FOLLOW THEM WITHOUT THEIR KNOWING IT THEY MAY LEAD US TO PAT!
WHATCHA LOOKIN' FOR, CONNIE?
Reg. U.S. Pat. Off. Copyright, 1936, by Chicago Tribune-N.Y. News Syndicate, Inc.
MUST GUZZLE COUPLE ASPIRIN TABLETS T' KEEP FROM GITTIN' DIZZY AFTER FOLLOWING SWAYING GENTS!
MILTON CANIFF

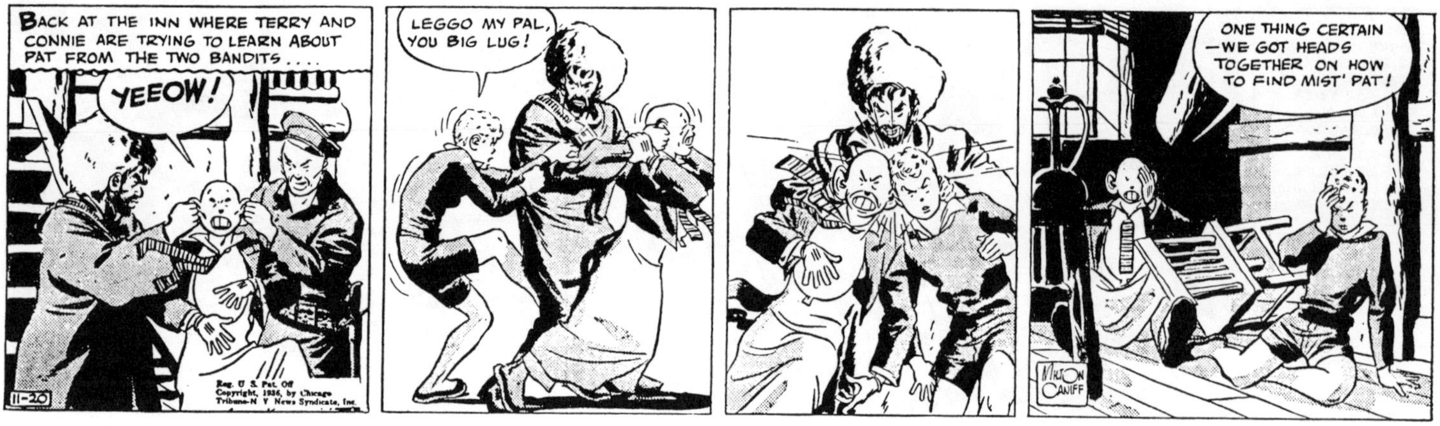
BACK AT THE INN WHERE TERRY AND CONNIE ARE TRYING TO LEARN ABOUT PAT FROM THE TWO BANDITS....
YEEOW!
11-20
Reg. U. S. Pat. Off. Copyright, 1936, by Chicago Tribune-N Y News Syndicate, Inc.
LEGGO MY PAL, YOU BIG LUG!
ONE THING CERTAIN —WE GOT HEADS TOGETHER ON HOW TO FIND MIST' PAT!
MILTON CANIFF

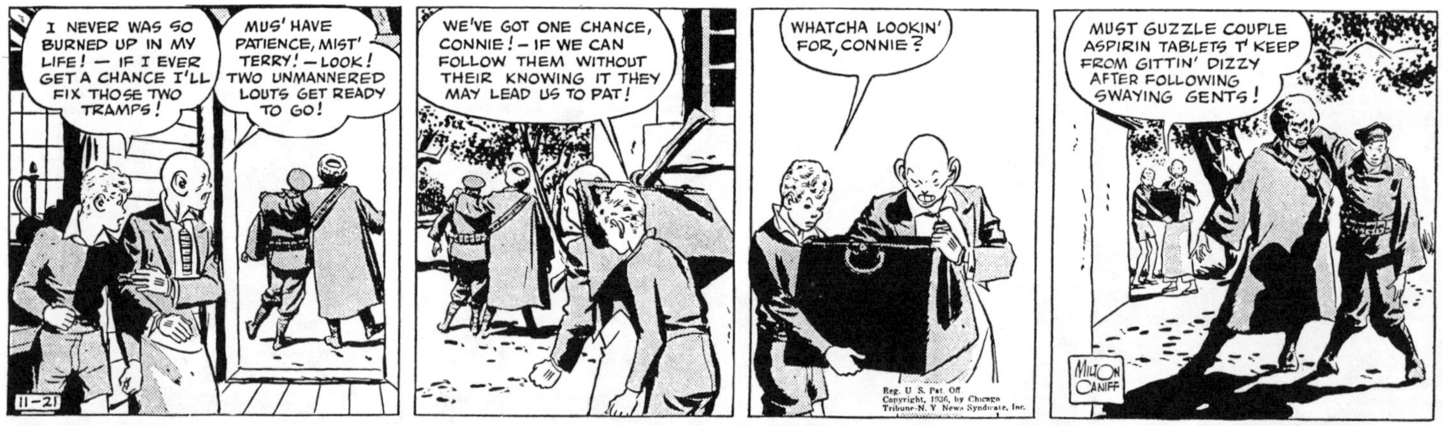
I NEVER WAS SO BURNED UP IN MY LIFE! — IF I EVER GET A CHANCE I'LL FIX THOSE TWO TRAMPS!
MUS' HAVE PATIENCE, MIST' TERRY! —LOOK! TWO UNMANNERED LOUTS GET READY TO GO!
11-21
WE'VE GOT ONE CHANCE, CONNIE! — IF WE CAN FOLLOW THEM WITHOUT THEIR KNOWING IT THEY MAY LEAD US TO PAT!
WHATCHA LOOKIN' FOR, CONNIE?
Reg. U. S. Pat. Off. Copyright, 1936, by Chicago Tribune-N Y News Syndicate, Inc.
MUST GUZZLE COUPLE ASPIRIN TABLETS T' KEEP FROM GITTIN' DIZZY AFTER FOLLOWING SWAYING GENTS!
MILTON CANIFF

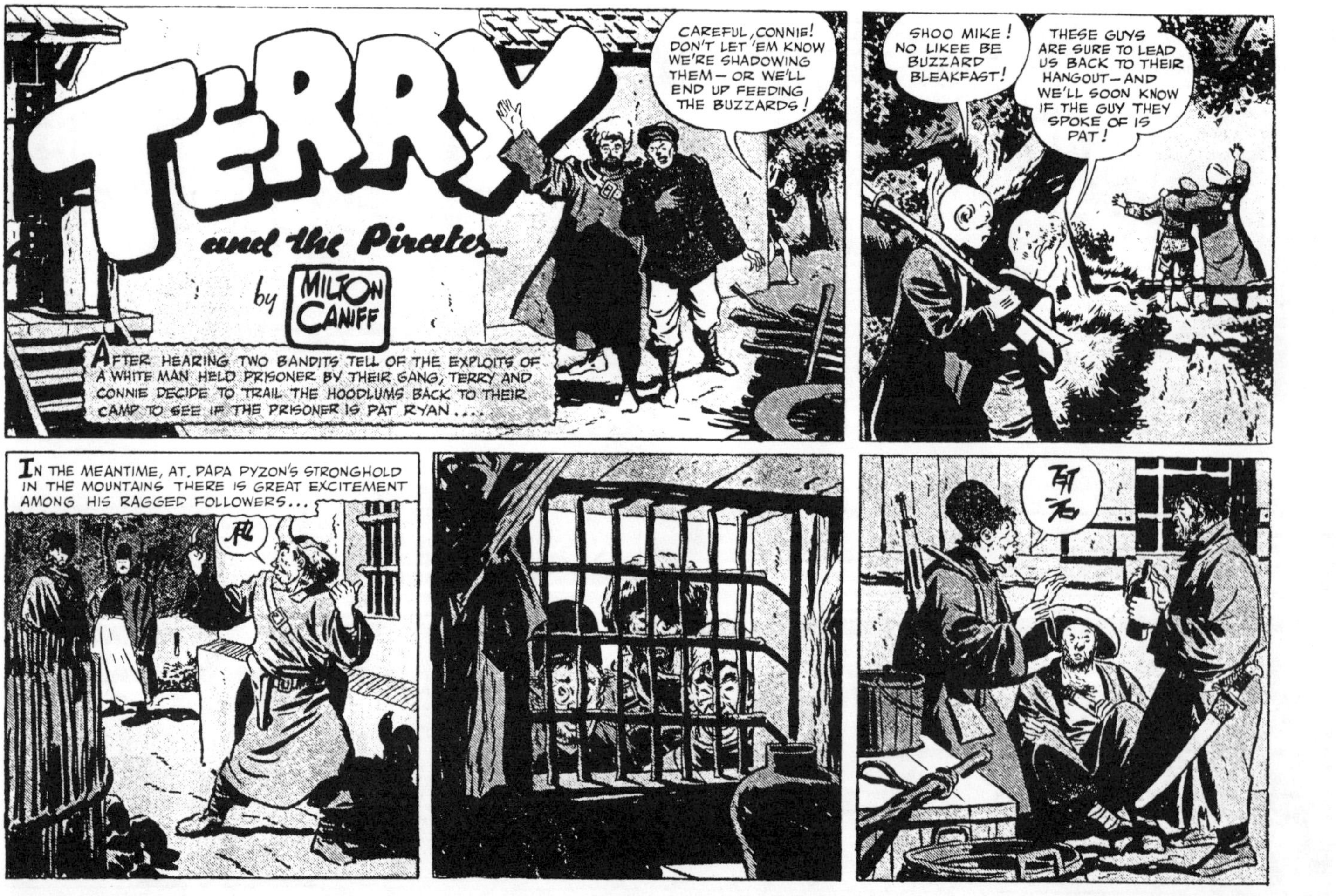
TERRY
and the Pirates
by MILTON CANIFF
AFTER HEARING TWO BANDITS TELL OF THE EXPLOITS OF A WHITE MAN HELD PRISONER BY THEIR GANG, TERRY AND CONNIE DECIDE TO TRAIL THE HOODLUMS BACK TO THEIR CAMP TO SEE IF THE PRISONER IS PAT RYAN....
CAREFUL, CONNIE! DON'T LET 'EM KNOW WE'RE SHADOWING THEM — OR WE'LL END UP FEEDING THE BUZZARDS!
SHOO MIKE! NO LIKEE BE BUZZARD BLEAKFAST!
THESE GUYS ARE SURE TO LEAD US BACK TO THEIR HANGOUT — AND WE'LL SOON KNOW IF THE GUY THEY SPOKE OF IS PAT!
IN THE MEANTIME, AT PAPA PYZON'S STRONGHOLD IN THE MOUNTAINS THERE IS GREAT EXCITEMENT AMONG HIS RAGGED FOLLOWERS...

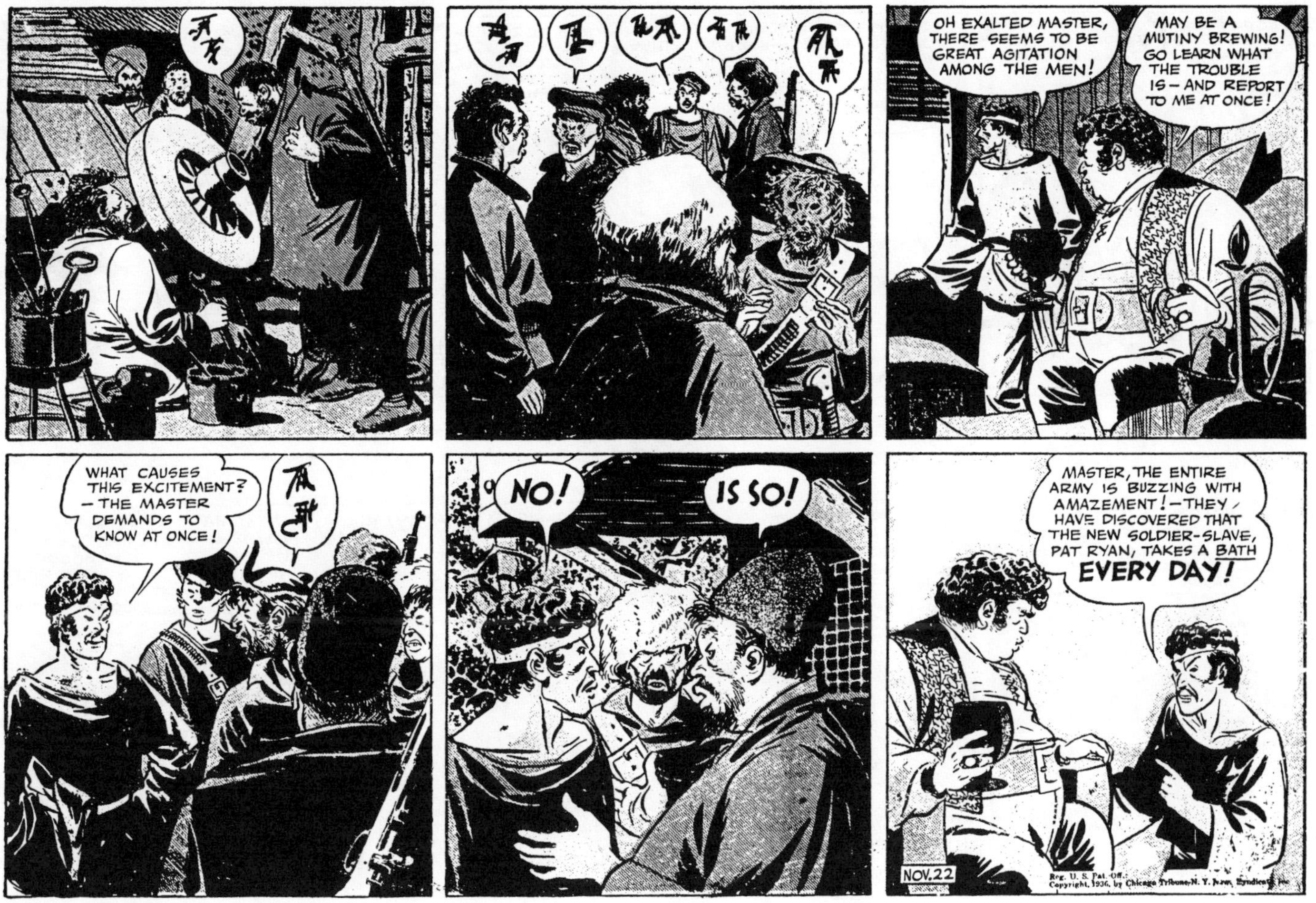
OH EXALTED MASTER, THERE SEEMS TO BE GREAT AGITATION AMONG THE MEN!
MAY BE A MUTINY BREWING! GO LEARN WHAT THE TROUBLE IS—AND REPORT TO ME AT ONCE!
WHAT CAUSES THIS EXCITEMENT? —THE MASTER DEMANDS TO KNOW AT ONCE!
NO!
IS SO!
MASTER, THE ENTIRE ARMY IS BUZZING WITH AMAZEMENT!—THEY HAVE DISCOVERED THAT THE NEW SOLDIER-SLAVE, PAT RYAN, TAKES A BATH EVERY DAY!
NOV. 22
Reg. U. S. Pat. Off.: Copyright, 1936, by Chicago Tribune-N. Y. News Syndicate, Inc.

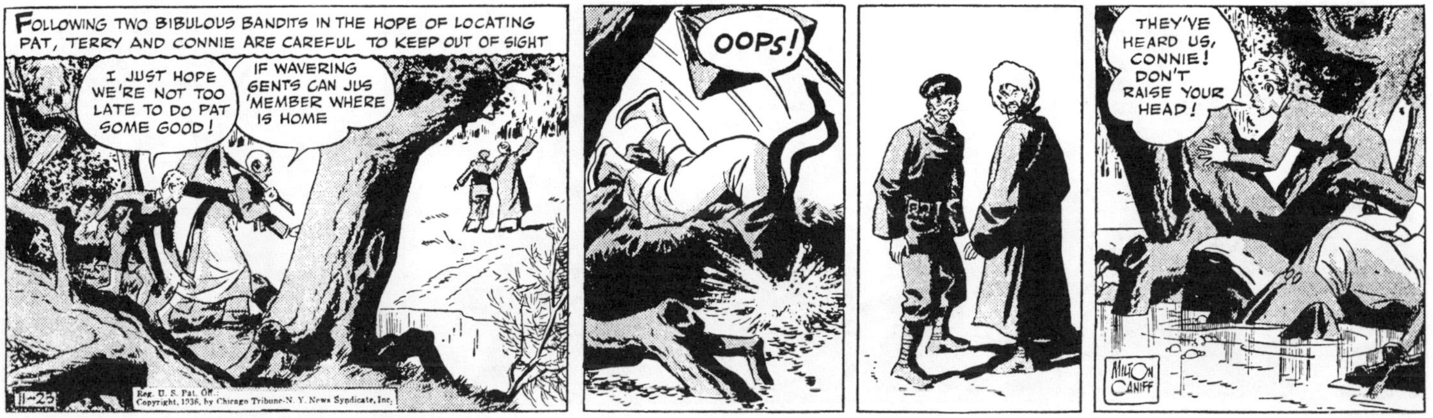
FOLLOWING TWO BIBULOUS BANDITS IN THE HOPE OF LOCATING PAT, TERRY AND CONNIE ARE CAREFUL TO KEEP OUT OF SIGHT
I JUST HOPE WE'RE NOT TOO LATE TO DO PAT SOME GOOD!
IF WAVERING GENTS CAN JUS 'MEMBER WHERE IS HOME
11-23
Reg. U. S. Pat. Off.: Copyright, 1936, by Chicago Tribune-N. Y. News Syndicate, Inc.
OOPS!
THEY'VE HEARD US, CONNIE! DON'T RAISE YOUR HEAD!
MILTON CANIFF

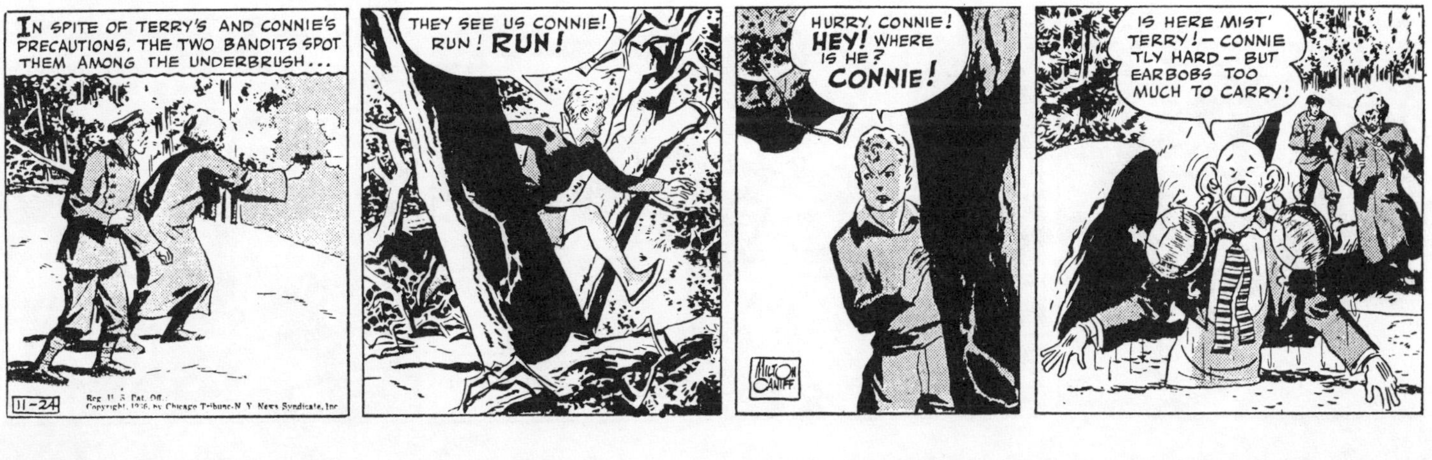
IN SPITE OF TERRY'S AND CONNIE'S PRECAUTIONS, THE TWO BANDITS SPOT THEM AMONG THE UNDERBRUSH...
11-24
Reg. U. S. Pat. Off.: Copyright, 1936, by Chicago Tribune-N. Y. News Syndicate, Inc.
THEY SEE US CONNIE! RUN! RUN!
HURRY, CONNIE! HEY! WHERE IS HE? CONNIE!
MILTON CANIFF
IS HERE MIST' TERRY!—CONNIE TLY HARD—BUT EARBOBS TOO MUCH TO CARRY!

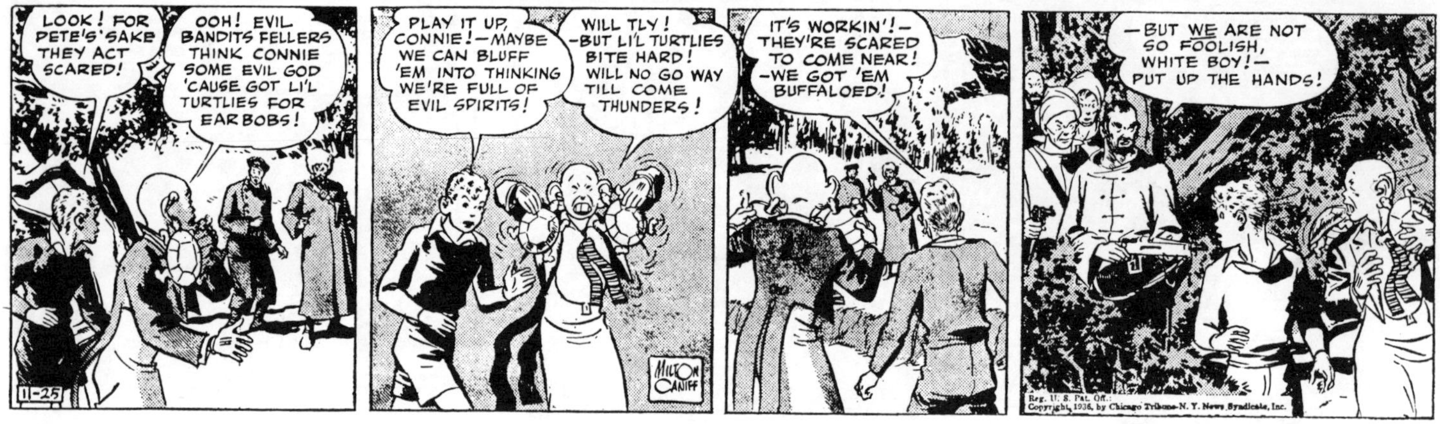
LOOK! FOR PETE'S SAKE THEY ACT SCARED!
OOH! EVIL BANDITS FELLERS THINK CONNIE SOME EVIL GOD 'CAUSE GOT LI'L TURTLIES FOR EAR BOBS!
11-25
PLAY IT UP, CONNIE! —MAYBE WE CAN BLUFF 'EM INTO THINKING WE'RE FULL OF EVIL SPIRITS!
WILL TLY! —BUT LI'L TURTLIES BITE HARD! WILL NO GO WAY TILL COME THUNDERS!
MILTON CANIFF
IT'S WORKIN'! —THEY'RE SCARED TO COME NEAR! —WE GOT 'EM BUFFALOED!
—BUT WE ARE NOT SO FOOLISH, WHITE BOY! —PUT UP THE HANDS!
Reg. U. S. Pat. Off.: Copyright, 1936, by Chicago Tribune-N. Y. News Syndicate, Inc.

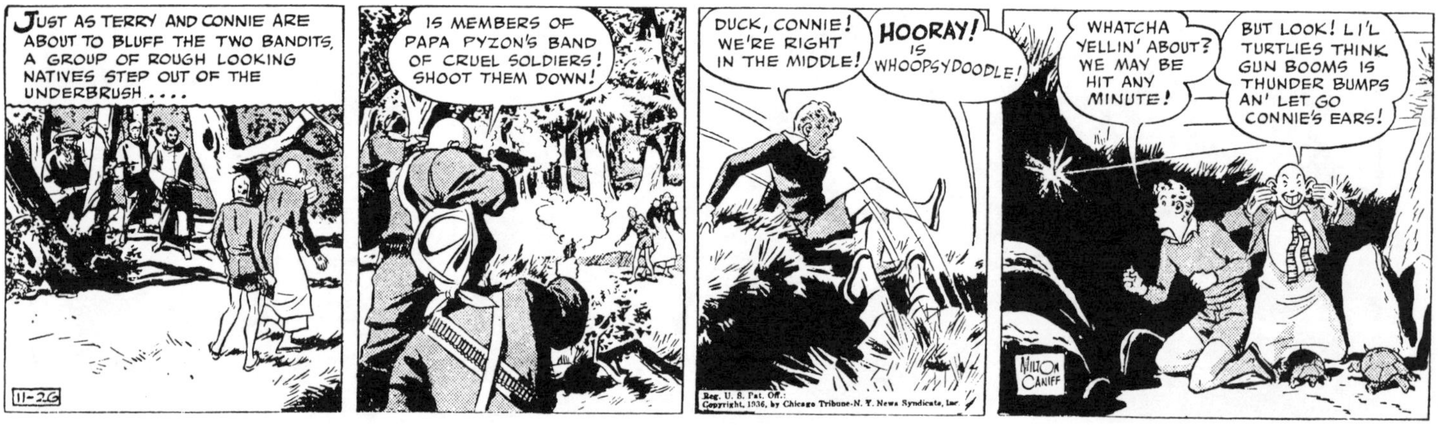
JUST AS TERRY AND CONNIE ARE ABOUT TO BLUFF THE TWO BANDITS, A GROUP OF ROUGH LOOKING NATIVES STEP OUT OF THE UNDERBRUSH....
11-26
IS MEMBERS OF PAPA PYZON'S BAND OF CRUEL SOLDIERS! SHOOT THEM DOWN!
DUCK, CONNIE! WE'RE RIGHT IN THE MIDDLE!
HOORAY! IS WHOOPSYDOODLE!
Reg. U. S. Pat. Off.: Copyright, 1936, by Chicago Tribune-N. Y. News Syndicate, Inc.
WHATCHA YELLIN' ABOUT? WE MAY BE HIT ANY MINUTE!
BUT LOOK! LI'L TURTLIES THINK GUN BOOMS IS THUNDER BUMPS AN' LET GO CONNIE'S EARS!
MILTON CANIFF

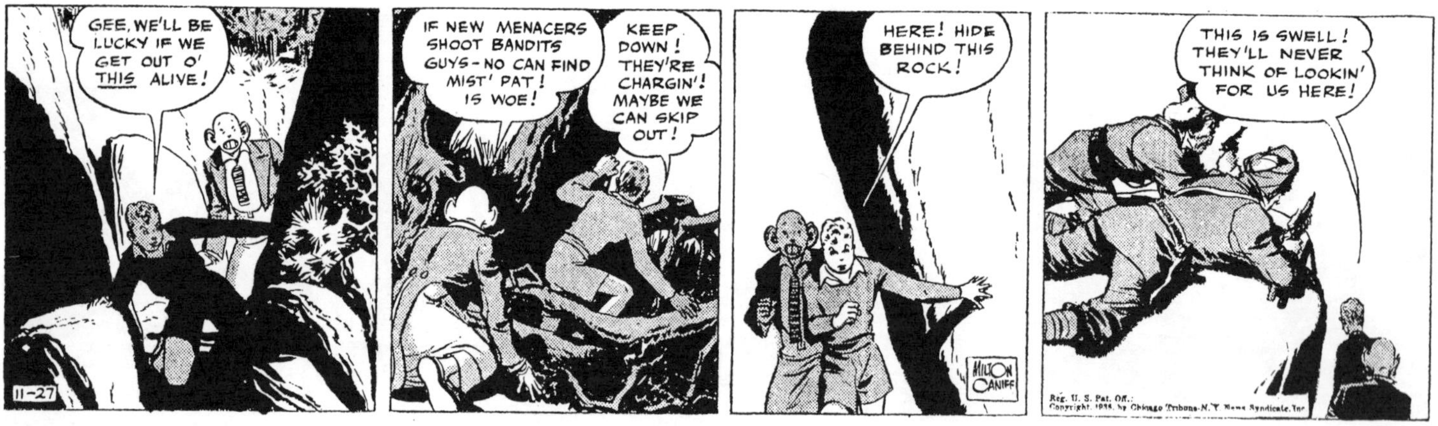
GEE, WE'LL BE LUCKY IF WE GET OUT O' THIS ALIVE!
11-27
IF NEW MENACERS SHOOT BANDITS GUYS—NO CAN FIND MIST' PAT! IS WOE!
KEEP DOWN! THEY'RE CHARGIN'! MAYBE WE CAN SKIP OUT!
HERE! HIDE BEHIND THIS ROCK!
MILTON CANIFF
THIS IS SWELL! THEY'LL NEVER THINK OF LOOKIN' FOR US HERE!
Reg. U. S. Pat. Off.: Copyright, 1936, by Chicago Tribune-N. Y. News Syndicate, Inc.

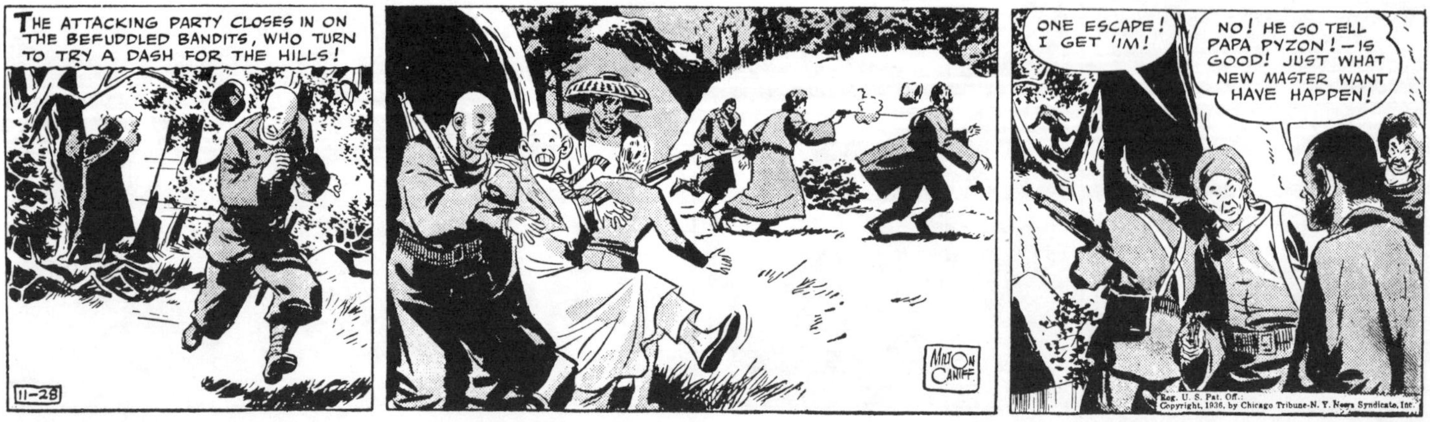
THE ATTACKING PARTY CLOSES IN ON THE BEFUDDLED BANDITS, WHO TURN TO TRY A DASH FOR THE HILLS!
11-28
MILTON CANIFF
ONE ESCAPE! I GET 'IM!
NO! HE GO TELL PAPA PYZON! —IS GOOD! JUST WHAT NEW MASTER WANT HAVE HAPPEN!
Reg. U. S. Pat. Off.: Copyright, 1936, by Chicago Tribune-N. Y. News Syndicate, Inc.

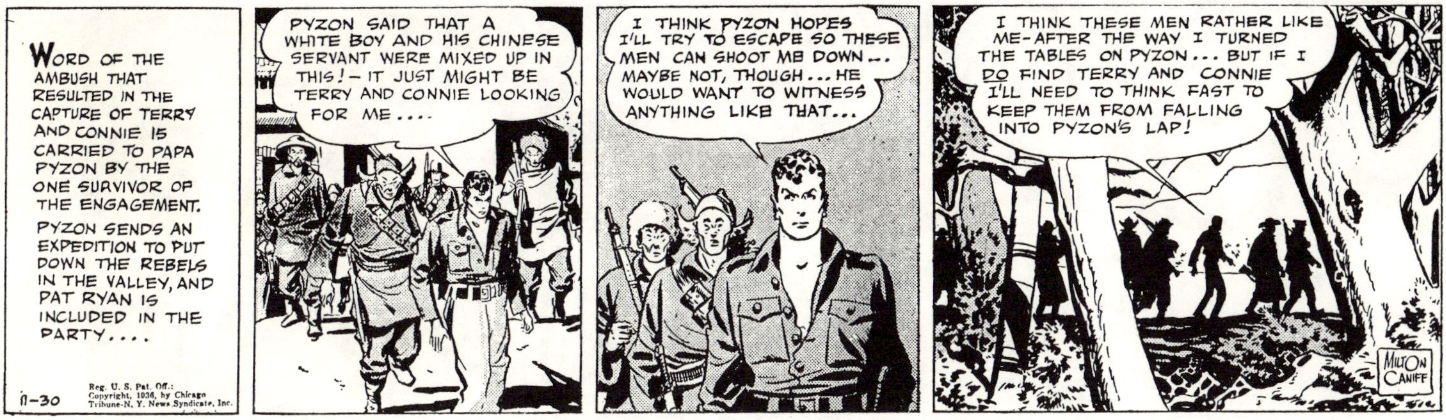
WORD OF THE AMBUSH THAT RESULTED IN THE CAPTURE OF TERRY AND CONNIE IS CARRIED TO PAPA PYZON BY THE ONE SURVIVOR OF THE ENGAGEMENT.
PYZON SENDS AN EXPEDITION TO PUT DOWN THE REBELS IN THE VALLEY, AND PAT RYAN IS INCLUDED IN THE PARTY....
11-30
Reg. U. S. Pat. Off.: Copyright, 1936, by Chicago Tribune-N. Y. News Syndicate, Inc.
PYZON SAID THAT A WHITE BOY AND HIS CHINESE SERVANT WERE MIXED UP IN THIS! – IT JUST MIGHT BE TERRY AND CONNIE LOOKING FOR ME....
I THINK PYZON HOPES I'LL TRY TO ESCAPE SO THESE MEN CAN SHOOT ME DOWN... MAYBE NOT, THOUGH... HE WOULD WANT TO WITNESS ANYTHING LIKE THAT...
I THINK THESE MEN RATHER LIKE ME - AFTER THE WAY I TURNED THE TABLES ON PYZON... BUT IF I DO FIND TERRY AND CONNIE I'LL NEED TO THINK FAST TO KEEP THEM FROM FALLING INTO PYZON'S LAP!
MILTON CANIFF

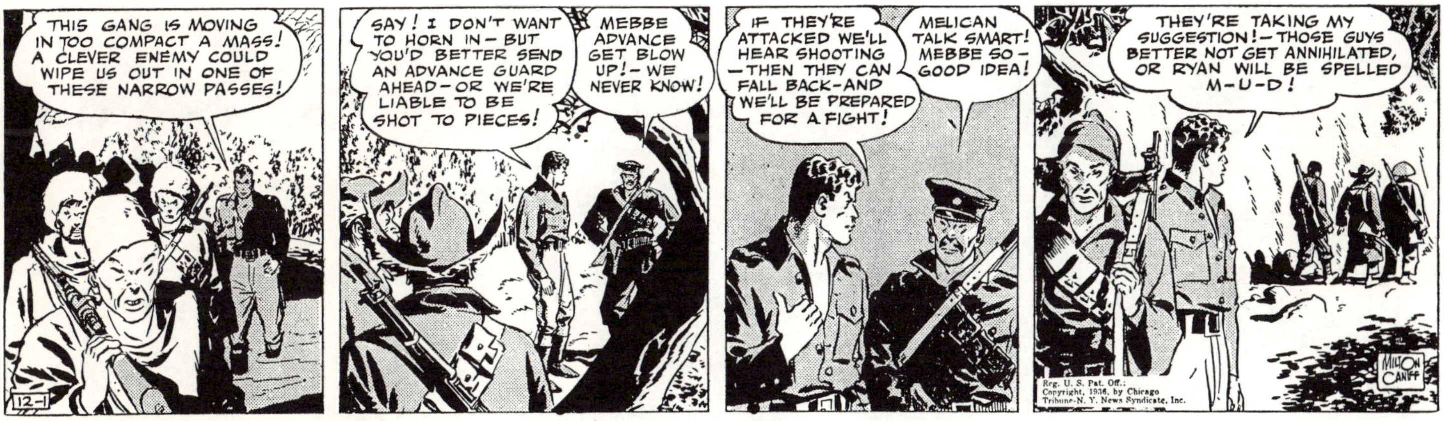
THIS GANG IS MOVING IN TOO COMPACT A MASS! A CLEVER ENEMY COULD WIPE US OUT IN ONE OF THESE NARROW PASSES!
12-1
SAY! I DON'T WANT TO HORN IN - BUT YOU'D BETTER SEND AN ADVANCE GUARD AHEAD - OR WE'RE LIABLE TO BE SHOT TO PIECES!
MEBBE ADVANCE GET BLOW UP! - WE NEVER KNOW!
IF THEY'RE ATTACKED WE'LL HEAR SHOOTING - THEN THEY CAN FALL BACK - AND WE'LL BE PREPARED FOR A FIGHT!
MELICAN TALK SMART! MEBBE SO - GOOD IDEA!
THEY'RE TAKING MY SUGGESTION! - THOSE GUYS BETTER NOT GET ANNIHILATED, OR RYAN WILL BE SPELLED M-U-D!
Reg. U. S. Pat. Off.: Copyright, 1936, by Chicago Tribune-N. Y. News Syndicate, Inc.
MILTON CANIFF

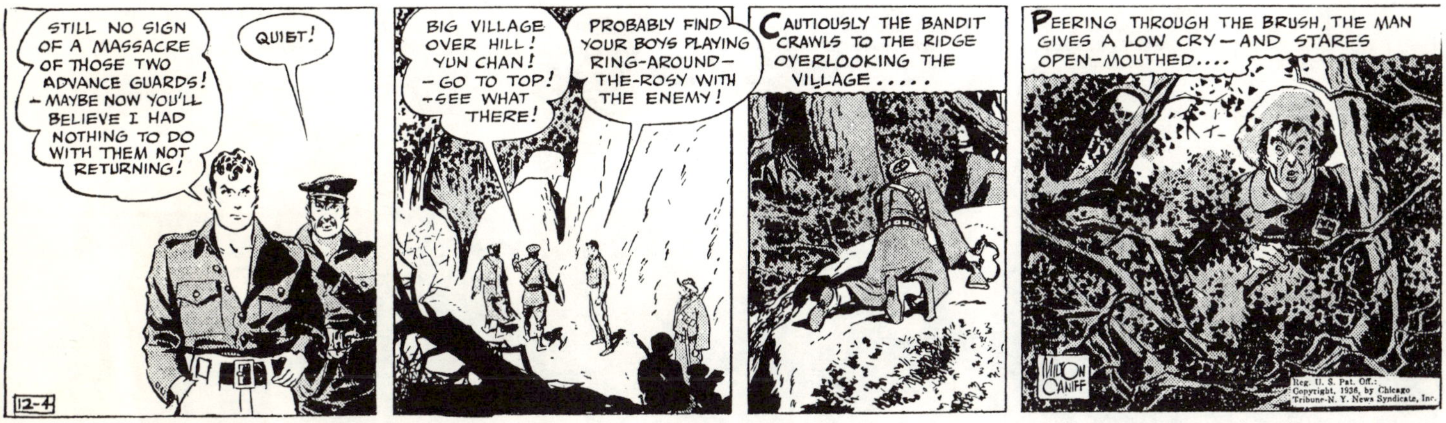
STILL NO SIGN OF A MASSACRE OF THOSE TWO ADVANCE GUARDS! - MAYBE NOW YOU'LL BELIEVE I HAD NOTHING TO DO WITH THEM NOT RETURNING!
QUIET!
12-4
BIG VILLAGE OVER HILL! YUN CHAN! - GO TO TOP! - SEE WHAT THERE!
PROBABLY FIND YOUR BOYS PLAYING RING-AROUND-THE-ROSY WITH THE ENEMY!
CAUTIOUSLY THE BANDIT CRAWLS TO THE RIDGE OVERLOOKING THE VILLAGE.....
MILTON CANIFF
PEERING THROUGH THE BRUSH, THE MAN GIVES A LOW CRY - AND STARES OPEN-MOUTHED....
Reg. U. S. Pat. Off.: Copyright, 1936, by Chicago Tribune-N. Y. News Syndicate, Inc.

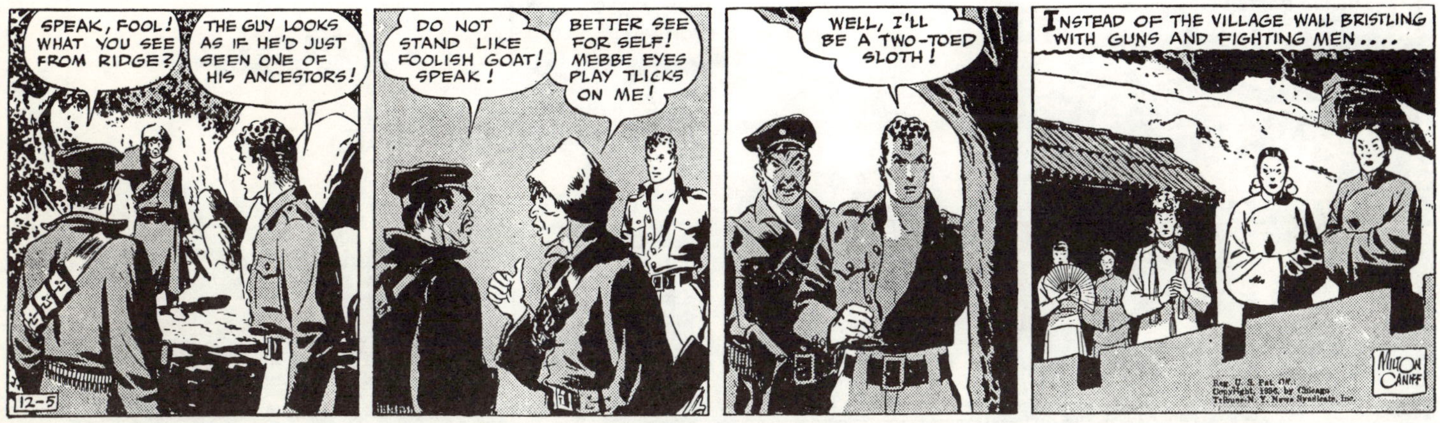
SPEAK, FOOL! WHAT YOU SEE FROM RIDGE?
THE GUY LOOKS AS IF HE'D JUST SEEN ONE OF HIS ANCESTORS!
12-5
DO NOT STAND LIKE FOOLISH GOAT! SPEAK!
BETTER SEE FOR SELF! MEBBE EYES PLAY TLICKS ON ME!
WELL, I'LL BE A TWO-TOED SLOTH!
INSTEAD OF THE VILLAGE WALL BRISTLING WITH GUNS AND FIGHTING MEN....
Reg. U. S. Pat. Off.: Copyright, 1936, by Chicago Tribune-N. Y. News Syndicate, Inc.
MILTON CANIFF

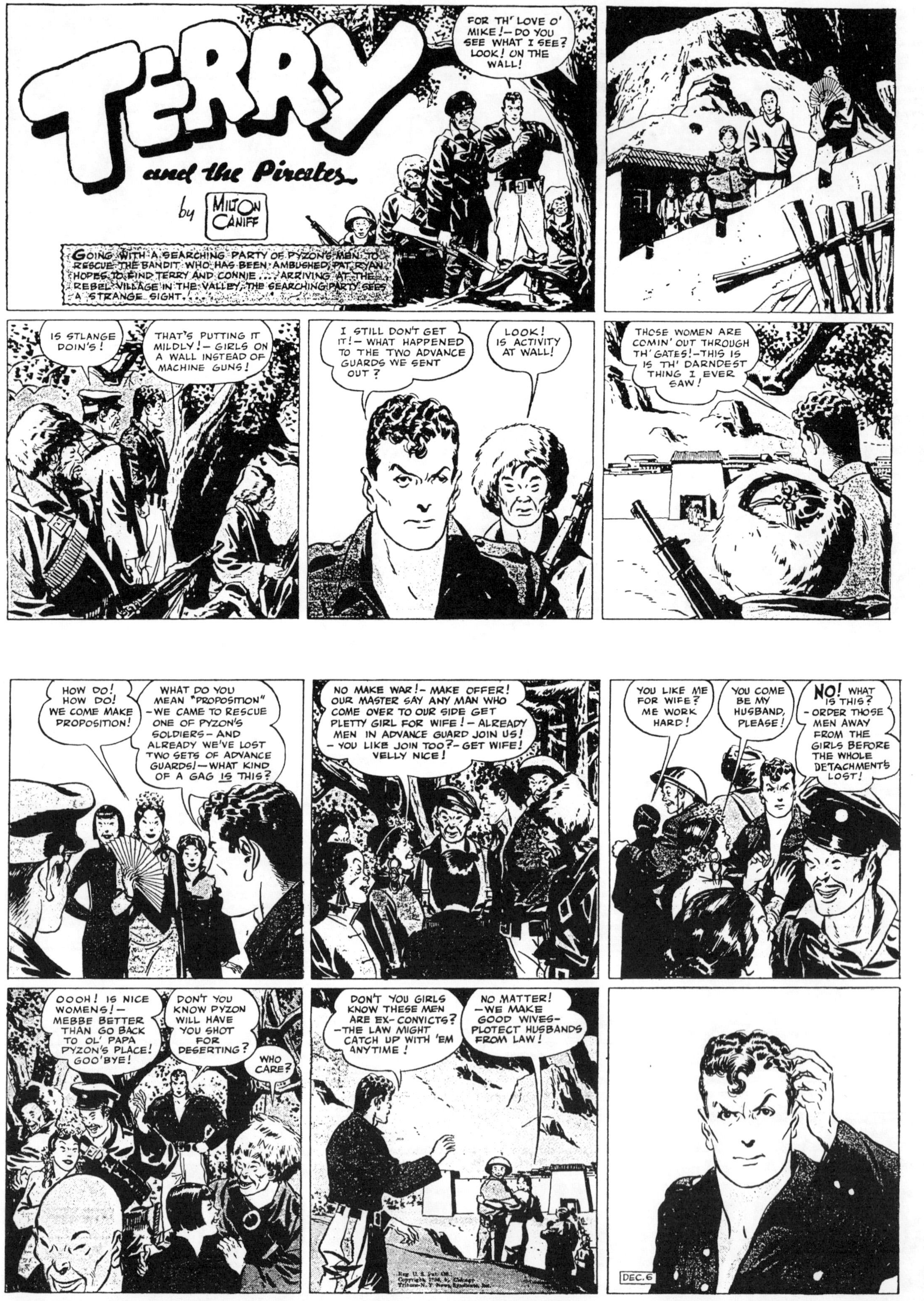
TERRY and the Pirates
by MILTON CANIFF
GOING WITH A SEARCHING PARTY OF PYZON'S MEN TO RESCUE THE BANDIT WHO HAS BEEN AMBUSHED, PAT RYAN HOPES TO FIND TERRY AND CONNIE . . . ARRIVING AT THE REBEL VILLAGE IN THE VALLEY, THE SEARCHING PARTY SEES A STRANGE SIGHT . . .
FOR TH' LOVE O' MIKE! — DO YOU SEE WHAT I SEE? LOOK! ON THE WALL!
IS STLANGE DOIN'S!
THAT'S PUTTING IT MILDLY! — GIRLS ON A WALL INSTEAD OF MACHINE GUNS!
I STILL DON'T GET IT! — WHAT HAPPENED TO THE TWO ADVANCE GUARDS WE SENT OUT?
LOOK! IS ACTIVITY AT WALL!
THOSE WOMEN ARE COMIN' OUT THROUGH TH' GATES! — THIS IS IS TH' DARNDEST THING I EVER SAW!
HOW DO! HOW DO! WE COME MAKE PROPOSITION!
WHAT DO YOU MEAN "PROPOSITION" — WE CAME TO RESCUE ONE OF PYZON'S SOLDIERS — AND ALREADY WE'VE LOST TWO SETS OF ADVANCE GUARDS! — WHAT KIND OF A GAG IS THIS?
NO MAKE WAR! — MAKE OFFER! OUR MASTER SAY ANY MAN WHO COME OVER TO OUR SIDE GET PLETTY GIRL FOR WIFE! — ALREADY MEN IN ADVANCE GUARD JOIN US! — YOU LIKE JOIN TOO? — GET WIFE! VELLY NICE!
YOU LIKE ME FOR WIFE? ME WORK HARD!
YOU COME BE MY HUSBAND, PLEASE!
NO! WHAT IS THIS? — ORDER THOSE MEN AWAY FROM THE GIRLS BEFORE THE WHOLE DETACHMENT'S LOST!
OOOH! IS NICE WOMENS! — MEBBE BETTER THAN GO BACK TO OL' PAPA PYZON'S PLACE! GOO'BYE!
DON'T YOU KNOW PYZON WILL HAVE YOU SHOT FOR DESERTING?
WHO CARE?
DON'T YOU GIRLS KNOW THESE MEN ARE EX-CONVICTS? — THE LAW MIGHT CATCH UP WITH 'EM ANYTIME!
NO MATTER! — WE MAKE GOOD WIVES — PLOTECT HUSBANDS FROM LAW!
DEC. 6

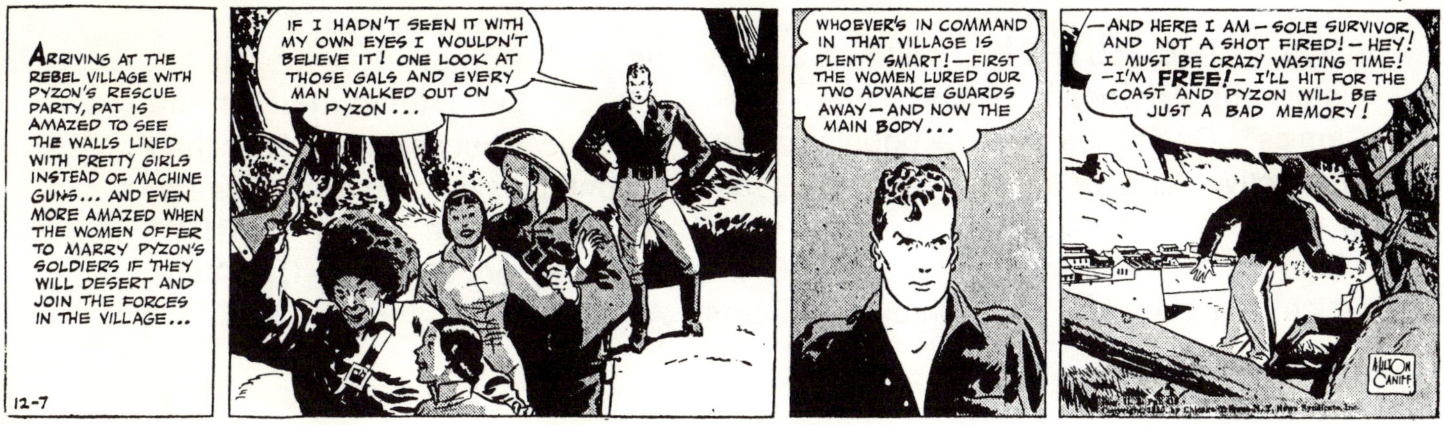
ARRIVING AT THE REBEL VILLAGE WITH PYZON'S RESCUE PARTY, PAT IS AMAZED TO SEE THE WALLS LINED WITH PRETTY GIRLS INSTEAD OF MACHINE GUNS... AND EVEN MORE AMAZED WHEN THE WOMEN OFFER TO MARRY PYZON'S SOLDIERS IF THEY WILL DESERT AND JOIN THE FORCES IN THE VILLAGE...
12-7
IF I HADN'T SEEN IT WITH MY OWN EYES I WOULDN'T BELIEVE IT! ONE LOOK AT THOSE GALS AND EVERY MAN WALKED OUT ON PYZON...
WHOEVER'S IN COMMAND IN THAT VILLAGE IS PLENTY SMART! —FIRST THE WOMEN LURED OUR TWO ADVANCE GUARDS AWAY—AND NOW THE MAIN BODY...
—AND HERE I AM—SOLE SURVIVOR, AND NOT A SHOT FIRED!—HEY! I MUST BE CRAZY WASTING TIME! —I'M FREE!—I'LL HIT FOR THE COAST AND PYZON WILL BE JUST A BAD MEMORY!
MILTON CANIFF

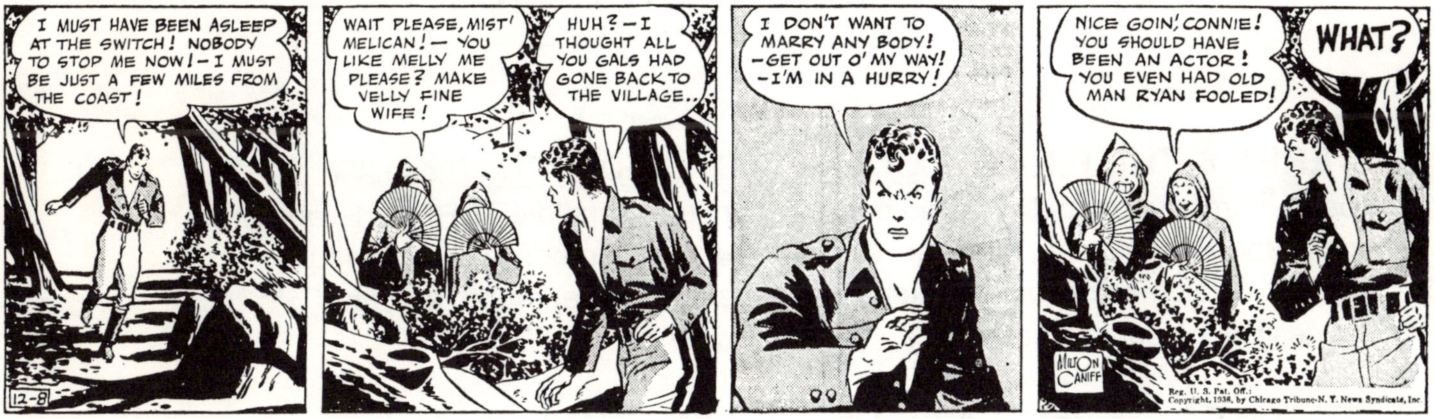
I MUST HAVE BEEN ASLEEP AT THE SWITCH! NOBODY TO STOP ME NOW!—I MUST BE JUST A FEW MILES FROM THE COAST!
12-8
WAIT PLEASE, MIST' MELICAN!—YOU LIKE MELLY ME PLEASE? MAKE VELLY FINE WIFE!
HUH?—I THOUGHT ALL YOU GALS HAD GONE BACK TO THE VILLAGE...
I DON'T WANT TO MARRY ANY BODY! —GET OUT O' MY WAY! —I'M IN A HURRY!
NICE GOIN', CONNIE! YOU SHOULD HAVE BEEN AN ACTOR! YOU EVEN HAD OLD MAN RYAN FOOLED!
WHAT?
MILTON CANIFF
Reg. U. S. Pat. Off.: Copyright, 1936, by Chicago Tribune-N. Y. News Syndicate, Inc.

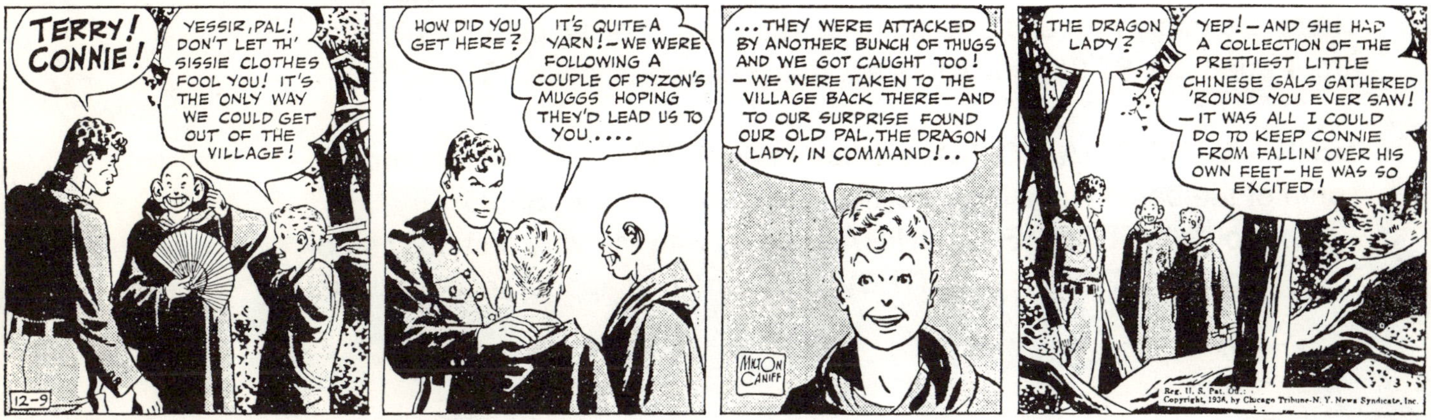
TERRY! CONNIE!
YESSIR, PAL! DON'T LET TH' SISSIE CLOTHES FOOL YOU! IT'S THE ONLY WAY WE COULD GET OUT OF THE VILLAGE!
12-9
HOW DID YOU GET HERE?
IT'S QUITE A YARN!—WE WERE FOLLOWING A COUPLE OF PYZON'S MUGGS HOPING THEY'D LEAD US TO YOU....
MILTON CANIFF
...THEY WERE ATTACKED BY ANOTHER BUNCH OF THUGS AND WE GOT CAUGHT TOO! —WE WERE TAKEN TO THE VILLAGE BACK THERE—AND TO OUR SURPRISE FOUND OUR OLD PAL, THE DRAGON LADY, IN COMMAND!..
THE DRAGON LADY?
YEP!—AND SHE HAD A COLLECTION OF THE PRETTIEST LITTLE CHINESE GALS GATHERED 'ROUND YOU EVER SAW! —IT WAS ALL I COULD DO TO KEEP CONNIE FROM FALLIN' OVER HIS OWN FEET—HE WAS SO EXCITED!
Reg. U. S. Pat. Off.: Copyright, 1936, by Chicago Tribune-N. Y. News Syndicate, Inc.

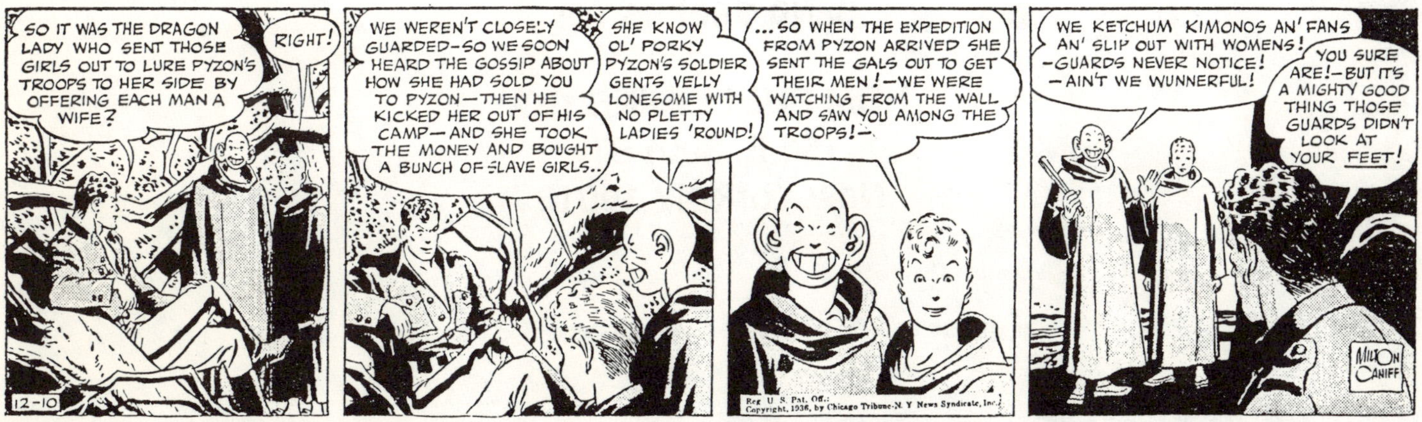
SO IT WAS THE DRAGON LADY WHO SENT THOSE GIRLS OUT TO LURE PYZON'S TROOPS TO HER SIDE BY OFFERING EACH MAN A WIFE?
RIGHT!
12-10
WE WEREN'T CLOSELY GUARDED—SO WE SOON HEARD THE GOSSIP ABOUT HOW SHE HAD SOLD YOU TO PYZON—THEN HE KICKED HER OUT OF HIS CAMP—AND SHE TOOK THE MONEY AND BOUGHT A BUNCH OF SLAVE GIRLS..
SHE KNOW OL' PORKY PYZON'S SOLDIER GENTS VELLY LONESOME WITH NO PLETTY LADIES 'ROUND!
...SO WHEN THE EXPEDITION FROM PYZON ARRIVED SHE SENT THE GALS OUT TO GET THEIR MEN!—WE WERE WATCHING FROM THE WALL AND SAW YOU AMONG THE TROOPS!—
Reg U. S. Pat. Off.: Copyright, 1936, by Chicago Tribune-N Y News Syndicate, Inc.
WE KETCHUM KIMONOS AN' FANS AN' SLIP OUT WITH WOMENS! —GUARDS NEVER NOTICE! —AIN'T WE WUNNERFUL!
YOU SURE ARE!—BUT IT'S A MIGHTY GOOD THING THOSE GUARDS DIDN'T LOOK AT YOUR FEET!
MILTON CANIFF

ABOUT THE AUTHOR: Milton Caniff is one of the greatest figures in the history of American conics. Often referred to as the "Rembrandt of the Comics", Caniff has been a popular as well as critical success. He has had one active strip or another appearing almost continuosly for over 50 years. In the early 30's Caniff produced **DICKIE DARE**; in 1934 he began **"TERRY"** which he wrote and drew until 1946 when he created **STEVE CANYON** which still appears in newspapers across America.

OTHER CANIFF BOOKS FROM NBM

TERRY & THE PIRATES COLLECTORS EDITION These 288-320 page, hardbound, gold stamped books reprint the complete TERRY. Every daily and Sunday strip, many never before been reprinted, is shown in full size. 10 volumes of this 12 volume series have been reprinted, and the series will be completed in 1987. Write for more information.

MILTON CANIFF-REMBRANDT OF THE COMIC STRIP The original version of this book appeared in 1946 as Caniff was finishing his work on TERRY. Comic historian Rick Marschall has updated this 1980 edition. There are many rare and beautiful illustrations and blowups of Caniff's art. Paperback $6.95, Collectors ed. (hardcover/dustjacket) $13.50

TERRY & THE PIRATES (paperback series) This series will reprint some of the best stories from TERRY. 64pp, color cover. $5.95
    vol.1 **WELCOME TO CHINA** - begins with the very first daily strip
    vol.2 **MAROONED WITH BURMA** - the first appearance of BURMA

SEND ORDERS TO:

NBM PUBLISHING CO.
156 E. 39th ST.
New York NY 10016

all orders add $2.00 per book for postage and handling